The Pain Artist

⊰ An American *Hikikomori* ⊱

E.E. "Doc" Murdock

H.O.T. Press

Published by
H.O.T. Press
Los Angeles
www.hotpresspublishing.com
Publishing fine books since 1983

ISBN: 0-923178-25-2
ISBN-13: 978-0-923178-25-3

Acknowledgments

I am indebted to the members of the Ojai Writing Workshop who provided valuable feedback as I worked through the many drafts of this book. I would also like to acknowledge the help of all my students at California State University, Long Beach who taught me so much. And of course, without the help of Zoe, this book would not exist.

Novels by E.E. "Doc" Murdock

- **My Vietnam War**
- **A Psalm for Cock Robin**: A Harp and His (Dead) Mother Mystery
- **Crueltown**: A Drew Steele Los Angeles-Las Vegas Mystery
- **The End of the Civil War**: A Drew Steele Civil War Mystery
- **Who Owns Arizona**: A Drew Steele Civil War Mystery

1
A Representational Proposition of Suicide

My story begins when I go out and close the front door real quiet so Grandma won't hear me leave. I jump down the front porch steps three at a time. No time to waste. It's now or never.

I head for the bus stop, moving fast. No regrets. Time to get it over with.

You think you are embracing a proposition, but are you sure you are not just embracing a representational version of it?

"So now you decide to pop up, Old Man. Well, it's more than a representational proposition. Look at me; aren't I out here acting in the real world? Aren't I walking on a real sidewalk, beside a real street? This time, I'm really going to do it."

Think about this. The act you are proposing is only relative to your current stream of consciousness.

Oh shit. Now he's going to do his stop-and-analyze-your-stream-of-consciousness routine on me. Over-analysis is the last thing I need right now. I'd better shut him up. "This is not just my current stream of consciousness. I've thought this out, and I'm determined to do it."

Self-determined as you think this act may be, it is actually—

"Oh no you don't. Not this time. I'm done thinking about it. Today is the day. I'm heading there right now to do it."

But being, actually being, means taking responsibility for your choices.

"I'm not lis-en-ing, Old Man. I don't have time for another one of your boring lectures about the responsibilities to the self right now. No matter what you say, this time you can't stop me. I'm going to do what I should have done a long time ago."

And that sets him off whispering inside my head: propositional representations, self-fulfilling attitudes and personal responsibility, social and historical contextualization. Blah, blah, blah. This time, I'm not going to let him get to me. I know better than to argue with him because that's what he wants me to do. Arguing with him only eggs him on. Argument is what he lives for. (That was a joke, one of my death jokes. Did you get it? No? Here's a hint: he's been dead for at least a hundred years.) I hurry on down the sidewalk. I'll just keep going forward and ignore him. Let him keep up his endless whispering inside my head if that's what he wants to do, but I don't have to listen to him if I don't want to. Really, I don't. If I try hard enough, I'm pretty sure I can turn him off. And besides, no matter what he thinks, this time I *am* taking full responsibility for what I'm doing.

The matrix of associations that link God to consciousness should not be taken lightly.

Now he's going to play the God card. No way I can let him get away with that. "Not that old God argument again. It's beneath you, old dude. Besides, haven't you heard? God is dead. A guy named Nietzsche—after your time— took God out behind the woodshed and killed him. Stabbed him in the back. So, too bad, God is now deadern a doornail. Tough luck for the old dude, but that's how it goes when you've outlived your era. Yep, Nietzsche did him in, and Camus helped, leading God to cry out, 'You too, Camus?'" (That was one of my intertextuality jokes. Did you get it? Probably not. People never get my jokes. Well, too bad. If you can't keep up, you might as well quit reading right now.)

"Hey, just look around, Old Man. Do you see any God-given perfection in this fucked-up neighborhood? Do you see any flowers? No. The few flowers that were here got trampled underfoot years ago in the Rodney King riots, and not one of them ever grew back (and who can blame them?). All that's left are run-down houses with poor people inside them."

But bad as it is, it's my neighborhood now. I've been here ever since my Mom took off and I had to move in with my old Grandma. Not that me and Mom were living in such a great neighborhood before she took off; it just wasn't quite as bad as this one.

Mom did her latest disappearing act because the fat, mean-spirited landlord who lived in the other half of our ratty old, leaky-roof duplex finally got bored with having access to her body in lieu of paying the *way* overdue rent and threatened to toss us out if we didn't come up with some actual money. So Mom did what she always did, grabbed the first guy who came along. Her new guy paid the rent for a while, and then she and that guy took off and left me all alone.

After she disappeared, the asshole landlord kicked me out and kept all my stuff. Even my clothes and my computer. In lieu of rent, he said. I didn't care that he took my clothes. You can get clothes at any thrift store. All you have to do is put on the clothes right there in the store, like you're trying them on, and then you walk out the front door. Nobody notices. You probably think that's wrong. Well, it isn't. They get all that crap for free, so if I take one or two things, why should it matter to anybody? Besides, aren't they supposed to be for charity? They should give stuff to me if I don't have any money to buy it.

So the bastard landlord was only stealing the clothes that I'd already stolen from those thrift stores. BFD. I didn't need those clothes, and I didn't need any of my other crap either. Except for my laptop computer. That computer gave me access to the internet, the only thing in this stupid world that I do care about.

I waited until he went out, and then I got into his place through a back window the idiot had left open. I took back my computer, along with a bunch of coins he had in a big glass jar. I used the coins to take the bus south to my favorite place in all of LA, Point Fermin Park, a little park right at the edge of the ocean. The weather was good, so I could sleep hidden in the thick bushes and just hang out. I'd sit on the edge of *my* cliff, with my back to the monster that is LA, and look out at the ocean all day. I'd watch the big ships coming in from who knows where, heading for the LA harbor. Most of them were container ships, loaded with big steel container boxes stacked up so high it looked liked they might tip the whole ship over. Other container ships were always there too, heading out from the harbor on their way back to China, or wherever. Probably on their way to get another load of crap to sell to the American suckers.

And there was something even better to look at: whales. Sometimes, I'd see the spouts of those whales way out there. They were great. I wish you could have seen them. You couldn't actually see the whales themselves, but if you kept a sharp eye out, you could see the sudden little white umbrellas of water spout up, and that told you a whale was out there. I liked to think about those whales, just swimming along, no problems at all, just doing whatever whales do.

Then one day, I was sitting at the edge of my cliff, watching the tourist whale-watching boats chase the poor scared whales around, when a truant cop showed up. He said the neighbors had called about a kid living in the park. (Stupid nosy neighbors; why should they care if I wanted to hang out in the park?) The truant cop asked why I wasn't in school. I told him I was a genius and had graduated from high school early. He didn't believe me, probably because I'm so short and skinny, I didn't even look sixteen, which was how old I actually was at that time. Anyhow, he said he was going to take me home. I didn't want to tell him I didn't have a home, so I gave him the address of my grandma who lives in Watts.

He said, Watts? What's a skinny white kid like you doing living in Watts? Only black people live in Watts.

I told him my grandma had been living in her ratty old house in Watts since the old days when white people used to live there.

He put me in the back seat of his car, drove me to Watts, and dumped me at my grandma's house.

After that, I mostly stayed indoors at my grandma's place. I spent my days surfing the internet, reading just about anything I could find: history, science, psychology, philosophy. Whatever.

But why am I boring you with all that? After tonight, none of that will matter anyhow.

Intentionality represents the aboutness of your mental state, a conception, not the act itself.

"What? Are you saying that I'm afraid, that I'm not actually going to do it? Well, I am. I going to do exactly what I said I . . . "

No! I've got to stop talking to him. I can't let him get to me like that. I'm going to go take care of this on my own. Then he'll see that this time it isn't just a mental representation. Sure, I may have conceived of this act before and didn't do it, but this time is different. This time, I'm not going to get hung up on the rightness or wrongness of it, or even the meaning of it. This time, I will go forward and do it, with or without his help, and that will be the end of it, the end of everything.

What, you think I'm kidding myself? You think I can't do this without his help? Well, I can. I don't need him, not really. All I have to do is stay out of my head and focus on what I'm perceiving in the external world.

Okay, what am I perceiving? I'm perceiving that I'm walking to the bus stop, walking through a really bad neighborhood known as Watts, which is part of a somewhat larger area in Los Angeles known as South Central, the "bad" part of LA. I'm perceiving small, run-down houses with dark-skinned people inside of them. (Except for me and Grandma, all of the people who live in this neighborhood have dark skin.) There is fear in this neighborhood. All you have to do is look around, and you see it everywhere. Bars on every window of every house. Metal fences with spikes on top. Glowering pit bulls lurking behind the fences.

What else am I perceiving in the external world? I pass a house with plastic toys abandoned in the flat dirt front yard. Must be kids inside that house. A little red dump truck without wheels. A squashed yellow duck. A naked doll with one arm missing. Once colorful, the toys are now faded and stained from years and years of being handled by little grubby hands. Those few toys are probably the only ones these poor kids have ever had.

I never had many toys either. We were about as poor as these people, and Mom didn't think I needed toys anyhow. She used to say, What's the point of playing? What good is playing gonna do you when you grow up and have to go out and survive in this fucked-up world? She was right. Who needed toys? Bunch of plastic crap, mass produced and imported from China. Fake shit, all of it. Waste of money, waste of time. Better for me to just spend my time on the internet looking up stuff. While she was out getting boozed up every night, I spent my time on the internet. It made me the person I am today. (I like sarcasm, don't you? It's one of my main tools, and I'm good at using it.)

Speaking of kids, you won't see any at this time of day. It's approaching the time of day novel writers call gathering darkness, and that means the gangs will be coming out to take over the streets: drug dealing, fights, shootings. Nighttime in this neighborhood is not a safe place for kids—not safe for anybody, actually.

Speaking of nighttime, did you know we make up time? Time is not real, you know. That's why a while back (actually, it's been quite a while back if you want to believe in made-up concepts like actual discrete units of time), I decided to set the date on my computer to a random date. Then, I threw all the clocks in the house into the garbage. From that moment on, for me, life has been *right now.* When you live in the right now, things like my mother running off and leaving me all alone exist only within a concept commonly referred as "the past."

Actually, now that we're talking about made-up concepts, did you know *reality itself* is not real? The fact is, reality is only a kind of dream, a sketchy manifestation of personal meaning that we turn into a reality that works for each of us. And I'm not talking about nighttime asleep-in-bed type of dreaming; no, I'm talking about the whole ball of wax, this thing we think of as life. Sure, I know it's pointless to go around making everything up, but it's what we humans do. You see, inside of our heads, there's a part of our brains that's called the cortex. It's a wily thing, that cortex. It's a specialized organ for creating reality. It's job is to trick us into believing that what we've created is real. Old Man taught me that. He said that to understand reality we have to completely exclude every assumption we have in our brain, including the assumption of objective time. Not only that, he said the feeling that experiences seem to take place in a linear sequence is also wrong. Einstein said it too. He said he could prove mathematically that time is imaginary. So now, here's how I look at time: I think we're nothing but inchworms crawling along a make-believe yardstick. The yardstick is our made-up concept of time. We go on and on, thinking we're going forward, thinking time is actually passing, but the truth is, none of it is real. Things don't actually happen one after another; that's only our *perception,* a thing made up by our wily cortexes. Silly inchworms, us.

Not only do our silly cortexes make up time, we even have a habit of breaking time down into discrete units—days, months, years. And then we try to make those time units even more important by creating repeated blocks of time like spring and summer, fall and winter. What a waste of time. (That's my time joke. I like those kinds of jokes, and I hope you like them too. They show how absurd everything is.)

Now, if I *was* to believe in time, I might have to start wondering if I'm somewhere near a time-related age milestone that other humans seem to enjoy celebrating, a birthday. My mother told me I was born in the springtime; therefore, if this *is* the period humans think of as springtime, I may have passed —or may be about to pass—my eighteenth birthday.

Birthdays! Dumb. Pointlessly grand events that only exist in the minds of those discrete-units-of-time people. Whether I'm now eighteen or still seventeen doesn't matter one whit. My having a birthday doesn't matter to one other person in this world, so why should it matter to me? Besides, eighteen is nothing but a number, a mark on *their* calendar. What difference does it make if I'm eighteen today or not? I'll still be the same person I was yesterday.

Uh oh, speaking of reality, now I'm hearing a real sound that's coming from outside of my head, out in the so-called "real" world. It's getting closer, coming from behind me. It's a sound I recognize, a sound that could mean trouble. Time to pay attention to the outside world—for a little while anyhow.

I turn to look. Yeah, just as I thought: it's a neighborhood low rider, a gang car, coming up the street from behind me. I quickly turn away. It's better to not make eye contact with gang dudes.

The car's rumble is getting closer. I tell myself to just keep walking. Ignore them, and hopefully, they'll just go on past.

Unfortunately, the car doesn't go on past. I hear it slow down to match my walking pace. I sneak a look at them out of the corner of my eye. It's a shiny black car, a customized old car, lowered almost to the ground. Tinted windows all around. Chromed dual exhausts, tuned to fart out a low rattling note. Unbelievably loud rap "music" is coming out of the car's windows. They've probably got speakers imbedded in the ceiling and in all of the car's walls, and they've got the volume cranked all the way up to make sure their rap "music" can be clearly heard by everyone within ten blocks. The bass background of the rap goes thump, thump, thump, vibrating the air, setting off car alarms all along the street (which, I suppose, is the goal). The young, dark-skinned occupants inside their cool ride are sitting so low they can barely see out. As they very slowly drift past me, all heads turn to stare, all minds thinking, Hey, white boy, what you doin' in our neighborhood?

One of them leans halfway out the back-seat window, his arm hanging down along the side of the car, and in his hand, a big black pistol. He does his menacing staredown, waggling his big black pistol in my direction.

I look away and keep walking. They don't scare me. Not tonight. Tonight, they mean nothing to me. Besides, they're not real. I can make them go away if I want to. That asshole with his stupid gun doesn't even exist. None of this exists. I'm making this all up. I can, if I want to, make them disappear. I think *Go away.* I think it hard.

And it works. The driver revs up the powerful engine of their cool ride and burns rubber to make a point about how much power he has. As the car rumbles on down the block, I hear the Doppler shift of their booming pseudo-music going away from me. They turn at the corner ahead, and away, away, they go, deeper into the horror show that is 21st century South Central Los Angeles.

Okay, so much for that stupid distraction. Back to thinking. What was I thinking about? Oh yeah, I was thinking about creating reality. I spend a lot of my time thinking about reality, the *fact* that we *create* reality with that cortex part of our brains.

The world can only exist with reference to a mind.

"Ah, so you're back, Old Man."

The mental activity of each person determines the form within which the world appears.

"I was just telling them that. My thoughts create all reality."

Anything else is ontological dogmatism.

"Right on, Old Man. And that means life is pointless, right?"

No response.

Oh well, forget him.

Speaking of creating realities, let's not lose track of the reality I'm creating for you. As we continue to head for that bus stop, I want you to remember those bare-dirt front yards and those wary-eyed pit bulls that watched us closely as we passed. And don't forget those sad, abandoned plastic toys we saw. They're all important to this story because they're all *symbolic*, representative of the physical and mental poverty that surrounds us. Hey, I know it's a bleak world I'm creating for you. If you can't take it, you should stop reading right now. You might as well face it right here and now: this story is not going to turn out "nice." Okay, warning posted. If you're still with me, let's continue on to the bus stop.

In the reality I'm creating for you, something is about to happen, something that happens most every evening at about this time: the neighborhood gang homies begin to gather on the street corners, and the next intersection we're coming to is the favorite hangout of a small group of teenaged wannabe gang dudes. But maybe, if I hurry, I can get past "their" corner and make it to the bus stop which is a (relatively) safe zone—too many witnesses.

Uh oh. No such luck. I look ahead and see that they're already arriving at their staked-out corner. They're all dressed in the neighborhood-standard sloppy T-shirts and hanging-down, butt-crack-showing baggy pants. Stupid to dress all alike like that. Might as well be wearing signs that say, Hey, look at me, I'm a bad *gansta.*

I stop a ways away from them to watch them go through their ritualized greetings, complicated non-handshaking handshakes and restless feet. I don't know why, but for some reason, their ritual handshakes are paired with a weird kind of agitated feet-shuffling. It's almost like a kind of dance they always do.

I hesitate. Should I go over to the other side of the street? I know I should, but tonight, I don't feel like it. I decide to just stay where I am and watch them. They think they're so cool, but I know them for what they are, school dropout do-nothings. I doubt if one of them even made it past the ninth grade. They survive by doing juvie mule drug runs for the older gang kingpins. Between those runs, they just hang out, lookin' for action, lookin' for trouble.

Let's say, this time, I decide *not to* cross over to the other side of the street. "What do you think, Old Man? It's up to me, isn't it?"

No response. Does that mean the old man thinks I *should* cross over? Aw, to hell with him. Today, I don't really care what he thinks. Even though I know it's safer over there, this time I'm not going to let those young gang dudes have the satisfaction of seeing me act scared of them. I start walking right toward them, but so far, they haven't noticed me. Now that I think about it, they probably would *prefer* that I do cross over to the other side of the street. That would be safer for all of us; safer for me so I don't have to get beat up again, and also safer for them so they can yell insults at me from a safe distance. Beating up a crazy white kid once too often might make them lose face with their gang elders. But tonight, that's their problem. This time, I'm going to walk right through them, like I don't even see them, like they don't even exist. With what I'm about to do tonight, I don't feel one bit like acting scared of them. Tonight, I own this sidewalk just as much as they do.

Getting closer now, but so far, they're still so caught up in their posturing with each other they haven't noticed me. I stop next to a wooden utility pole that smells like old sun-burnt oil and listen to them go through their endless and pointless South Central ritualized greetings: "Yo, nigga. How goes?"

"Safe, bro."

An even younger one arrives to join their scene. He's walkin' cool like they all do: step, lean to one side, next step, lean to the other side. Exaggerated coolness. Stupid. Do they practice such nonsense at home in front of their mirrors? The young dudes already at the street corner greet the newcomer with the usual hand-slapping and nervous tap-dancing feet. "Sup, Lil G?"

Ah, so this one is nicknamed Little G. He looks to be no more than thirteen, and he's small for his age.

He pulls up his floppy white T-shirt and flashes a sliver pistol that's stuck in his waistband.

Uh oh, better be careful of that one. He's smaller than the others, and that means he's probably more dangerous—like one of those little snarly dogs that attempt to deny their tinyness by barking and biting, trying to make the great big world aware of them.

His buddies all lean in closer, admiring the pistol, oo-in and aw-in over it. He gets his reward: hand slapping, more restless feet dancing.

After all the approving of his new pistol is done with, Lil G takes out a joint and says, "Hey, how bout a bomb?" (I've read about that on the internet: it's a special Watts version of a marijuana joint that's laced with crack cocaine). He lights it up. Big inhale, then he passes it around to the others. He says something I can't make out because he's talking in a clenched whisper as he tries to hold down the smoke. They pass the bomb around, laughin' and grinnin' and leanin' forward, one after the other, to do their knee-slappin' holy-shit-this-is-good-shit jive talk in their raspy hold-the-smoke-down whispers.

I've had run-ins with these wannabe gangsters before. Even though they're a couple of years younger than me, they always try to prove they're tougher than me. They assume I'm weak just because my skin is lighter than theirs. Well, maybe I am weak, but it's not because of the color of my skin; it's only because I don't waste my time pumping iron like they do, something they probably learned in juvie detention.

These gang dudettes think this particular corner is their "turf," and to prove it, they make it a point to hassle me every time I pass by. Well, why not? Hey, I'm the only white kid in the neighborhood, so who else do they have to hassle? It's a ritual: they're dark-skinned, I'm light-skinned; therefore, hassling required. But I also know these wannabes are not as dangerous as they like to let on—not yet anyhow. They'll spend a bit more time in the reformatory where they'll learn meanness, and sooner or later, they'll end up in prison where they'll learn hardness and heartlessness. And then, once they're back here on the mean streets of South Central LA, as soon as they've proved they don't give a shit about anybody or anything, the older gang members will teach them how to deal drugs and fight and steal.

Uh oh, the dudettes have finally notice me. They all turn to stare. They're probably wondering why I didn't go over to the other side of the street this time. So, here we go. Time for another one of our little neighborhood dramas. They'll pretend to be tough little gangbangers, and I'm supposed to play the role of the scared white kid. We all have to play our part. Or so they think. But not tonight. Tonight, these young gang wannabes are in for a surprise.

As I approach, the one who must see himself as the leader—probably just because he's the tallest and has the most tattoos—leans forward and puts one hand above his eyes, like he's trying to be sure his eyes aren't deceiving him: a white boy is actually entering their turf. "Well, would ya look at this," he says. "Here come the crizm."

They all laugh at his joke, calling me a crizm. I've heard it before. Some kind of Watts insult for whities like me. Very funny. Acting like he's wondering who I might be. Oh, ha ha. He knows me. All the gang homies around here know me. I'd be an anomaly even if I wasn't crazy; when you're the only light-skinned boy in the neighborhood, you stand out, and when you're the kid who's always mumbling to himself, you *really* stand out. They must see me as totally different from them, *opposite* from them, actually, a skinny white out-of-place ghost among the dark shadows that rule this neighborhood. Okay, so they *do* rule this neighborhood. But tonight, I rule because tonight I'm not scared of them. Because of what I'm about to do this very night, I have no reason to be scared of anybody.

They continue to stare at me as I walk right up to them. I like this feeling of not being scared. Feels *good*. Feels *damn good*. In fact, it feels so good, maybe I should have a little fun with them. I hold my arms out toward them and say, "Well, if it isn't the triplets. Hey, dudes, did your mommies dress you all the same like that?"

At first, they look truly shocked. Am I dissing them? Dissing somebody in this neighborhood can carry the death penalty. But then they look at each other and come to a realization: it's only the crazy white kid. They crack up. Knee slapping. High fivin'. Ha, ha, ha. It's the crazy white kid. Always good for a laugh. Next, they commence showing me some of their stupid hand-twisting gang signs, fingers twisted into something like letters, I guess, or symbols of some sort. I don't know what those hand gestures mean, and they know I don't know. They think that makes them so cool. The truth is, it actually makes them laughable—brainless mimics of each other, self-absorbed cartoon cutouts.

But even while they're laughing at me, they're gradually forming a semicircle barrier in front of me to keep me from going forward.

They are no longer laughing, so it must be time for the threats. And after that, it'll be time for the getting beat up part. Maybe I *should have* gone over to the other side of the street, and I probably *shouldn't have* made fun of them because tonight I don't want to be bothered with them. I really should have kept my focus on getting to that bus stop.

Maybe I can just push right on through them. That might work if I don't make any more eye contact; eye contact makes them think I'm challenging them, and they'd have to respond to that and I'd have to waste even more time getting beat up.

But I can't seem to make myself ignore them. Tonight, for the first time ever, it feels like it would be more fun to continue the game. On this night of all nights, why not? So I stand my ground and make up some of my own weird hand-twisting signs. They don't mean anything to me, but I act serious, as if they do.

They look puzzled. They look at each other, but none of them can figure out what I'm up to. Maybe they're not even smart enough to realize I'm making fun of them.

I laugh real loud to make sure they know it's a joke, and then, I do make eye contact, a kind of so-what-are-you-going-to-do-about-it kind of eye contact.

My little hand-twisting trick seems to have gotten their attention. Now, they're starting to wonder if this crazy white kid *really is* making fun of them They're starting to look pissed off.

Damn, why did I do that? I really don't have time for this nonsense tonight. So, what's driving me? Is it because tonight is the end, the real end of it all? But what if they decide to really hurt me? I might not be able to make it to the bus stop to get to where I need to go. I'd better knock it off. No more eye contact, no more fun and games. I'd better just get going to that bus stop.

I try to edge around them, but the leader dude jumps in front of me. He puts a ridiculous grin on his face and sticks out his fist like he wants to bump fists. He says, "What say, ooo-fay?"

His voice is shrill, artificial, a jokester's voice. He says it friendly-like, and he's still grinning; it's as if he's saying, Hey, let's let bygones be bygones. So what if we beat you up a few times in the past?

Stupid. Pretending to be friendly. He's no friend of mine. I know it, and he knows it. And his little pals know it too. The gang he's hoping to soon join would probably throw him out, or worse, if he really did get friendly with a white boy. In this neighborhood, it's understood to be a joke if you act friendly to a white person.

I try to ignore him. The darkening sky to the west tells me I really do need to hurry up and get out there to San Pedro. These idiots mean nothing to me. Why am I wasting time with them? Tonight, nothing should matter to me except getting down there to Point Fermin Park, the end of land here in LA, and the end of the world for me. It's only a bit of a bus ride away, and then, it will all be over. Compared to what I'm going to do out there tonight, these gang nitwits are nothing. They are mere specs of dust on the sidewalk. I can walk right through them if I want to. I try to push through them, but the tattooed guy steps quick to block my way. And then he starts bouncing from one foot to the other, his fists up.

What the hell is he doing? Oh, now I get it. He's ducking and bobbing like some kind of idiotic prize fighter: duck, bob, jab. It's stupid. No other word for it. Is this going to be just some dumb clowning around, or will they decide, once again, to beat the shit out of me? The others are grinning, watching, waiting.

But I will do nothing. If he wants to dance, fine. I'll just ignore him and talk to the old man. "What do you think of these idiots, Old Man?"

Each individual must share in the collective responsibility of the society.

"What? You think I'm responsible for them? Like I *owe it* to my society not to cause a ripple in the pond? Bullshit. Take it from me, you old fart, life in this society is no lovely pond. Life in this society is shit, and if you lived in this fucked-up time period, you'd know it."

The gang dude leader has suddenly stopped dancing. He's staring at me. He turns back to his friends, a question on his face. They're all staring at me. The one they called Lil G does a circular motion with his finger around his ear.

Oh, I get it: they think my whispering means I'm nuts. They don't understand that I'm exploring an important philosophical concept.

"Ow!" Damn. That dancing gang dude hit me in the stomach. I guess my whispering to myself pissed him off.

It hurt when he hit me, but I pretend it didn't. This asshole kid can't hurt me. Not tonight. From this moment on, I will not recognize him as part of my reality. He doesn't even exist.

He goes back to ridiculous dancing, fists up, ducking and bobbing.

One of his jabs hits me in the shoulder. That one hurt too, but I don't let on. I've been hit harder. A lot harder.

He's still dancing, and he hits my other shoulder. I don't react. I ignore him. Let him duck and bob like some kind of idiotic grinning Mohammed Ali. It means nothing to me. I'll just think about other things. Like . . . words! I should think of some really good words to describe these idiots. Let's see. How about moronic? Or brainless? That's a good one. How about . . . dimwitted? That's another good one. Or ludicrous. That's an even better one. What are some more? Asinine. Mindless. Witless. Yeah, I should use that one on him. The next time he hits me, I look right at him, grin, and say, "Witless."

He hits me in the stomach again.

The blow doubles me over, but I quickly stand up, look straight at him, and calmly say, "Asinine."

He's ready to hit me again, but he hesitates. He seems confused. He stops dancing. He's trying to figure out if my words could possible be aimed at him. I can almost see some kind of slow clunky wheels turning inside his head. He's thinking, Could this white dude possibly be making fun of me? Me who is so cool, being made fun of by this skinny little white kid who is not cool at all? Naw, couldn't be.

His pals can't figure out why he stopped dancing and hitting. They wait. There's a bad silence.

But then, he recovers and goes back to dancing. Maybe he doesn't know what else to do. Hitting me isn't doing any good; I just started saying odd words. He thought he was the cat toying with the mouse, except the mouse is not cooperating. The mouse is not acting scared. For some reason, tonight the mouse is acting downright weird. It makes me think of something I read on the internet. It was about a theory of human motivation called "cognitive dissonance." It said cognitive dissonance is created when you're confronted with information that conflicts with your beliefs. So, you have to reduce the dissonance. Maybe if I can convince him that I'm just a crazy person, not worth bothering with, he'll be able to reduce his cognitive dissonance about how I'm acting by deciding I'm not worth the bother. I say, "Attunement is correlated with authentic existence."

He stops dancing and stares at me.

I say, "Being appropriated by the event of appropriation is not an individualistic way of living. The world becomes visible as a communication structure."

The dancer turns back to the others for help. They also look puzzled.

Okay, that worked pretty well. Now, I should just eliminate them from my reality. I push forward through the middle of them and head on down the sidewalk.

So far, so good. They're not chasing me. I bet the dancing dude is glad I got him out of a situation that was causing him too much cognitive dissonance.

But then, I hear one of them yell, "Hey, motherfucker."

I look back. It's the youngest one, the little snarly dog kid they called Lil G. He's got his stupid pistol out, and he's aiming it at me.

So he's got a gun. BFD. I will not be scared. Not this time. With what I'm going to do tonight, I no longer have to give a shit about what any of these half-wits do. I give him the finger and keep walking, casual like. That little gun-toter won't take kindly to me giving him the finger, so maybe I'll get a bullet in the back. Fine with me. I'll be dead, and he'll spend the rest of his life in prison. He probably would have anyhow.

In this particular reality I'm creating, I don't get shot in the back. I guess I convinced them that it wasn't worth the bother to kill me.

Okay, let's say I make it to the bus stop. A tired-looking dark-skinned lady in a tired-looking old black dress is there with her two little girls. The lady keeps looking at her watch like she thinks the bus is late (which it always is), but I know it's just a way for her to keep from looking at me. The dark-skinned folks in this neighborhood—at least the adults—never look directly at the weird light-skinned kid if they can help it. But the little girls *do* stare at me. I'm sure they've seen plenty of light-skinned people on TV, but never around here. Maybe they wonder why I'm not on TV instead of in *their* neighborhood.

The bus comes, and the dark-skinned family gets on ahead of me. They sit up front, and I go to sit in the back. Except for me, it's only dark-skinned people on this bus: the lady with her two girls and some old folks. Two older women who are sitting up behind the driver have their heads together, whispering. They both have hair that's dyed a weird dark red color. It makes me think about my mother's hair. But her red hair is real, and she's damn proud of it. She once told me her father was suspicious of her red hair. He'd get drunk and say, Who in our family ever had red hair? How did a redhead get in our woodpile? Then, he'd put on a fake scowl and say, Now that I think about it, that damn milkman had red hair, didn't he? Mom said he would always laugh at his own joke, but maybe he really was suspicious. Maybe he had good reason to be. I never met that boozing old grandfather. Mom said he was quite a character, well known at the local bars. But eventually, he took off and was long gone before I came along. He left Grandma all alone, and according to Mom, Grandma was pretty pissed off about that. And I never knew my own father either. Mom always made a point of saying she never knew "which one" it was. She always said it with a laugh, and then, she'd hold up her glass of booze and say, Let's drink to the bastard, whoever he was.

And now Mom is gone too. Took off like my grandfather. Took off like my unknown pop. I guess running off is in my family's genes. Mom did her latest disappearing act with some Hispanic-looking guy that was always showing her maps of South America and telling her they should go down there so she could see how beautiful it was. I guess that means he must have come from down there. I never trusted that bastard. He pronounced his name something like Ahnhel. I looked up Hispanic names on the internet, so I guess his name must have been spelled like "Angel." But I can guarantee you he was no angel. He had nervous eyes and a mean laugh, and when he got extra drunk, I didn't like the way he looked at me. Kind of spooky. So to myself, I called him "An-hell," and whenever he came over to our house, I stayed in my room. But I could still hear him and Mom out there in the kitchen through the paper-thin walls. They'd get home from the bars late at night, drunk as skunks, and sit at our kitchen table looking at that map of South America. He was always going on and on about how great it was down there, all green and everything. I guess he was trying to lure her away to an alcoholic life down there in South America that was better than the alcoholic life she was living here in LA. Anyhow, one night after looking at that map for a long time, she took off with him, and she never came back. I guess they must have somehow scraped up enough money to get themselves down there. At first, I missed her. A lot. I kept on wondering when she would come back. All the other times she took off, she always came back, sooner or later. But this time, she didn't. I guess she'd rather be down there in South America with that jerk than be here with me. Well, good for her. I hope she and that and that stupid old An-hell are having a ball down there. Now, I don't miss her anymore. In fact, now I'm glad she's gone because now I can do anything I want to. I don't have to go to school, and there isn't anybody who gives a shit about me, so I don't have to give a shit about anybody either. After that stupid truant cop dropped me at Grandma's house, I told her Mom had run off to South America, so Grandma made a deal with me: she'd let me stay if I'd take care of the house and bring her stuff to eat. That way, she can stay in bed and watch her stupid TV soap operas all day long, and I can just be on the internet.

I bring my focus back to the reality of the bus. All of the dark-skinned people on the bus are ignoring me, so I ignore them too. I look out the window. This part of LA looks as tired as the people on this bus. We pass by one run-down neighborhood after another. This is the part of LA that everybody else would like to forget about. No mans land. The forgotten place where "those" poor black people live.

The bus takes us through one of the few South-Central business districts. Not many businesses left in this part of town. They all closed down and ran away after the Rodney King riots. A lot of the businesses got burned down during the riots, or else they got burned out later by their owners to collect insurance so they could get the hell out of here. The few ragged businesses that still exist around here seem to be barely hanging on. We pass an open-air car repair shop that used to be a Shell gas station. The gas pumps are gone, and it looks like the place was partially burned out. The Shell sign is still there, with the day-before-Rodney King 1992 gas price: 89.9 cents per gallon. The big yellow Shell sign is full of bullet holes. Gang kids taking target practice, I guess. A rough-plywood sign has been nailed up over the open car-repair bay: "BODY SHOP"—hand-painted in clumsy dripping-down red letters. They probably mostly do insurance scams. Inside the darkness of the place, sparks from some kind of grinding machine bounce off of the greasy concrete.

We go on, passing block after block of vacant weedy lots that are strewn with garbage and half-buried old tires. Scraps of dirty paper rise up and flip over from the wind of our big square bus as we roar by.

We pass a liquor store and a really big gun store, and then, a used car lot with a handful of dusty cars that nobody will ever buy. A string of tattered plastic red and white triangular flags sag down on top of the cars. The whole neighborhood seems as worn out as those used cars: shabby buildings, sun-faded cars, streets full of potholes—all of it beat down, bushed, bone-weary. Smog always hangs over this area, muddying the sunset, turning the air a weird yellow-brownish color. We all live in a place where the air stinks. It stings our eyes and makes it hard to breath, but everybody's too tired to care anymore. It's on us and inside of us, but it's become so much a part of us that we don't even notice it anymore. We probably all smell like LA smog. If the Star Trek people beamed us out to Iowa or some place like that, the people that live there would say, "What's that smell?"

We finally get to the Carson bus terminal where I get off and transfer to the southbound bus that will take me down to San Pedro. I sit at the very back, as usual, and a group of bummed-out-looking men sit up front near the driver. Do they feel safer up there? Are they staying away from me? They're all wearing the same kind of gray uniform. Harbor workers, I guess, night shifters, heading for work with their lunch pails and their sour attitudes.

Theoretical attitude versus objective perspective.

"Didn't I say I was going to ignore you, Old Man? I know I'm perceiving things in my own unique way, but so what?"

The harbor workers turn to stare at me, like they think I'm talking to them. Then, they quickly turn away. I bet I make them nervous. Crazy people always make the "normal" people nervous. They think crazy means unpredictable, and unpredictable makes them nervous. They prefer it when things are predictable. That's why they make sure nothing ever changes in their boring lives. But if they work together at the harbor, I wonder why they don't talk to each other. They must not like each other. Nobody likes anybody anymore. You-versus-meism has become the norm of the world now.

I stare out the window at the cars that surround us. This bus and about a zillion cars are all creeping along on the freeway, getting nowhere fast. We move forward a little, stop, move forward, stop again. Typical LA traffic. They keep on adding more and more lanes to LA freeways, but the traffic still barely moves. Nobody can get to where they want to be, so every driver in every car is impatient.

Not moving is making me feel impatient too. If those asinine gang homies hadn't held me up so long, I would have been there by now. I lean my forehead against the bus window and stare down at the people in their cars. Light-skinned people mostly. All heading out of the city from their downtown jobs, just like they do every day, escaping to their expensive homes up in the Palos Verdes hills. So many cars. One person in each car. A lot of them talking and texting on their cell phones. They look bored, and none of them look happy. Hey, I'll tell you something I read on the internet. I read that psychologists say time seems to move more slowly when you're unhappy. I bet those people in their fancy cars must exist in a constant state of slowed-down time. No wonder they're unhappy: getting up in the morning, suffering through the same old slow, slow morning rush-hour drive to work, somehow getting through yet another day at their same old boring jobs, and then doing the reverse slow, slow drive back home every evening. They're like that Sisyphus guy I read about. In Greek legend, a guy named Sisyphus was this crafty king who killed a lot of people in misguided wars (sound familiar?). Eventually, he got too big for his britches and betrayed one of the Greek gods, so Zeus, the chief god, ordered him chained up and sent down to Hell. But once he was down there, crafty old Sisyphus asked the Devil to demonstrate how the chains worked, and as the Devil was demonstrating, Sisyphus managed to get *him* chained up. Now, *that* caused a real problem up on Earth because with the Devil chained up down in Hell, the rulers couldn't conduct a decent war because their enemies wouldn't die. Also, no old people were dying, so things were getting too crowded. And the rulers could no longer do human sacrifices because the human sacrifices wouldn't die either. So, the other gods had to intervene. They released the Devil and vowed to make life so miserable for Sisyphus that he would wish *he* was dead. They made him push a giant boulder up this really steep hill, and once he got the boulder to the top, they made it roll right back down, so he'd have to go down and start pushing it up all over again. Those people in all those cars are just like Sisyphus, going through the motions, pushing their particular boulder over and over again, until they finally get out of this slo-mo nightmare by dying.

But not me. I won't get caught living a life like that. The solution is in my own hands, and tonight is the night I will take that option.

The search for meaning in life is futile.

"That's exactly what I was telling them, Old Man. The secret to life is to realize right from the start that there's no meaning to any of it."

Belief provides hope, and hope provides the meaning.

"Oh no, you're not gonna go into that old God argument again, are you? Talk about absurdity. Listen, Old Man, believing in something for which there's not a shred of evidence is the real absurdity. You want to know what I think? I don't think anybody actually *believes* in religion anymore; they just use it to justify what they want to do. Like over there in the Middle East where the nut cases use religion to suppress their women and to justify killing people in endless so-called religious wars. So, you might as well forget about God making up our reality for us."

Reality is no less real just because we make it up.

"You and I know that, but what about these people?" I point at the men sitting up at the front of the bus. "They have no clue."

Uh oh. The guys in the harbor worker uniforms are turning around to stare. They look pissed at me. I guess I was I talking a little too loud.

I go back to looking about the window. Who cares if those guys stare at me. We're almost to San Pedro anyhow. I would have known where we were even if I had my eyes closed because we're going past the oil refineries. Even with all the bus windows closed, the smell of the refinery is overpowering. Those big oil refineries are right next to the freeway, and they let off acidic, choking smoke. Orange flames from the burn-off pipes lick at the dark sky. It kind of reminds me of Mordor, which is an imaginary really bad place I read about in a book called *Lord of the Rings*. Have you read it? I read it in the school library when I was supposed to be studying. In the book, Mordor was described as a barren wasteland with fire, ash, and dust, a place where the very air you breathe is a poisonous fume. Sounds like here, doesn't it? I can't imagine how the people who live near here can stand it.

At the end of the freeway, most of the cars head up into the hills to their houses. Our bus turns down the hill toward the harbor. As we go along next to the harbor fence, I look out the bus window at the big container ships that are in the process of being unloaded. It's almost completely dark now, and the high-up bright yellowish lights of the harbor are trying to burn through the smog. The tall cranes look like huge, awkward preying mantises as they pluck the big steel boxes off of the ships and lower them down onto waiting flat-bed trucks. As soon as a truck is loaded, it drives away, and the next one pulls up to take its place. A long line of empty trucks are waiting for their turn to get loaded, all of them idling and putting out puffs of black diesel smoke to help create even more smog.

The bus stops by the entrance to the harbor. The harbor workers get off the bus and head for the harbor gate. I get off and go the other way, up the hill. I'm heading for Point Fermin Park where *my cliff* is waiting. Point Fermin Park is the furthest south part of LA. Look at a map. See that tit of land sticking out into the ocean? That's Point Fermin Park. It's where LA ends and ocean begins.

When I get to the park, I head straight for my cliff. I've taken this walk before, but this time is different. This time, I've thought it through, and nothing is going to stop me.

It's completely dark now, and it's especially dark in this park because most of the lights along the sidewalk have long ago burned out, or were knocked out, and no one has bothered to fix them. Doesn't matter; I've been here so many times, I could probably walk this sidewalk with my eyes closed. I decide to try it. I close my eyes and walk normally. It works. I come to the fence next to the cliff without ever once stepping off the sidewalk. Pretty good, eh? I lean against the fence and look out at the dark ocean. There are moving lights out there. Must be a ship coming in from somewhere far away, heading for the LA Harbor. Too dark now to see the ship itself, so its lights seem to float along on top of the sea. Only a few lights. That means it's not a cruise ship. Cruse ships are always lit up like a fucking Christmas tree when they pass by here at night. I wonder if they only do that when they're coming into a harbor. To put on a big show. So, this one must be one of the big container-carrying monster ships, like the ones I saw being unloaded down there in the harbor channel.

I look at the part of the sidewalk that's on the other side of the fence. A few feet out, it's broken clean off. I wonder how long ago it broke off. You can tell the sidewalk used to go out a lot farther. In fact, I bet this whole park used to be a lot bigger. It's like some giant monster is constantly gnawing away at the edge of the cliff, making the park smaller and smaller. I wish the protective fence wasn't here. Then the broken-off sidewalk would just end, sticking out into space like a diving board. If people tried to go for a walk in the park when it was real dark, they would just walk out into mid-air like Wile E. Coyote. That would be *funny*. I think about how many times I've leaned against this shaky old fence. Once, I actually climbed over the fence and edged my way out to the end of the broken-off sidewalk. I half expected the sidewalk to collapse from my weight and fall all the way down to the bottom of the cliff with me still standing on it. But it didn't. From out there, standing right at the edge, I was able to look straight down. A hell of a long drop down there to the rocks and crashing surf below. I got that feeling of how easy it would be to just take one more step. Just one more step, and it would be all over. But that night, I didn't take that one more step. I got a scared feeling and hurried back to the safety of the fence. I was shaking. I guess that was the first time I really thought about doing it, thought *seriously* about dying, about not existing anymore. Stupid. Why should anybody be scared of dying?

The true existentialist is aware of the absurdity of existence.

"Exactly right, Old Man. But most people don't get the fact that life is absurd, and death is the only escape. They don't even realize that death is the end. Kaput. All that hocus pocus about heaven and hell is nothing but a bunch of crap made up by people scared of dying."

The concept of life-ending is sense-giving in that it provides choice.

"Right. But I do have choice. In the reality I'm creating right now, I have the choice not to live in this reality anymore."

Choice creates meaning.

"Okay, then this is my meaning. I'm tired of pushing a stupid boulder back up to the top every day. To hell with it."

No response.

I guess he finally realizes that this time I'm serious. Old Man has given me some good advice in the past, but this time I'm not going to be changing my mind. Tonight, I *will* take that last step into nothingness. What better way to celebrate my eighteenth birthday, if I really am close to my eighteenth birthday. It's my way to "celebrate" my last day on this stupid earth. Let me tell you something. As soon as I got up this morning, I knew this was going to be my last day. After I finished fixing Grandma her breakfast, I got on the internet to look up the subject of suicide. There are *a lot* internet sites that talk about suicide, but mostly, they're dumb suicide-help sites. I did finally find some more interesting sites that talked about the long history of suicide and laws about it. Did you know that some countries still have laws against killing yourself? In countries like India, you can get up to a year in prison for trying to kill yourself (assuming you don't succeed). North Korea has the strictest laws against it. In North Korea, you don't even get off scot free if you successfully commit suicide; frustrated that they can't punish a person who successfully commits suicide, they punish the surviving relatives instead. I bet my grandma will be surprised if tomorrow morning they come to haul her away to jail. But here in the United States, killing yourself is no longer against the law. Good to be on the right side of the law. (I told you I like sarcasm, didn't I?)

If I would have told anybody about what I'm going to do tonight, the "authorities" might have tried to diagnose me as suffering from depression or something stupid like that. I can guarantee you I'm not depressed. And I know *exactly* what I'm doing. Their little rules are only made up to make themselves feel better. They want to make out that killing yourself is a crazy thing to do, but I'm amazed a lot more people don't do it. The way most people live their miserable lives, what's the point in staying alive anyhow?

This morning, knowing what I was going to do today, I started looking on the internet for what psychologists and psychiatrists might have to say about suicide. Turns out, they were pretty negative about it. Figures. They make a lot of money off of people by convincing them they're crazy, and they wouldn't want to lose any paying customers. They've staked out a pretty profitable place in our good old pay-money-to-get-help system of American capitalism, and they aren't about to let go of it. The whole absurd idea of paying money to fix your head reminds me of a funny old Peanuts cartoon I saw on the internet. In the cartoon, a little girl named Lucy has set up a wooden stand next to the sidewalk with a sign that says "Psychiatric Help – 5 cents." I bet she gets a lot of kid customers these days; life in the 21st century is hard for kids in the city, so I bet they'd gladly cough up five cents for any kind of real "psychiatric help." But no matter how much they pay the shrink, I know it won't work. If people act crazy, it's because it works for them. It's their way of surviving in a mad world. The *really* crazy thing would be to go to a shrink doctor to get help because all they do is talk to you. How is just talking to you supposed to help? The very idea is absurd. It's pretty obvious to me that the shrink business is just another American capitalist scam. And I should know. Back when I was going to school, they said I had mental problems. What a joke. I didn't have mental problems. I was the only one who was seeing things clearly. Everybody else has the shared mental problem of thinking everything is *so* real. But it's not, even though those shrinks will try to convince you that it is. And they'll try to convince you that mental illness is an actual thing. Ha! The term, mental illness, only describes a certain degree of deviation from a society's preferred norms. The result is that the definition of mental illness changes from society to society. Here's an example: if you talk to God, that's fine, you're just praying, but if you say you're talking to your own special God, the one you just now made up, they'll say you're nuts and send you to a psychiatrist who will give you expensive pills to make sure you only pray to the God *they* made up. Don't you think that's funny? Giving you pills to make you pray only to the "approved" God. Besides, if God really existed, He wouldn't have much time to listen. He'd be too busy helping athletes win races and such. (I told you to expect sarcasm.)

Well, no matter what people say, I'm not crazy. Maybe I do things different from other people, but that doesn't mean I'm crazy. Not really. Back when I was still (occasionally) going to high school, they sent me to the school counselor. I assumed they'd sent me to him because the other students were always calling me the crazy kid. But when I got to his office, he said that wasn't it. He said he'd called me in because some stupid teacher had complained to him about my sarcasm. He put on his fake sympathetic look and said my sarcasm was going to give me nothing but trouble in life. He went on and on with that kind of crap. I refused to even look at him. I kept my eyes locked on his idiotic bowling trophies that were on the shelf behind him. When he finally wound down, I told him I wasn't worried because most people were so dumb they didn't even get that I was being sarcastic. He said I should look at him when he was talking to me, but I wouldn't do it. I just kept on looking at his stupid trophies. He was a pretty fat guy, and I could just imagine him at some bowling alley trying to knock down a bunch of stupid bowling pins that were almost exactly the same shape as him. Picturing it made me laugh out loud. That got him red-faced pissed at me, but I couldn't stop giggling. Then, he tried to hide his anger. He pulled himself together and went back to looking "professional." He said that just because my IQ test said I was supposed to be some kind of hotshot genius, it didn't give me the right to make fun of people. Then, I did look at him. I looked right at his fat face and asked him what other kind of fun do I have? I said, What's the use of being a genius if you can't make fun of everybody who isn't? I could tell he was disgusted with me. But I didn't give a shit what he thought. He didn't really care about me. He was just pretending. It was his job to pretend to care. Then, he leaned across his stupid desk and told me I should use my gift to better the world. I looked back at his moronic bowling trophies and told him fat chance of that happening, the world was going to hell in a hand-basket, and there was nothing I or anybody else could do about it. He shook his head and dismissed me from his office. I never got called in there again. I bet he just wrote me off. BFD. I wrote him off too.

Anyhow, that was then and this is now. Doesn't matter anymore. Now, it's time to do what I came here to do. I hop over the fence and move out to where the sidewalk is broken off. I can see black rocks and white waves way down there. I look out at the blackness of the ocean. It brings home what I'm about to do, and it comforts me. So, this is really it. This time, I want to be sure I'm really, really aware of what I'm doing. It will be almost like a celebration. I'll "celebrate" my almost eighteenth birthday in style. Make a big splash, so to speak. But not really. I don't want to hit the water, that's for sure. I'll have to jump straight down to be sure I land on rocks, not out in the water. I lean way out and look down. So close now. Almost ready. I put my arms out to the side with my fingers spread out as if I'm about to fly away like a bird. I feel a slight breeze coming up off the ocean. It's almost like an invisible hand holding me back, keeping me from leaning out too far. I hear the ocean waves down there smashing into the rocks, making an ominous rumble. Ominous. That's a good word. The rhythmic sound of those waves hitting the rocks down below *is* ominous, hypnotic, like it's calling to me: come down, come down here with us. Come on, jump.

"Yes, I hear you. I am going to jump. I'm ready to jump. That's why I'm here." I realize I said that out loud, and I said it pretty loud. I look around to see if anybody heard. But there's nobody in the park.

Figures. Point Fermin Park is not a place anyone would want to go to at night. Gangs hang out here. You can tell by the gang graffiti all over the place. But tonight, the gangs must be off causing trouble somewhere else. Thank goodness. I want to do this all by myself. I'm not trying to make any kind of statement. I don't need an audience.

I lean forward a little more and look straight down. Old Man once told me I should look into the abyss and think about meaning. Well, that's what I'm doing, and guess what? I'm not afraid. Not at all. I can even imagine myself falling. I'll be exceptionally brave all the way down, and I'll be glad to feel the wind on my face as I fall. I'll actually enjoy the cooling mist and the smell of the sea air, and I'll be happy to finally get it over with. That reminds me: as I fall, I should try to do a perfect swan dive to be sure it's my head that hits the rocks first. As I think about that, I realize I've never actually done a swan dive, or any other kind of dive. While the other kids at the pool were showing off their bravery and their swan diving skills, I was hiding my pasty-white skin in the shade of the building, sitting cross-legged on a chair made of hard plastic that stuck to my sweaty legs, reading an important book—maybe Kafka or Dostoevsky—to show them I was a brainy kid, and a brainy kid like me didn't have time to do any silly swan diving. I remember their excited squeals as they jumped off of the high board. And I still have that image of them, as if they're still stuck up there in mid-air, all knobby knees and cleverly pointed hands reaching out to meet the water, sort of like they were doing some kind of upside-down praying. I bet they all thought they were real swan-diving pros. Well, if those kids were here tonight, I'd show them how to do a *real* swan dive, a perfect swan dive that none of them would have the guts to try. I bet they wouldn't even dare get this close to the edge. Odd, I haven't thought much about those kids since the day I dropped out of high school. They're probably all graduated by now, probably all working at dumb jobs, flipping burgers, or delivering pizzas. I used to hear some of them talking about joining the Army after they got out of high school, so maybe they're over getting their asses shot off at wherever the current American war of invasion is (I no longer bother to keep track of this country's endless wars). And even though the high school I went to was right in the middle of a big fat slum—mostly poor whites and poor Mexicans—it's possible that maybe a few of them even went off to college. I wonder what those kids would think of me swandiving off of a cliff. I can see the headline: "Young man commits suicide by jumping off cliff at Point Fermin Park." But they probably won't even remember me. Or if they do, they'll probably say, Oh him, the weird kid.

Suicide. That's what the newspapers will call it. A negative term. A head-shaking-and-mouth-frowning term for what is actually a brave thing to do. They won't think of it as brave though; they'll probably think of it as dumb. But what do they know? They don't know a thing about it, and don't want to. Me, I know a lot about suicide. Like I said, I looked it up on the internet. Some of the internet sites quoted "experts" on the subject, most of them saying the same dumb thing, that suicide is a permanent solution to a temporary problem. Bullshit. This shitty existence they call life is not just a temporary problem; it's something you have to put up with every Goddam day, day after day, year after year. The "experts" also said it was a mean thing to do, a way to get back at anyone who loves you. Even if that was true, it doesn't apply to me because I don't have any of that. Nobody loves me. Even my Mom didn't really love me, even though she was always saying she did. She'd come home real drunk in the middle of the night and wake me up to slobber all over me with her drunken kisses and tell me how much she loved me. She'd call me her smart little genius boy and say how proud she was of me. I wish that damn school counselor had never told her about that stupid IQ test he gave me. And my grandma, Mom's mother, doesn't love me either. She pays less attention to me than Mom did. The truth is, poor old Grandma's forgotten how to love anybody or anything except her TV soap operas and her pills. She's so out of it, she doesn't even know what day it is. A while back, I tested her by asking her if she even knew who the president of the United States was. Without taking her eyes off of her stupid TV, she said it was that cowboy actor who used to advertise Chesterfield cigarettes. She was talking about Ronald Reagan! That's how far caught in the past Grandma is.

I wonder if she'll miss me when I'm dead. She'll probably only miss having somebody there to make her three-times-a-day toasted cheese sandwiches and her cup of canned mushroom soup, not too hot because she might burn her delicate old lips, and it always has to be in her little fine-white China cup, the one with the stupid pink flowers all over it. Oh no, I'd better not even *try* to bring her soup in a different cup. So, I have to carefully wash that fragile little cup as soon as she's done with it, so it'll be ready when she tinkles her stupid little bell for her next meal, her bell of command, her bell of dominance, her bell that reminds me who is paying the bills. When that bell calls me, her loyal servant—loyal slave is more like it—better come running to her bedroom for whatever she wants this time.

Wait a minute. Did I just feel movement under me? I think I hear a creaking sound. Is this piece of old sidewalk about to break off?

No! I jump back away from the edge.

Jesus, that creaking was scary.

But I didn't jump back because I was afraid. It's just that I don't want to go like that. When I go, I want it to be because I'm ready. And I don't want anybody to think it was an accident, some stupid old sidewalk breaking off. For some reason, I'm out of breath. You probably think that means I'm going to chicken out again. But I'm not. Not this time. This time I really am going to do it. Being out of breath only means I'm having a good solid realization of what I'm about to do. When I jump, I want to feel the significance of what I'm doing, all the way down.

I turn to look back at the park, the world I'm about to leave. The stupid old park will be the last thing I'll see before I die. I bet you didn't know there's even such a place as Point Fermin Park. It sure isn't anything like what you'd think of when you hear the word *park*. There are no swings for the kiddies, no grass for playing softball or for kicking around a soccer ball. In fact, the grim little "park" looks like it was specially designed to be a gang hangout, a place nobody else would want to go. There's nothing but flat dirt, that's rarely trod upon, except for when the gangs show up to do their stupid planned beatings that welcome a new member to the group. I used to watch them do it from my hiding place in the bushes. It was an interesting idea, beating a guy up to show you like him, that you accept him. It made sense, in a weird way. Anyhow, the reason there's no grass here is because the whole damn park is under huge brooding trees that somebody must have planted about a hundred years ago to make sure no sun ever got in. There aren't even any leaves to shuffle through because an old Mexican guy with a smelly gasoline-powered blower strapped to his back comes once in a while to blow them all away. He was the only person who knew I was sleeping in the bushes back then, but he never said anything to me, and I'm sure he didn't tell the cops either. He didn't give a shit if I wanted to live in the bushes, and I liked him for that. It made me feel like we were probably alike: neither of us giving a shit about anything. Sleeping in the bushes was as good as sleeping anywhere else, even if it did get a little cold at night. In fact, I liked being there a hell of a lot more than when I had a home to go to. No drunks with their stupid arguing and screaming that kept me awake all night. Before she took off, my mom and her drunken friends were always fighting. Who knows about what. Yeah, it was a lot better to just hide out in the bushes and listen to nothing but the ocean waves hitting the shore way down below.

Thinking back on those days makes me think I should take one last walk through the old park before I jump. But if I do go for a short walk, it's not to look for anything redeeming. I know there's nothing that's going to convince me that life is actually worth living. Hell with that. I'm still going to do it, and tonight is the night. If I go for a walk now, it's just for one last look around. This old codger of a park will be my last memory, and that's okay with me.

I hop back over the fence and follow the cracked and tree-root-buckled sidewalk toward the other end of the park. I keep an eye out as I go: never know when you might run into some of the local gangbangers. They wouldn't take kindly to somebody my age being on their turf, even if I'm not wearing colors. (Living in Watts, I've learned to wear only dumb plaid shirts that have no red or blue in them. And no baggy pants; only thrift-store plain brown corduroy pants. In other words, I've learned to wear clothes that make me look like a nerd because if you look enough like a nerd, sometimes the gangs will ignore you.) But tonight, there aren't any gangbangers around, only silence and darkness under the big old brooding trees. As I walk, I notice the only thing that might legitimize this place as a real park, one lonely old concrete picnic table. But the old table is so totally covered with gang tagging and over-tagging, it looks like a painting by that Jackson Pollock guy, the one that threw paint all over his canvases and then sold 'em for about a million bucks apiece. Have you seen those paintings? Weird.

As I walk, the old park is telling me exactly what I need to hear: it's telling me there's nothing of value here. The park is like everything else in this stupid country, worn out and stupid and worthless. I stop in front of the old used-to-be white-but-now-gradually-turning-smog-gray lighthouse. The old place looks like it's about to fall down. The top part used to be glassed in, but the glass is all broken out now. Kids throwing rocks, I guess. I suppose this old lighthouse was put here at the edge of the cliff to warn sailors away from the land, back before they had radar on ships. It probably used to have a really bright light up top that flashed out a warning: Hey, sailors, this is land I'm sitting on, so don't run into me if you know what's good for you. The lighthouse has a bronze plaque on the side of it saying it's on the historic register. Well, wahoo. So it's historic. Big deal. Nobody cares about that kind of shit anymore. These days, the past is past, gone and forgotten. The old lighthouse is good for one thing though: it's a billboard for gang graffiti. Some new tags have been added since I was last here. Lots of RSP, which stands for the Rancho San Pedro gang, and there's some PWL 13, the gang from San Pedro. But now, most of that has been crossed out and over-tagged with DRO. It's spray painted in red, and that means the Bloods are moving into this territory. It means they're threatening death to anybody who gets in their way. If the local kids try to defend their turf, some of those kids are going to die on the streets of San Pedro. Welcome to gangbanging, San Pedro. Well, I hope they have lots of fun shooting the shit out of each other. Doesn't matter to me. I wish I had my own can of spray paint. I'd cross them all out and make up my own "DIE" message. See how they like that. Oh, the hell with it. I turn away from the lighthouse and head back for the cliff. Time to get it over with. Time to do my leap into nothingness.

I pass the building that houses the restrooms, a concrete block of a building that reminds me of every other building in LA—artless boxes that nobody would ever look at twice. On the internet, I used to like looking at pictures of beautiful buildings in really interesting places like Rome, or Paris, or Sidney, Australia. When I was little, I used to dream of someday having enough money to go to places like that. Maybe I'd go to Florence, or Venice. You should see the amazing buildings they have in those places. But now, I know I never really had a chance to go there, no chance really to even get out of LA. It takes money to go anywhere else in this world, and there's no way I could ever get my hands on that kind of money. The stupid concrete restroom building does remind me that I haven't peed since I walked out of my grandmother's old termite-ridden house in Watts. I might as well go in and pee before I jump. I'm on the women's side of the building. Should I go in there to do my peeing? Well, why not? Old Man once told me social norms were only concepts, stuff made up by the powers-that-be in order to control us. So, I go into the women's side, and I'm surprised to see that compared to most men's restrooms, it isn't all that dirty. It has two stalls, and both doors are still attached. Amazing! And there isn't even much gang graffiti. Odd that the gang boys haven't come in here to deface the girl's restroom. I guess they wouldn't want to be seen going into a girl's restroom. They might be willing to sell drugs to little kids and shoot people, but they aren't quite ready to break the social norms about which restroom you're supposed to use.

I change my mind. Better not defile this girl sanctuary with my boy piss. I go around to the boy's side to do my business. I'm feeling impatient now to finish this last human act and get on with the jumping-off-the-cliff part. As I walk into the boy's side, my assurance that everything in the world has gone to shit is once again confirmed. Not only is the door still missing from the one graffiti-covered stall, but now, the toilet's porcelain is all cracked, as if somebody came in to beat on it with a hammer. And now there's no toilet seat, so you'd have to sit on the cold cracked pot itself if you had to do anything (but you'd better not actually have to do anything because there's no toilet paper). I go to the urinal. Since the last time I was in here, the bolts that held the rusty metal urinal to the wall have come loose—probably kicked loose—and as a result, one end of the thing has fallen down to the cracked concrete floor and is leaking. The result is a slippery and smelly mess. I get on with the peeing process, pissing into the upper end of the tin urinal and watching it run down to the other end where it dribbles to the floor, adding my piss to the piss that's already there. I'm still focusing on watching my pee flow down the chute and onto the floor when this big dark-skinned guy comes in through the door. He walks right up to me and stands there stone-faced, staring down at my little thing. I hurry to finish, and then I try to edge around him to get out the door quick. But it's no use. He puts his big hand against my chest and holds me back. He says, "Hand it over, whitebread." He doesn't seem angry at me. Not at all. It's almost like he's bored with the whole mugging process, but he has to do it. It's boring, but it's a living. I hand over what little money I have without a word, thinking, What does money matter anyhow if I'm going to kill myself in a few minutes? He points his big finger at me and snarls, but then he lets me go with only a few slaps to my face.

I get the message: don't tell anybody about this or you're dead. I think about telling him he doesn't need to worry, I'll be dead soon enough anyhow, but I keep my mouth shut and head back for the cliff edge. As I walk, I'm asking myself why I bothered to go take a piss if I was going to kill myself anyhow. Does it mean I'm not serious? Is this night going to be like all those other nights when I chickened out? No way! That dark-skinned mugger appeared out of the night like a dark angel to tell me I was doing exactly the right thing. His role in this little drama was to assure me that there was absolutely nothing to live for in this piece-of-shit world.

I follow the cracked sidewalk to the fence and climb over it. I move out close to the edge. No moving lights out there on that dark ocean now. I guess all the ships are safely in the harbor for the night.

So, this is it. All I have to do is take one step forward, and it's so long world. So long big ships. So long all you big old whales.

I lift my foot.

I close my eyes and put my foot down.

And then I'm falling.

I open my eyes.

Yes! I did it, I really did it. I'm falling down, down, and down through the darkness. Weird, it feels like it's all happening in slow motion. I have the funny thought that I should have practiced swan diving with those kids at the pool because I'm not doing any kind of dive at all; in fact, I'm flipping end over end which is making me feel panicky, and I don't want to feel panicky. I want to feel calm and do a perfect swan dive, but for some reason my hands are grabbing at the air, and maybe I made some kind of high-pitched sound that I didn't want to make, and I can't stop my flipping, and I can't tell which way is up and which way is down, and I keep thinking why is this taking so long?

And then, there is darkness.

It feels like I'm lying in water.

And there is pain. *A lot* of pain. Does this pain belong to me? What could it mean? If I'm dead, why would I be feeling pain?

A bright light, shinning in my eyes.

Behind the light, a vague shimmering face. Eyes looking at me.

"Holy shit, the motherfucker is still alive."

2
Conception of the Phenomenal Present

Pain. The whole world is pain. Nothing in this reality but pain.

But then, there was light.

Then, darkness again.

Light, then dark, then light again. Keeps repeating.

But always, there is the pain. And now, sounds. I'm hearing sounds. Is it people talking? Was I sleeping? It feels like I'm in a bed. Maybe I'm still sleeping. Maybe this is a dream.

My eyes are seeing something. Something white. A ceiling?

I turn my head to the side. Movement. Vague images of white-clad things drift past. Are those shapes people?

It was dark, but now, it's getting light again. I think I understand: light must mean daytime, dark must mean nighttime.

And then, there is a very bright light above me. A circle of masked men hover over me, looking down at me. Are they doctors, or is this still the dream? If it is, it's a dream about darkness, and getting darker.

I open my eyes. I must have been asleep.

I see a white ceiling up there. I remember that white ceiling, I think.

I try to remember other things, but pieces of the puzzle seem to be missing. There are scenes, but they all run together: jumping off of a cliff, falling and falling, people, sirens, doctors.

But wait! If I jumped off of my cliff, why aren't I dead?

Or am I dead? Is this what it's like to be dead? If I am dead, why does there have to be so much pain? Pain in my legs. I'm feeling like the pain in my legs means I'm not dead. And if I'm thinking about whether I'm dead or not, I must not be dead.

Think about this proposition: whatever is conceived by the mind is, by definition, true. If you think you are alive, then you are alive.

Oh, now I remember. It's the old man. I guess he's still with me. He's telling me the pain I'm feeling means I'm not dead. Okay, let's say I'm *not* dead. What am I seeing? I'm seeing people. The people are moving past the foot of my bed. They're dressed in white. Hospital workers? Yes, I must be in a hospital. That means, apparently, that jumping off my cliff didn't kill me after all. Damn, fucked up again.

A man in a white doctor-type coat is suddenly next to my bed. Where did he come from? He has one of those stethoscope things hanging around his neck. He seems real enough. More evidence: I must be alive, in a hospital. Only logical. He's asking me what I said. Did I say something out loud?

Suddenly, he's gone. How odd. How do they come and go so fast?

Darkness, but the pain is still there. Some white thing comes drifting through the darkness. It does something to a tube that seems to be attached to my arm. The pain goes away. Some of it, anyhow.

I open my eyes. Light again, and the pain is back. Does the light bring the pain? The pain is everywhere, inside of me and outside of me. No, that can't be. The pain must only be inside of me. I have to focus. I have to figure out where the pain is. I'm supposed to be smart, so be smart. Be logical. Focus on the pain. Where is it? Okay, now I have it figured out: the pain is in my legs. That must mean I still have legs. Or do I? If I wiggle my toes, it will tell me if I still have legs. Only logical. I wiggle my toes. That causes pain. It means I still have toes, and that means I still have legs. Logical. Good to be logical. Being logical, I decide the men in white must be doctors, and the women in white, the ones who come and go, must be nurses. Some of them talk to me sometimes, but usually I can't quite remember what they said. But I do remember that one of them showed me a machine that's on a pole next to my bed. She said the machine is hooked to the tube that leads to my arm. She said there was morphine inside the machine. She showed me how to push a button that makes the morphine go into my arm. Whenever I push that button, some of the pain goes away. For a while, anyhow. And it makes Old Man go away too. I don't know why. I'll tell you something else about that morphine. It makes you have weird dreams. In some of the dreams, I jump off of my cliff and fly out over the ocean. It's so easy. I fly like a bird without even having wings.

In other dreams, the lights are very bright and a bunch of doctors in masks are gathered around me. They're doing something to my legs. But maybe those aren't dreams.

I open my eyes and see a white ceiling. But in this white ceiling, there's a silver metal vent up there. It must mean I'm in a different room. Only logical.

But there is still pain. Lots of pain. Then, I remember something: if I push the pain-go-away button, some of the pain goes away. I push the button, and then I count inside my head to see how long it takes for the pain to go away. The pain fades, but then I have to start the count again to see how long it takes to come back. The pain slowly creeps back into my legs. It's like an invading army of tiny little pain guys. They march up from my ankles, slow at first, but then they start moving faster, spreading out to take over and occupy new territory. I know I can kill them off, or at least wound them, by pushing the morphine button again, but I try to resist doing it too often. I want to learn more about the little pain soldiers before I attack them with the morphine. Unfortunately, sometimes I push the pain-go-away button too many times, and the pain does not go away. The army of little pain guys comes back to invade and occupy both of my legs, especially my left leg. I push the morphine button and nothing happens. The army of little pain soldiers laugh at me. I'm out of ammunition, and they know it. They increase their attacks, digging in deeper. I try to get help by pushing the other button, the one that calls the night nurse, but no help comes. Waste of time. The night nurse never comes. I push the pain-go-away button again. Nothing. Damn. I have to force myself not to push that button. It reminds me of an experiment I read about on the internet. They put rats in a cage that had an electrified floor. The only way the rats got to escape the shock was to learn how to push a lever. They only had to push it once in a while, but once they learned about that lever, they keep on pushing it over and over again, even after the electric floor had been turned off. I tell myself I *will not* be like those rats. I tell myself not to push the pain-go-away button when the machine is empty. I'm smarter than a rat, aren't I? I have to learn how to control the pain with my mind.

And I also refuse to be like that guy down at the other end of this ward who lies awake screaming all night. Actually, he may be the smarter rat: he's learned that if he screams loud enough, the night nurse will eventually get tired of his screaming and come to give him a shot of something that shuts him up. But I *will not* do that. If the night nurse doesn't want to help me, then fuck her. Fuck them all. I'm going to learn how to control the pain all by myself. The smart-ass doctors and mean nurses would probably be yelling their heads off if they had to deal with this much pain, but not me. I *will* learn how to control it. But how? Let's see, I seem to remember reading somewhere on the internet that some Eastern gurus have learned how to control pain. But I can't look that up on the internet because I'm stuck here in this hospital. All I have to draw on is what I have stored in my brain, and I can't seem to find much about Eastern philosophy in there. I have a few stored words: Confucianism, Taoism, but they lead to dark places with no further information. I give up searching inside my brain about that and tell myself to think about something else. But what? I should think about my mother. Where is she when I need her? I'm in a hospital, I have pain, and she's not here. A mother should be with her son when he's hurt. But no, she likes it better down there in South America with that jerk, An-hell, while I have to lie here battling the little pain guys. It means she doesn't care about me. It means nobody cares about me. But I can't stop thinking about her. I keep on wondering where she might have ended up. I remember her and that An-hell bastard sitting at our kitchen table looking at a map of South America. It seems like he was showing her something in the northern part of that map. Where he used to live, supposedly. To get away from the pain, I should try to recreate that map in my mind. Maybe he was pointing to Columbia. I'll go there, to the deep dark Colombian jungle. I have to get through it, but the thick green jungle plants and the brown hanging-down vines are almost impenetrable. They grab onto me, hold me back. Why are they trying to keep me from finding her? I know, it's the pain in my legs, trying to get my attention. I have to ignore the pain because I have to fight my way through the jungle to find her. She might be right on the other side, but the pain won't let me go to her. It says I should quit trying to find her and pay attention to it. It's telling me I should forget about her because she forgot about me. But I don't believe she would forget me. Maybe she did run off and leave me, but I bet she'd come back if she knew I was in this hospital. The little pain guys laugh at that. They remind me that in all the time since she left, she hasn't sent me a single letter. Not even a postcard. They remind me that she'd figure out that I'd end up at Grandma's house—I had nowhere else to go. But maybe that mean old An-hell bastard is holding her prisoner down there. He probably wants her all to himself. Maybe when she tries to send me a letter, he stops her. That would be just like him. I never trusted that bastard. I have to stop thinking about Mom. It only makes me feel sorry for myself. I focus on the sounds of people coming and going. I wish I could see them, but I can't see them because they've pulled the curtain around my bed all the way closed. Maybe I'm so messed up, nobody wants to look at me. I wish I had a mirror to see how bad I look. Or maybe I don't want a mirror. Maybe I'd look so bad it'd freak me out.

A woman comes in to ask me about payment for services rendered. I laugh and tell her that I don't have a single cent to my name. I start to tell her about the big dark-skinned guy in the Point Fermin Park restroom who robbed me just before I, uh, *fell* off a cliff, but she's not interested. She makes me sign some kind of welfare paper, so I scrawl Micky J. Mouse. Why should I give them my real name? They don't care, and I kind of like the idea of not having a real name anymore. It's almost like not existing anymore. About the only person on this earth that knew I even existed before they brought me in here was Grandma, and I'm sure she wouldn't want to get out of her bed to come see me. She wouldn't want to miss a single episode of her TV soap operas. As the woman gets ready to leave, I ask her if she could pull back the part of my curtain that's down by my feet so I can see who goes past.

She does it. Good. At least now I have something to look at besides the ceiling up there. I discover that I'm close to the door to this ward. Nurses come in through that door, scuttle past, then come back. To keep the pain at bay, I try to imagine what they're doing out there.

But then, a doctor comes in and pulls back the sheet to look at my legs. I have plaster casts on both of my legs, so what is he looking at?

He says "Hmm" and puts the sheet back over me. He pats me on the shoulder, and tells me I'm doing fine.

I don't know what he means by that. Doing fine? In what way? Is any of this under my control?

He leaves, but thankfully, he doesn't close the part of the curtain that's open down by the end of my bed. I see more people coming in, maybe visitors coming to see the other patients. I won't be getting any visitors because nobody knows I'm here. As far as the world is concerned, I'm dead. Well, okay, that was the idea in the first place.

Existence equals perception. What is, is what can be experienced.

"Oh, so you *are* still here, Old Man. Good to hear from you again. I need some distraction. Do we exist only if we believe we exist?"

Conscious awareness of the self is always present.

"But what about other people's awareness? If my mother has forgotten about me, do I still exist for her?"

No answer.

I wonder why that question always shuts him up. If my mother still has a consciousness, shouldn't I still exist for her?

My thoughts are interrupted by someone laughing. Now that's a sound I haven't heard since they brought me into this place. I wonder who is doing the laughing. Surprising anybody on this ward would be laughing because I know who is on this ward. When they pulled back my curtain to mop the floor, I saw I was in a long narrow room with lots of beds in it. A man was in every bed, and none of them looked very happy. Now, with the curtain next to my bed back in place, I can no longer see them, but I can still hear them. They're a complaining bunch. They complain about the food, they complain about the doctors, they complain about the night nurse who never comes when you push the call button. So many different men's voices. What are they all doing here? They could be all injured, like me, but most of the voices sound old, so maybe they had heart attacks or something. I'd hate to be stuck down at the other end of this big ward. At least here by the door, I can watch the people come and go. It helps divert my attention away from the pain in my legs and helps me hold off a bit longer before I have to push the pain-go-away morphine button.

When the daytime nurse comes in to refill my pain-go-away box, I ask her how many men are on this ward.

She's distracted, but says, "Too many. I've never so many indigents. Must be the economy. Beds even out in the hallways." She hurries out.

So, I'm on the *indigent* ward. A big ward full of men that can't pay the hospital. No wonder they're not very happy. Hearing their sad voices, makes me feel sorry for them. I even feel sorry for the harried doctors and nurses who have to take care of them. But then, when I was still out in the world, I didn't know anybody who was all that happy either. My grandma isn't happy; she's just surviving, lost in her TV world of dumb soap operas. And the gangbangers in my neighborhood aren't happy either. They too are just surviving, going through the motions, getting by from day to day. Maybe they do their violence to keep from thinking about how shitty their lives really are. It's a wonder they don't all shoot themselves in the head with their fancy pistols. It's a wonder that everybody in the whole damn world doesn't get a pistol and shoot themselves in the head.

But I don't like thinking about the world out there; I know it's all going to hell, so who cares? That kind of thinking only makes the pain in my legs worse. If I'm going to get through this, I have to use the one functional thing I have left, my brain. Even though that counselor didn't like me, he said I was the smartest kid in the school. So I'd better start using my smarts to figure out how to deal with all this pain. I know I can do it. If I'm smart enough and logical enough, I should be able to put my mind somewhere where the pain isn't. The awareness of pain must take place somewhere inside the brain; therefore, pain is all in the mind. No reason why I shouldn't be able to control my own brain.

Several doctors come in to interrupt my being logical. They surround me and one of them pushes the button on the pain-go-away machine.

Why did he do that? Are they going to hurt me?

They pull back the sheet and start doing something to my legs. I keep my focus up there on the ceiling and wait for the pain to start.

But it doesn't. I hear a buzzing sound, but no more pain than usual. What the hell is that buzzing sound? Seems like I've heard it before, but that was back in the dream days, back when I first was brought in here. Does the buzzing sound mean they're cutting some part of me off? No, they wouldn't do that here. For that, they'd have to take me back to the surgery room, wouldn't they? Well, who cares? Let them do whatever they want. I focus on the ceiling and practice being logical. I will feel no pain. No such thing as pain.

One of the doctors holds up something. Looks like a plaster statue of a leg. Actually, half a leg. More buzzing, and he holds up another plaster statue of half a leg. I guess they're cutting off my leg casts. As soon as they get them both off, my legs feel cold. Haven't felt that in a while.

They all lean in closer. They say things to each other. The younger doctors are behind, and they lean forward too, trying to get a better look at my legs. One of the older doctors in the front row says, "An interesting case. Minimal bone available for the reconstruction. Notice the tight spacing of the screws and plates."

So, I must have screws and plates in my legs. Am I going to be some kind of mechanical man? I wonder if it means I'll be able to walk when they get done operating on me. I hadn't thought about that. I hadn't really thought anything about the concept of "after." I was supposed to be dead, but I'm not, so maybe there really will be an "after."

Another voice interrupts my thinking, a younger-sounding voice. The voice says, "Will they hold?"

An older-sounding voice says, "Who knows? With this amount of damage, it's all uncharted territory."

They go away, talking among themselves. I watch them go out through the ward door. They're passing around x-ray negatives, holding them up to the light.

After they're gone, I realize that not one of them had looked at my face or said a single word to me. To them I'm just a pair of fucked-up legs, an interesting case. Actually, they're not even interested in my legs; they're only interested in the screws they put into my legs.

I feel the coolness on my legs down there. It means they left the casts off. I realize this is my first chance to get a look at my legs. I throw back the sheet and lift my head enough to see them. What I see looks pretty horrible: both of my legs look all bumpy and scarred, with stitches all over the place. The left one seems to be the one that has been hacked on the most. I wonder if them leaving the casts off means they're done with me. One of the doctors seemed worried that the screws and plates might not hold. What did he mean by "hold"? And what if they don't? Would that mean I'll never be able to walk again? Does that matter? If I can't walk, how would I get back to my cliff to do a better swan dive? But do I still want to do that? Something feels . . . I don't know . . . different. Maybe now that I understand the concept of dying better, maybe I don't want to do it. Not sure. I'll have to think about that. Later.

As I listen to the complaining voices on the ward, I stare up at the silver vent in the ceiling, trying to distract myself from the pain. I see something move up there inside that vent. I watch and wait. It moves again. Now I see what it is. It's a spider. Black, but not very big. So, a spider is living up there inside that vent. I've never seen him before, but I have seen a few wisps of cobwebs. I whisper, "Hello Little spider. How are things up there?" I like the idea of him living his life up there while I live my life down here in this bed. I'll keep an eye out for him. Maybe it'll help me not think about the pain so much. It must be dark inside that vent. I bet spiders like the dark.

Dark. That word reminds me of something I read on the internet. A dark philosopher. He wrote something about pain, didn't he? What was his name? A German name. Schopenhauer. That's it. What did I read about him? Seems like he thought everybody lives in a state of constant dissatisfaction. (Well, that's obvious.) He believed life is nothing more than an endless search for satisfaction. It also seems like I read that he was into Eastern philosophy. Maybe he knew something about how those gurus control pain. I stare up at the ceiling, trying to remember what he wrote about Eastern religion. Something about all philosophy being based on principles of Eastern religion. Maybe the old man knows about that. "Hey, Old Man, tell me everything you know about Eastern religion and controlling pain."

Siddhartha set out to learn about the human experience. When he left the luxury of his father's palace, he chose a life of extreme asceticism.

"Well, that's all fine and good, but what's it got to do with pain?"

Extreme asceticism led Siddhartha to an answer, and the answer was that he should abandon extreme asceticism and find a middle way.

"Okay, the middle way. What does *that* have to do with pain?"

No answer.

Shit, I'm stuck. All I can find inside my brain is stored remnants of a few vague concepts. Why didn't I spend more time studying Eastern philosophy when I had all that time to read stuff on the internet? All I can remember are a few things I happened to run across on the internet by accident. Stuff about Buddhism and the eightfold path. I also read some of the old Vedic stories. They were pretty interesting. Maybe I should ask Old Man about that. "Uh, the eightfold path thing, does it have anything to do with pain?"

Shiva set up a race around the world between his two sons, Ganesha and Murugha. The first one to get back would be the winner. Murugha was very fast and took off riding like the wind on his peacock. He was back in no time, but Ganesha was already there. Ganesha had a bunch of arms and a big fat head like an elephant, so Murugha didn't believe Ganesha could have made it all the way around the world and back so fast. Ganesha replied that his father was his only world, so all he had to do was walk around his father.

"What the hell does that story have to do with pain?"

No answer.

Waste of time talking to Old Man. He'll just lead me into the dark parts of my own brain. And what makes me think Eastern thought has anything to teach me about pain anyway? Maybe all this pain in my legs has made something go wrong with my brain so it just keeps leading me into things I haven't read about yet. Damn, maybe by trying to turn off the part of my brain where the pain is, I've turned off the part of my brain that was good at remembering. I sure hope it hasn't knocked out all the things I worked so hard to store in there.

My thoughts are interrupted when two weird-looking guys come in through the ward door and look around. One of them points at me, and the other one nods.

What are these two weirdos after?

The guy who pointed at me comes right over and sits on the edge of my bed. The other one stays by the door.

What the hell? Why is this guy sitting on my bed?

He just stares at me, arms crossed, head tipped a bit to the side.

He doesn't say anything, but there's something about him that seems gay. But he's not dressed gay—more like angry street tough: tight jeans and a street-typical stained gray T-shirt with the sleeves cut off to show his two matching dragon tattoos, one on his left bicep, facing right, the other on his right bicep, facing left. I'm sure those two inward-facing dragons means something to him, but I can't imagine what. His head is mostly shaved, except for a stripe of green spiky hair down the middle. It looks like one of those old Roman crested helmets. I bet he has no idea how ridiculous it makes him look.

I check out the other guy, the one who's staying by the door. He's wearing a black leather jacket that has silver chains attached at the shoulders, and he also has a shaved head, but no stripe of hair down the middle. Instead of hair, he's got some poorly-made tattoos, strange symbols, all over his head. I can just imagine him making those ugly tattoos himself, standing in front of a mirror, using the point of a knife dipped into a bottle of black ink. But the most noticeable of his head tattoos is a more professionally done one, a tattoo of a very weird third eye in the middle of his forehead. I guess it's supposed to be a vampire eye or something like that. I try to imagine going through life with a thing like that on my forehead. What would I be trying to say? How would I be wanting people to react to me? It's downright weird. In fact, these two are so weird, it's almost like one of the weird dreams I get after I push the morphine button in the middle of the night.

Unlike the calm guy sitting on the edge of my bed, the one by the door is acting real nervous. He keeps on leaning out the door to look. Is he keeping watch? For what?

Green hair, still sitting on my bed, says: "So you *are* alive."

He says it with a *sort of* friendly smile. I get the impression that he isn't very practiced at being friendly. But why did he say that thing about me being alive? What does he know about it? Is he unhappy that I'm alive? Are they here to kill me? But why would they want to do that? One thing for sure, I don't know them. I'm sure I'd remember a couple of weirdos like them.

Green hair waves his hand in front of my face. "Hey, you in there?"

In there? Of course I'm in here. At first, I think about just ignoring him, but I'm curious about what he said about me still being alive, so I say, "I guess so." But then, I realize that was not a very clever response for a smart kid whose IQ is supposed to be off the scale. I should have said something clever and sarcastic. The problem is, I'm out of practice. The doctors and nurses in this hospital don't give you very many opportunities for sarcasm. The guy looks like he's about to say something else, but before he can get it out, I quickly say, "Now that you mention it, you seem to be alive too. Sort of."

Green hair doesn't seem to get my joke. He looks puzzled, then irritated. He leans closer and whispers, "Hey listen, dude, we went to a lotta trouble to save ya."

They saved me? What the hell is that supposed to mean?

Green hair turns to the other guy by the door. "He's out of it."

"Give him a smack," says mister tattooed third eye. "Maybe that'll snap him out of it."

I say, "No need to give me smack, sweetie. I'm fine without it. But what do you two weirdos mean, saved me?"

"We did," says green hair. "We're the ones who called nine-one-one. You had bones sticking outta your leg. Blood comin' out like crazy. Youda died, dude, if we hadn't called it in."

"Yeah," says weird-third-eye, coming closer, "youda died."

He looks pissed off. I wonder why.

He points at me and says, "We shoulda got a ree-ward."

Green hair waves him off. "What he means is, we went to a lot of trouble to save you. And here you are, alive and all. We could use, you know, like a little reward for our trouble."

So that's it. They called for an ambulance, and now they want money for doing it. A ree-ward, as they call it. But I don't have any money. That big dark-skinned guy in the Point Fermin restroom took what little money I had. Or was that part of the dream? Now that I think about it, just about everything that happened that night is starting to feel like a dream. But that dark-skinned mugger guy had to be real. He took all my money and called me a "whitebread." I remember that. And there was a leaking urinal. I remember that too. Piss all over the floor.

Green hair says, "Did you hear me. I said—"

"I heard you." I figure it must be about time to explain the facts of life to these two. I sit up a little, trying to ignore the increase in pain it causes. I reach out and pull back the curtain. I point at the other men on the ward. "See all those men? They're indigents. This is the indigent ward. We're all just a happy bunch of indigents here." I lie back, feeling proud of myself. My sarcasm is starting to come back.

Tattooed third eye takes another step into the room. "What the fuck is an indigent, asshole?"

He seems even more pissed off now, which, with that stupid tattooed vampire eye in the middle of his forehead, strikes me as funny. How can you even try to look angry with that comic-book eye stuck in the middle of your forehead?

I decide to respond in kind. "No, not an indigent asshole, just plain old indigents, asshole."

He takes another step toward me. "You trying to be funny, asshole."

The guy doesn't seem to have much of an insult vocabulary. I'm about to help him out with a few clever ones of my own, but his green-haired partner, the one still sitting on the edge of my bed, raises a hand to shut him up. "Don't pay my friend any mind. He's still upset that he didn't get to finish that night because of you. He was about to come when he saw you jump. He said, 'Jesus, that motherfucker just jumped off the cliff.' Stopped him cold, and I can guarantee you he wasn't happy about it. Can you blame him? You know what that's like, don't ya? Being almost ready to come when something stops you?"

I put on what I hope is an exaggerated sympathetic look and say, "Of course. Terrible. Just terrible. You should have finished him off."

"Yeah, well, he wanted me to, but I said we'd better go down and check on you."

Tattooed third eye is still pointing at me, obviously still pissed off. "You didn't have no money in yur pockets."

So did they go to all the trouble to go around and take the path down to the shoreline just to help me, or was it to rob me? I stare at the guy's weird third-eye tattoo. If he was to ask my opinion, I would have told him that getting that tattoo was a mistake. It turns his otherwise hard-ass facial attitude into a joke. In fact, looking at how silly it is actually cheers me up a bit. I decide to keep the entertainment going. "Sorry about that, fellas. If I'd a known you went to all that trouble to rob me, Ida gone to the bank before I jumped. In fact, if my legs weren't so fucked up, I'd go out right now and rob a bank or something, just to help you two idiots out."

Now the real two eyes of the guy with the fake third eye are looking *really* pissed off. He comes toward me.

Maybe I should be scared of him, but the more I look at his stupid third eye, I can't help grinning at how pathetic he is. I mean, trying to act like a mean person with a silly tattoo like that right in the middle of your forehead? Impossible. I feel sorry for him.

He arrives at my bedside, both fists up in the air. He's got a letter tattooed on each of his fingers, but I can't make out what they're supposed to mean.

Suddenly, the whole scene gets to me, and I start laughing. With his fists held up high like that, he looks like some kind of ridiculous three-eyed toy robot. I realize I'm actually feeling a bit grateful to both of them: their weirded-out haircuts and tattoos and their stereotypical tough-guy attitudes are so ridiculous it's making me feel more like my old sarcastic observer self again.

Green-hair tries to hold third-eye back, but the crazy bastard isn't having any of it. He comes to the bed and grabs my leg through the sheet. "How about if I squeeze the shit out of your fucked up legs, asshole. You want me to do that?"

His squeezing my leg hurts like hell, but I try to keep a straight face and pretend like I don't even feel it. "Why, yes," I say, as calmly as I can, "do. That would be so clever of you. You could tell all your queer friends how you went to the hospital to hurt a cripple. That would make you quite a hero, I bet."

Just then, a doctor comes in through the ward door. He's holding some x-ray negatives up to the light.

Green-hair quickly jumps off the edge of my bed and pulls third-eye away. As they hurry out the door, the doctor stares after them. Then, he turns back to me. "Who was that?"

I shrug. "Just a couple of well-wishers."

The doctor frowns, but then he puts on his well-practiced sympathetic doctorly look. He points to the x-rays. "Your scans are looking a lot better. There's a chance you might be able to walk again after all. I mean . . . someday."

"Well, thank God for that," I say, acting very serious. "It's a long walk from the bus stop to that cliff."

The doctor seems startled, but then he regains his doctorly look. "Now, son, don't be talking like that. You think we went to all the trouble to put your legs back together just so you could try it again?"

"You're right, doctor. First, I need to go to a swimmin' pool somewhere so I can practice my swan diving."

He stares at me. He's not sure if I'm kidding or not.

I decide to let him off the hook. "Just kidding, doctor. I'll be a good boy and learn to be a productive member of society. Maybe I'll go back to high school and become a track star."

His face shows relief. He comes forward to pat me on the shoulder, smiling now, grateful to me, I think, for not messing up his morning with any unsettling pessimism. "Well, I don't know about running track. We didn't have much intact bone left to work with, especially in your left leg. I'm afraid it's going to be a little shorter than your right leg. But you never know. I've seen cases like yours where . . . maybe with crutches or something, you might be able to get around. You know, eventually."

By now, I've been in this damn hospital long enough to learn that doctors have absolutely no awareness that such a thing as sarcasm or irony even exists in this world, so I know it's not going to upset him when I keep my little self-entertaining game going by saying, "Golly, that would be great."

After the doctor leaves, I wonder if his words mean they're done with me. Maybe if I had some money, they'd keep on trying, but it doesn't matter much to me one way or the other. All their endless surgeries seem to be doing is giving me more and more pain, and now this doctor is telling me I might never walk again, except maybe "someday," with the help of crutches.

I turn onto my side to pee into the ridiculous plastic box-with-a-neck thing they give you so you can pee lying down. I'm still in mid-stream when a prim, sour-faced woman, who I'm sure has never smiled once in her entire life, comes in. I ignore her and continue peeing.

She waits until I finish and put the pee container back onto the side table, then she comes to the side of my bed and shoves a page full of small print into my hands. It has the words "John Doe 43379" handwritten on the top of the first page.

She hands me a pen, and without cracking any kind of expression at all, says, "Sign where it says to sign."

Some of the papers have little yellow stick-ons with the words "Signature" or "Initials." I leaf through the papers. Lawyer stuff, probably saying I can't blame them if they've totally fucked me up.

I look up at her. She's staring off into the distance and clutching her clipboard to her bosom as if it's some kind of protection against me.

"Now hold on," I say. "Are you kicking me out? The doctor told me I wasn't supposed to put any weight on my legs until that last round of surgeries heals up."

She still won't look at me. "You can heal up at home."

"But I live with my old grandma. She can't take care of me. She's all but bedridden herself and—"

"Listen," she says, finally looking directly at me. She uses her clipboard to point toward the door. "Didn't you see those people out there in the hall? We've got people in beds in just about every hallway, and they're a lot worse off than you are. You have to go home and heal up there. It's the rule."

"Well," I say, "if it's the rule, then you'd better just toss me out with the trash. I guess that's the way it is in the hospital business. When you've used up your dole money, you're out the door."

She doesn't seem much impressed with my clever sarcasm.

"Just sign the paper," she says. "Somebody will come with a wheelchair. They'll take you home."

I scrawl an unreadable "Donald J. Duck" signature in the appropriate places and hand the papers back to her.

She quickly clips the papers to her precious clipboard and hands me a prescription form.

I can't read the doctor's scrawl. Some kind of pain killer, I guess.

The woman hurriedly leaves the room, and soon, a nurse comes to unhook the tube from my arm. Although she doesn't act very friendly, she does push the morphine button twice before she pulls out the IV.

I'm feeling a lot better with those two shots of morphine running through me when a young Hispanic-looking girl comes in with the wheelchair. She smiles shyly and hands me a shirt. I recognize it. It's the same shirt I had on the night I jumped off the cliff. It hasn't been cleaned, and it's kind of stiff. Maybe because of the sea water. I decide to try to get the hospital gown off and the shirt on by myself while the morphine is still working. I say, "Crank my bed up, please."

She presses the button to raise the bed, and I close my eyes to try to push away the pain as I'm slowly brought up into a sitting position. It's the first time I've been allowed to sit up since they brought me in here. Although it hurts my legs like hell, I somehow manage to get the damn hospital gown off and my shirt on. But just doing that much has exhausted me. Man, I must be really weak. I lie back, and I'm still trying to catch my breath when she brings the wheelchair close to the edge of the bed and reaches out to help me.

I look at her, and she looks at me.

I say, "No pants," and throw back the sheet to show her.

She doesn't seem as embarrassed at my nakedness as I thought she would be. I have the thought that maybe another part of her job is washing the bedridden patients. Nobody ever washed me. Maybe those of us on the indigent ward don't get special privileges like being washed. I probably stink like hell.

"I need some pants," I say.

She shrugs. "No pant in *bolsa*. You come with pant?"

"They probably had to cut them off of me."

"Oh," she says, and again she reaches out to help me out of bed.

I refuse to take her hand. "No way," I say. "Not without pants."

She looks concerned, but she doesn't move.

I point toward the door. "Can't you go find me some pants?"

She thinks about that, frowning. Then, she brightens. "Mr. Mason. Now he no need . . . I mean, wait minute." She hurries out of the room.

While I wait for her to come back, I think about what it's going to be like to get out of this damn bed. How long have I been here lying flat on my back? I look down at my naked legs. What a mess they are. There's hardly any place that hasn't been cut on, and there are several bumps under the skin where I guess they must have put in stuff to try to hold my shattered bones together.

Soon, the Mexican girl is back with a pair of gray pants.

She helps put them on me, and even the touch of the cloth on my legs hurts more than I would have believed possible. I lie still until the pain subsides a bit, and then, I sit up. Uh oh, woozy.

She holds onto me to keep me from tipping over, then she helps me inch my way to the edge of the bed. My new pants bunch up around my waist. They're way too big for me, but luckily they have a belt. I cinch it up, and then she helps me slide out of bed and into the wheelchair. The sudden shot of pain in my legs takes my breath away. I can absolutely guarantee you that despite the morphine that's supposedly still inside me, that move into the wheelchair is the most pain any human being in history ever felt.

The girl places my bare feet on the cold metal foot plates of the wheelchair, and off we go. She wheels me down the hall, and then we ride down in the elevator while I grit my teeth and try to put my mind where the pain isn't. Even the slight weight of my feet on the wheelchair footrests feels like it's killing my legs.

When we get down to the first floor, she wheels me out of the elevator, across the wide lobby, and out the main entrance where a really big guy in a white uniform is waiting. His uniform looks fairly clean, but it has brown spots on it (dried blood?). He snatches me up out of the wheelchair and carries me out to a small bus that has the name of the hospital on the side. The big dude is carrying me so easy, it makes me feel like I'm a little kid. Jeez, how much weight have I lost?

Ignoring my whimpering, he carries me onto the bus and drops me into a seat. I'm pretty sure that drop just broke anything that wasn't already broke, and I want to give him a sarcastic comment like, Thanks a lot, asshole, but I can't get a word out because I have to keep my teeth clenched to try to ward off the incredible pain. The whole process of getting me onto the bus took only a few seconds, but it hurt so much I can't hold back the tears. I don't want the other people on the bus to see the tears coming out of my eyes, so I turn away and pretend to look out the window. I feel ashamed at my weakness. Here, I thought I'd been getting better at not hitting that damn morphine button so often, but now it hurts so much a bunch of stupid tears are coming out of my eyes. Aw, hell with it. I've got to quit feeling sorry for myself. After all, who was it that jumped off of that cliff? It was me. I only have myself to blame for not learning how to do a better swan dive.

As the bus starts to move, I wipe away the tears with the backs of my hands and check out my fellow passengers. Three down-and-out looking light-skinned guys, and a very skinny dark-skinned woman who's wearing a dirty blue bathrobe. I wonder if that bathrobe was what she was wearing when she came into the hospital.

The bus driver is a burly guy who looks kind of Italian. He's glancing back at me in his rear-view mirror. He probably thinks it's pretty funny to see a grown up guy crying like a little baby.

I could give a shit what he thinks. I turn away and look out the window again. It looks like we're heading downtown. We turn onto San Julian Street. I've heard of it. It's LA's skid row. The driver stops the bus next to a row of cardboard lean-tos. The whole area looks like a garbage dump: scattered plastic bags and plastic bottles, broken glass, torn-up cardboard, and lots of wadded up, wet and filthy pieces of cloth.

The driver looks back at us in his rear-view mirror. "Welcome home, folks. Everybody out."

The other men, indigents all, I suppose, get up and shuffle forward. They all look as weak as I feel, but it looks like they know the routine. They silently help each other down the bus steps and onto the street.

I look out the window and see that some of the local vultures are crawling out of their cardboard mansions. They systematically go through the pockets of the new arrivals, but they find only wadded up tissues which they angrily throw to the ground. One of the new arrivals is wearing a fairly new-looking pair of pants, so they make him sit down on the sidewalk while they jerk them off of him. The guy has a yellowed catheter sticking out from his underpants. When they're through with him, he gets up and wanders off down the street, holding onto the catheter tube to keep it from dragging on the ground. Another one of the new arrivals is wearing a fairly serviceable pair of brown shoes. They take those off of him and let him go without bothering to take his holey socks or his worn out clothes. The last guy to be shaken down has a used-to-be fancy western-style shirt with shiny pearl-like buttons down the front and on the cuffs. They strip the shirt off of him and push him away. Next, they gather around the bus door. They help the woman in the bathrobe down the bus steps. I'm thinking it's nice of them to help her down; at least they still respect a women. But as soon as she's down to the sidewalk, two tough-looking dark-skinned women come forward. They tear the bathrobe off of her, and even take the time to knock her down before they run off with their prized new blue bathrobe. The poor woman is left sitting on the curb in her ragged underpants and yellowed bra, sobbing into her hands. The rest of the vultures crowd around the bus to look through the windows. They're looking at me.

The bus driver turns to look at me. "Hey, buster. Everybody out."

I shake my head. "This is not where I live."

"Your discharge papers didn't have no address. No address, and this is where you go."

I look out the bus window at the gauntlet of homeless men waiting out there for me. Now, I realize it was a mistake not to put down my grandma's address on those hospital papers. I don't want to end up sitting naked on the curb next to the dark-skinned lady, so I say, "Mistake. Some kind of mix up." I try to look really pathetic so the driver won't just grab me and throw me out. "I live close to here. Can't you take me home?"

"What am I, your mother? You want me to drive you all the way to your damn house?"

"It's only a couple of miles," I say. "Just down there in Watts." I tell him my grandmother's address.

"Watts? You expect me to take you all the way down there?"

"It's not far. Besides, isn't that your job?"

"What the hell you doin' livin' in Watts anyhow? You're not black."

"White people live there too. A few anyhow."

He grumbles something under his breath, closes the bus door, and drives away

I look back at the group of vultures. They're standing in the middle of the street watching us go. I can tell they're really disappointed.

At my grandma's house, the driver stops abruptly and again looks at me in his rear-view mirror. "Okay, here you go, your highness."

"I can't walk. Legs all fucked up. That's why I was in the hospital."

"So what?" he says. "You expect me to carry you? Get the fuck off my bus." He stays right where he is, still looking back at me in his rear-view mirror. I get the feeling he's learned not to look directly at his charges. Maybe it means he does still have a heart, but if so, by now it's buried so goddam deep inside of him he's probably forgot that such a thing as sympathy still exists in this world.

"Can't. The doctors told me not to put any weight on my legs."

"Then crawl," he says.

I know there's no way I can crawl on my shattered legs. That would just about kill me. But I do manage to lower myself down onto the floor. I find that if I sit down and use the bus seats to drag myself backwards on my butt, I can make a little progress. It hurts more than I would have believed anything could hurt, but I'm determined to show him I can make it all by myself. I drag myself along that dirty bus floor until I get up next to him. I say, "Thanks so much. You've been such a big help."

"Fuck you," he says, looking straight ahead out his front window.

I decide I might be able to get myself down to the sidewalk if I use the same backwards technique to lower myself down using the chrome handrail. By moving slowly and carefully, I manage to do it, using my anger at the asshole bus driver to motivate me and to mask the unbelievable pain every movement causes. As I go, I tell myself to remember that in the future: anger makes some of the pain go away.

I'm barely out of the bus when he takes off, fast.

I sit there on the sidewalk watching him go. "Thanks again," I yell, waving cheerfully. "You're a prince among men."

He gives me the finger in his trusty rear-view mirror.

3
Perceptual Belief

It takes some time to accomplish it, but using the sit-down-and-scoot-backwards method, I drag myself up the sidewalk to Grandma's front steps. I keep my mind focused on the task, not on the pain. I make up a mantra and recite it just before each new move: over the river and through the woods, to grandmother's house I go. Just a little farther now. Over the river and through the woods. I tell myself, pain does not exist. You'll be inside soon, and you'll be able to lie down in your own bed. The hardest part is getting up the old wooden steps and onto the sagging boards of Grandma's porch. Somehow, I make it, still moving backwards, but now, the pain in my legs is so intense it doesn't feel like injury pain anymore, it feels more like pressure pain, as if both of my legs are being crushed in a giant vice. I do finally make it to the front door, but I'm totally exhausted and soaked with sweat. I lie back and stay still, hoping that if I don't move at all, some of the pain will subside. I stare up at the hanging strands of what's left of the paint on the ceiling of grandma's old porch, trying to focus on anything other than the pain. I'm out of breath, almost panting. I feel more weak than seems possible. I was in pretty good shape before I jumped off that cliff, but my time lying in that hospital bed has apparently weakened me more than I thought. Damn, before that night, I could walk all over the place. When I was hiding out in Point Fermin Park, after Mom took off, I used to walk up the hill to that little Korean Bell memorial park, and then I'd hike across the grassy field to where the World War Two coastal defense gun emplacements are. The big guns are gone, but the concrete tunnels where they kept the ammunition are still there, and despite all the scary gang graffiti in the dark tunnels, it's still a pretty interesting place to go to think about how things used to be back then. Sometimes, I'd walk even farther, way up into the Palos Verdes hills. From way up there, I could look out all the way to Catalina Island. Back then I was such a good walker, I could practically walk all day and hardly feel it. But now, after hardly ever going out of Grandma's house for a few years, and then being in that hospital bed for so long without moving, it feels like all my muscles have turned to Jello.

I hear a sound and turn my head toward it. A little dark-skinned girl with her thumb in her mouth is staring at me through the wooden slats of the neighbor's front porch. She's cute. Little kid eyes, wide with curiosity. I give her a wave, but she doesn't wave back. She probably wonders why I'm lying on this porch. I decide I'd better get inside before one of her older brothers comes out of her house. I've never talked to them, but I've seen them come and go, acting all loose and cool like they do, wearing their backwards baseball caps and their neighborhood-cool baggy pants that are about to fall off. I don't think they're gangbangers, but with the way they dress, you never know.

Ignoring the pain, I somehow get myself up onto one elbow so I can reach the doorknob. I turn the handle, push on the door, and it swings open. A miracle! The door wasn't locked. I wonder why Grandma left it unlocked. I roll inside. Holy shit! That roll move was a mistake. Now that was *real* pain, full-on, all-consuming, all-enveloping pain. I hope I haven't done any new damage to my legs. I'll have to remember not to try anything like that again. I manage to push the door closed, and then I lie on my back trying to catch my breath. I stare up at Grandma's old chandelier while I wait for the pain to subside. But the little pain guys in my legs seem to be digging in for the long haul. Where's my morphine button now when I really need it? And why didn't they give me any pain pills before they threw me out? All they gave me was one lousy prescription, and that won't do me any good if I can't get to the drugstore. But I guess I know why they didn't give me any pain pills: pills cost money. Sorry buster: no money, no pills. It's the wonderfully capitalist American way.

I hear Grandma's TV back there in her bedroom. I guess she did all right without me, but I wonder what she's been eating.

Okay, time to take stock. I'm safe inside Grandma's house. All I have to do is lie here on the floor and wait for the pain to subside. Then, maybe I can make it to my bed. I try to convince myself that if I keep my focus on that old chandelier up there, some of the pain will go away. I tell myself that pain only exists in my brain, so if I concentrate hard enough on something that's outside my brain, the pain will not be there. I try to think about nothing but what I'm looking at, that old chandelier. It's made out of dangling-glass beads, dull now with years and years of dust. But the glass beads still try to reflect what little light there is in the room. Maybe I can use those glass beads up there to hypnotize myself into not feeling any pain. The chandelier may be old and covered with dust, but at least it's a familiar thing, and right now, old and familiar is a lot better than the sterile white fakeness of that damn hospital. The old chandelier tells me I really am still alive, right back to where I started, before I took that bus ride out to Point Fermin Park. I'm all fucked up and in terrible pain, but I'm alive.

So now that I'm back home, what happens next? I can't walk. I can't even crawl. All I can do is drag myself around backwards like some kind of weird backwards-moving crab. I'm like the guy in that Kafka story where he wakes up one morning and discovers he's been turned into a giant insect. I guess it was some kind of metaphor about the kind of lives most people live, a bug's life. At least that's the way I took it, and I guess I am sort of like that now. But at least an insect could get around. I'm like some kind of broken-down worthless life form that's even lower than an insect. I can't even crawl. Damn it, why couldn't I have done at least that one thing right? As I fell through the air, I was flipping all over the place, so why did I have to go and land on my feet? I could have just as easily landed on my head, and that would have been the end of it. Why did it have to turn out this way? I have a brief thought that maybe I wasn't destined to be dead. But I quickly push that kind of thinking away. I don't believe in fate or any of that other woo-woo crap. Not logical. And it's for damn sure God didn't have any other purpose for me because if there's one thing I know for sure, it's that there *is no* God. It's all *made up!* I read on the internet that even the primitive humans created gods to try to convince themselves that there was something more to life than this endless, day-after-day shit. They created gods that looked something like themselves, only more powerful, and then they turned it on its head to say it was God that created *them* in *his* own image. Hey, how about this? I bet if those whales swimming around out there in the ocean have created a god, it will look like them. He'd be *big!* and He'd be a hell of a good swimmer.

I lie still and listen to the sound of Grandma's TV coming from the back of the house. I wonder it I can coax her out of her room long enough to at least help get me into my bedroom. "Hi, Grandma," I shout, "your favorite grandson is home."

No answer. She must be totally caught up in her TV soap operas, she's not hearing anything else. It means I'm on my own, as usual. Even the Old Man has abandoned me. I haven't heard from him since I left the hospital. I wonder why.

I'm totally worn out, but I need to get to my bedroom. All I want to do is sleep. I force myself to get back up into a sitting position. But then I have to stop moving again while I wait for the pain to die down. I look at Grandma's old dining room table and try to think about that instead of the pain. It's a heavy old thing, that table. With four fancy wooden chairs around it. There's a thick layer of dust on the table and on the chairs too. I wonder when was the last time that table got used. Not since . . . I don't know, maybe not since the last time Mom and I came here for Thanksgiving. When was that? A long time ago. I was pretty young. Grandma was still getting around pretty well back then. We had turkey. Mashed potatoes too, I think. And some kind of cranberry stuff. I can't say I remember much about the meal, but what I do remember is that the occasion turned into yet another one of their stupid shouting arguments. Mom and Grandma always argued when they got together, and it was always about the same thing, Mom's lifestyle, her drinking, and why she couldn't ever hold onto a good man. Grandma said something that got Mom really pissed off. She got red in the face and jumped up so fast, she knocked her chair over backwards. She grabbed her purse and pulled me out the front door. That was our last Thanksgiving with Grandma. Mom never went back to Grandma's house after that, at least as far as I know.

Hard to imagine us ever having had a normal enough life to come here for Thanksgiving to sit at that old table. It's so covered with dust now it's like a museum, a museum of what our life used to be like.

Grandma has no need for things like dining room tables now. All she needs now is her bed and her TV. And somebody here to make her meals. Since Mom left and that truant officer dumped me here, that somebody has been me.

I look toward the kitchen. Dirty dishes piled in the sink. She hasn't been washing any dishes, but it looks like she's actually been getting out of bed long enough to fix herself something to eat. I guess even TV soap operas have to be put on hold if you get hungry enough.

I decide the pain has calmed down enough for me to try to make it to my bed. I use my backward scooting method to inch my way along. Luckily, my bedroom is close by, the next room right off of the dining room, what used to be the living room.

Moving one scoot at a time, ignoring the incredible pain, I finally make it. I stop in the doorway to catch my breath. Looks like nothing has changed in my room. My laptop computer is still on the old card table. That's the most important thing. After the truant cop dumped me here, I turned this room into my bedroom. Grandma didn't care because she hardly ever comes out of her own bedroom which is at the back of the house.

The ratty old mattress that I fished out of the dumpster at a nearby apartment house is still in the middle of the floor. Slowly, I make my way to it. Lucky it's a very thin mattress, or I'd never be able to get up onto it.

I take a couple of deep breaths and with one more really painful move, I'm on it. Made it! Breathing hard, I lie on my back and stare up at the ceiling waiting for the pain to die down. Even with all the pain, it feels good to be back in my own bed. Damn, how many days and nights have I laid here awake staring up at that black ceiling?

Why is my ceiling black? you ask.

It's black because I painted it black. I wanted it to look like the night sky. I did it all by myself. I went to the hardware store and shoplifted a paintbrush, a can of flat black paint, and a little can of bright white paint. I hid it all in my school backpack and walked right out of the store. Shoplifting is easy if you just act normal. When I got back from the hardware store, I stood on the old wooden dresser and painted the whole ceiling black with that little tiny brush. I moved the dresser all around the room to do it, and then I looked up on the internet where the major constellations would be in a winter sky, and I put little white dots up there to make those patterns: Scorpius and Orion and Taurus. I used nine white dots to make Scorpius's claws and to make his legs stick out to the side. I added a few more dots to make up his dangerous stinger, cocked, ready to strike out at whoever needs to be punished. But I think I like Orion the best. I like the way he stands up there so proud, and how his sword hangs down next to him, ready to be used to vanquish his enemies. Maybe, if I can just concentrate on old Mister Orion, I can make some of the pain go away. No such thing as pain up there in that nighttime sky. Nothing but cool darkness and old Mister Orion. Maybe if I focus hard enough on him, I might actually be able to fall asleep.

Daylight. It seems like I've been lying here awake in the dark all night trying to fight off the pain, but I must have slept. A little. But now that I'm fully awake, the pain is right back. And strong! It's in both of my legs and some in my lower back. The intensity is amazing! How can there be such pain? If I still had access to that pain-go-away button, I bet I'd be pressing it like crazy. And like those trained mice, I bet I'd keep right on pressing it.

I hear a sound, like the creaky opening of a door. Is it the front door? Did I forget to lock the front door when I crawled in last night? Now that I think about it, why was that door unlocked in the first place? Why would Grandma ever leave it unlocked? She's scared to death of the neighborhood gangbangers since that time they crawled in through a window and stole her money. They threatened to kill her if she called the police. That was before I moved in here. Maybe they're scared to break in again now that I'm living here. Ha! I hope you realized that was a joke. They're not afraid of me. More likely, the only reason they haven't come back is that now they know there's nothing in this house worth stealing.

I listen. Footsteps, coming closer. For some reason, I have the sudden thought that maybe it's those two weird characters that tried to shake me down in the hospital. Now they're coming to try again. But how would they have found me? I didn't even tell the hospital people where I live. I'd better yell. Scare off whoever it is. "Who's there?"

The footsteps stop. Then they come closer, and a dark-skinned woman's face peeks around edge of the doorway. A thin face. A scowling face. Eyes deep in their sockets. Tired eyes, the eyes of an old woman, but somehow the face doesn't seem old. In fact, it might be a fairly young face. The face says, "Who you be, boy?"

"I live here," I say. "Who the hell are you?"

"You live here? Since when?"

"Since yesterday. I mean since . . . before that too. The last couple of years, I guess."

The dark-skinned woman comes into the room. She stands there staring down at me, hands on her hips. She really is skinny, scarecrow skinny. A faded blue dress that hangs loose on her skinny shoulders like the patient gowns hung on the very sick people back in the hospital. Is she sick? Or just very tired?

"Oh, you must be the grandkid."

"That's right. Did Grandma tell you about me?" I try to sit up, but the pain is so intense, I can't do it.

"Yeah, she tell me 'bout you. She go on all the time 'bout you. She ask me where you gone. How'm I suppose to know where you gone?"

"I was in the hospital. An . . . accident."

She stares at me, frowning.

Do I look that bad? I realize I'm still wearing the sea salt-stained shirt I had on that night, and the giant gray pants that Mexican girl gave me at the hospital.

"Well, now that you back, you can fix the old lady her meals. She always goin' on 'bout how you be the only one who know how to do it right. Soup, she says. She want some kinda soup. She think I make her soup? Let me tell you, boy, I don't make no soup. They didn't say I had to make no soup."

"I know how to make her soup, but I can't walk."

"You can't walk? What the matter with you, boy? You on crack or somethin'?"

"My legs are all fucked up. That's why I was in the hospital." I lean forward, pause until the pain dies down a little, then pull up my pant legs.

Her eyes widen. I can't imagine what all those red scars and bumps under the skin must look like to her.

She leans closer. She points at the lumps. "What those?"

"Screws. That's what the doctors said, anyhow. Screws and plates and shit to hold my legs together."

She stands back and shakes her head. "Well, don't spect me to take care of you. I only sign on to take care of the old lady."

"I just need a drink. Can you get me a drink?"

"So you an alky? I ain't gettin' you no drink. I seen enougha that kinda thing ta last me a lifetime, believe you me."

She turns to walk away.

"No, I mean water. Can't you get me a glass of water?"

She turns back. "You not hear so good, boy? Like I say, I only sign on to take care of old lady." She points with her thumb toward the back of the house, toward the sound of Grandma's TV.

"Please. Just a glass of water. That's all I need."

She shakes her head in disgust and walks out of my bedroom. But in a few moments, she's back with the glass of water.

Ignoring the pain, I manage to almost get myself up into a seated position. I drink the whole glassful non-stop before I thank her. Damn, I was thirsty.

"So how you hurt those legs, boy?"

I hand her back the glass. "Like I said, an accident. I ended up in the hospital, but they booted me out because I didn't have any money. They said they were short of beds."

"That's what they would say. No money and out you go. That's the way of it. Believe you me, I know about that."

Her words make me wonder if she has some kind of experience with the hospitals in this part of town.

She's still staring at me, but she doesn't seem quite so irritated. Finally, she comes a little closer and looks down at me. "So you gonna be here a while?"

"Fraid so."

"Well then, I'm goin' back to the welfare people. I wasn't sposed to take care of two. I got my own kids to take care of."

"You have kids?"

She shrugs. "Who don't have kids?"

"Listen, missus, maybe I can make a deal with you. If you can get me a wheelchair, I could probably get around enough to take care of Grandma myself."

"Wheelchair? Where I get a wheelchair?"

"Uh, I don't know. Maybe from the welfare people?"

"No way. Last time I done say somethin' I want from them, they say they might hafta do a site visit. Said they'd see what the old lady thinks of the job I'm doin' here. Now I stay away from them welfare people. I doan bother them, and they doan bother me."

"But the doctors said I can't put any weight on my legs until they heal up. Maybe you can get a wheelchair from . . . from a thrift store . . . or someplace."

"You want me to pay for a wheelchair? Out my own pocket?"

"Maybe your husband could get one."

That gets a laugh out of her. "That son of a bitch? He long gone. Sorry, boy, you on your own." She starts to turn away.

"Wait! I can't even crawl. I'll starve to death lying here."

She turns back and stands in the doorway looking down at me. "Boy, I think you best go back to that hospital. I call 'em."

"No, no. Please don't call them. I don't want to go back there. I just need time for my legs to heal up. They said I might even be able to walk after they heal up for a while."

She stares at me, and I stare back at her. I know it's not her job to take care of me. If she's been taking care of Grandma just to get her welfare check, that's all she should have to do. I have to think this through. I'm supposed to be good at thinking, so think. What's the solution? There has to be a solution. I look around the room, and I see it: my computer! The solution is right there on the ratty old card table I've been using as a desk. I point at it. "Listen, ma'am. See my computer over there? If you could bring it and put it on the bed here next to me, I can get online and order a wheelchair."

"You got that kinda money, kid?"

"I don't have any money. But I've got an account set up at Amazon. It's tied to Grandma's bank account where her Social Security checks go."

"Amazon?"

"Amazon dot com. It's a web site. They have all kinds of stuff. I bet they have wheelchairs too."

The woman thinks about that, and then she goes to get my old laptop. She puts it on the bed next to me.

I say, "I'll get on right now and order a wheelchair. But it'll take a few days to get here. If you could fix me a few things to eat until it gets here, then I can use the wheelchair to get my own food."

"You want me to fix you *and* the old lady food?"

"Only until the wheelchair gets here."

"I think I best call the hospital."

"No! I don't want to go back there. Besides, they wouldn't let me back in. I don't have any money, and they're overcrowded. Beds in all the hallways. The wheelchair will be here in a few days. Then I can get up and help out."

"You pay me?"

"Like I said, I don't have any money. Only Grandma's Amazon account."

She shakes her head and turns to leave. "I got to go make the old lady her food."

"Wait! Instead of money, I could order you stuff. From that Amazon place. What do you need?"

She looks down at her dress. "Can you get clothes there?"

"Sure I can. What do you need?"

"My kids need clothes. For school."

"Sure. I can get them some clothes. And clothes for you too. As long as it doesn't cost too much. My grandma's monthly Social Security check isn't all that much."

She thinks about it. "They need new pants. And new shirts too."

"Sure, we can get that. Whatever you want. You go get me some food and some more water, and I'll fire up my computer. Deal?"

The woman nods.

"And don't tell Grandma. This will be our little secret."

"I don't bother her. There was bread and cheese, so I make her that. Cheese sandwiches. I put 'em in the fridge and that's it."

"And she gets up and gets them herself?"

"Guess so. They get et. That's all I know. And those jars of peanut butter get gone too."

I'm surprised to hear Grandma has actually been getting out of bed. I guess it means the extra food I ordered from Amazon before I left was enough to tide her over while I was gone. That, plus all the cookies and crackers I ordered and left on her bedside table.

I say, "Well, don't tell the welfare people she's able to get out of bed. She's supposed to be disabled. Bedridden."

"You think I dumb, boy? If I tell 'em she can make her own fixins, they'll send me somewhere else."

"Somewhere where the work is harder."

She shrugs.

"I get it. Don't worry. I won't say anything."

She nods and leaves the room.

I get the computer going and dial into one of the corporate dial-up accounts I've been using. They never use their dial-up accounts. All I had to do was look in a phone book for the names of some LA businesses and hack into their internet accounts using default passwords. They never bother to change them.

I get into the Amazon site and type in "wheelchair." The Amazon site shows a bunch of them. There's a cheap one for ninety-nine bucks. I'm sure Grandma has a lot more than that in her account. I bet this cheap wheelchair will work well enough for just getting around the house, and I'm not planning to go outside anyhow. I click to put that one in my shopping basket.

The dark-skinned lady comes back with a cheese sandwich and a glass of water for me. She also brings me a clean shirt and a pair of pants she says she found in the hall closet. I guess she must have smelled the clothes I'm wearing. She also hands over a bottle of Motrin she says she'd found in the hallway bathroom.

I thank her very politely and chew up a half dozen of the ibuprofen tablets and wash them down with the water.

"You need so many? she says.

"I need to concentrate," I say. "The pain in my legs is fuckin' up my thinking." But as I say those words, I realize the pain isn't as bad as it was last night. So it does help to be distracted. Important for me to remember that.

She sits down on the mattress next to me. As I type in the search words for kid's clothes, I ask her what her name is.

"Denesa."

"Oh, like Denise."

"No!" She says it kind of sharply. "Dee-ness-a. Denise a whitebread name."

Whitebread. That's what the dark-skinned guy called me out in Point Fermin Park when he was robbing me. It must be some kind of currently-popular insult for light-skinned people.

"Oh, sorry," I say.

"What your name, boy?"

"Scotch. My mother named me that because it was her favorite drink."

"That not true. Your grandma call you Fitzgerald."

"Aw, don't call me that. Or Gerald either. You can call me Scott, my middle name. My mom chose my names from that author, F. Scott Fitzgerald, and turned it around."

"Who?"

"He was an old-time writer. When she'd get depressed, she'd sit up at night reading old-time novels like that. She'd curl up on the couch reading and work on a bottle of booze she'd suckered some guy into buying her. Sometimes, she'd read those books out loud, whispering to herself."

"Your grandma tole me your ma run off."

"Yeah."

"You miss her, I bet."

"Naw. Well, sometimes. I used to anyhow."

She stares at me, and I wonder if she's really seeing me for the first time. Maybe she doesn't talk to many light-skinned boys. Maybe not any.

The computer shows me a selection of kid's clothes at the Amazon.com site. She leans closer to look, and that makes me realize that even though I've been living in the middle of a neighborhood full of dark-skinned people for a couple of years now, I've never once talked to a single one of them—except for the gang homies who only talk to me to hassle me.

"There," she says, pointing. "They like that."

She's pointing at T-shirts with Disney Cars cartoons on them.

"You've got little boys?" I ask.

"Yeah. Two."

"Well, how about this shirt here? It's got a funny cartoon picture of Tow Mater on the front of it."

"Okay. Good."

What size?

"Seven."

I put that one into my shopping cart and point to another T-shirt with a cartoon picture of Lightning McQueen on it. "How about this one?"

"Good. My little one. He'll like that. Size six."

I put that one into my shopping cart. "Pants?"

She nods. "Yeah, they need pants. You sure it's not too much money?"

"Naw, it looks like kids clothes at Amazon are cheap. Let's look at pants."

I get the pictures of kid's pants on the computer screen.

Denesa says, "No shorts. They think they're too old for shorts now."

I scroll down through the pictures of kids' long pants until I get to boys' jeans.

She shakes her head. "No way. You think I'm gonna let 'em wear that kinda thing? They start wearin' them kinda pants, next thing they'll be lettin' 'em hang down low showin' off their butts like them damn gang kids do. Just let 'em try gettin' involved with them gangs, and I'll move 'em straight outta the projects, even if we have to live homeless. I swear I will."

"I understand. It's like a war zone out there."

"No, you don't. You don't know nuthin about it." She keeps her eyes on the computer screen and won't look at me.

She's right. There's no way I could imagine what it would be like trying to raise two little boys in a place like Watts. The news is full of horror stories about living in the projects: rapes in the dark hallways, kids getting hit by stray bullets in the project playgrounds. I hope she can find a way to get them out before it's too late and they either join a gang or get hurt because they refuse to.

I continue to scroll down through the pictures until she again points. "There."

She's pointing at plain brown pants with a crease in front. They're like something a kid might wear to church. No gang kid would be caught dead in uncool pants like that.

"Size seven and eight," she says. "I roll the pant legs up. They grow out of stuff so fast."

"What about you?" I ask. "Don't you need anything?"

She looks down at her worn dress. "I could use a new dress. Not for normal. That don't matter. For when I have to go out. Like church or . . . "

I realize she's shy about asking anything for herself. Interesting. She comes on strong at first, but she's actually kind of a shy person.

I search the Amazon site for women's dresses, and she points to a blue dress that's not all that different from the one she's wearing, except that it has fancy-looking white lace around the collar. It's not very expensive. Maybe she only chose that one because it was cheap.

I click to put that dress into my shopping cart. I add my usual order of bread and cheese and peanut butter and honey and canned goods, and just before I click on the PAY NOW button, I remember to add two really big bottles of ibuprofen pain killer tablets. I select the "pay by electronic check" button, and we're done.

She stands up and looks toward the door.

I say, "You have to go?"

She nods.

I try to think how to get her to stay a little longer. I don't want to be left all alone with my pain. But then, I realize it's more than that. She's somebody to talk to. She's actually about the only human being I've talked to in a long time. Except for Grandma, and that's like trying to talk to somebody who's lost inside a TV. I realize that even though I'm normally not interested in talking to anybody, I haven't minded talking to Denesa. Not at all. She started out kind of gruff, but when we were looking for clothes for her kids, she revealed her softer side. And she stopped using as much of the exaggerated black talk. I'm not sure why that is. I hope it means she's stopped thinking of me as the enemy.

Before she can head out the door, I say, "I saw something on an internet news site. It said some Grape Streeters got killed. Did you know those kids?"

"Yeah. Seen 'em around. Knew their mammas." She won't look at me. She keeps looking toward the door. "Hey, I gotta go. Things . . ."

"Sure," I say quickly. "Your kids."

She turns back. "They say I gotta be here to make food for the old . . . I mean for your grandma. Mornin' and night. Else they cut me off. Morning, like now, is okay, but what am I supposed to do when my kids get home from school?"

"You don't have anybody to watch them?"

"A neighbor does. She works in a hotel downtown. Cleanin'. But sometimes the buses run late, and she don't come home until after my kids are already home from school. I hate it when my kids get home and there's nobody there. Not safe. Not safe atal."

I say, "Well, here's what I'm thinking. When I get my wheelchair, maybe I can take care of the evening shift for you."

She turns to look into my eyes. "You think so?"

I nod. "Tell you what, that wheelchair should be here in a couple of days. You keep me alive for that long, and I'll see if I can take care of making Grandma's evening meal."

"But what if they do that site visit thing, and I'm not here?"

"I'll just tell them you went out for a minute. Like . . . you went to the drugstore to get her some pills or something. Anyhow, if they show up, I'll handle it."

She stares at me for a long time. "You're a good kid." She pauses, and then adds, "for a whitebread." She smiles to let me know the insult has now turned into a friendly joke.

It's the first time I've seen her smile. She's missing one of her front teeth, and the other front one is chipped. I can't help but wonder how that might have happened, but I don't ask. None of my business, and besides, I'm starting to feel a little better, and I don't want to make myself sad right now.

4
Non-Intentional Units of Consciousness

This morning, I'm still in bed, but I'm back to my normal routine, exploring internet sites. It's frustrating to be stuck in bed for so many days, but at least I've got my computer. I've been reading everything I can find about the philosophy of pain, but I'm not finding much.

Pain is a non-intentional unit of consciousness.

"Oh, so you're back again, Old Man. I never know when you're going to disappear for a while and then pop back up again."

Pain is a non-intentional unit of consciousness.

"Yeah, I heard you the first time, but what does it mean? All I care about is getting some control over all this damn pain."

Given the structure of consciousness, pain cannot be an exception.

"The structure of consciousness? How does that help me deal with my pain?"

Pain is a conscious experience. Consciousness can be intentional or non-intentional, but it is still consciousness.

"Well, I damn sure do feel all this pain. Is that the conscious experience you're talking about?"

Pain is part of being in the world.

"Yeah, I guess I am still in the world, even though I didn't want to be."

To fully accept our place in the world, we must realize that human pain is part of that reality.

"Yeah, well, do you think I have any choice?"

Life is pain. Humans are born, they suffer a life of pain, and then they die.

"Oh, so now you're gonna to go existential on me. It's a concept I could get into, if I wasn't already into the actuality of it. You try lying here feeling all this pain and see how good you are at accepting it."

The weak man denies the miseries of life. He pretends that this life is not the ultimate state of reality.

"Right, right, we've been through all this before. But that was a discussion we had in the abstract. Now I'm dealing not with the concept of life's pain, but Goddam real physical pain."

Solace can be found in the concept of a better world awaiting.

"No, no, no, I won't let you get back into all that God crap. Like I told you before, there is no God. He's dead and gone, and there is no better world awaiting anybody."

No answer.

I guess that shut him up. I don't know why I even bother to try to talk to him when he gets on his God kick. So, it looks like this is one situation where the old man isn't going to be much help to me. He wants me to get in touch with my pain, embrace it, when I've already learned that the only way to lessen the pain is the opposite, to focus on something else. I have to learn how to put my brain in a place where the pain isn't. That *has to* be the best approach, no matter what Old Man says. Actually, I should conduct experiments to find the best way to do that. I start by focusing on my black sky ceiling. I try really hard to focus on those white dots up there while I think about how unbelievably gigantic the universe is. I read on the internet that there are as many stars as grains of sand on the earth. That doesn't make sense to me. Seems like too small a number. Something that somebody made up. It seems more likely that the universe is infinite. No beginning and no end to it. That means there must also be an infinite number of planets, planets with people on them. I bet the people on some of those worlds are so advanced they don't have to suffer pain. They're probably so advanced they don't even know what pain is. I should be like those people on those planets. I take several deep breaths and concentrate: I'm living on another planet; there is no such thing as pain on my planet, no pain at all.

Well, that didn't work. My legs still hurt like hell. I'd better get back to looking up stuff on the internet; the internet is about the only thing that can distract me enough to push my pain into the background for a while.

For about the hundredth time, I Google "philosophy of pain," and one of the links mentions the name "Nikola Tesla." Wait a minute, I know that name. Tesla wasn't a philosopher. He was an inventor. He invented alternating current. I click on that link anyhow, and find out it's the story of how he was able feel the pain of others. When one of the workers in his laboratory burned his hand, Tesla said he instantly felt the worker's pain. Aw, that doesn't help me. It just makes me think more about feeling pain. I might as well go back to reading about cosmology and the infinite universe and alternate worlds that don't have pain. I Google "alternate worlds," and it gives me a lot of astronomy links. At one site, they're discussing the possibility that there are parallel worlds to ours that are right here next to us even though we can't see them. They call them "branes," short for membranes. They're supposed to be parallel planes, flat, like sheets of paper that are infinitely close to each other, but maybe twisted. They say the inhabitants of one brane wouldn't be aware of the inhabitants of the other branes, even through we'd be right next to them. I like that idea. Other worlds, other types of reality, right next to us all the time, and we can't even see them. I sure wouldn't mind stepping into another reality where pain doesn't exist, but I can't, so I should quit wasting my time reading about that and look somewhere else.

When I was in that hospital, I remember wondering if Eastern philosophy had any solutions for dealing with pain. Now's my chance to check that out. I Google "gurus that can control pain." Google mostly comes up with sites that talk about all the pain and suffering that being human involves, but there are a few sites that talk about some guru in India who supposedly can stick his hand into a fire and not feel any pain. But it doesn't say anything about how he does it. I keep looking, and I find a lot of sites with general info about Eastern philosophy. Most of them tell me I should embrace Buddhist philosophy and use meditation to face up to all the "issues" I'm harboring within myself. Supposedly, that will help me "become one" with whatever is causing me the pain. Embrace Buddhist philosophy, eh. What do you think of that, Old Man?

When Lord Vishnu was very young he was lying on a big banyan leaf, wondering what the purpose of life was.

"Lying on a banyan leaf? What does that have to do with pain, Old Man? You know, I'm beginning to think you don't actually know very much about this Eastern religion stuff. You're just reciting random stuff you saw me reading on the internet. You might just as well go away and let me read about it myself. I stare at the computer screen. Why isn't the old man helping me? Am I going to have all this pain forever? It's a damn depressing thought.

I hear a creaking outside on the front porch. Is must be Denesa. But what if it's not? I have the sudden memory of those wannabe young gangbangers that hassled me that night when I was on my way to the cliff. I disrespected them. Are they coming to take revenge on me for that?

The front door opens, and thank goodness, it *is* Denesa. She's dragging in a couple of big Amazon packages. Good. It means my Amazon order has finally arrived. If that wheelchair is in one of those boxes, maybe I can finally get out of this damn bed.

I wave at Denesa, and she waves back before she heads for the kitchen. I listen to her out there making Grandma something to eat. Grandma hasn't come out of her bedroom once since I got back, so I guess Denesa has been taking pretty good care of her.

Pretty soon, Denesa brings me in a sandwich and some water. Next, she drags the boxes into my bedroom and unpacks them while I watch. She shows me the kids clothes first, and I can tell she's pretty excited to get them. Next, she holds up her new dress for my opinion. I tell her it will look good on her.

Then, it's time to tackle the big box that I assume holds my new wheelchair. She unpacks it and gets it set up. It looks pretty good, but right away I can tell that without the use of my legs, I won't be able to get into it. It looks unstable, like it would just tip over if I tried to pull myself up into it.

Denesa says she'll help me up, but I say no, I have to figure out how to do it by myself when she's not here.

She thinks about it for a minute, and then she says, "Be right back. I got somethin'."

I hear her leave by the front door.

I reach out and drag the wheelchair over closer to the bed to check it out. It's kind of flimsy-looking, but I expect it'll work. But I still can't see any way I'll be able to get into it without using my legs.

Denesa is soon back. She shows me a piece of rope, a pair of pliers, and a fairly large screw hook that she says she happened to have at her place. She drags in a dining room chair and gets up on it to attach the screw hook to the top of my bedroom door sill. Finally, she attaches the rope to the hook. She's pretty handy. I guess being on her own, she's learned how to fix things around her apartment.

Now it's time for me to try it out. She wants to help get me over to the doorway, but since I've got quite a few ibuprofen in me, I feel like I might be able to do it by myself. I have her place the wheelchair in the doorway, and even though it hurts like hell, I'm able to use my backwards scooting method to make it over there. I reach up and grab the rope. I clench my teeth and try not to let Denesa see how much pain this kind of movement gives me.

On the first try, the wheelchair just rolls away, but Denesa figures out how to lock the wheels. I try again, and using the rope, I manage to pull myself up into the chair. Despite the pain it causes, I figure out I can use my hands to lift my legs up onto the footrests.

Well, I guess I'm ready to go. I reach down and unlock the wheels and try a few short spins around the bedroom. It hurts, but I keep my focus on maneuvering the wheelchair. "By damn," I say. "Look at me, Denesa, I'm mobile."

Denesa smiles her big broken-off tooth grin.

I wheel myself into the dining room and take a spin round the old table. No problem.

I look down the hallway toward Grandma's bedroom. I guess I should wheel myself in there to say hi. I'm not sure if Denesa even told her I was back.

I arrive in Grandma's bedroom to find her half sitting up in her bed, propped up with fat pillows. As always, she's watching one of her soap operas on her old TV.

She glances at me, and then turns back to the TV.

Didn't she even miss me? I decide to try to sound cheerful. "Hi, Grandma. I'm back."

She says, "What are you doing in that wheelchair?" She's talking to me, but she's keeping her eyes on the TV.

"Well, the reason I was gone for a while was because I got into . . . a kind of accident."

She still won't look at me. "Figures."

I guess that means she knew I'd be back sooner or later, and that I would have somehow fucked myself up. If she only knew.

As soon as I wheel myself back out into the dining room, Denesa asks if I think I can actually fix my grandma her food.

I wheel my way into the kitchen and open the refrigerator. I can reach all but the top shelf, so I ask Denesa to bring everything down to the lower shelves.

Next, I ask her to take all the packaged food and canned stuff out of the kitchen cabinets and arrange it all on the kitchen counter. I tell her to put the dishes and the toaster and all the pans there too.

Once, she's got that done, I show her that I can now reach everything. And I can even operate the stove with no problem. I'll be able to open cans and heat up Grandma's mushroom soup. I'll bet she's been missing it.

Denesa nods her approval. "Okay then, I guess I won't be seeing you for a while." She packs up her new clothes and heads for the door.

I'm not so sure I like the idea of her leaving for good. Not that I need company, but I hadn't really thought through the idea of her never coming back. I say, "Uh, I think you ought to come by and check in once in a while. I mean just in case the welfare people come by."

She thinks about that, and then she nods. "Good idea. I'll run over here whenever I can. Just in case, like you said, in case them welfare people came by."

She leaves, and I do a few more practice spins around the dining room in my new wheelchair. It all works pretty smooth. Even though sitting up causes me plenty of pain in my legs, it feels good to be mobile. Damn good. I wheel into the kitchen to look for something to eat, and that makes me realize how much I used to take little things like walking into the kitchen for granted.

I fix myself a peanut butter sandwich and wolf it down. Then, I wheel myself back into my bedroom and get my computer and set it up on the card table. That done, I'm back in business. Although it does hurt more to be sitting up, just the simple act of sitting upright in front of my computer makes me feel more human, less like that damn bedridden bug of Kafka's. Now, where was I? Oh right, I was searching the internet for Eastern religion stuff. But maybe I don't want to read about numbered lists of different paths to enlightenment anymore. They may lead to enlightenment, but they don't seem to be leading me to a way to get rid of my pain.

"Hey, Old Man, if I start meditating, will that Lord Vishnu get up off of his damn banyan leaf and give me a hand with my pain?"

No answer. He doesn't like it when I make fun of him. Staid old bugger.

But I did notice that there was one thing all the Eastern religion sites have in common: they all talk about the benefits of meditating. Maybe I should try that. I decide to start meditating one hour in the morning and one hour at night, specifically on how to deal with pain. Maybe that way I can get in touch with whatever "issues" are making my pain worse. All it takes is time, and I've got plenty of that.

5
Epistemological Relevance

The days go by. Actually, I suppose weeks and weeks are going by. Who knows? Time doesn't mean anything to me. I spend my days on the internet, and I when get deep into internetland, the days seem to melt one into the other. My internet-searching routine is interrupted only by my three trips per day out to the kitchen to fix Grandma her meals. Denesa comes by occasionally and talks to me about her kids and whatever trouble is going on over at the projects. I wouldn't mind if she came by to talk to me a little more often, but now that I'm back to taking care of Grandma, why should she?

Some days, I fix myself something to eat, but I'm not much interested in food. What I want is information. Knowledge. I want to know absolutely *everything* there is to know. Sometimes, I talk with the old man, but mostly I just read and think and then read some more. Mostly, I study philosophy, but lately, I've been reading a lot about world history. Of course, that means I end up reading a lot of stuff about wars. Man, it sure seems like humans have always had a hard time getting along with each other. I also read about the history of art and culture and medicine and technology, and lately I've been reading about astronomy and physics, especially quantum physics. I like that kind of stuff. I have to admit there's a lot of it I don't get, but that just makes me want to read more.

But you want to know something? Just about everything I read leads me right back to philosophy. It makes me realize that philosophy underlies everything. Odd that nobody at the high school I went to ever mentioned philosophy. During the few years I was actually attending that school, I may have heard the names of a few of the old time philosophers, like Plato and Aristotle, but that was it.

I notice sunlight is coming in through my window. It means somehow another whole night has gone by, and I haven't moved from in front of my computer. My legs are hurting, and I know I should lie down to take some of the pressure off of them, but my brain is so full of the new things I'm learning, I don't want to stop. As soon as I finish reading about one subject, my mind says, what's next? I go to the Google site and get ready to type in another search about philosophy, but then I notice that above the Google search box is a Google doodle that shows different countries as if they were islands. Each little island has its own flag. They must be commemorating something about world geography. Maybe it's telling me I should take some time to look up something about world geography. I've already learned that countries, and their boundaries, and even their names, change all the time due to wars and shifts in world power, and I've also learned that the real reason there are so many wars is because politicians start them in order to get themselves reelected. Studying history has taught me that a politician will do *anything* to get reelected, even send armies off into other countries to kill a bunch of foreign people. Nothing like a good war to boost the popularity ratings. And because of that, this country has been involved in one war or another for just about all of my life. Soon as one war dies down, the politicians, with prodding from what the internet calls "the military-industrial complex," go looking for another one. They not only use up a lot of soldiers, they also use up a lot of airplanes and ships and lots of other cool—and incredibly expensive—weapons. One of their coolest new weapons is known as a "drone." For a long, long time, it was obvious that sooner or later, we'd get robots to fight our wars for us. Hollywood made lots of movies based on that idea. They showed hoards of human-looking evil robots marching in the same kind of formations the old British Redcoats used, disintegrating everybody in sight with their loud, and very cool, zappers. But when militarized robots actually showed up in our real world, they didn't look like us at all; they looked more like cute little airplanes. And they didn't kill people by zapping them; instead, they killed people by shooting rockets down on them from twenty thousand feet up. The government liked drones as soon as they were invented: if they want to kill a "suspect," they can just blow up the house where the suspect is supposedly hiding. Kill everybody inside, just to make sure. No need for time-consuming trials and defense lawyers and all that courtroom drama; just aim at "the target" and pow! they're all instantly dead. Gone and forgotten. The controllers of those drones, operating them from somewhere in Nevada, halfway around the world, don't need to know who is in a house—just aim and pull the trigger. It's like some real-life (and really-fun) video game. On the internet, I find a site that shows a map of Pakistan, and it marks all the places where houses have been blown up by those satellite-controlled robot airplanes. Man, there are a lot of blown up places on that map.

But I don't want to get caught up reading about that stuff. Nothing I can do about it anyway. It gets too sad if you starting thinking about everybody who "got in the way" in one or the other of our endless wars. I guess nobody else in this country cares, but the whole idea of robot airplanes killing nameless foreign people who are just sitting there inside their houses really bothers me. It just doesn't seem right.

The same site that has that terrible map of Pakistan has other maps you can look at. One of the maps on their list is South America. That reminds me: An-hell was always showing my mom some place on his big map of South America. I'm pretty sure he was pointing at the farthest northern area, so I click on that part of the map. It looks like the furthest most northern country of South America is Colombia. I click on that map and it says Colombia is big, over 439,700 square miles. That's a lot bigger than Texas. But it's not very populated. It says almost half of the country is rain forest with no cities. I try to imagine my mother living with An-hell in that rain forest, but that doesn't make sense. She's a city girl, and I bet they wouldn't have any of the good-times bars she likes to hang out in. Not in the middle of some damn rain forest. And what about TV? She was totally hooked on watching the entertainment news on TV. I bet they don't have very good TV reception down there in the middle of a damn rain forest, so how would she keep up with the doings of the Hollywood movie stars? It doesn't make sense that she'd stay down there this long without her TV and her good times bars. And doesn't she even miss me a little bit? I keep on wondering why she didn't at least leave me a note before she left. But maybe that An-hell guy talked her into their big traveling adventure while she was really drunk, and she just went for it. She's done that before, but until this time, she always came back. Because she doesn't at least write or call, I can't shake the thought that An-hell could be keeping her down there against her will. The site says Columbia is one of the world's leading producers of cocaine. That could be it. Maybe An-hell got her hooked on cocaine, and that's why she doesn't come back. She probably tried cocaine in the past. She was always big on trying new things, but her main drug has always been booze. The only time I ever saw her happy was when she was drunk.

I give up on looking at maps of South America. Worrying about my mother going away and leaving me alone is making me feel sorry for myself, and that always makes the pain in my legs worse.

That reminds me. If I'm on the internet day and night, why haven't I looked at anatomy and medical sites to find out more about what they did to my legs? Maybe those kinds of sites will give me an idea as to whether there's any hope of me ever walking again. I find a medical site that shows pictures of orthopedic surgeries. It shows the four main types of surgical screws that are used to hold human bones together. The most common type is the *cortical screw*. It has thin threads the full length of the screw, and they say it's used to anchor together bones when you have dense material to screw into. There's a completely different type, called a *cannulated screw,* that usually gets buried deep inside a large bone. It's supposed to be guided into place using a wire guide, but I'm not quite sure how that works because the article doesn't show me any pictures of that. A smaller screw, called the *Herbert screw,* is used to hold small bones together. It's hollow, like the cortical screw, but it's threaded on both ends, and in an opposite way so that when you turn it, the two connected pieces of bone get pulled tight together. Seems like they might have used something like that to hold my leg bones together. Finally, there's the *cancellous screw* which is used when you don't have as much hard bone to work with. It's coarser threading requires less thread contact to hold securely. They said they didn't have much to work with on my fucked-up legs, so maybe that's the kind they used on me. The way they talk about it on the internet sites, it all sounds more like woodworking than surgery. I'm surprised they didn't use super glue on me. But who knows, maybe they did.

Anyhow, even though my legs still hurt a lot, they do seem to be holding together pretty well. I guess those screws worked. But will they continue to hold? And do they stay in there forever, or am I supposed to go back someday and have them taken out? Why didn't anybody at that stupid hospital tell me anything like that?

6
Intentional Awareness, Interpreted Experience

Today, I'm reading about psychology. It's not that I'm looking for answers about why I jumped off that cliff (I know why I did that), but I am curious about why they sent me to a psychologist back when I was in high school. When I started my search for info about psychology on the internet, it showed me a lot of sites about Freud. They say Freud created a technique called psychoanalysis, a method for treating psychological problems by talking to the patient. Talk therapy they call it. Well, I know about that. Not long after that school counselor threw me out of his office, they made me go see a psychologist and did he talk. Talk, talk, talk. That's all that guy did. Booring! He said it had been reported to him that I was always mumbling to myself. I told him I was reciting the pledge of allegiance. Honoring my country. Despite his slow brain, he figured out I was pulling his leg. He kept on asking questions so I told him that actually I was praying, asking God to save me from the boring people all around me. That's when he got all up tight and said the teachers at my school had been telling him I was a smart aleck kid who would never give a straight answer to their questions. I asked him why those dumb teachers kept on asking me questions if they didn't like my smart aleck answers? The psychologist stared at me for a while, and then he said that would be enough for today. I never saw him again. I wonder if that guy was trained in Freudian psychoanalysis. According to the internet, Freud thought every psychological problem had something to do with repressed sexuality, when people haven't worked out their infantile sexual feelings. Like the Oedipal complex, which is when little boys are jealous of the attention their mothers gave to their fathers instead of giving it to them. Well, since I never knew my father, and I have no interest in sex, that must be why I'm not crazy. (Between you and me, it sounds like Freud was the real nut case.)

I read on, and it says Freud had a long-term friendship, then a long-term feud, with another famous psychologist named Carl Jung. I look up Jung and it says he was also into the concept of mental illness being related to repressed sexuality, but he was also into the occult and something called the collective unconscious which he thought was a special part of our brains that links us all together. He also believed in precognition, which is seeing what is going to happen in the future. He went to a lot of seances, which is where a person called "a medium" is supposed to be able to talk to the dead. Jeez, this Jung guy sounds nuttier than Freud. Were all those old-time psychologists a bit off?

But that stuff about Jung does give me another word to look up. Precognition. Can that really happen? I Google "precognition," and it leads me to sites that report on research that has been done on precognition and ESP. It says that for a while there was ongoing government-supported research that investigated whether or not some "special" people had precognition. For a while, it looked like they did. But then, one by one, the research studies were shown to be either flawed or outright fraudulent, and that kind of research gradually died out. Despite the failure of the research, the site I'm looking at says the idea is still popular in movies. It says movies often use the idea that police departments use the so-called "mediums" to help them find missing people. But according to this web site, there is no known case in which a medium ever actually helped a police department find anything.

I'm glad I followed that link about the discredited research on nutty stuff. It reminds me that if I'm ever going to make any real progress in my goal of learning everything about everything, I'm going to have to stay logical and not get distracted by all the nutty stuff that's scattered all over the internet. If I read something that doesn't make sense, I should immediately go looking for research on the subject (and not the fake research on sites that have something to prove).

At any rate, I'm ready to give up on psychology. Too weird even for me. What I need is information about the brain. Specifically, how pain works in the brain.

I Google "the neurology of pain," and it leads me to a site that says many different areas of the brain are involved in experiencing and processing pain. It says the reason I feel pain in my legs is because certain "afferent nerve fibers" are carrying the pain information from my legs to my spinal cord and then up to my brain. Then, my brain informs me, Hey, bud, your legs are hurting! So, one way to look at it is that it's not actually my legs that are hurting, but a system of nerve actions that are telling my brain that I have pain. And like I said before, if it's all in my brain, I should be able to figure out how to turn off that part of my brain. Only logical.

I keep looking and find another web site that talks about the "gate control" theory of pain. It says that both pain-responsive nerve fibers and touch-responsive nerve fibers carry information from the site of pain, so the more touch-responsive activity there is in that area, the less pain-responsive activity there can be. In other words, if I rub my leg, it should interfere with the transmission of pain information to my brain. Worth a try. I lean forward and put some weight on my left foot. Of course, that causes pain. I try it again, but this time, I rub the least hurtful part of that leg, not hard, but enough, I hope, to stimulate the touch-sensitive nerve fibers in that area. Did it work? Maybe a little. Hard to say. Maybe it takes practice. I'll work on it. The site goes on to say that the method worked better on athletes that had experienced pain as part of their sport, like boxing or football. Well, I've experienced a hell of a lot of pain in my legs. Doesn't that mean that I too should also be getting better at controlling my pain?

I go back to searching the internet, and I run across another web site that discusses how pain is dealt with by the brain. Unlike those other sites, this site focuses on what's going on inside the brain. It says new brain-imaging studies are showing that more than one area of the brain is activated when any part of your body is hurting. It says there is pain-stimulated activity in an area of the brain called the parieto-insular cortex, and there is also activity in the medial frontal cortex. So, it looks like I'm going to have to figure out how to get control of more than one area of my brain. That may not be so easy.

This morning, when I was in the bathroom, I happened to look into the mirror and notice how thin my face looked. I normally don't look at myself in mirrors, but this time I did, and it told me I must be losing a lot of weight. I decided to ignore that information. I'm hardly ever hungry, so what's the big deal? There's so much to learn on the internet, who has time to eat, or even sleep? I want to learn everything, and I won't let anything stop me, not even hunger. What I'm really starving for is knowledge. I now understand what an addict feels like, always desperate for more and more, and no matter how much you get, it's never enough. The great thing about the internet is, there *is* always more. Once you learn everything you can about one subject, there's always another subject there for the taking. It makes me wonder how much knowledge a human brain can hold, and how long it would take to learn everything about *everything!*

Other than fixing Grandma's food, and grabbing a few bites of food for myself, about the only breaks I take from studying on the internet is to do my pain-control meditation. I don't know if I'm doing it right, but I'm keeping at it, doing it twice a day, always focusing on finding the area in my brain where the pain isn't. At first, I thought meditation might put me to sleep, but as it turns out, it does just the opposite. After a few minutes of meditating, I'm energized and ready to go back to studying on the internet. I will admit to you that sometimes the pain forces its way into my consciousness, and when that happens, nothing works but to eat a handful of ibuprofen tablets. Taking those pills frustrates me though: ibuprofen threatens to make me sleepy, and I don't want to sleep. I just want to stay on the internet and keep on studying. If I could somehow hook my brain directly to the internet, that would be the best solution. Wouldn't it be great to have everything that's on the internet dumped directly into your brain?

Unfortunately, I'm stuck with the reality of sequence, and the fact that there are only twenty-four hours in the day. So I try to forget about days and nights, try to avoid sleeping, and just keep studying. I feel like that Sisyphus guy I told you about earlier, except that my boulder to push up the mountain is studying.

And speaking of Sisyphus, let me tell you about something I read this morning. Albert Camus wrote a book called "The Myth of Sisyphus." In the book, Camus said Sisyphus would actually have been the happiest person in the universe. Why? Because his life had purpose.

Without purpose, life is meaningless.

"Yeah, Old Man, I guess that's the main idea: an endless task would give life meaning. Since Sisyphus knew his life had no promise of anything different, he had no decisions to make. He had no chance of *success*, so he had no chance of *failure*."

A man's purpose defines him.

"Right. While regular humans have free will, and therefore, have to decide whether or not to roll their boulder up their own particular hill, Sisyphus would have no such decisions to make. There would be nothing for him to be happy or unhappy about."

Purposes are values projected into the future.

Values projected into the future? An interesting idea. But what if the future is known? What if I knew, for sure, that I was going to spend the rest of my life right here in this old house, studying on the internet? I guess I wouldn't have any reason to be unhappy.

In his book, Camus wondered what Sisyphus would think about as he walked back down to the bottom of the hill to retrieve his boulder. He sure as hell wouldn't be thinking about what he was going to do later that day (the future). He wouldn't be thinking about food or romance or worldly gain (values); he would only be thinking about getting back down to bottom of the mountain where his boulder would be waiting for him. For him, life was simple and straightforward and decisionless.

I think I should take the lesson of Sisyphus to heart. I should focus on my task and nothing else. I shouldn't worry about my learning having any purpose in the world; it is simply my task, and that's all there is to it. In the past, if I studied long enough to master some new type of learning, it gave me a sense of accomplishment. But then, I would stare at the computer screen trying to decide what to do next, and that made me suddenly notice how much pain was in my legs. My mistake was taking on the emotional feeling of accomplishment. I need to be more logical and get rid of all emotions, all feelings. I should realize that whenever I've managed to get my boulder to the top of the hill (new learning), it only means that another learning task is waiting for me. There is nothing to *feel* about it; it just *is*. I bet if I can somehow get rid of all feelings, good or bad, the feeling they call pain will also go away. From now on, I will try to be more like Sisyphus and realize that my life is what it is, studying stuff on the internet and nothing more.

That thought makes me wonder if anybody else might be doing what I'm doing, spending all their time on the internet. Out of curiosity, I go to Google and type in "spending all your time on the internet." Google shows me a lot of links to sites that talk about "internet addiction," but they all see it as a bad thing. (Get the joke? Internet sites saying being on the internet is a bad thing.) But I know they only see it as an addiction because they think it takes time away from whatever else they think a person should be "accomplishing."

I'm about to give up when I run across the word "*hikikomori.*" It seems to be a Japanese word that's related to internet addiction. I look the word up on Wikipedia, and it tells me the Japanese word translates to "pulling inward," but in Japan, it refers specifically to a set of young people, mostly boys, who have withdrawn from society and spend all their time on the internet, refusing to go out and interact with other humans. I'm amazed! There are actually others out there in the world that are like me. Am I an American version of *hikikomori*? But I doubt that those Japanese *hikikomoris* are like me. They may have withdrawn from the world, like I have, but I bet they use social media, Facebook and stuff: they may not go out of their parents' houses, but they're probably interacting with other people using the internet. Or else they're playing against other *hikikomoris* on those group internet games. Still, it's an interesting idea that there's actually a name for young men like me: *hikikomori*. From now on, if anybody asks me what I do, I'll tell them I'm an American *hikikomori*. That is, if I ever meet anybody who would ask me anything, which is not very likely. But so what? We *hikikomori* don't care what anybody else thinks. We *hikikomori* don't need people. We *hikikomori* prefer to be by ourselves. The internet is enough for us. For this *hikikomori,* at least, studying philosophy and science and neurology and history and stuff like that is enough of a life.

Like Sisyphus, I have my purpose, and my purpose *defines* me. And besides, if I need to interact with anybody, I can talk to people on the internet. Like Old Man, and smart people like Camus and Kafka. But I only want to talk to people who are dead. I don't want, or need, to establish any relationships. That would only distract me from my task of pushing my boulder up my the hill.

So, what is my boulder today? What haven't I learned about?

What about those Eastern gurus who are supposed to have learned how to completely turn off their pain? I haven't looked them up on the internet lately. I read about them after I got out of the hospital, but it sounded like a bunch of baloney.

But now that I've learned so much more about how pain works and how it's controlled by the brain, I should go back and take a closer look at them.

I Google the two words, "guru" and "pain." One web site talks about this one guru in India who's supposed to be able to put his hand into a fire and not feel any pain. Maybe he's learned how to turn off the part of his brain that feels pain. But as I read on, it says the flesh on the guy's hand doesn't get burned.

Normally, I don't pay much attention to such nonsense. I'm not one of your "true believer" types, and I know the world is full of quacks and fakers. But this guy seems to have a lot of followers, so I keep on reading. When he was asked how he was able to keep the flesh of his hand from burning, he said there was such a thing as the "transcendental position," which means you put yourself in a place that's outside the material world. Interesting.

The other day I was reading about some physicists who say there are worlds parallel to ours, worlds that are right there next to us, but we can't detect them. Maybe that's how that guru guy puts his hand into the fire without it getting burned. Maybe he's just putting his hand into a parallel universe. But then I remember my pledge not to go for things that don't sound logical. More likely, he's just lying.

I keep searching and find another site that's about an Eastern guru who says he doesn't eat anything at all. He says he lives on air. Weird. The more I read about Eastern gurus, the more they sound like nonsense. More like magic than fact.

And sure enough, I find another site that talks about "eating" the sun, getting nutrients from the sun by staring at it. Sounds like a good way to damage your eyes. But some people seem to be going for it. Here's a thing I'm learning: the more far out something is, the more strongly some people want to believe it. But despite how nutty most of the Eastern religion sites are, I think they're onto something with their meditation idea. I'm willing to keep on trying that because it seems to help me focus. I'm not about to sit around meditating all day long, but I can spare an hour or so everyday to give it a fair trial.

Here's a thought: in a way, the things those gurus are telling me sounds a lot like what some of the existentialist philosophers have been telling me for a long time. Maybe I should go back to reading about the existentialists. I liked them the very first time I read about them. I especially liked the existentialist writers that wrote stories, writers like Kafka and Dostoyevsky and Sartre and Camus. When I was in school, I used to go to the used book stores and steal their books, but now, I've discovered that just about all of their stories are available for free on the internet at sites like Project Gutenberg, or at some of the university web sites. For example, I recently read an existentialist play online named "Waiting for Godot" that was written way back in 1952 by an Irish playwright named Samuel Beckett. The characters in the play seem to find the very act of living so exhausting and so meaningless that they can hardly face the concept of going on. It felt very true. I'm surprised everybody in the world doesn't feel like that most of the time.

Right now, I'm reading Dostoyevsky's story, *Crime and Punishment*. I downloaded it from the Project Gutenberg web site. In the story, a character named Raskolnikov kills another character named Alyona Ivanovna, and wonders if murder is permissible if it serves the "greater good."

It's a more important question than you might think. I mean, isn't that the whole idea behind killing people in a war? For example, in World War Two, they trained young American Air Force pilots to drop bombs on innocent foreign people in Germany and in Japan. They say they did it in order to bring the war to an end. Supposedly, it was for "the greater good," at least if you're looking at it from the American point of view. The way I look at it, a lot of innocent people had to die just because they happened to live in a country we were at war with. Near the end of that war, those young American pilots dropped an atomic bomb on a Japanese city called Hiroshima. The bomb killed hundreds of thousands of innocent people, including, according to the internet, thousands of innocent babies asleep in their cribs. Was that a bad thing to do? Did the people in America feel bad that those babies had to die? No, not at all. Those babies *had to* die because they happened to have been born in a country we were trying to defeat in a war. We killed them for "the greater good, " to end the war.

Supposedly, we killed all those babies because we hoped it would lessen the chance that more American solders would have to die. I guess they believed American humans were more important than Japanese humans, more important even than little Japanese babies. The American president, Harry S. Truman, said he had been "guided by God" to drop the atomic bomb on Hiroshima.

Unfortunately, even after they dropped the atomic bomb, the Japanese still refused to give up, so three days later, other young American pilots "had to" (still for the greater good) drop an even more powerful atom bomb on another Japanese city, Nagasaki. That bomb incinerated even more babies in their cribs, but the Japanese *still* wouldn't give up. They were determined to get even with the U.S. for killing their babies. But it wasn't long before the Soviet Union took advantage of the situation and declared war on Japan. That convinced the Japanese that they were outnumbered, and they'd better give up before even more of their babies got blown up.

So, if the greater-good concept is valid in war, why can't an individual make the same argument? That seems to be what Dostoyevsky is saying. But maybe the greater-good concept was only Raskolnikov's justification to steal money. And maybe dropping an atomic bomb and killing all those innocent Japanese babies was just an excuse to use a cool new weapon that had taken a lot of time and money to develop.

Anyhow, where was I?

Humans make decisions based on their personal realities.

Oh right, I was talking about going back to study the existentialists. I read on the internet that both Camus and Sartre talked about the existentialist concept of "existence precedes essence."

Humans are born with an essence. It is called human nature.

"What? No, I think they're saying just the opposite, Old Man. I don't think the existentialists believed in God."

If there is something universal about humans, a way to be. We are all made according to a predetermined model.

"Nice try, Old Man, but there is no such thing as 'human nature,' just like there is no such thing as God. Humans are all different because we all grew up experiencing different things. Do you think the gangbangers who rule this poor neighborhood have the same 'human nature' as the rich kids who live out there in those million-dollar houses on the beach? No way. They are very different. They became what their experience dictated them to be. Based on everything I've learned about people and societies and human history, we're all products of our environments and our experiences. End of story."

No answer.

Apparently, the old man doesn't want to talk about what the existentialists have to say about God. But I do. The existentialists that I've talked to on the internet say we're condemned to be free. That means there is no God telling us how we have to be. Except for a few genetic minor differences, we're all born with the same characteristic human capabilities that pretty much dictate what we can and can't do. Even our brains are pretty much all the same when we're born—a clean slate. But from that point on, our environments and our experiences change who we are. I think of it like growing new branches on a tree. We all start from the same type of seed, the human seed, but as we add new branches to our tree, pretty soon we're all different from each other. We still look pretty much alike, but our brains have been changed by our experiences. The fact is, the only difference between us humans is what we have taken into our brains through learning. Therefore, it is logical that I should use my "freedom" to stuff as much learning into my brain as possible. The more I learn, the more different I'll be from all other humans. I'll know things that none of them will ever know.

7
Deconstructing Primordial Intuition

Guess what? Today, I ran into a completely new branch of philosophy called "deconstruction." The internet tells me it's a new approach to philosophy developed by a current-day French philosopher named Jacques Derrida who is creating a philosophy of language. It says Derrida is known for "semiotic analysis." I look that term up, and it says it's a way of looking at what has meaning in a culture and what's behind our cultural practices. Interesting stuff. I go to some other links about this Derrida guy, and it tells me he's considered controversial in the field of philosophy. I'm not sure why; his philosophy of deconstruction seems a lot like what I've been doing on my own— deconstructing everything, trying to understand what's real and what isn't.

I'm really getting into this new deconstruction philosophy when I hear somebody come up onto the creaking front porch. Is it Denesa? I hope so. She hasn't been by in a while. I hurriedly wheel my way to the front door and open it. It is Denesa, and she's holding a wadded-up blue towel. Did she think I needed a new towel? Doesn't she realize that if I need a new towel, I can just order it on Amazon.

She walks right in without a word, closes the door behind herself, and unfolds the towel. A little blue and white bird flies out. I watch it fly around the dining room until it eventually lands up on the end of a curtain rod. It's a parakeet, a damn parakeet. It sits up there on the curtain rod, turning its head sideways to look down at me.

"Stupid bird flew in my bathroom window," says Denesa. "I tried to chase it out, but it wouldn't go."

"It's a parakeet," is all I can think to say.

"Yeah," she says. "I asked around my neighbors, but nobody said they'd lost it, so I figured you could use some company."

What? Why would she think I needed company? And even if I did want a bird for company, what would I feed it? I turn back to Denesa. "Uh, what do parakeets eat?"

"Bird seeds I guess. Can't you order some on that Amazon computer thing of yours?"

"Yeah, I guess so. But why don't you just keep it? I could order some birdseed for you. Wouldn't your kids like a pet bird?"

"Actually, that's why I wanted to hurry and get it out of my place before the kids get home from school. Sure, they'd wanna keep it, but they're gone all day at school, and now that I'm makin' a little money helping out mothers that got babies, I don't have time to take care of it."

I think about that. I'm sure her kids would really like to play with it. What little kid doesn't like having a pet? I remember when I was little, I found a stray puppy and brought it home. But Mom said we couldn't afford to feed it, so she made me tie a piece of rope around its neck and take it to the nearby school playground. I tied it to the bottom of the monkey-bars and ran away. The poor little thing looked so sad when I left it there. The next day, I went back, and the dog was gone. I always hoped some kid took it home and got to keep it. Lucky damn kid.

"Well," I say, "how about this. How about I keep it here and you can bring your kids over to play with it?"

She doesn't respond. She's still looking up the silly little bird.

I'm wondering why I said that. Am I lonely? Do I need company?

Denesa frowns and looks toward the door. "Well, we'll see. Anyhow, I got to go." She heads for the door.

"Thanks," I say as I watch her go down the porch steps. "I guess."

She waves one hand without looking back, and I watch her hurry away down the sidewalk.

I close the door and look up at the little parakeet. It's still sitting up there, turning its head from side to side, as if it's trying to get a better look at me. It's interesting that birds have their eyes in the sides of their head. To watch out for danger, I guess. On the internet, I've seen pictures of predator birds, like hawks and owls, and they have their eyes in the front of their heads. Better for looking for prey, I guess. I bet they'd love to eat this little bird if he ever got outside where they could catch him. It looks like the parakeet isn't going to budge from his high perch up there on the curtain rod, so I let it be and go back to my computer.

I'm hardly starting to read again, trying to figure out what this deconstruction philosophy is all about, when the damn bird startles me by flying in and landing on my shoulder. I turn my head to try to look at it, but it's so close I have to just about cross my eyes to see it.

It says, "Pretty boy."

I laugh. "Pretty boy? Is that your name? Are you a boy?"

It turns its head to look at me out of its little black eye, and then it repeats those same two words: "Pretty boy."

"Is that the only thing you know how to say?"

"Pretty boy," it replies. And adds a few shrill tweets.

I guess whoever owned it before taught it to say that, and they must have also let it stay on their shoulder. Okay with me. I let it stay there as I go back to studying this new type of philosophy. Pretty soon I'm hardly even aware that the little bird is still there on my shoulder.

"Check this out, Old Man. What do you think of what this Derrida guy is saying? He's talking about communication systems and the fundamental nature of language. I think he's asking whether human language can be seen as a functional system capable of communicating organized content without considering human experience.

No answer.

The old man is talking to me less and less these days. It seems like the more I learn, the less I hear from him.

I notice that the parakeet has managed to pull some threads loose from my shirt collar. I brush the silly little bird off my shoulder and say, "Quit that, Pretty Boy."

But after one fast-flying circuit around my bedroom, he comes right back. He lands on my shoulder and again starts pulling at threads in my collar. I give up and let him do it. Who cares? I guess that's his entertainment. So what if my shirt collar ends up looking ragged? Nobody will ever see it, except for Grandma and Denesa, and if I ever do decide to go out, maybe I'll start a new ragged-collar shirt style.

I go back to reading about the philosophy of deconstruction. It's not easy to understand, but that's exactly what I'm looking for: complex new things to learn, new things to think about. I continue reading until I hear Grandma's tinkling bell. I look at the angle of the light coming through the bedroom window and realize it must be lunch time already. How could the time go by so fast? I roll into the kitchen to fix her something to eat, and the bird stays right there on my shoulder, staying busy tearing apart my shirt collar. Even when I roll into Grandma's bedroom with her food, it doesn't budge from my shoulder. It takes one look at Grandma and says, "Pretty Boy."

That causes Grandma to tear her eyes away from her TV long enough to glance at me. She says, "What's that on your shoulder?"

"It's a parakeet," I say. "That welfare lady brought it."

She looks back at her TV and says, "What do you want with a bird?"

I don't know how to answer that question. I shrug and the little bird flutters his wings to keep his balance on my shoulder. Good question. What do I want with a bird? Denesa thought I needed company. Do I?

Grandma isn't paying any attention to me now. The commercial is over, and she's back to focusing on the her soap opera. On the TV, some actress is overacting, trying to look really sad. She's dabbing at the corners of her eyes with a tiny white handkerchief. An older man in a gray suit is sheepishly staring at his shoes. The usual nonsense.

I roll back into my bedroom. "Well, Pretty Boy, let's see if we can find some food for you. Pretty Boy stops pulling at the threads on my shirt collar long enough to look at me. Maybe my mention of food reminded him that he's hungry.

At the Amazon.com site, I search for birdseed, and it shows me a variety of different types of seeds for wild birds, but it also lists a type of seed that it says is specially formulated for parakeets. "Look here, Pretty Boy. Apparently, you need a special kind of food. Well, since you're so special, how about I put in an order for a big bag of this here parakeet seed for you?"

Pretty boy says, "Pretty boy?"

"Yep, that's what it says. Special food. But you'd probably eat wild bird seed or any other kind of seed, wouldn't you?

He says, "Pretty boy."

"No, no. Don't thank me. Nothing but the best for Mr. Pretty Boy."

I put the parakeet seed into my Amazon shopping cart ,along with my usual order of food, and click to send it off.

Pretty Boy tweets his approval.

I go back to reading on the internet, and Pretty Boy goes back to pulling at the loose threads in my shirt collar.

I'm finding this new deconstruction philosophy really interesting, but so far, I'm still not quite sure what it's all about. It talks a lot about cultural "texts," which as I understand it, can refer not only to printed words, but also to any form of communication. A "text" could be the words in a book, but it could also be a TV news bulletin, an advertising billboard, or even something like a Disney cartoon: they all harbor information and therefore can be defined as texts. It says that the way information is transmitted and received depends on the society you live in, and the semiotic analyst's task is to identify the signs within the text and deconstruct the codes within the texts with reference to the values and beliefs of a society. There are different kinds of textual codes, such as the kind used in making movies (like close-ups to draw attention to something), and social codes such as facial expressions and hand gestures. It says the semiotic analyst must also understand the relationships between "signifiers," the linguistic units used in language. Examples are phrases or phonemes. It says once you put it all together, you get meaning.

I can see right away that this new deconstructive philosophy is going to take me some time to figure out. But that's just what I'm looking for, something involving enough to keep my from thinking about anything else (like the pain in my legs).

That thought makes me notice how much my legs are hurting. I've been sitting in my chair without moving for way too long. That always happens when I get too engrossed in something new. I lean back to stretch and Pretty Boy has to flap his wings to keep his balance.

He says, "Pretty Boy," and he lets out a few shrill tweets right in my ear.

"Jeez, not so loud, Pretty Boy."

He turns his head sideways to look at me, but he doesn't say anything else. Did he understand that I wanted him to pipe down a bit? Maybe he's smarter than he looks.

"Well, Mister Pretty Boy, what should we look up next?"

He says, "Pretty Boy."

I'm not sure what that means, but it sounded sort of like a question. "You're probably wondering why I'm in this wheelchair, aren't you?"

He says, "Pretty Boy."

"Well, the why of it is not important, but now that you mention it, you've got me wondering why my legs are taking so long to heal. Or maybe they *are* healing, even though I'm still having a lot of pain. What say we do a little research on that subject?"

He gives me a tweet of approval, and I turn back to the computer. As I've done many times before, I do a Google search on leg injuries. Mostly, the sites I find talk about broken bones and tendon injuries. This time I type in a more specific question, "How long should it take shattered leg bones to heal?"

I hit a couple of different sites, and the consensus seems to be that it can take anywhere from six weeks to six months, depending on the extent of the injury.

I'm not sure how long I've been out of that hospital, but it must be at least six months. I do some more searching and find a site that provides pictures and instructions about how to do certain leg exercises to strengthen damaged legs—even, it says, while the patient is still in a wheelchair. It says the patient should begin by pushing down on the wheelchair footrests several times a day. It says you should be able to gradually build up enough strength to stand up for short periods.

I try pressing down on the chair's footrests.

Ouch! That hurts like hell.

Pretty boy stops tugging at the loose threads on my shirt collar and digs his little claws into my shirt so he can lean forward to see what I'm doing. He turns his head to look at me and says, "Pretty boy?"

"What am I doing? I'm testing my legs. This internet site says they should be mostly healed up by now."

He says, "Pretty boy!"

I guess that means he's encouraging me.

"It says here that if I do these types of leg-strengthening exercises, someday I might actually be able to stand up."

He says, "Pretty boy."

"Yeah, I know I'm not doing anything close to standing up yet, but we have to be optimistic, right?"

He says, "Pretty boy!"

See there. He agrees with me.

I hear somebody come onto the front porch. Now who could that be? I quickly get up and get into my wheelchair. I roll to the front door, and when I open it, I see that it's Denesa, and she's got a surprise for me: she's brought along her two little boys. So these are the two boys she's always talking about. She's got them dressed in those outfits we bought on the internet, and boy, are they a couple of cute little kids.

I give them a big grin and say, "Well, hello there, fellas."

They pull back and stand against their momma, shyly staring at me.

I keep on grinning at them. And I'm not just acting happy to see them, I really like that she brought them to see me. I don't know why I should be happy to see a couple of kids, but I am. Being an only child, I don't know much about little kids, so maybe I just like the idea of them. Or maybe I like them because they haven't had time yet to start believing in all the crap adults believe in. I roll my chair back out of their way and say, "Welcome. Welcome. Come on in."

Denesa herds the two boys in and closes the door. She rests her hands proudly on the shoulders of the boys. She nods toward the older boy and says, "This one is Javon, the man of the family."

Javon stares at me without smiling. He certainly seems solemn for a seven year old. I give him a serious salute.

She tousles the hair of the younger one. "And this is Zyrell. We call him the zipper cause he won't ever sit still."

I roll my chair forward toward them, but not too fast; I don't want to scare them. They're probably not used to seeing light-skinned people, at least not this close up. I start to put out my hand to shake, but then I change my mind.

Instead, I lean forward to look at the older boy's shirt. "Well, look at this. Isn't that Tow Mater on your shirt there?"

The boy nods and smiles, but he's still acting shy. He's still holding back against his mother, warily keeping his eyes on me.

"You like Tow Mater?" I ask.

He nods again, and smiles a little more broadly this time.

I turn to the younger boy. He's a lot thinner than his brother. I hope he hasn't been sick or something.

I point at the front of his T-shirt. "And I bet this is good ol Lightnin' McQueen right here on your shirt. I'd recognize him anywhere."

The little boy takes a step toward me and points to the front of his own shirt. "He's a car."

"Well, he sure is," I say.

I look up at Denesa. She seems quite proud of her two boys, but she doesn't seem all that happy today. I wonder if she's having some kind of problem.

"He's got eyes," Zyrell adds, pulling his shirt out for me to see.

Looks like Zyrell is the more talkative one. He doesn't seem all that shy now, but his older brother is still holding back. Maybe they get more cautious around us light-skinned people as they get older.

I look closer at the zipper's shirt. "Why you're right. That car does have eyes." I pretend to be amazed. "How can that be?"

"He's fast."

I can't help but laugh. "I bet he is."

I look up at his mother. "And how's momma today?"

Denesa hesitates, and then says, "Momma's got a problem."

She has an unsure look on her face; I might even call it a scared look. And then I realize why she brought her kids. "You want to leave them."

She clasps her hands together, like she's begging. "Only for a little while. I'd never ask, but school's out for the holiday break, and I got to go down to the welfare office. They say I gotta get a job or they'll cut me off. I tried to tell 'em I can't get no job because of my kids, but it's so noisy on that damn hallway pay phone, I couldn't tell for sure what they were sayin'. They were talkin' about some kind of form I gotta fill out. I tried to tell 'em I deserve what little bit of welfare money they give me 'cause I got two little kids to take care of and no husband. But they keep on sayin' I hafta come down there and fill out some paper that lays out all my "resources." That's what them welfare people called it. Resources. As if I got any of them."

It seems like she's about to burst into tears.

"Hey," I say, reaching out toward her, "it's no problem. No problem at all."

"They won't be any trouble," she says. "Really." She still sounds like she's begging.

I point toward my bedroom. "Hey, I bet we can find some cartoons on my computer. Maybe even one about cars."

"I'm real sorry," she says. She's wringing her hands nonstop now.

I notice her nails have been bitten down really short. She must be under a lot of stress.

"My neighbors are all gone out. I don't know where they went today. Normally, they'd keep an eye on 'em for me, but I didn't know I was gonna have to go out. And if I don't get down to that welfare office before they close . . ."

I wave toward the door. "Go. Go. We'll be fine. Take your time getting back. We'll have fun, won't we boys?"

They don't look so sure. Like his momma, the older boy seems about to burst into tears.

Denesa kneels down in front of them and tells them they have to be very, very good boys. She tells them they have to be very quiet and do everything mister Scotty tells them to do. She tells them she won't be very long, kisses them both on their foreheads, and hurries out the door with only one regretful glance back at me.

The boys and I stare at the door after she's gone. It's a little daunting to be suddenly in charge of two little boys, but I'm feeling good that she trusts me. I have the odd thought that it's maybe the first time anybody other than my mother ever trusted me with anything, let alone trusting me with kids. But I realize I don't mind being in this situation. Not at all. I bet I can make these two boys like being with me if I try hard enough. I decide to take it as a challenge.

I turn to look at them, and they shyly stare back at me.

Then Pretty Boy saves the day, by speaking up: "Pretty Boy."

Both of the boys turn and look up to see him. He's looking down at them from up on the top rim of his favorite lampshade.

"Go on over and say hello," I say. "His name is Pretty Boy. He'll talk to you."

Pretty Boy confirms what I said with an extra clear, "Pretty Boy."

"Go on," I say. "If you stand over there under that lamp, I bet he'll fly down and sit on your shoulder."

The older boy looks doubtful, but Zyrell doesn't need to be told twice. He hurries over and stands with his back to the lamp. He looks back at me expectantly.

"Just wait," I say. "He'll come down."

Pretty Boy lets out a few good tweets, but doesn't seem quite ready to come down just yet.

Zyrell sure is a skinny little boy. And Javon isn't much heavier. I wonder if maybe they're hungry.

"Okay," I say, "whose hungry?"

They both seem interested, but they're still acting a bit cautious.

Damn, now that I've said that, I wonder if I've got anything kids would like to eat. I wish I had some ice cream or something. Maybe I shouldn't have said anything about eating. I look toward the kitchen. But there must be something.

"Well, come on, then," I say, spinning my chair around. "Let's go see what we've got." I wheel my chair toward the kitchen, hoping they'll follow me. They could just run out the door. Then what would I do? I'd never get my chair down off the front porch to chase after them.

Luckily, they both do follow me, but they're holding back, still a bit cautious.

I open the refrigerator and look inside. Not much. They wouldn't want cheese and bread. Kids probably don't like stuff like that. I glance at them. They're watching me, sticking close together.

Nothing but bread. And it's just regular white bread, the only kind Grandma will eat. Do kids like white bread? And would they accept white bread from a whitebread guy? Maybe they'd like some of Grandma's honey. I bet all kids like honey.

I take out the loaf of bread and show it to them. "How about some toast and honey? That sounds good to me. How about you guys?"

They seem interested, so I pop two slices into the toaster, and while we wait, I decide the place to start making friends is with the younger one. He seems the most accessible. "So, you're Zyrell. What a great name."

He ignores me. He's standing on his tiptoes trying to reach the plastic bear-shaped jar of honey. I reach up to get it and put it in his hand. "You want to put the honey on the bread yourself?"

He nods excitedly. I think he really is hungry. Maybe his momma didn't have time to feed them after she talked to the welfare people on the phone.

I take the two pieces of toast out of the toaster and hold them both out to him. He sticks the corner of his little tongue out of the side of his mouth as he carefully squeezes the honey onto the bread.

I can hardly keep from bursting out laughing at the sight of that little tongue poking out of the corner of his mouth as he carefully aims the squirts of honey at the bread.

He hands one piece to his big brother before he bites right into his own piece.

His older brother also starts eating right away, but then pauses to bop his little brother on top of the head. When Zyrell looks up at him, frowning and rubbing the top of his head, the older boy whispers, "Say thanks," and nods toward me.

Zyrell says, "Thanks," without bothering to look up. He goes right back to eating.

"Thanks, Mister Scotty," says the older boy.

"You're certainly welcome, Javon. Now, I think I should put some more bread in the toaster. What do you think?"

They nod, both smiling now.

Pretty Boy chooses that moment to fly down and land on Zyrell's shoulder.

Both boys squeal with pleasure.

Pretty Boy goes right to work searching for loose threads on Zyrell's T-shirt.

I can tell this is going to work out just fine. Thanks to Pretty Boy and that little bear-shaped jar of honey, we're all going to become great friends.

By the time their mother comes back, we've gone through several more pieces of bread and half of the jar of honey. We had a nice talk about which are the best Disney cartoons and a more serious conversation about how school isn't much fun except for recess.

Denesa comes in to find us gathered around the computer watching cartoons.

They run to hug her, and Pretty Boy retreats to his lampshade.

I ask her how it went.

She frowns. "Okay. But they say from now on, I got to try to make some money. Lady says to me, 'Why not take in laundry or somethin'.' I says to her, 'Hey, I got to pay quarters down in the laundry room even to do my own laundry. How I gonna make any money that way?' Anyhow, they make me fill out a bunch of papers and let me go. They say I get to keep my dole. For now."

Zyrell looks up at her and says, "We had honey."

Denesa looks at me.

"Toast and honey," I say. "They were hungry."

She shakes her head and frowns at them. "They're always hungry. I think they both got hollow legs."

The kids giggle. It must be a family joke.

She pats them both on top of their heads and stares down at them lovingly. "I hope they weren't too much trouble."

She glances back toward Grandma's bedroom. "Did?"

I shake my head. "Naw, she's all caught up in her TV. Didn't hear a thing."

"Thank you so much, Scotty. It's just that I had no other . . . "

I wave off her concerns. "No problem. We had fun, didn't we boys?"

They both nod and smile at me.

She continues to thank me as she herds them out the door.

I wheel to the door and watch them go down the steps and onto the sidewalk.

"Thanks again," she calls.

"Anytime," I say, and I mean it. I hope she *does* bring them by again. They're both cute as can be, and very polite.

She takes them by the hands and hurries away down the sidewalk.

I lean out the door to watch them go. The little family seems small and fragile. I think of all the dangers in this damn neighborhood, gangs, child molesters, rapists. I wonder how often she dares take them outside. Probably not too often. Then again, maybe she's used to all the shit that goes down in this neighborhood.

As I watch them go, I try to imagine what life is like for them. I can't seem to shake a nagging feeling of worry about them over there in those dangerous projects. I wonder if it means something has changed inside me since I tried my fouled-up swan dive off that cliff. I really did enjoy having those two kids around. I wouldn't have expected that. I've never had anything to do with kids. Not ever. So, why did I like being with them so much? After all, they took me away from my internet research. But I now realize that all the time they were here, I never once thought about what I was missing on the internet. I must have been getting bored with my usual research, and they gave me something new to think about.

I wheel my chair into the kitchen to start fixing Grandma's meal, but I stop when I see the bear-shaped jar of honey sitting on the counter. Who am I kidding? It wasn't because I was bored; I really did enjoy being with those two kids. It was something to see the eager way they went after that toast and honey.

I have the sudden memory of that cluster of gang homies down at the corner. I look toward the front door. Denesa is going to have to walk through that bunch. Will they hit on her? She always seems completely tired out, and that makes her look a lot older than she really is. And except for her broken teeth, she's not really all that bad looking. Those guys *might* give her trouble. On the other hand, maybe having two little kids gives her cover. Maybe none of the young men in this neighborhood want to take on the responsibility of a ready-made family. Besides, they've probably got plenty of girls to have sex with in their own gangs One thing for sure, Denesa sure as hell won't want them to come anywhere near her precious little boys.

That leads me to a frightening thought: in this neighborhood, little boys grow up to become gang members, no matter how cute they are at age six or seven.

8
Grand Narratives and Personal Meaning

It's past noon, and I'm hurrying to fix Grandma her mushroom soup. I see that the salt shaker has somehow gotten pushed to the back of the kitchen counter. I can't reach it. Grandma will give me no end of shit if I forget to put a goodly amount of salt in her mushroom soup (even though the label says it already has a shitload of salt in it), so I grab the edge of the counter to pull myself up to get it. But as soon as I'm back sitting down in my wheelchair with the stupid salt shaker in my hand, I realize that for a brief moment I was essentially standing up. Apparently, the leg strengthening exercises I've been doing really have made them stronger. I try to think through how I did it. It seems like I must have put most of my weight on my right leg, my better leg, and actually, it didn't hurt as much as I would have thought. I decide to try it again. I get a good grip on the edge of the counter with both hands and pull myself up. It works. I'm standing!

Pretty Boy, who is pecking away at his torn-open bag of birdseed on the counter, notices me up above him. He lets out a surprised tweet. I realize this is the first time he's ever had to look up to see me.

I keep a tight grip on the edge of the counter, wondering how long I can stay standing. I soon discover that as long as I keep most of my weight on my right leg, the pain eventually begins to fade a bit. It proves I actually *can* stand up if I want to. I've been babying myself by staying in my wheelchair all the time. But no longer! From now on, I'll do a bunch of standing up sessions every day. It hurts, but so what?

Pretty Boy looks up at me and says, "Pretty boy?"

I nod to show him I understand his question. "You've never seen me do this, have you? It's called standing. It's what most humans can do, and from now on, I'm going to be doing it more often.

He says, "Pretty boy!" to show me he approves.

"Why thank you, Pretty Boy. Nice of you to say so."

I sit back down in my wheelchair and take Grandma's food in to her. And then I wheel back into my bedroom to get on the computer. I'm still thinking about my success at standing up, but I'm anxious to get back to reading about my latest discovery, this new philosophy of deconstruction. I hit a bunch of web sites related to deconstructionism and discover this Derrida guy has written a bunch of books. One of them is titled *The Problem of Genesis in*

Husserl's Philosophy. A book reviewer says that despite the title, Derrida is quite complimentary of Husserl's ideas. I'm starting to think this new type of French philosophy might have mainly come out of the ideas of the early phenomenologists like Husserl and Heidegger. I've always liked reading about phenomenology because it talks about the concept that reality is not perceived in the same way by all humans. And this deconstructive philosophy also seems to have incorporated some of the ideas of existentialists like Nietzsche and Sartre, so I'm pretty sure I'm going to like learning about this new way of looking at philosophy.

As I continue the internet research, I keep running into Jean-Francois Lyotard's name. I look him up on Wikipedia and discover he's a pal of Derrida's. It says he and Derrida started the International College of Philosophy together. It's a teaching institute designed to take the teaching of philosophy away from the constrictions of the university system and focus on "intersections of thought," mainly referring to the intersection of philosophy and science. I read on, and it says the most amazing thing: it says attendance at their seminars is open to the public and free. They don't even give grades. What a concept. A place that teaches philosophy for free. It says the school has some of the top philosophers in the world as the teachers. Wow, wouldn't that be great? If I was in France, I could go to that school and take any philosophy class I wanted to. Why the hell don't we have anything like that in this country? Here, it costs a damn fortune to take any college class. The thought about not having enough money to take philosophy classes in this country is so upsetting, I have to stop thinking about it. I'm stuck here, and I don't have any money, so that's the end of it.

I go back to reading and find out that Lyotard says societies get fucked up by what he calls "grand narratives." He says grand narratives are *really* big ideas that are accepted by a whole society. He says common grand narratives like religion and patriotism are instilled in us when we're young, when we don't even know we're being indoctrinated by them. Religions, for example, claim to have *the* truth. All you have to do is go along with it, and you'll be saved. But you also have to renounce the "false truths" of all the other religions. He says wars have been fought over those kinds of religious grand narratives throughout history, and they're still fighting over them today. He points out that people also fight over nationalistic beliefs. Some societies push the idea that communism is the true answer, while other societies believe capitalism is the best solution. Back during the "cold war," those who held those kinds of opposing beliefs were ready to go to war over them, even if it meant wiping out all life on Earth with nuclear bombs.

I think this Lyotard guy has it exactly right. It's not just that people are deluded by their closely-held beliefs, they're compelled to act on them. It seems related to that stuff I read before about reducing cognitive dissonance: people have such a strong belief in their own grand narratives, they need to reduce the cognitive dissonance caused by the thought that any other competing grand narrative might have value. Like the Christian Crusaders back in middle ages: they went out to kill people who believed in a different version of God than they did. I guess that's one way to reduce your cognitive dissonance: kill anybody who disagrees with you. But did those Crusades really happen? I decide to look it up on the internet. It says the Crusades *did* happen. They started in 1095 when the leader of the Catholic Church, a Pope named Urban the Second, sent out armies of crusaders to hunt down and kill any and all Muslims, promising that anybody who took up arms against the "infidels" would get to have eternal life in God's Kingdom. And if that wasn't enough, he personally guaranteed that they would get God's pardon for their worldly sins, which meant they would avoid punishment in purgatory no matter what bad things they had done in their lives. So, the "crusaders" went on a Muslim killing spree, and they kept on killing those "evil" Muslims for two hundred years. But it didn't work because the Muslims had their own grand narrative religion, and they weren't about to change their minds, no matter how many of them got killed. In revenge, they killed any Christian they could find. Interesting. Looks like that kind of religious grand narrative based killing must be what's causing a lot of today's wars. It seems like a new war starts up every other day by people who believe in their own grand narratives so much they're willing to kill anybody who disagrees with them. Our government has a different grand narrative, so it calls them "terrorists" and tries to kill all of them.

Okay, enough of that depressing stuff. Time to go back to studying this Derrida guy. I again Google his name and find there are a heck of a lot of web sites that talk about him, so I guess he must be pretty famous.

I find one web site that summarizes his theories. I should say they "try" to summarize his theories: I'm still finding his ideas hard to understand. He mostly talks about signs and signifiers in language, and he's interested in the influence of experience on meaning, how each of us has different experiences and that changes how signs and signifiers are received. I like that idea. It goes along with my belief that we are only what we have stored inside our brains.

I go to several other sites to read about Derrida's philosophical theories, but no matter how much I study him, I still feel like I'm not fully "getting" his ideas. That pisses me off. After all, I've been studying about philosophy for a long time, so why should it be so hard to understand this new one? Is he intentionally trying to make it overcomplicated?

I keep searching the internet for more info about him, and I discover the most amazing thing: he's close by! The internet tells me he's currently a visiting professor at the University of California's branch campus in Irvine. Irvine! That's a city just south of LA. It's really close. There's probably a bus that goes from here in LA right down to that campus. That gives me a very exciting idea: I could actually go right down there and talk to him! The more I think about it, the more I think I should do it. I should go down there and ask him to tell me exactly what he's talking about. That would be so cool. Talking to a famous philosopher, in person, instead of just on the internet.

I sit back to think about it. The idea of going down there to see him has, for the first time in a long time, got me thinking seriously of going outside this house. That's funny. Only this morning I was thinking how logical it was to be a *hikikomori* in this twenty-first century, how it's so much better to just stay inside your house and study. Why should I go outside and have to deal with all the crap that's going on in the world? I mean, with Amazon.com delivering my food, and anything else I need, there shouldn't really be any reason for me to ever go outside. But now, the idea of getting a chance to talk to a real live famous French philosopher has got me intrigued: I wonder if he would actually talk to me if I just showed up at his office. What would he think about me, a kid who didn't even finish high school, wanting to talk philosophy? But what the hell. It wouldn't hurt to try. If he would talk to me, just think how trippy that would be.

I click on Google maps and ask it to show me the route between Watts and that university campus down there in Irvine. It says it's only 37.4 miles. Next, I go at the Southern California bus service site, and sure enough, I could get down there with only a few bus transfers.

But then, I stop to think how I'd even get started. Like, how would I get my wheelchair down off of Grandma's front porch? And how would I get on and off the buses? Do they help people that are in wheelchairs? Probably not. But what if I could learn to walk at least enough to get to the bus stop? I just proved I can stand up by holding onto the kitchen counter. Doesn't that mean I should be able to learn to walk again? So what if it hurts? All I have to do is learn how to ignore the pain.

I decide to test it. I swallow an extra large number of ibuprofen tablets and get ready to try the next step. (Did you get that "step" pun? Of course you did.) I wheel out to the kitchen and use the counter to pull myself up out of my chair. Pretty Boy is on my shoulder, busy with his usual task of dismantling my shirt collar, and he has to sink his claws into my shirt to hold on. He lets out a loud questioning tweet.

"Nothing to worry about, Pretty Boy. I'm just going to try that standing up thing again, but this time I'm gonna let go of the counter."

He says, "Pretty Boy?"

Well, no matter what he thinks, I'm still going to try it. Keeping one hand on the counter for balance, I'm able to use the other hand to turn the wheelchair around. "Okay, Pretty Boy, here we go." I let go of the counter and grab the wheelchair handles.

The wheelchair tips over backwards, and down I go. Pretty boy hops off of my shoulder just in time to avoid getting smashed. He stands there on the floor, close to my face, saying "Pretty boy!" over and over.

"Yeah, right, I know. I fell down."

I let loose a long string of cuss words that Pretty Boy has never heard before, and that scares him. He flies away and lands up on the top rim of his lampshade.

"Well, that didn't start out so good, did it?"

Pretty Boy cocks his head to the side and says, "Pretty Boy?"

"Yeah, you're right. That method didn't work, but how the hell am I going to get down to Irvine if I can't figure out some way to walk?"

Pretty Boy lets out a couple of loud tweets.

I guess that means he thinks I should keep trying.

I lock the wheels of my wheelchair and crawl back up into it. Out of breath, I sit there trying to think of some other solution. At that hospital, one of the doctors told me I might be able to get around "someday" by using crutches. But where would I get crutches? Actually, the more I think about it, I don't think I would need *two* crutches. It's only my left leg that's weak. I can stand on my right leg, for a little while anyhow. Maybe I could get around with a cane. Worth a try. Seems like I saw one of Grandma's old canes in the hall closet a while back.

I wheel to the closet and dig through all the junk. Sure enough, I find a cane. In fact, I find three canes. Grandma must have used a cane for a while, before she decided to stay in bed all the time. They're all made of wood, and one of them has a hooked handle that looks like a bird's beak. "Look at this, Pretty Boy," I say, holding up the cane. "Looks like a bird's beak, doesn't it? Pretty cool cane, eh?"

He flies down from his high perch to land on my shoulder. He digs his claws into my shirt and leans forward to look the cane over.

"Okay, what say we try it again?"

He tweets what I think is his approval, but it wasn't a very confident sounding tweet.

I grab what looks like the sturdiest of the three canes and wheel back into the kitchen. Once again, I use the counter to pull myself up.

Pretty Boy is tweeting nonstop.

I guess he's asking if I'm sure about this.

"What the hell, Pretty Boy. It's either figure out how to walk or be stuck in this house for the rest of my life."

I put the cane in my left hand and let go of the counter.

Well, at least I'm still standing. I'm balanced on my right leg with the help of the cane that's in my left hand. Despite the intense pain, I'm ready to take my first step. Using the cane for support, I cautiously put some weight on my weak left leg.

And down I go again.

Pretty Boy flies back to his lampshade and lets out several more loud tweets. He's looking down at me and shaking his head.

"Oh yeah? You think I can't do it? I almost took a step. You just watch. I'll figure out how to do it."

I pull myself up into my wheelchair again. Okay, one last try.

Pretty Boy is still tweeting, still sounding nervous.

"Don't be scared, Pretty Boy. I can do it. Are you with me?"

He hesitates, but then comes down to take his place on my shoulder.

"Good boy. We'll do this together, or die trying."

He cocks his head to the side to stare at me out of that little black eye, and lets out a feeble tweet.

That either means, Sure, let's try it again, or Are you crazy?

But I'm going to try it, no matter what he says. I pull myself up onto my right leg again and get a good grip on the cane in my left hand. This time, I won't try to actually walk; I'll just try shifting my weight back and forth between my stronger right leg and my weak left leg.

I let go of the counter and try it: one quick shift of weight, right to left, and then I'm back onto my right leg again.

By damn, at least that works.

Pretty Boy lets out a loud tweet of congratulations. And he's being brave, staying on my shoulder, even though he's got his claws dug deep into my shirt, just in case.

No dummy, that bird.

"Now, how about I try again to actually take a step?"

Pretty Boy keeps his mouth shut. He's being noncommittal, but he's sticking with me, staying put on my shoulder.

Staying close to the counter, I reach out just a little bit with my left leg, still using the cane to support most of the weight. One quick little step, and I'm back on my right leg.

"By damn, Pretty Boy. Did you see that? I'm walking! Well, almost."

He lets out several tweets of congratulations.

By God, it hurt like hell when I put any weight on my left leg, but I *did* move forward a little.

"You know, Pretty Boy, with practice, I think I might actually be able to make it to that bus stop."

Pretty boy responds with a few less-than-confident-sounding tweets.

"Well, you're right. I didn't move forward very far, but I'll get better at it. Just give me time."

"Pretty boy!"

He's encouraging me to keep trying. Okay, if he's willing, so am I. I'll be walking in no time.

For the rest of the day, I keep practicing. And despite the pain, I'm able to use Grandma's old cane to get myself the few steps back and forth from the refrigerator to the stove. It takes several of my cumbersome little moves to cover what is really only a few yards, and it hurts like hell for the brief moments I put weight on my weak left leg, but it feels like a major accomplishment to actually be getting around the kitchen without resorting to the wheelchair. I can tell that my right leg's getting stronger, and that's starting to give me hope that soon I might actually be able to make it to the bus stop. From there, I can ride the bus down to Irvine to talk to Professor Derrida.

But to get ready to meet with him, I know I need to do more studying. I've learned a lot about his philosophy, but I'm not sure I'm quite ready to talk to him intelligently. I do some internet searches about the books he's written. One of his books is titled *The Gift of Death*. Now that's an interesting title. I look that book up on Amazon.com, and it shows me the book's cover, a very detailed drawing of a picture of an angel hovering over an old bearded man who's holding a knife. It says the cover picture is a Rembrandt etching called "Abraham's Sacrifice." I've heard that Biblical story. The old man in the picture must be Abraham, the old guy who God told to prove his belief by killing his own son. I guess the picture is the angel who came at the last minute to tell him not to actually do it. I look the story up on the internet and discover it's in Genesis, Chapter 22. I read the whole thing. It's interesting because it's written like a short story with the actual dialogue God has with Abraham. God wants to test Abraham's faith, so He tells Abraham, in a kind of matter-of-fact way, to go to the mountain and kill his only son and burn him up as an offering. The way the story's told, Abraham doesn't complain or question it at all, he just gets his kid up early the next morning, saddles the donkey, gathers some wood to use for the burning, and heads for the mountain. Along the way, the kid gets a bit suspicious about it all. He understands the part about doing a burnt offering, because in those days it was a fairly normal thing to burn up living things as an offering to God, but where is the lamb? Abraham tells him not to worry about it, that God will provide the lamb to be burnt. When they get to the mountain, Abraham builds an altar, lays out the wood, ties the kid up, and puts him on top of the wood. He takes out his knife and is ready to kill the kid and burn him up, when an angel calls down from heaven to say, Hold off, don't kill your kid, and a ram magically appears for Abraham to burn up as the offering to God instead of his only son. It's an interesting story on many levels, but it gets me to wondering what kind of a real God would tell somebody to do something horrible like that? I guess, in the Christian religion, a willingness to prove your faith by killing your kid and burning him up is supposed to be a good thing, but the whole idea seems pretty weird to me. It tells me a lot about how religions change over time: apparently, when the Bible was being written, it was a normal thing to burn up poor innocent animals as a sacrifice to the Christian God, but now, apparently, Christians don't think God likes that anymore. Anyway, for some reason, they don't do it anymore.

I guess I just don't get it. I mean, the whole idea of killing and burning up your only son to prove your loyalty to God seems pretty bogus to me. If this kind of Christian God wants people to go out and kill their kids, wouldn't that make the people dislike Him? But then, in the story, the angel tells Abraham it was all just a test, like a fire drill or something. Wouldn't that part of the story also get out? If the people knew that God would just send an angel to intercede at the last minute, it wouldn't be such a great demonstration of belief after all. Seems to me that it would have been a much more powerful demonstration of belief if God would have gone ahead and let the guy kill his kid and burn him up as an offering. That would let everybody know that when God tells you to do something, He isn't messing around.

I decide to do a Google search for "God and Abraham" to see what others think of the story. Surprisingly, the first link that comes up is not about the God and Abraham story from the Christian Bible; it's about one of Islam's great annual festivals, "Eid-ul-Adha." It comes about two months after Ramadan, and it's the time when Muslims are supposed to sacrifice some living thing in memory of Abraham's willingness to sacrifice his son. Apparently, the

Abraham story and the idea of killing things as a sacrifice to God is not only an important part of the Christian religion, it's also an important part of the Muslim religion.

I stop reading about all that stuff. Too weird for me. I shouldn't have let myself get distracted by that kind of shit. Back to studying about Derrida. He says that although humans communicate with words and symbols, getting ahold of any "true" meaning is a tricky business. He says trying to understand the meaning of a word is like trying to hold onto a slippery squirming fish: although we may think we know what a word means, it's only our personal interpretation of it. He says only the person who wrote or spoke the word can really know what it was supposed to mean, and even then, the thought that was in his mind when he wrote or spoke the word might not come out the way it was meant to. Even after a writer writes a word, later, when he looks at that word again, he might see it differently because time has passed since that instant when he wrote the word, and he's had new experiences since then that have changed him.

And then there is the reader. How will the reader react to the word? The reader will have had different experiences than the writer, so the reader will interpret the word differently.

One of Derrida's main ideas is that once a writer writes down words and sends them out into the world, they no longer belong to him: once written, they belong to the reader and are subject to each readers unique interpretation. (Like right now when I'm giving you my story. What you do with it, how you react to it, is up to you.)

Another interesting thing Derrida talks about is the idea that every word has a relationship with other words. Take one of our most basic words, a word that exists in every human language from the ancient humans living in caves to modern humans living in big cities like LA. The word is "good." We all think we know what that word means, but what if there was a human society whose language did not include the word "bad"? The result would be that the word "good" would have no real meaning; good is a concept that only has meaning in terms of its relationship with the concept of bad.

Pretty interesting stuff. I can't say I'm actually getting everything he's saying about linguistics and logocentrism and *bricolage* (every discourse is bricoleur), but I am getting enough to get me interested in the man himself. I like the way he looks at things. He always seems to find a new way to look at any subject. And I get the feeling, that he's not the kind of guy to make a big deal of that, even if he is supposed to be this big-time famous philosopher. Maybe that means when I get down there to that university in Irvine, he'll actually take the time to talk to me. In fact, it feels like he thinks a lot like I do, how I question everything and want to deconstruct everything, how I want to tear people's ridiculous ideas and beliefs down by showing them how the component pieces of their beliefs don't hold up when you look at them closely. That said, I doubt that his definition of "deconstruction" is the same as mine (remember, the reader's interpretation of a word is never exactly what the writer intended), but I still feel like we might have a lot in common, especially in how we look at things. I'll have to ask him about that when I get down there to Irvine and meet him.

9
Deconstructing Hierarchies of Value

Today is the day. For the first time in a long time, I'm going to go out of this house. Today is the day I'm going to get on a bus and go to that university down there in Irvine to meet with Professor Derrida. I've been so excited about it, I haven't slept much for days. Instead, to get ready for the big meeting, I've been staying on the computer day and night, studying every internet site that had anything to say about Derrida and his philosophy of deconstruction. In between my study sessions, I've been practicing walking. Now, I think I'm ready.

I make Grandma's breakfast and quietly wheel it into her room. I'm careful to put her food down on her bedside table without waking her. Then, I slip into her closet and raid her money stash, taking only enough to pay for the bus fare to get me down there to Irvine and back, plus only a little more, in case I run into anything unexpected. She'll never miss it. In fact, I doubt if she's looked in that old tin box for years.

I wheel back into my bedroom and stop to think if I've forgotten anything. I've been practicing getting around the house using Grandma's old cane, and I've developed a technique that might look weird, a sort of step, drag, and step again technique, but it works well enough that I think I can make it to the bus stop, as long as I take it slow and easy. On the internet, I studied the bus routes that will take me to Irvine. My plan is take the bus down there to that university, find Professor Derrida's office, and wait there for him. He has to show up at his office sooner or later, and the way I figure it, there's no reason for him not to talk to me. All I have to do is tell him I'm thinking about taking his class (and that's the truth; I would love to take his class). I've studied about him on the internet, and I've studied his ideas, so I think I can talk intelligently to him. If I show him I'm smart, I bet he'll want to explain more about his theories to me. After all, he's a teacher, isn't he? But I'm a little worried that he'll be so smart he'll see that I'm not really getting the full import of his ideas. His approach to philosophy isn't as straightforward as the philosophy of all those old guys I've met on the internet, so maybe he'll tell me it can't be explained in one sitting. Maybe he'll say I have to sign up for his class. Okay, I'm willing to do that. Why not? So what if I never finished high school? I bet I've actually read more about his ideas than the other students in his class.

I put on one of my old plaid shirts and a plain pair of pants. No use standing out; I'm going to be standing out enough as it is, what with my step-drag-step method of *sort of* walking. I look at myself in the mirror. I figure I probably look like any other college student (if they only knew).

I go back to my bedroom and look around. What else do I need? Nothing that I can think of. I wheel out into the dining room, but before I open the door, I remember to brush Pretty Boy off of my shoulder. He flies over to his usual lampshade perch.

He cocks his head at me and says, "Pretty boy?"

"Yep, that's right, Pretty Boy. You're about to see me do something brand new. I'm going out. Keep an eye on the place for me."

He's very confused about that. He asks, "Pretty boy?"

But there's nothing more to tell him; I'm going out, and that's all there is to it. I ignore his concerns and open the door. I use the door handle to pull myself up out of my wheelchair, and I get myself balanced on my right foot. I use my cane to help me take a small step with my left foot, and then I'm quickly back on my right foot again. So far, so good. I manage to get out onto the front porch. I look up and down the street. Nobody around. Good.

But how am I going to get down those steps? Hmm. I hadn't though about that. Staring at the steps, I realize the solution is obvious, even though it will look kind of dumb: I'm going to have to sit down and scoot myself down the steps. No use falling down and busting my head right at the start of my journey.

Once I've scooted my way down to the sidewalk, I get a good grip on my cane again and stand up. Well, here goes, my first step outside of the house.

It turns out that I didn't have so much to worry about: I've practiced my step-drag-step technique enough inside the house, I find it works just as well outside. I'm making progress, even though it's damn slow.

I head for the bus stop. I know it's not going to be easy. It used to only take me a few minutes to get to the bus stop, but now it's going to take me a lot longer. And I also know there's going to be plenty of pain in my legs all the way. But like Sartre said, whatever doesn't kill you makes you stronger.

It takes a lot longer than I thought it would, but I make it to the first intersection. There's not much traffic this early in the morning, so I'm able to limp across without getting flattened by any of the mean-spirited drivers.

I keep trying to hurry, but I soon learn that hurrying doesn't work: if I take bigger steps, it puts me on my weak left leg for too long, and that causes a hell of a lot of pain. Better to be patient and just take small steps. There's no hurry.

Up ahead, I see that there's only one gang dude on the hangout corner. Thank goodness. Today, I don't have time to play games with those idiots. The gang guy is leaning up against a wooden utility pole. This early in the morning,

I know there can only be one reason for him to be out here: he's waiting for the schmecks (heroin users) to show up. As I pass, he vaguely looks me over and chuckles at my step-slide method of locomotion.

"Morning," I mumble and keep on moving.

He seems about to say something to me, but just then a haggard-looking, middle-aged woman in a fairly-new tan-colored Mercedes pulls up to the curb. She rolls down her window. He walks over to her car, real casual and friendly like. She hands over some bills. He looks in both directions, and then hands her a little white plastic package. Within seconds, her electric window is rolling back up and she's zooming away down the street. The gang dude puts the money away and heads back to his waiting spot.

I watch the Mercedes disappear around the next corner. Pretty brave of a light-skinned woman to come down here to get her fix. But I guess she has to go where the drugs are.

The gang dude watches me as I shuffle my way across the street. He seems curious about me, but that's all. Maybe now that I'm a full-fledged cripple, I won't have as much trouble with the gangs as I used to. Maybe even gangbangers have a little tiny bit of sympathy for a cripple. I wonder how other regular people will react to me. Maybe they won't like to look at me. That would be good. I'd rather be left alone anyhow. But maybe some of them will make fun of me. Just in case, I'd better work on some good sarcastic rejoinders. If they make fun of me for being crippled, I'll make fun of them for having such tiny brains.

I finally make it to the bus stop, but I'm totally worn out. I plop down on the bench to wait for the bus. Despite my well-practiced technique of putting my mind where the pain isn't, my legs are screaming with pain. I dig into my pocket and get out some ibuprofen tablets. I work up some spit in my mouth to swallow them whole. Maybe I should have brought along a bottle of water, but no matter; I know there's a drinking fountain at the bus transfer station (if you don't mind the taste of LA's heavily chlorinated water), and I'm sure there will be drinking fountains down at that big fancy university. Maybe they'll have better tasting water down there in Irvine.

When the bus pulls up, I already have a plan for how I'm going to get on. I stick my cane into my belt, as if it's a sword, and use the chrome handholds to pull myself up onto the bus. The driver, surprisingly, is light-skinned, even though it's not likely there will be any other light-skinned people on this bus route. He doesn't even look at me as I put the correct change into the glass money box. Unfortunately, he starts the bus moving before I can get to a seat, and that means I have to keep a good grip on the seat rails to keep from falling down. At first, I'm pissed off at the driver, but then I wonder if it might mean he didn't even notice that I'm a cripple. It would be fine with me if nobody notices. Or maybe the bus driver did notice and doesn't care if he makes me fall down. Maybe nobody will care. These days, nobody gives a shit about anybody else's troubles.

Every individual is, at end, alone with himself.

So now Old Man decides to start talking to me again. Why does he think I need his help now? I ignore him.

There are no empty seats near the front of the bus, so I slowly work my way toward the back, holding onto the seat rails. With the bus moving, it's a challenge to keep my balance, but I keep moving. Unfortunately for me, the bus suddenly turns a corner, and I'm not ready for it; I go down and end up on my butt, sitting smack in the middle of the isle.

I hear laughing from the back of the bus. I look in that direction. Uh oh, dark-skinned gangbangers. Two of them, wearing the usual floppy plain white T-shirts and baggy dark pants that are always about to fall off their fat butts. But I don't see any red kerchiefs. At least they're not Bloods.

I stay where I am, sitting on the floor, while I check them out. One of them has the word "Criminals" tattooed around his neck. It's like a printed necklace. Looks like they're from a gang that calls themselves Criminals. Haven't seen them before. Wonder what they're doing on a bus in this neighborhood?

Normally, I'd make some kind of wisecrack to put them down, but I know if I say anything they might react, and I damn sure don't want to get distracted from getting down there to Irvine.

I get ahold of a seat rail and try to pull myself up. One old dark-skinned guy surprises me by reaching out like he's going to help me. I wave him off. "I'm okay," I say. "Just practicing my falling down and getting up technique."

He turns away and looks out the window.

One of the gangbanger dudes hollers at me: "Whattsa matter, whitebread? Never learn how to walk?"

There's that derogatory *whitebread* term again. When did that become the standard insult for us light-skinned folks?

After a couple of tries, I manage to pull myself back up onto my feet. The only available seats are just in front of the two gangbangers. Not surprising. The other passengers are smart enough to stay away from them. In fact, I'm a little surprised the other passengers didn't immediately get off the bus back at whatever stop those gangbangers got on. But maybe everybody thinks that because there are plenty of other passengers on the bus, it will keep the gang dudes from getting too far out of line.

As soon as I finally make it to an empty seat and sit down, one the gangbanger dudes starts in on me again. "Whattsa matter with yur legs, asshole? Got the wobblies?"

I turn to face them. I know I should keep my mouth shut, but this is a chance to use a line I've had ready for a long time. "Well, look at you two boys. All dressed up in your cool hanging-down pants. Say, why do you guys all like to show off the cracks in your butts? Trying to get the attention of the queers?"

I quickly turn back to face the front.

That stops their laughing. Good. They can't do anything to me because there are too many witnesses on this bus. Besides, this neighborhood is probably not part of their turf.

But the talker gets up and comes to hover over me. "Whad you say, motherfucker? You some kinda smart ass?"

The dude can't be more than twenty or so, but he's had time to acquire quite a few tattoos: the usual snakes and knives, plus a bunch of letters and numbers that must mean something to him.

I grin at him. "Just a bit of social commentary, dude. Nothing to worry your pea brain about."

Say, that wasn't bad. It's been a while since I've been around people and had a chance to try out some good insults, but I think I've still got the knack for it.

The guy leans down and puts his face in mine. "You be asking for it, motherfucker. You hear me?"

I look him right in the eyes. Interesting that I'm not scared. I don't feel the slightest bit of fear, and that feels good. Damn good. I just cross my eyes and grin at him.

The guy pulls back and stares at me. He can't figure me out. But he does realize I'm not afraid of him, and I see the slightest ripple of anxiety cross his face. He can't figure out what to do if this crazy whitebread cripple isn't scared of him.

I decide to help him out. "Why don't you just go back there and sit down with your little twin bro before you embarrass yourself anymore."

That finally *does* get a reaction out of him: he reaches into his pocket and pulls out a switchblade. He snaps it open and shows it to me. "You lookin for some of this, motherfucker?"

I laugh at him, really loud so everybody on the bus can hear. "Why, look at that. If it isn't a switchblade knife. Don't you realize what a cliche that is these days? How nineteen fifties. Where's your big bad pistola?"

He reacts by pushing the point of the blade against my neck. I hear a gasp from a woman a few seats ahead.

For a moment, I wonder if I've gone too far, but the fact that he doesn't actually stick me with the knife means he's just trying not to get shown up by a light-skinned teenager in front of his buddy.

I let him keep the knife against my throat and hold out my hands toward the other passengers and say, "Look here, folks. This little boy has a knife. Isn't that cute?"

None of the other passengers will make eye contact with me, and several hands go up to hit the button to tell the driver they want to get off at the next stop. I can see the driver eying us in his rear-view mirror. I've read on the internet that some of the buses in LA now have a panic button that calls the police. I wonder if this bus has one, and if so, did he push it? Oddly, I realize I don't care one way or the other.

Then, I catch myself. What do I think I'm doing? I'm on my way down to a university in Irvine to meet with a famous French philosopher, so why am I wasting time getting these two idiots all riled up? I hold up both hands. "Hey, listen, dude. I was just kiddin' ya. Forget it. You're right, I was being dumb. I admit it. I make too many jokes."

He hesitates, but then seems to relax a little. "You sure the fuck do, asshole. If you doan wise up, you gonna get stuck. You hear me."

"Oh yes, sure. I hear ya. This here mothafucka be hearin ya loudn clear."

Uh oh, now the knife is back against my throat.

Shit. Why didn't I just let it drop? Nobody likes to have somebody make fun of the way they talk, especially a dimwit like him.

"Hey," yells the driver. "Sit down back there."

The driver is being surprisingly brave. I bet he *has* called the cops.

Then I notice something else: he's not stopping at the bus stops. The people waiting out there at those bus stops stare at us as we go by, surprised that the bus didn't stop for them like it was supposed to.

The driver again yells, "I said, sit down."

But this tattooed gangbanger isn't about to take that from a white bus driver. "Fuck you, driver," he yells. "Mind your own business for I come up there ta mind it for ya."

Uh oh, looks like the dude is gettin' a little bit hot under the collar.

"Now, now," I say, grinning, "it's not polite to speak harshly to our loyal driver. After all, he's only doing his—"

I don't get to finish my clever comment because the other gangbanger has come up behind me and has his arm around my neck. He just about pulls me up out of my seat and says, "You lookin' to get hurt, motherfucker?" His breath smells like old garlic and tomato sauce. I feel the point of his knife in the middle of my back.

I shake my head no, and he lets his arm relax enough to at least let me breathe. I twist my head around to look at him. He's older than the other one, and he's got more tattoos. Not only does he have the "Criminals" tattoo, he's also got weird-shaped letters and numbers on both sides of his neck, almost all the way up to his ears. Anybody who would deface themselves like that probably doesn't know, or care, much about the world outside of his gang. And there's something else different about this one, a vacant look in his eyes. He might be stoned on something hard. Maybe he doesn't even realize he's on a public bus.

The big question is, do I want to die this way? Do I really want to end it here and now? I guess being killed on a city bus actually wouldn't be such a bad way to die—might was well go down in flames. It would make all the papers: white boy killed by black gang members. People would remember me as *that* white kid, the one that got stabbed on a city bus. I'd be famous.

While I decide what to do, time seems to have stopped. Everybody seems frozen in place: me, this hard-ass gangbanger with the bad breath, the other gangbanger, the passengers, the bus driver—nothing moves, not even time; nothing *can* move because I've stopped it all with my mind. A flurry of thoughts are all competing for my attention. I can still feel the point of the knife blade in my back, so maybe this guy really is going to stab me. I'm not feeling scared, but now I'm not sure why I pushed them so hard. Am I actually trying to get these gangbangers to kill me? What happened to my idea of going down to Irvine to talk to Professor Derrida? Was that just a fantasy?

Cognition precedes action. Action precedes consequences.

He's right. My actions in this moment will determine what happens next. First the cognitive part: do I want to live? Is it worth pushing my boulder up my hill one more day? What about all that philosophy and science and history I've been reading on the internet? If I'm going to die here on this bus, what was the purpose of all that learning?

Sisyphus was not seeking fame. His task was his purpose, his only purpose.

The old man is right. I guess I do have a task to complete. I have more to learn, and as part of that learning, I have to get down to that university in Irvine to meet with Professor Derrida.

I start time moving again.

"Listen," I say, trying to make my voice seem more friendly, "I was just kidding around. I don't know why I do that. Bad habit, I know. Let's just forget about it, okay?"

The dude removes his arm from around my neck.

I turn around in my seat to face him. He's still holding his knife, but he seems confused. Despite my rational thoughts about needing to bring this confrontation to an end, his hesitation gives me an amazing feeling of power. I've never felt anything like it before. Have I learned so much that I now have control over people, even over this idiotic gang dude?

I use the handrail to stand up and face him. I point toward the back of the bus. "You know you aren't going to do anything on a public bus, so why not just go back and sit down."

He just stares at me, his mouth open.

"Go!" I shout. "Sit!" I push him away.

Did I really push him? Did I really just shout those words at him? It sounded like I was telling a bad dog to go to his doghouse.

So he stabs me. Right in the chest.

I hear a woman up near the front of the bus scream.

I look down at where he cut me. It doesn't really hurt all that much, so I suspect the blade didn't go in as far as he wanted it to. Maybe it hit a rib or something. I look up at him. He seems to be as surprised as I am, as if he can't quite believe what he just did in front of all these witnesses.

He turns toward the front of the bus and waves his knife at the people who are now all facing toward us, all of them wide-eyed and scared. "Quit lookin at me!," he yells. "You, driver, stop this fuckin bus!"

But the bus driver doesn't stop, and some of the people are getting up out of their seats and moving toward the front of the bus to get away from the situation.

Now the stabber and his gangbanger buddy are both holding their knives out toward the other passengers, as if they think the other people will try to rush them. But I know that's not going to happen. All of the other people on this bus are dark-skinned, same as the gangbangers. Some white kid getting stabbed is none of their business. I know I'm on my own, but despite the fact that this jerk has just stabbed me in the chest, I'm still not feeling one bit of fear. In fact, I'm not feeling much of anything. Have I gotten that good at not feeling pain? It gives me even more of a feeling of power, as if it's all just so stupid it's beneath me, not worthy of my attention.

But I am feeling a bit woozy. I look down at my shirt. There's a lot more blood than there was before. How long ago was that? Can that much blood come out in only a few seconds? Maybe this idiot's knife went in farther than I thought.

The gang dude who stabbed me pushes me down to the floor and steps over me. Oh well, I guess now he's going to go forward and kill the other people too. Does that matter to me? Maybe, maybe not. I stare up at the bus ceiling and have the funny thought that a stained bus ceiling will be the last thing I ever see. I wonder what made those stains up there.

But wait, it feels like the bus just stopped. Did the vacant-eyed gang dude with the big knife just kill the driver?

I hear the hiss of the front bus door opening. I hear a very loud voice: "Drop it motherfucker, or you're dead."

Cops. Must be the cops. I guess the driver did call them. Must have driven his bus to where they were waiting.

Okay, fine. It means this little drama is over. Now to see how bad I'm hurt. I'm not feeling much pain, so maybe the asshole's knife didn't hit anything serious inside me. Maybe if I can somehow get up and get back into my seat, the cops will take the gangbangers away, and I'll be able to resume my trip down to Irvine to meet with Professor Derrida. At least I'll have a hell of a good story to tell him. I'll tell it to him in detail. I'll act out what the gang dudes said and what I said back to them. I'll bet Professor Derrida will like my story, especially when I tell him how those gangbangers didn't scare me at all. I'll tell him how I made fun of them, and how I could see confusion and fear in their eyes. He'll be amazed: gangbangers with knives scared of one skinny little white guy.

I try to get up, but things aren't working very well. I don't seem to be able to figure out a way to get up on my feet, and that's got me a bit confused. To get up, I need a cane, don't I? What happened to my cane? I feel a rising panic from somewhere inside the middle of my brain. How am I going to be able to get all the way down to Irvine without my cane?

I hear shouting. What is all the shouting about?

And now somebody is grabbing ahold of my arms. "No!" I say. "Leave me alone. I have to get down to Irvine. Professor Derrida is there. He's an important man, and he's not going to hang around all day waiting for me."

10
Incompatible Trajectories of Awareness

Light.

Too bright.

Pain.

In my chest.

"So, you gonna wake up now?"

A voice. A voice asked me a question. Wasn't I on a bus? Where am I? And it feels like my wrists are tied down. Why would that be? Is this some kind of weird dream?

"They knocked you out good, didn't they?"

I turn my head.

A kid. Red hair. Pimples.

Who is this kid? And why is he looking at me? I say, "Where?"

"Where? You mean where are you? You're in a hospital, man. Jeez, they must have loaded you up good with that shit. Not surprising though. You were still fightin' 'em when they brought you in here. You were yelling somethin' about Dare-e-da. Gotta go see Dare-e-da. That's when they strapped you down and shot you up with their knock-out juice."

A shot? Knock-out juice? Why don't I remember that? And why is my chest hurting so much?

"Hey, you listening to me?"

"Don't . . . remember."

"Oh, yeah, that happens to me too. They shoot you up with that shit, it calms you way down, but then later, you don't remember anything about it."

"Who shot me up? And why are these things tied on my wrists? Get 'em offa me."

The kid looks around. "No way. I'd get in trouble."

I lift my head off the pillow to see what is holding my wrists. Looks like strips of some kind of strong cloth. Maybe canvas. I jerk at them, but they feel pretty strong.

I look around. Only one door, with a little window in it. Thick metal screen covering the little window. I turn my head to look behind me. A blank wall. Painted plain hospital light green. There's one window, but it's also covered with the same kind of thick metal screen that's covering the little window in the door.

I look back at the kid. He can't be more than sixteen, or so. Maybe only fifteen. He's acting nervous. Why is he so nervous? I'm the one tied down.

"What's your name, kid?"

"It's David. And don't call me kid. I'm as old as you, I bet. Almost."

"No, you're not. You're probably only about fifteen."

"So what? I can take care of myself. I been on my own. Lots of times. This time, I was on the streets for over a month before they caught me."

"So you're old for your age. BFD."

I ignore him and try to figure out how to slip out of the cloth things that are holding my wrists, but the more I pull at them, the tighter they get.

I look at the kid again. He's watching me try to get loose, and he's not making a move to help me. "God damn it, David. Just untie me."

He folds his arms across his chest. "Maybe I will, and maybe I won't. I told you my name, so now you gotta tell me yours."

"It's Scott. Now untie me, or when I do get loose, you'll be sorry."

He looks around again. What's he looking for? There's nobody else in the room, and only one other bed. Is that his bed?

"Untie me. Now!"

The kid goes to the door and peeks out through the little window. Then, he comes back and quickly unties my wrists.

I rub my wrists. They're red and damn sore. Was I struggling against the tie-downs when I was knocked out? Why can't I remember? And why the hell did they have to tie me down in the first place? Did they think I was dangerous or something?

I sit up, and that sends a jolt of pain from my chest that goes right up to my brain. It brings a memory: I got stabbed. Some asshole gang jerk stabbed me in the chest when I was on a city bus.

I pull up the white smock I'm wearing and see a square white bandage, with something red in the middle. Must be blood leaking through.

David leans closer. "Looks like you got hurt."

I swing my feet over the side of the bed, and that sends another clenching pain through my chest. Damn, that shithead gang guy must have stuck me deeper than I thought.

I pull away a corner of the bandage and see a short row of stitches. At least he didn't slice me, just stuck the knife straight in. It doesn't look like they had to do any surgery on me, just stitched me up.

David leans closer to look. "Stitches. What happened?"

"Some stupid asshole stuck me with a knife. On a bus."

"Gangs?"

I try to stick the corner of the bandage back down, but the tape doesn't seem very sticky.

"Was it a gang?" he repeats.

"Of course it was a gang. What other kind of dimwit jerk is going to stab somebody on a public bus."

"Did the cops nab him?"

"Sure they did. They were waiting at the next bus stop."

"Maybe the dude didn't care if he got caught."

"Guess not. He was covered with tattoos. Probably got 'em in prison. Maybe he was ready to go back in to get some more."

"Jeez. He coulda killed ya."

"Yeah, well so what?"

He stares at me. "So is that why they locked you on the psych floor? Were you trying to get yourself killed?"

"This is the psych floor?"

"Sure. You didn't know that?"

"How could I? I was out like a light, wasn't I? So, why are you on this psych floor? Are you some kind of nut case?"

He holds out his arms. There's rows of thin scabbed-over lines on both wrists, from side to side. So, this kid tried to kill himself, and they locked him in here. Looks like he didn't do a very good job of it. I should talk. But at least when I jumped off that cliff, I was doing it for real. I didn't make some halfhearted attempt to cut my wrists. "Listen, kid, hacking away at your wrists is a cliche. I read on the internet that most people who cut their wrists are just trying to get attention. A cry for help."

He jerks back his arms and holds them behind his back. "No way. It was for real. I meant it. You know those plastic disposable razors? If you break 'em open, the blade inside has a real sharp edge. It cuts deep, and you hardly feel it. And it woulda worked too, if they hadn't a found me."

"If you didn't feel it, you must of been stoned out of your gourd."

"I wasn't stoned. Not all that much anyhow. You know those hills up in Griffith Park? I went way up there. Hid in the bushes. That's where I did it. And it woulda worked too if those two guys hadn't come along. Hikers. Just my luck for a couple of hikers to come along."

"So they brought you here. Why aren't you wearing this smock kind of thing they've got on me? You're dressed in regular clothes."

"Cause I'm supposed to get let out today. As soon as my mom comes for me. But who knows when that'll be. She'd probably rather I rotted in here."

"Why's that? She mad at you 'cause you cut yourself up?"

"She doesn't give a shit what I do. But she'll come. Eventually. Maybe they just haven't found her yet. She's hardly ever home."

"Well, there are better ways to do yourself in than hacking on yourself. Besides, if you want to bleed to death, you don't go side to side. You got to find a vein. You've got to get down in between the tendons to find a vein. Or an artery, the ones what carry blood away from the heart. Those are even deeper down. Under the tendons."

"You seem to know a lot about it. You a medical student or somethin'? My sister's studyin' to be a med tech."

"No, I just read a lot. On the internet. But never mind that. How do I get out of here?"

"You don't. The shrink has to say you can go."

He holds out his wrists toward me. "So, explain it to me. I should cut my wrists the long way? And deeper?"

I gingerly try standing up, but I'm dizzy.

David grabs my arm to stabilize me, and I sit back down on the bed. My legs! I tried to stand up without even remembering my legs are all fucked up. What kind of drugs did they give me that would make me forget that?

David is drawing his fingernail along the underside of his wrist, as if it was a knife. "Like this? The long way?"

"Forget the wrist cutting. There's better ways."

David again puts his arms behind his back. "Okay, so I'm not smart like you. Maybe I did screw it up. Tell me how to do it."

I stare at him. What an idiot. No wonder they locked him up on a psych ward. But that thought gets me wondering if this the same hospital I was in before. Do they have a record on me?

"Well?" says David.

If this kid wants to knock himself off, he probably will. And I guess it's up to him. Like the existentialists say, everybody has free will.

"Listen, David, all I know is what I read on the internet. They say the best way to do it is with downers. You take a lot of downers along with a lot of booze, like gin or vodka, and you just go to sleep. You just don't wake up."

"Yeah sure. I heard about that. But where would I get that many downers?"

"You can buy them on any street corner. Anything you want. Even heroin. An overdose of heroin is a good way too. Probably more fun, at least for a few seconds."

He seems excited about that. "Heroin? Cool. Can you get me some?"

"Me? Not me. I got my own problems. First thing I got to do is get the hell out of here. I was on my way to . . . an important appointment."

"To see that dare-e-da person? That's what you were yelling."

"Yeah. He's a philosophy professor. Down at UC Irvine. I've got to get down there right away. I wonder what time it is."

The kid looks toward the window. "Just past dawn, I guess."

Dawn? I've been in here all night? They must have really knocked me out with whatever shit they shot me up with. But it's still a weekday. I could still make it down there to Irvine today, if I get moving right now.

Holding onto the bed, I stand up again, but the bolt of pain in my legs doesn't want me to do that. I sit back down again.

"What's the matter?" says David. "Are you dizzy? Maybe you'd better hang around here for a few days. Let that stab wound heal up better."

"No, it's my legs. I had a cane. Did you see it?"

He shakes his head.

Damn, this is not going to be easy. How the hell am I going to walk without my cane? I need to get back in control, move my mind away from the pain. Maybe I can replace the old pain in my legs with this new pain in my chest.

David takes ahold of my arm. "You'd better lie back down."

I shake off his hand. "No, I've got to get out of here." I point at the door. "Is that door locked?"

He looks toward the door. "No, but you'd have to get past the nurse."

"Okay, lets go."

He laughs an abrupt little laugh. "You can't just go out and get on the elevator. The nurse will see you and stop you."

"Help me get to the door. I want to see what it looks like out there."

He shrugs. "Okay." He starts toward the door.

"Wait!" I say. "I can't walk."

He stares at me. "Why not?"

"Like I said, my legs are all fucked up."

"What happened to them?"

"It's a long story. Just help me."

"Okay, sure." He comes back, and by putting my left arm over his shoulder, I'm able to make progress using my step-slide-step method, using him as if he was my cane.

"I had some bus money in my pants. What would they have done with my clothes?"

"Oh, your clothes are safe. There's a little room with lockers in it. Right behind the nurse's desk. Your stuff will be in there. But they take your money. At least they always take mine."

"Okay, let's go there and get my clothes."

"We can't. Like I said, it's behind the nurses station."

This weird kid, David, with his hacked-to-shit arms, seems to know the routine here. I wonder how many times he's been in here for trying to kill himself. "Listen, David, you may be willing to wait around until your mom comes to drag you out, but not me. If there's a way out of this nut house, I'll find it." I nod toward the door. "Check it out. See if anybody's looking."

I lean up against the wall while he opens the door a crack and looks out.

He shakes his head. "Looks like the other patients are still asleep. Nobody out in the hall, but there's one nurse at the nurse's station."

"Let me see." I peek out. The long hallway is fairly dim, except there's a counter about halfway down with a bright desk lamp on it. A nurse is sitting behind the counter, writing something.

Nearby, I spot just what I need: a metal stand on wheels, the kind they use to hang IVs from. I could use that stand as a rolling cane.

I turn back to David. "Listen, you distract her while I go behind that nurse's station to get my clothes."

"Distract her? How?"

"I don't care, just get her away from that station."

He peeks out again. "Maybe I can make her chase me."

"Good. Do it."

He goes out and starts tiptoeing down the hallway toward the nurses station. He looks ridiculous, sneaking along next to the wall with his hands held out in front like he's some kind of weird mouse walking on its hind legs. He may be off of his rocker, but he's willing to try stuff. You have to give him that.

As soon as he makes it halfway to the nurse's station, I go out and put both of my hands against the wall. Going hand over hand, and hopping on my right leg, I make it to the metal stand. But I soon learn that it doesn't make a very good crutch because it tends to roll away when I put weight on it. Still, it's the only cane I've got, so it'll have to do.

David has reached the nurse's station, and so far, she hasn't noticed him.

Then she sees him. She stands up behind her desk and says, "David! Where do you think you're going?"

He takes off running down the hallway.

"Hey!" she yells. "Come back here." She goes running after him.

Using the rolling metal stand for support, I hop to the nurse's station and duck into the room behind it. It's pretty dark in the room, but I see the row of lockers against the wall. I start pulling them open. Most of them are empty, but I finally find one with clothes in it, a pair of dark gray pants, probably from a suit, and a white dress shirt. I quickly take off the smock and put on the too-big dress pants. But the white shirt has something dark spilled down the front of it. Blood? Just my luck, the only shirt I can find has blood on it. I pull open other lockers until I find a ridiculous green shirt with white cuffs. An old man's shirt, I bet. But who cares? I put it on. There's also a pair of white tennis shoes. They're a little too big for me, but I don't care. I've gotta move fast.

I peek out the door. The nurse is dragging David back to that room we were in, scolding him. He's going along with her, but he's resisting. I think he's making sure she keeps her focus on him. Good going, David.

As soon as they disappear into that room, I use my rolling cane to hop toward the elevator. It's slow going, but I finally make it. I press the down button, and as soon as the elevator arrives, I slip inside. I press the button for the first floor, and as the elevator doors start to close, I figure I've got it made. But then a hand slips into the crack before the doors can close completely. The doors spring back open. It's David. "Hey," he says, "weren't you gonna wait for me?"

As the elevator starts down, my hopes sink. "Why did you have to do that?" I say. "Now the nurse will call somebody, and they'll be waiting for us down there."

He pouts. "I wanted to go with you."

"Well, you can't."

"You said you'd get me some heroin."

"I never said that."

"Yes, you did."

"No, I just said it would be a good way to knock yourself off, if that's what you want."

"Yes, it is what I want. I want to—"

I cut him off. "Well, it doesn't matter now because they'll be waiting for us downstairs."

The elevator doors open, and amazingly, there's nobody there waiting for us. I lean out. People are going about their business; nobody is paying any attention to us.

David says, "Wait here." He runs out of the elevator.

Where the hell is he going? Then, I see what he's after: a wheelchair.

He brings it back. I sit down in it, and David wheels me toward the front door. Nobody is paying any attention to us. I still can't believe that nurse hasn't called anybody to stop us. David runs me to the glass doors, and they open automatically as we get there.

There's a cab outside, and the foreign-looking driver is leaning up against the car's front fender, reading a newspaper.

David runs my wheelchair to that cab and opens the back door for me. He helps me in and then runs around to the other side.

The driver gets into the driver's seat and looks back over his shoulder. "Where to, fellas?"

"Just go!" I yell.

He turns to look at me. "In a hurry?"

"Yes, just go. Go. I'm late for . . . for an important appointment."

"I need an address, boys."

I give him my grandma's address, and he frowns at me. "Watts?"

I nod. "That's where I live."

He stares at me, and then at David. I can tell he's sizing us up. "Listen, guys, they don't let us carry cash anymore. You got exact change?"

"I've got the money," says David. "Just go."

The cab driver shrugs and starts the car. As he rolls out of the hospital driveway, I realize it *is* the same hospital I was in after I jumped off the cliff. I remember pulling out of this same driveway on that hospital bus with the damn sadistic driver that tried to dump me on skid row. It seems like years ago, but I guess it really hasn't been all that long.

I lean close to David. "I can't believe that nurse didn't call down to stop us."

David grins and whispers, "You know those cloth straps they used to tie you to the bed?"

I stare at him. "You tied her to the bed?"

He nods, still grinning. "Why not? They did it to you. Did it to me once too. Let them see how it feels."

"Jesus," I say, looking back toward the hospital. I hope they never figure out who I am.

I turn to David. "Do you really have money?"

"Yeah," he whispers. "I've got a twenty hidden in my shoe."

"Okay. Good You can drop me at my grandma's. It's not far."

He shakes his head. "No, I'm coming with you."

"You can't come home with me. I stay at my grandma's.

"You said you'd get me some heroin."

I glance at the driver who seems to be listening to us.

I whisper, "Quit saying that. When we get to my grandma's house, you can't come in. You're on your own. I got my own problems without trying to help you knock yourself off."

He folds his arms and pouts.

As we go along, my stomach clenches in response to every bump in the road. Maybe the damn knife wound is going to take longer to heal up than I'd hoped. What if the semester ends before I can get down there to that university to talk to Professor Derrida? I guess I'll just have to get better at turning off the pain. I'll rest for a day or two and then try it again.

When we arrive at my grandma's house, a few of my dark-skinned neighbors are out sitting on their front porch steps like they always do when it's a warm day.

The cab driver keeps glancing at them. He seems nervous. When I ask him to come around and help me get out, he says, "No way." He points at the meter. "Just pay up and get the hell out of my cab. I'm not gonna hang around here."

"I'll help you get into your house," says David.

He opens his door, but the driver reaches back and grabs his arm. "Oh no you don't. I gotta get paid before anybody gets out."

David reaches down into his shoe and fishes out his twenty-dollar bill.

The driver grabs it.

David holds out his hand. "Give me the change."

I push down David's hand and say, "No, the kid is going on with you. I can get out on my own." I open my door, but before I can get out, David jumps out and runs around to help me.

No," I say, "let me do it. You've got to go."

But he gets ahold of my arm and puts it over his shoulder and lifts me out. The kid is stronger than he looks.

We are hardly clear when the driver speeds off, even though both of the cab's back doors are still open.

"Well, there goes your twenty," I say. "Now you're gonna have to walk home."

He looks around. He seems scared. "You want me to walk home from here? A white person? In this neighborhood?"

Despite the pain I'm feeling in my chest, that makes me chuckle. "What, you never been to Watts before?"

"Are you kidding? Who comes to Watts? You have to let me stay here with you." He nods toward my neighbors who are staring at us. "They'll kill me as soon as you go inside."

I laugh again. "They won't kill you. They're just . . . people."

"But they stabbed you."

"That was a gang dude. And I gave him a reason to. These are just regular people. They're as scared of the gangs as you are."

"You gave the gang a reason? What does that mean?"

"Never mind. Just go that way." I point. "There's a bus stop. Couple of blocks down."

He looks in that direction, but then he shakes his head. "I don't have a dime on me. You can't leave me out here. You gotta let me stay with you, Scotty. Can I call you Scotty?"

"You can't call me anything because you have to go now. My grandma won't allow any visitors, even if I wanted you hanging around. Which I don't."

"Please, Scotty." He looks like he's going to cry.

"Aw shit. Help me inside, and I'll try to get you some change for the bus."

He helps me up the porch steps, and as soon as I open the door and get inside, I hear grandma's little bell tinkling. It sounds frantic.

I point to my wheelchair. "Bring me that."

He goes to get it, and helps me sit down. I again put my finger up to my lips to tell him to keep quiet.

He nods and puts his finger up to his own lips.

Ignoring the new pain in my chest, I wheel into Grandma's room. She's immediately on me. "Where the hell have you been? I've been ringing for you all night."

"I had to go out."

"All night?"

"I got held up."

She shakes her little bell at me. "Listen, Fitzgerald, I don't have to let you stay here, you know. It's not my fault your mother took off. The rule is, you're supposed to be here when I need you." She shakes the bell at me again. "I'm hungry. Right now."

Uh oh, she never calls me by my real name unless she's really pissed at me. I'd better not come back with any smart aleck response. "Okay, Grandma. I'm sorry. It was unavoidable. I won't let it happen again."

But I'm not sure she even heard me. She's already gone back to watching her TV. She presses the volume button on her TV flipper to turn the sound up louder.

Good. The louder the better. If she hears David out there, she might really throw me out.

I wheel back out to the kitchen to get her something to eat and catch David looking in the refrigerator. He closes the refrigerator quickly and jumps back.

I roll up next to him and whisper, "Sit down at the table and don't make a sound. I've got to get my grandma something to eat, then I'll fix something for us. Then I've got to rest. I got stabbed, remember?"

"I can get the food," he says. "You're hurt. You just rest, and I'll take care of everything. What should I fix us to eat?"

"Shhh!" I shake my finger at him. "If you have to talk, whisper. Better yet, don't say a word. Just sit down and be quiet."

Pretty Boy comes flying in from my bedroom and makes a fluttering landing on my shoulder. He stares at me, and I bet his look is saying, Where the hell have you been? But I guess he forgives me because he goes right to work pulling threads from my collar. I think he's a bit excited to have a brand new shirt to work on, even if it is a dumb old man's green shirt.

David is staring at the bird. He giggles, and I shush him.

I gulp down a bunch of ibuprofen tablets and quickly fix Grandma her breakfast. I wheel it into her room, but when I put in on her bedside table, she's so caught up in her TV soap opera, she hardly seems to notice. Maybe she wasn't all that hungry after all. I can see she's been busy eating from the packages of cookies I order for her on Amazon. The big package of chocolate chip cookies looks to be about half empty. I'll have to put in another order soon.

When I roll back out into the dining room, I see that David is still sitting meekly at the table. He runs a finger over the old wood and holds it up to show me the dust. "I could help you around here," he whispers. "I could clean the place up."

I ignore him. No way I'm going to let him wiggle his way in here. He has his own home to go to. Even if his mother doesn't like him, at least he actually has a mother that sticks around, so she'll be looking for him at that hospital.

I fix us cheese sandwiches, and he devours his. I wonder how long since he ate.

I fix him another one, and he wolfs that one down too.

Even though he's about as skinny as me, he seems to have a big appetite.

I'd like to get him some bus money to get rid of him, but I can't raid Grandma's box full of change until she goes to sleep.

I shoo Pretty Boy away and gesture for David to grab a chair and follow me into my bedroom. He does it, and I close the door. I tell him to put his chair in the corner and be quiet.

He does as he's told and sits there, his arms crossed, staring at me.

I ignore him and lie down on my mattress. Finally, I can get a little relief from the pain in my chest. I close my eyes and try to put my mind where the pain isn't. But after only a few minutes, I know I'm not going to be able to sleep. I open my eyes and pull up my shirt to see how bad my wound looks. Thankfully, it's not bleeding anymore.

I look at David and see that he's staring up at the ceiling. "Why is your ceiling painted black?" he asks.

"Because I painted it black."

"Well, then what are all those white spots?"

"It represents the night sky. Those white spots are the main constellations."

"No Shit? What's that one?" He seems to be pointing to Orion.

"Orion."

"Those dots are Orion? How do you know?"

"Damn it, David. I'm trying to get some rest here."

"Oh, sorry." He again crosses his arms and goes back to looking up.

If I can't sleep, I might as well look up something on the computer. Maybe that will make me sleepy. "David. Do me a favor and bring me my computer."

"Oh sure." He jumps up. He goes to the table and grabs my laptop. "Where do you want it?"

"Just put it here on the bed next to me."

He does it, and I turn onto my side to look at the screen. It's still on one of the sites about Derrida. Good as anything.

But as I start to read, David asks, "Checking your Facebook?"

"Don't have Facebook."

"What?" He seems genuinely surprised. "Email?"

"I don't have email either. Why should I? I don't know anybody."

He grins. "You could email me."

"I doubt it. As soon as you're out of here, you're gonna go kill yourself, remember?"

He shrugs. "Maybe now that I have a friend, I won't have to. At least not for a while."

I shake my head. "I wouldn't count on me, if I was you. I might not be around all that long either."

"Really? You gonna kill yourself too?"

"If I decide to."

He stares at me, probably not sure if I'm serious. Am I? If so, what am I waiting for? I push those kinds of thoughts away and focus on the internet.

But my inattention to David doesn't deter him. He keeps right on talking. He rambles on, telling me about how his old man got arrested for beating up his mother because he caught her with another guy, and now his mother has a restraining order against his father, but she won't agree to a divorce because she's dependent on the money in their joint checking account. He tells me how the kids at school picked on him until he quit going and how his mother was never at home, so she didn't even know he'd quit until the school truant cops came to his house and told her. So she made him go back to school, and that's when he started his wrist-slashing trick, which is what got him committed to the psych ward at that hospital. He says that after he got out the first time, he lived on the streets until the cops got him and took him home. He ran away again, but eventually, living on the mean streets of LA got to him, and that's when he went up into the bushes at Griffith Park to try to do a better job of wrist slashing.

I'm only half listening to his long-winded story because I'm trying to focus on an article about Derrida that says the task of deconstructionists is not only to analyze word and concept dualities, but also to find new perspectives that take human communication beyond its surface implications and "reauthor" texts to find new stories within them.

I'll have to remember to ask Derrida about that when I see him.

It seems like only minutes have gone by when I hear Grandma's tinkling little bell again. Lunch time already?

I get up and get into my wheelchair. I tell David to stay put while I go fix Grandma's lunch. I'm hoping that maybe after she eats, she'll fall asleep so I can grab some bus money for David out of her old tin box.

But when I take her food in to her bedroom, she seems wide awake. She's all caught up in some TV soap opera about a woman who's boo-hooing into the usual dainty little handkerchief as she confesses that she just had an abortion. An abortion? her husband says. But how can that be? I've been away on that job in Saudi Arabia for the past year. The moment is so dramatic, Grandma doesn't seem to notice I've brought her lunch in.

I go back out and find David waiting for me in the dining room. I fix us a couple more sandwiches, and then I go back to my mattress and get on the computer again.

David sits on my mattress next to me, eating his sandwich and jabbering away about this and that.

I try to keep my focus on a web site that says Derrida is often criticized for saying there is nothing outside of the text. They're saying he's denying the reality of the world, but I don't think so. I think what he's saying is that there is no reality outside of the reality we overlay on what we perceive. I can hardly wait to talk to him about that to see if I'm right. Another article says he had a running argument with Michel Foucault, so that means I have to look up this Foucault guy. The internet says Michel Foucault was a French philosopher and historian. It says, like Derrida, he was into literary criticism and linguistics, but he was also very interested in how societies create their own unique punishment systems to deal with crime. As for the reason he and Derrida didn't get along, it turns out Foucault accused Derrida of being intentionally obscure, unwilling to explain his theories in simpler terms. Well, I do have to agree that

Derrida is not easy to understand, but I doubt if he's being intentionally obscure. I mean, as a teacher, wouldn't he want his students to understand what he's trying to teach them? It also says Derrida dissed Foucault for advocating metaphysics, and Foucault dissed Derrida right back because of how Derrida was interpreting Descartes. Anyhow, this Foucault guy sounds like an interesting person. I'll have to study more about him after I get through studying Derrida.

A while back, I read that Derrida also had a disagreement with that other French philosopher, Jean Francois Lyotard. It said Derrida picked apart (deconstructed) Lyotard's analysis of pronouns and syntax, like when we're saying how great a departed friend was, we're actually saying we must be great too. It's starting to sound like Derrida makes a habit of alienating other philosophers by "deconstructing" their ideas. Also, he revealed how most philosophers fall into the trap of using a "we" subject in the nominative, or an "us" subject in the accusative, or the dative, without it becoming self-referential, rather than being other-referential as they were intending.

Did you understand that? I didn't. Derrida can be really hard to understand. Just when I think I'm getting what he's talking about, he throws in a confusing sentence like that. To even begin to understand what he's saying, I have to go figure out what each of the terms he's using means. But whenever I do that, I usually just find other terms that I also have to go look up. It feels like a never ending process, like opening up one of those little Russian dolls that always has another doll inside.

But I'm not complaining. It's interesting stuff, and what else do I have to do?

Maybe the old man can help me. He's been quiet lately, and he usually doesn't like to talk about "modern" philosophers, but it's worth a try.

"Hey, wake up, Old Man. What do you know about this stuff? It all seems self-referential."

"Are you talking to me?"

David is staring at me.

I point at the computer screen. "I'm just trying to understand this stuff. It's complicated."

"Jeez, man, do you always whisper to your computer like that? It's weird."

"Like I said. It's complicated stuff. I'm just thinking out loud."

He gets up and leans over my shoulder to look at the screen. "What is it?"

"It's an article about deconstructive philosophy."

"The what philosophy?"

"Deconstructive. But never mind. Leave me alone. I need to concentrate."

"Why are you reading that kind of shit?"

"It's what I do. I'm studying."

"You takin' a class?"

"No. I mean, not yet. Maybe I will."

"In college?"

"Where else? They don't teach philosophy in high school. It's the most important subject there is, and they don't teach it in high school at all."

"But you said you didn't even have enough money to give me bus fare. How're you gonna pay for college?"

"I'll figure it out. In the meantime, I can study it all I want on the internet. Now leave me alone so I can get back to it."

I go back to reading about Derrida, but out of the corner of my eye, I see David heading out of my bedroom. I tell him, "You can get something to eat out there in the kitchen if you're hungry, but don't make a sound. If Grandma hears you, she'll kick you right out of here."

He puts his finger to his lips and whispers, "Quiet as a mouse."

I can hear that Grandma's TV is still blasting away back in her bedroom, so she probably won't be hearing anything until whatever soap opera she's watching gets over. But then I start to worry that David might wander into her room. I sit up to see what he's doing. Looks like he's dusting. Somewhere he's found a cloth, and he's busy dusting everything in the entire dining room. If Grandma came out of her bedroom—which she hardly ever does—she sure would be surprised to see some skinny, moody-looking boy dusting her house, with a parakeet riding along on his shoulder.

I turn my attention back to the computer. I wonder why Derrida is seen as such a rebel? Are all of the French philosophers seen as philosophy rebels? Maybe I need to get a better idea of what the general concepts of so-called French philosophy are. To start, I Google that Foucault guy, and I find out he believed you could tell a lot about a society by studying their laws and their punishments. He was especially interested in looking at society's ever-evolving views on morality. He pointed out that laws and punishments for breaking "morality" laws, like homosexuality, change as a society changes. Like in the United States, not all that long ago, every state in the union had strict laws against any and all homosexual behavior. But gradually, as homosexuality became a more open life style, those laws disappeared.

Reading that makes me wonder if Foucault was gay. I Google his name along with the word "homosexual," and Google leads me to a web site that says he came to America in the seventies to teach at UC Berkeley, and it didn't take him long to go across the bay and get involved in the San Francisco gay scene.

Uh oh, the site says that a few years later Foucault died from AIDS. Strange. Here was a famous French philosopher who came to America to teach, and apparently, to study the San Francisco gay scene, but he ends up dying because he got *too* involved in it.

Following up on his idea about understanding a society by studying its laws and punishments, I do a Google search for law and punishment in the United States. The first site I find says Americans that identify themselves as black or as African-American comprise only about twelve percent of the total US population, but they comprise nearly forty percent of the total US prison population. It says Hispanics make up another twenty percent. That gets me to wondering if the people in this country with darker skins really *are* committing most of the crimes, or are the police just more likely to arrest them and juries more likely to convict them. I sit back to think about it. Here I've been living in Watts for quite a while now, and I have to admit I don't know much about the dark-skinned people who live all around me. My neighbors all have dark skin, but they don't seem like criminal types. Of course the gangbangers in this neighborhood *do* commit crimes; it's how they make their living. But I doubt if gangs are committing enough crimes to fill up all the prisons.

David comes back and parks himself on the mattress next to me. I guess he's finished his mad cleaning effort, and now he's bored, so he's come back to bother me.

I try to ignore him and continue my studies.

But sure enough, after only a few minutes, he's leaning over to try to see what's on the computer screen. "What are all those numbers?"

"Those numbers are statistics," I say. "They indicate that while Americans represent only about five percent of the world's population, nearly one-quarter of all the world's prison inmates are in United States prisons."

David looks doubtful. "That can't be. What about places like Russia? Or China? I heard they lock up people just for saying things the government doesn't like."

"Yeah," I say, "but according to this, they don't lock people up near as much as we do. Let me check."

I go to the Wikipedia web site and enter, "world incarceration rates." It shows me a table of data. I point at the screen. "It says the United States has the highest documented incarceration rate in the world, seven hundred and fifty four per hundred thousand people, fifty percent more than Russia. And listen to this, more than seven times as many as in China."

David frowns. "That's fucked up."

"Sure is. And look at this. It says we have seven times as many people locked up as in Canada, a country that's only separated from us by a dotted line on a map."

David looks puzzled for a moment, then snaps his fingers. "Drugs. I bet in this country they're filling the prisons up with pot smokers and crack addicts."

I look that up. "Yeah, it says drug-related arrests increased from forty-one thousand a year before President Reagan started the war on drugs to more than half a million arrests per year now."

"Told ya."

"But it says imprisonment for all kinds of other crimes has also been increasing too."

"Does it say why?"

"It lists two main causes, tougher sentencing and privatization."

"What's privatization?"

"It says privatization was another thing President Reagan and the Republicans in Congress started. They turned a lot of the prisons over to private companies, and those companies have been lobbying Congress for stiffer laws and longer sentences. That makes sense: the more people they have incarcerated, the more money they make."

David says, "So it's all about the money, as usual."

"Yeah. It says the private prison companies have been lobbying Congress and local elected officials like crazy to try to stop the legalization of marijuana. Their lobbyists are even trying to put a stop to medical marijuana."

"What the hell? Medical marijuana?"

"It's basic capitalism, David. Capitalism is where lobbyists line up to put money into the pockets of the politicians to protect their interests, and because the politicians will do *anything* to get reelected, they do whatever gets them the most money for their reelection campaigns."

David frowns. "Why do you waste your time reading that stuff? There's nothing we can do about it."

I try to think how to answer him. He's right. There is nothing we can do about it; it's just the way the system works. I say, "I just want to know about it, David. I want to know how things work. It's all right here on the internet. Don't you want to how know things work?"

"So that's what you do all day? Study how things work?"

"Sure. I study everything. Damn, David, don't you realize what a miracle the internet is? Can you imagine living without it? We wouldn't know anything. They could tell us anything they want, and we'd have to believe them. Don't you get that, at least?"

He shrugs and looks away. "Aw, I got other things to worry about."

I tap on the computer screen. "Just stop worrying long enough to think about it, David. Every damn thing in the world is on the worldwide network we call the internet. More and more stuff is being added every day. All it takes is a few clicks of the mouse, and there it is, right in front of you. Nothing like this has ever existed on this planet. The internet tells us what's *really* going on. When my mom was still around, we used to watch the TV news every night, but there was nothing on it. A few headlines and tons of commercials. We only watched the news because she wanted to know what the Hollywood celebrities were up to. Besides that celebrity news, there wasn't much else, nothing but stories designed to get you to watch the commercials and buy things."

David shrugs again. "Yeah, but what can we do about it? They have all the power."

"Who is *they*?"

"You know, the ones with the power."

David may not be all that smart, but he has a point. There is *us*, and there is *them*. The *them* has all the power, and it's important for *them* to keep it like that. They know that as long as they feed us enough "good-life stuff," like cars and clothes and whiz-bang movies and TV shows and fake crap about flying saucers and secret societies, the peons will stay pacified and not ask too many questions.

I can see that I've lost David's interest. I'm about to explain to him that today's politicians hire big propaganda corporations to spread dirt on their opponents, when I hear Grandma's bell tinkling.

I look toward the window. Damn, it's already getting dark outside. I'd better get Grandma her supper.

I start to get up, and when I wince from the pain in my chest, David scrambles to help me.

After he gets me seated in my wheelchair, I say, "You hungry?"

"You bet." He jumps up and gets ahold of the push handles on my wheelchair. He zips me out into the kitchen, and as we go by the hallway to Grandma's bedroom, I call out, "I'm fixing it right now, Grandma. Be there in a jiffy."

I don't hear any response. Just the blaring of her TV. Good. She still doesn't suspect I've got a visitor.

I down more ibuprofen tablets and start fixing Grandma's meal. When I take it in to her, I see that she's watching a sitcom that has the usual "canned" laughter that cues you when you're supposed to laugh. I put her food tray down on her bedside table, but she won't take her eyes off the TV where some skinny guy dressed in clothes that are too big for him says something about the butts of the women at his workplace. His words are followed by a blaring, volume-turned-up laugh track. I don't see anything funny about what that the guy said, but Grandma laughs when she's told to. Oh well, as dumb those programs are, I guess it keeps her entertained.

I wheel back out to the kitchen and find David putting together a couple of peanut butter sandwiches. Pretty Boy is on his shoulder, closely watching what he's doing.

When the sandwiches are ready, I grab mine and retreat to my bedroom. I turn on the desk lamp and point it toward the wall. Then, I carefully lie down on my mattress, trying not to aggravate the pain in my chest too much. Damn, that little wound is really starting to hurt. Maybe I should have taken more of those ibuprofen tablets.

David sits down on my mattress next to me to eat his sandwich. "So, this is all you do? Spend all day reading stuff on the internet?"

"Yeah. Now let me concentrate."

"Okay," he says. "Cool. No problem."

He concentrates on eating his sandwich, and it only takes me a few minutes to get completely caught up in reading about all the strange laws different societies have had and the weird punishments they made up. It says the world's first legal code was developed in some place called Mesopotamia about a thousand years B.C. The code they made up legalized the punishment concept of an eye for an eye, a concept that later turned up in the Christian Bible. The internet also says that in the old days, China and India had punishments like tattooing and disfigurements to let people know who had committed a crime. Some crimes were cause for castration or mutilation, and until recently, almost all societies had the death penalty. In the Roman empire, the manner in which the death penalty was carried out differed for different sorts of crimes. The worse crime was treason. For that, you got stripped naked and whipped until you were dead. The next most serious crime was killing your father. For that, you were sewed up inside a sack and thrown into a river. Sometimes, to make it more uncomfortable inside the sack, they threw in a snake or a dog. For infidelity, you got to be buried alive. Roman emperors could also make up their own death penalties, such as tearing the accused apart by tying them between two horses, or feeding them to wild animals. And of course, everybody who's ever seen a Christian history movie knows about another form of the death penalty that was practiced in Rome, crucifixion. But crucifixion was only supposed to be done to slaves or non-citizens. All of the Roman punishments were carried out in full view of the public, and the punishment days were like big festivals. They were so popular, I'm surprised they don't still do it that way these days.

I find another web site that says that in five hundred B.C. Greece invented the jury system. Before that, what was legal or illegal was dictated by the king. Since then, most countries have adopted some sort of jury system. In some societies, it's a jury of your peers, and in others, it's a jury of government officials, or a combination of peers and trained jurors. But in almost all cases, the punishment you get depends on your social class. Sometimes, it's written into the law, but sometimes it's just because richer, higher-class people can afford a better lawyer.

I keep on reading about crime and punishment until I hear Grandma turn off her TV. I don't have any idea what time it is, but it must be late. Hopefully, she took a sleeping pill. I don't know what's in all those pills she takes, but they seem to knock her out good. I wonder how old those pills are. No doctor has come to see her since I've been staying here, but she still seems to have quite a stash of them.

I read a little longer, then I get up and David helps me get into my wheelchair. I say, "I'll go see if I can get you the money for the bus. You stay here and keep quiet."

He gives me a thumbs up, and I wheel into Grandma's bedroom, trying not to make a sound.

I needn't have worried; she's snoring away. I go to her closet and take enough change out of her tin box for David's bus fare, and a little extra for myself, to make up for the amount I lost when they took my clothes at the hospital. I'll need it for bus fare as soon as I'm ready to again head down there to that university in Irvine.

I wheel back into my bedroom and shoo Pretty Boy off of David's shoulder. He flies back out into the dining room, and I close the door behind him.

I hand David enough money to pay the bus fare.

He looks toward the window, then back at me. "It's dark out there, Scotty. You can't send me out there in the dark. Not in this kind of neighborhood."

He looks like he's about to cry, and I suppose he's right to be scared. He's so dumb, he might actually manage to get himself killed out there. Even if they don't kill him, the local gangbangers are sure to relieve him of the money. They might even take his clothes and shoes just for the sport of it. It wouldn't be the first time the cops found some beat-up white kid wandering around this part of town totally naked.

He's looking at me with his watery puppy-dog eyes, so I know I'm going to have to relent. "Well, all right, but only 'til morning. Then you have to go. I've got important stuff to do."

That cheers him up. "Oh thanks. Don't worry, I'll be quiet as a mouse."

"You'd better be. And I have no place for you to sleep."

"Sure, sure. Don't mind me. I'll just sleep . . . " He looks around. "On that rug out in the other room?"

"No, Grandma might come out in the night and find you. You have to stay in here."

He puts his finger up to his lips. "Don't mind me. I'll just go to sleep . . uh, right over here." He goes into the corner and lies down on the old hardwood floor. He turns away from me and pretends to go to sleep.

I stare at his back. He's a weird kid, but he's a gentle guy, and pretty out front. Kind of surprising, considering what he's been through.

I slip out of my wheelchair and ease myself down onto my mattress. I'll just try to sleep for a few minutes and then get back on the computer. But man, as soon as I lie down, the old familiar pain in my legs reminds me that it's still there. And now, I have a brand new pain in my chest where I got stabbed. Shit! Why did that idiot have to go and stab me? Now, I have to wait for this new wound to heal before I can go talk to Professor Derrida. I focus on my usual task of putting my mind somewhere where the pain isn't, and I'm almost asleep when I feel something jiggle my mattress. I look over and see that it's David trying to quietly sneak in.

"Okay, David, what the hell do you think you're doing?"

He sits up and looks at me. "Oh, sorry, Scotty. I thought you were asleep."

"Well?"

"Uh, that floor is too hard."

"Yeah, I bet it is, but you can't come crawling into my bed. What are you, gay or something?"

"Not really. But I'll suck your dick if you want me to." He grins.

"What? I don't do any of that gay shit. Go back to your corner, and go to sleep."

But David doesn't leave. He just lies there staring at me.

"You know, he says, "I really don't think I'm gay. I only sucked a few dicks to get money. Like I told you before, I was on the streets for quite a while before they caught me and took me back home. I was . . . uh, desperate."

"That's the only way you can think of to get money? Sucking dicks? There must be a thousand better ways to get money."

He shrugs. "Like what? Stealing stuff? I tried to steal some food at a grocery store, but they caught me. Said if I ever came in there again, they'd call the cops. Sucking dick is not so bad. Not really. You just open your mouth and let them do whatever they want. You think about something else."

I shake my head. What an idiot. He has a home to go to, and he's out on the street sucking dicks. He's lucky he didn't get himself killed.

David shrugs again. Shrugging seems to be his main way of expressing himself. "Besides," he says, almost whining now, "I'm not smart like you. I had to do it. The first time, it was just some old guy. He said he'd give me some money if I did it, so I did it."

"Well, keep away from me. I've gotta get some sleep."

"So you prefer . . . uh, girls?"

I turn over and face away from him. He's keeping me from moving my mind away from the pain in my legs and in my chest. I mumble. "How would I know?"

"No shit?" he says. "You're a virgin?"

I turn back to face him. "Shh! Keep your damn voice down, David. What's it to you whether I'm a virgin or not."

David frowns.

What is he thinking now?

He whispers, "I'm not much good at talking to girls, but a girl in my neighborhood showed me . . . you know, how to do it. But you . . . hey, jeez, you're smart. You know all that stuff from the internet. And other stuff. You could probably get a girl anytime you wanted to."

I turn away from him again. "Why would I want to? Who needs it? Just shut up and go to sleep. And you have to stay all the way over there on the other side of this mattress. Or I swear, I'll throw you out on the street, whether it's dark out there or not."

He's silent for a while, but then he whispers, "I can get you a girl."

"Go to sleep."

"No, really. My sister. She'd fuck you if I told her too. She's about your age. And real cute too."

"God damn it, David. I'm not interested. Go to sleep."

"And she's smart like you. Goes to college and everything. But she got involved with this jerk who knocked her up and then left her. My mom made her get an abortion, even though she didn't want to."

"Your sister doesn't sound all that smart."

"Yeah, that's what she says too. Now she's down on herself and won't go out with guys. But she'd fuck you if I told her to."

"Why should she?"

"Because I say so. We have this rule. We always have to do what the other one says to do."

I turn back over and stare at him. This kid is not only a weirdo, but he's also got a weirdo sister. "Yeah, well she'd take one look at my fucked-up legs and run the other way. I pull up my pants legs.

He leans closer to look. "Jesus, your legs *are* all hacked up. What the hell happened?"

"Buncha surgeries. Doesn't matter anyhow. The point is, no girl is gonna get in bed with a cripple."

"My sister would. She's studying to be a nurse. Or medical tech. Something like that. I'll bring her over. She'd like you cause you're smart."

"No, David, you won't bring her over. In the morning, you'll take the bus back home to wherever you live—"

"Hawthorne."

"Fine. In the morning, you'll go back to Hawthorne and tell your mom and your sister you're sorry and you'll never try to hurt yourself again. For Christ's sake, David. You've got a home to go to. With food. A warm bed. And a nice house, I bet. Be glad for it. From now on, just keep your head down and stay out of trouble."

David doesn't answer.

"Did you hear me?"

"I'm going to sleep."

"Well, fine. You can take my advice or not, but in the morning you're outta here."

I turn over and start working on putting my mind where the pain isn't. But this damn kid has got me thinking about his so-called cute and smart sister who'll do whatever he tells her to. I can't let my mind go there. I need to get some sleep.

But now, I don't feel sleepy. I can't stop my mind from thinking about what he said. Would she really do anything he tells her to? It might be interesting to see how she'd react to my legs. Maybe she'd want to study them, like it was a class assignment or something.

No, that's a stupid idea. It's probably not true anyhow. If he does have a sister, there's no way she'd be interested in me, a kid who can't even kill himself properly. And that gets me to thinking about what happened on that bus. Was I trying to make those gangbangers on the bus do me in? Does it mean I still want to die? If so, what am I waiting for? Like I told David, there's plenty of good ways to do it, any of them better than getting myself stabbed and ending up with even more pain.

I push those kinds of stupid thoughts away. I have to remain logical. I am a *Hikikomori*, and I have a purpose. My purpose is learning. It's my particular boulder to endlessly roll up the hill. I must focus on that and nothing else.

For most of the night, I just stare up at the ceiling, but maybe I doze a little. When I see it's starting to get light outside my window, I wake David and tell him he has to go.

He gets up, but he says he's hungry and heads for the kitchen.

I get into my wheelchair and chase after him. "God damn it, David, I'm not your mama. Go home and get your own mother to feed you."

"She won't be there. She's never there."

"Fine, all the better. That way, you can do whatever you want. Go home and raid the refrigerator. Like I said last night, David, be grateful for what you have. Now go, I've got work to do."

I herd him out the front door.

He hesitates there on the porch for a few moments, but finally he does his usual shrug and goes down the steps and out to the sidewalk.

When he looks back, I point in the direction of the bus stop. He looks worried, but he starts off in that direction, walking fast now.

I watch him go. I think he'll be all right. It's too early for any of the gangbangers to be out. He'll make it to the bus stop, and then he'll go home. At least, I hope he'll go straight home. He's not the brightest bulb in the socket, but he's not such a bad guy. Maybe he'll straighten himself out and go back to school. Maybe his sister will help him, if he really has a sister.

I close the door and go to the kitchen to fix Grandma's breakfast. I take it in to her. She's still snoring away. How many sleeping pills did she take last night?

I wheel back to my bedroom and stare at my mattress. Should I lie down again? My wound is hurting, but not all that bad. No use being a wimp and lying around all day. I decide to eat a few more ibuprofen tablets and stay in my wheelchair. I grab my laptop and put it back on the table.

Pretty Bird is happy to see me back in my chair because it means he can fly down and go back to work pulling threads out of my shirt collar.

"Well, Pretty Boy, what should I study today?"

Pretty Boy looks up from his thread-pulling and says, "Pretty Boy."

"Derrida? Yeah, you're right. I'd better work really hard to understand even the most complex subtleties of what he's saying. That way, as soon as my wound heals and I go down there to meet with him at his university, he'll be so impressed with my knowledge, he'll have to let me into his class.

11
Epistemological Constructs

Today is the day. Time to head back down there to that university in Irvine to see Professor Derrida. I'm still having some pain in my chest, but I can't sit around here forever waiting for the stupid stab wound to stop hurting. Am I going to forever be a slave to my pain or its master? I choose master. It's just a matter of putting my brain where the pain isn't. I pull up my shirt to look at the wound one more time. It worries me that there's so much redness and swelling around the stitches. I wish I had somebody to ask about it, but Old Man only deals in the philosophical, not in the physical.

Pretty Boy gets a grip on my shirt and leans forward to see what I'm looking at. He turns his head to look at me and says, "Pretty Boy?"

"Good question, my little friend. I've been asking myself the same thing: is all that redness normal?" Maybe I should put some salve or something on it. But I don't think there's any salve in this house, so I might as well quit worrying about it and get on with my trip. Whatever is causing the redness is not going to kill me, and if I'm ever going to get down there to that university, I can't keep putting it off. I look out the window. The sun is just now coming up in the east. If I make Grandma her breakfast and lunch, and take both of them in to her right now, I could head out and catch an early southbound bus. That way, I'll be sure to be there to catch Professor Derrida, whatever time of day he shows up at his office.

Pretty Boy lets out a few loud tweets. He seems to understand I'm about to do something different.

I roll out into the kitchen and get busy making Grandma's breakfast and lunch. I consider slipping one of her sleeping pills into her soup, but decide she'll probably be so caught up in her TV soap operas that if I make it back here before dark, she won't even miss me. I take the food in to her bedroom. She's still snoring away. Good. When she wakes up hungry, she'll see I've already brought her food in and not go calling for me. She'll probably be upset when it's lunch time because her soup will be cold, and she'll start ringing her little bell, but when I don't come, she'll just eat it and then get caught up in her TV programs again. I go back to the kitchen and make myself a quick cheese sandwich. I wolf it down as I'm getting dressed: innocuous plaid shirt, innocuous gray pants, old worn running shoes. I bet it's exactly what a student at that university would wear. Next, I go to the hall closet to dig out another one of Grandma's old canes. I decide on the one that's shaped like a bird's beak. I push my wheelchair aside and stand up to test it. The cane seems strong enough. I go to the front door, but stop to take one last look around. Pretty Boy is on the kitchen counter, pecking away at his bird seeds. I call to him. "See ya later, Pretty Boy. Keep an eye on the place." But as soon as I open the door, Pretty Boy comes flying in to land on my shoulder. I have to quickly step back and close the door. "No, no, Pretty Boy. You can't come with me. What you don't understand is that the world out there is much bigger than your little world inside this house. You wouldn't last a day out there in the big bad world." I brush him off my shoulder, and he flies back to the kitchen counter and starts pecking away at his seeds again. I can tell he's pissed off at me. "Well, you have to stay inside, no matter what you think. I'm doing it for your own good."

He ignores me and keeps on pecking away at his seeds. So be it. I go out and do my usual sitting down and scooting method to get down the porch stairs. Then, I get a good grip on my cane and begin my slow shuffle toward the bus stop. I look ahead to the corner. Looks like none of the young gang homies are there. They must all be out doing drug runs for the gang. Good. This time I don't want to get stopped for any reason.

But when I get to the corner, I see that they *are* there; it's just that this time they're over on the other side of the street. The usual threesome of young wannabe dark-skinned gangsters are there, but this time there's somebody else with them, a somewhat older dark-skinned guy, and he's not dressed like the local gangbangers usually dress. He's wearing a dark brown leather jacket and tan pants. And expensive-looking running shoes. It looks like he's giving the young wannabes some kind of lecture, and they're all paying close attention to him. I bet he's a senior member of the *real* local gang, the one those kids want to join. I realize I'd better get on past them quick; don't wanna mess with any real gangbangers. I had enough of that when I got stabbed on the bus.

I try to hurry up, but that just makes me stumble, and one of the young dudes sees it. He laughs and yells at me: "What's the matter, crip, forget how to walk?"

I keep on going, hoping they don't try to follow me.

The kid who yelled at me holds up his hand to stop the traffic, and they hurry across to my side of the street.

Damn, looks like they think today is a good day to hassle me. Maybe they're trying to impress that older gang member. I decide to stop and wait for them. I'm not about to let them think I'm afraid of them. I turn around stand my ground, trying to look as bored as possible.

"Hey," the kid says as he approaches me, "we heard about how you got yourself stuck. On a bus, no less. What'd you do, say something smart ass to 'em?"

Now I recognize him. He's the snarly little jerk, Lil G, who just *had to* threaten me with his fancy new pistol the last time I was here.

"Listen," I say, "no time for your nonsense today. I got to go."

I start to turn away, but just like last time, the little twerp pulls up his floppy white T-shirt to show me his fancy silver pistol. "You don't got to go nowhere til I say so, asshole."

"Oh," I say, "did your mommy buy you a new toy? How cute."

He pulls the gun out and points it at me.

I raise my hands. "Oh my, I'm sooo scared. Whatever shall I do?"

Immediately, the older guy pulls the kid back and gets in his face: "What the fuck's the matter with you? Showing a gun right out here in the Goddam street?"

The kid looks chagrined to be called out in front of me. He leans around the older guy and says to me, "I'll get you later, motherfucker."

I say, "You know where to find me, punk. I'll meet you right here in the middle of the street. High noon." I reach down and slap my hip like I'm on old-time cowboy slapping leather.

The older guy chuckles at that and comes closer to me. He's still smiling, and I take that as a good sign.

"Sorry about that," he says. "Kid's a hothead."

I size up the guy. He's tall, lean, but strong looking, maybe in his early thirties. He's got the usual gangbanger tattoos, and one that's especially noticeable on his neck, a very well-done face of snarling pit bull with big teeth and startling red eyes. Under the pit bull's face is the number 99 in the kind of fat wobbly style graffiti street artists use. I've seen that graffiti style 99 before in this neighborhood, but never along with an angry dog tattoo.

He may be a gangbanger, but there's something different about him. His eyes seem wary, but also more alive, more . . . thoughtful. I wonder why he wants to talk to me. Whatever it is, I've got no time for it. I've got to get down to Irvine, and this time, I'm not going to let anybody make me late.

I turn away and hurry on down the sidewalk—if you can call my painful step-drag-step locomotion method hurrying. But I don't make it much farther on before the guy jogs up beside me, and the other three gang dudettes are right behind him. Damn. Why did I have to mouth off to these guys? Now they think they have to go through some ridiculous routine to save face.

But the older guy still seems to be trying to act friendly. "They tell me you live around here. On this street?"

Is he really interested in me, or is this some kind of trick?

"Name's Jake," he says. He sticks out his hand.

Does he really want to shake hands, or this another one of their stupid gang games? I give his hand an intentionally limp shake and try not to wince at his iron grip. But I don't think he meant to hurt my hand; he's just very strong. Despite his calm manner, I suspect he's actually one tough son of a bitch. He's at least six inches taller than me, and he's got that loose and lanky look, the kind of look all the really tough guys have. I give him a little salute of respect and resume my shuffling, limping walk toward the bus stop.

But he falls in beside me again. The guy moves quick. He's light on his feet for such big guy.

"Why you limpin'?" he asks. "What happened to your leg?"

I should have known he wasn't done with me. I glance at him, but I don't slow down. He seems calm and serious, as if he's really waiting for my answer. And it dawns on me that he's not using the normal black ghetto talk; instead, he's talking to me like we're just two normal people. I have the feeling he might even be educated beyond the eighth grade, as unlikely as that is in this neighborhood.

"Happened on a bus?" he asks. "Like the kid said?"

Lil G, the kid who pulled the gun on me, decides to squeeze in between us and butt in. "Yeah, it did. Serve the whitebread right. I bet he was doin' some —"

Jake, if that's his real name, turns on the kid. "Shut the fuck up, Lil G. I'm talkin' here."

All of a sudden, the gun totin' kid doesn't seem so brave. He frowns and looks down at the sidewalk. "Well, he deserve it. That's what I hear. He mouth off to some Criminals on a bus near here, so they—"

Jake turns fast and grabs the front of the kid's shirt. "On a bus *near* here? Is that what you just said?"

The kid looks scared, and his hand goes down to his waistband. For a just moment, I think he's going to pull his gun on Jake. If he does, will the other two young ones back up his play against the older guy?

No, the other young dudes move away from the little gun-toter, and that lets the kid know he's on his own. He keeps his eyes down, and he's nervously scratching at the back of his neck. He mumbles, "Well, I heard he start it. On that bus. "

"He started it?" yells Jake right into the kid's face. "Some outsiders come in here and stab one of our unarmed citizens? On one of our local buses? For Christ's sake, that's like coming in here and stabbing people right in our own Goddam front yard. You okay with that? You okay with them coming into our hood and pullin' shit like that?"

The younger kid has no answer, so I decide to help him out. "He's right. I mouthed off to those guys. They couldn't back down, not in front of all those people on the bus."

Jake turns back to me and puts a finger up close to my face. "No, it's not alright. It's not the way we do things here. This is our turf, not theirs." He points toward the bus stop. "And if I ever run into those guys . . . when they get out of jail, I'll say it right to their face. Let's see if they wanna try'n pull a knife on me."

"Forget it," I say. "I'm all right now. I got to go." I start walking again, and this time, thankfully, they don't follow me.

But Jake calls after me, "You live in my neighborhood. You remember that. This is my turf. You run into any more of those Criminals on a bus, or anywhere else in this area, you tell 'em you live in Big D Jake's hood. Got it?"

Without turning around, I give him a thumbs up and keep going.

As I go, I'm thinking about what he said. He seems to think I need his protection, but I wish I'd of never run into him. I'd rather just hide out in Grandma's house and be an anonymous *hikikomori*. The last thing I need is to get caught in the middle of some kind of gang war.

The way he talked down to the those wannabe gang dudes, I suspect he might be one of the leaders of whatever gang controls this neighborhood. He said to tell 'em this was Big D Jake's hood. I wonder if Big D and that tattoo of a snarling pit bull on his neck might stand for big dog. Is he the big dog in this neighborhood? I decide to worry about it later. Right now, the main thing is to get on that bus and get myself down there to Irvine.

When I get to the bus stop, I sit down on the bus stop bench, and only then does the pain in my chest really start to gnaw at me. I pull up my shirt, suddenly afraid that my walking, or my leaning on my cane, has pulled loose the stitches. But the wound isn't bleeding; it looks about the same as it did back at Grandma's, sort of red and swelled up. No big deal. I should just forget about it. Think about something else.

I lean back and close my eyes. I tell myself, there is no pain, there is no such thing as pain. I'm having some success at pushing the pain into the background when the screeching brakes of the city bus brings me back. I struggle to my feet, and use the bus's chrome handholds to pull myself aboard.

I pay my money and quickly find a seat before the driver can get the bus moving. I look toward the back of the bus and see that none of those Criminals gang members are on the bus this time. For a moment, I wonder if they got the word that the Big Dog was after them. But then I realize they'll still be in jail for stabbing me. Maybe I won't have to worry about them coming after me for revenge, at least not for a little while.

At the main bus station, I find the southbound bus to Irvine. I get on and get seated. Thankfully, there are no gangbangers on this bus either.

A few more people get on, and then we pull out of the station and head for the southbound freeway. So far so good. This trip shouldn't take too long. I stare out the window, but there's not much to see, nothing but the usual zillions of cars and trucks all around us.

I close my eyes and try to review Derrida's theories. I think I have it down pretty well, but how should I start out? Which aspect of his deconstructionism should I focus on? Or maybe I should just start out by telling him how much I enjoyed reading his works. No, I'd better not waste his time. I should talk about something specific, like how he's been accused of putting the final nail in the coffin of epistemology.

Epistemology presupposes a philosophical construct of knowledge. The road to knowledge lies inward, not outward.

"Yeah, I know that, Old Man. He made a good argument against the need for a God or any other "outside" explanation, but what if he's not interested in his original arguments anymore? He might just dismiss me as not up to date."

Truth cannot be distinguished from unfocused objects of thought.

"Sure, sure, I know that. But what if he sees the representational view as only being related to linguistic representations of thought?"

Beliefs must be examined as separate from representative ideas.

"I guess you're right. I'd better just stick to the main thrust of his ideas about deconstruction. Get him to talk to me about that."

I hear someone giggle. I turn to see that two young girls across the aisle are glancing at me. They're whispering to each other behind their hands. I guess they think my mumbling to myself is funny. Well, the hell with them. But maybe I'd better keep my thoughts to myself. They might be students at that university.

Okay, the important thing is to come up with a good plan and stick to it. I keep on going over it, trying hard not to whisper out loud, and before I know it, I realize the bus has left the freeway, and we're coming to the university campus.

Okay, this it it. I get off the bus, along with the two girls. I guess they really were students. I stall for a few minutes at the bus stop, and then I follow them up the hill toward the university buildings, just as if I was one of them.

I'm impressed at how nice the campus looks. Manicured green sloping lawns, neatly trimmed bushes, colorful flowers next to the sidewalk. As I slowly shuffle my way along, I start to imagine what it would be like to be a student at this university. I'm about the same age as those two girls, and I bet I'm just as smart as they are. Maybe even smarter. When I talk to Professor Derrida, I'll tell him my high school counselor said I had the highest IQ in the whole damn school. And then I'll start right in telling him what I've learned from the internet about his ideas. I bet that'll convince him to let me take one of his classes.

Two guys, students I bet, are sitting on the lawn talking. I stop to ask them where the philosophy department is, but they say they don't know.

As I go on, I realize they didn't look at me like I'm a weirdo or anything. They didn't even seem to notice my funny way of walking. That encourages me. Maybe the students at this university don't like to make fun of cripples.

I head for what seems to be the center of the campus, and I see a guy who's somehow managing to read a book while he's walking. I figure somebody who can do that must know where the philosophy department is.

I ask him for directions to the philosophy department, and without even looking up from his book, he points to a close-by building. I don't bother to thank him because he's so into his book he probably wouldn't even hear me. Man, if that guy is any indication, the student here are . . . well, studious. But I'm studious too, even if my studying is only on the internet instead of in books.

I shuffle my way to the building he pointed to, but inside, I find only empty hallways. Where is everybody? I have the horrible thought that maybe this university is not in session right now. Why didn't I think to check that? The university schedule is probably on the internet somewhere, so why didn't I look it up? Is this all just some kind of stupid dream? Did I think I could just show up and Professor Derrida would be there and welcome me with open arms. Maybe I should just turn around and get the hell out of here.

But then I tell myself not to go getting pessimistic before I've even found his office. I might find him there, reading, or grading papers. I bet he'd welcome the chance to take a break and talk to a potential student who's eager to learn.

Feeling more confident now, I work my way down the deserted hallway, checking the name cards on each faculty office. I reach the end of the hall. No Derrida. Is his office not in this building?

An older woman with gray hair comes out of an office down at the end of the hall. She looks like the professor type, so I call out to her. "Can you help me?"

She turns to look at me and waits as I limp down to her as fast as I can. I'm a bit out of breath, but I manage to stammer, "Which office is . . . I mean, where can I find Professor Derrida?"

She looks at me oddly, and asks, "Are you a student here?"

Her manner is not exactly accusatory, but I have the feeling that she knows I don't really fit in here.

I say, "No, but I'm thinking of coming here. I want to take some of Professor Derrida's classes."

"Oh," she says, and then she hesitates. She seems disturbed by my question. I wonder why.

She looks back down the hallway, and says, "I'm afraid he's gone."

"Oh, damn. I mean . . . shoot. I was afraid I took too long to get here. I live . . . a long way from here. And I had to wait to change buses, and . . ."

She just stares at me.

Here I am blathering on, wasting her time. A big-time professor like her probably doesn't have time for a wannabe student like me. It's not her problem that I didn't get here in time to meet with Derrida. I have a quick thought about the possibility of finding a place to sleep somewhere on campus so I can be here early in the morning. That way I'll be sure to catch him tomorrow. She looks like she's about to turn away, so I quickly say, "Uh, what time does he come in tomorrow? I mean, does he . . . have a class tomorrow?"

She shakes her head. "No, young man. I'm sorry I didn't make myself clear. You hadn't heard? He'd been ill for some time. He went back to France, and he recently passed away there."

I stare at her. I think I heard her clearly, but my mind doesn't want to believe what she's saying. Or maybe I didn't really hear it correctly. She said he'd been sick for a long time. Maybe he's just very sick. I've been preparing to meet with him for so long, he can't really be dead, can he?

She glances at her watch and says, "I'm afraid I have to go now. I'm sorry."

I mumble something about it being okay, but as she walks away down the hallway, I realize it definitely is *not* okay. How could he be dead, and I didn't know about it? Why wasn't there anything about him dying on any of those internet sites I've been reading? It must mean it just happened. Maybe he just died in the last few days. Oh no, that could mean that if those stupid gangbangers hadn't of stabbed me that other time when I was trying to get down here, he would still be here and everything would have been different. Maybe he would have liked me. Maybe he would have invited me to come and stay with him at his house. Maybe everything would have turned out different. Maybe he wouldn't have even died.

I shake my head to get rid of such stupid thoughts. People don't just up and die. That woman professor said he went back to France and died there. He probably went back to France some time ago. That means my whole idea of coming down here to meet with him and take classes from him was just a stupid dream. A fantasy. What the hell is the matter with me? I must be getting soft in the head. Living in Grandma's crumbling old house with nothing to do but study on the internet must be making me crazy. More important, it's making me forget what the world is really like. In the real world, dreams never turn out the way you want them to. In the real world, people get sick, and they die. In the real world, everything is just shit, and when everything is shit, nothing ever turns out the way you want it to.

I lean my forehead against the wall. I feel like crying, but I don't want to because crying would be stupid and because it wouldn't do the slightest bit of good. Derrida is dead, and that's all there is to it. So what was the point of all my studying about him? There was no point. Of course there wasn't: there's no point to anything. The old man has been telling me that for a long time. And he's right. I might as well take a bus straight back to that cliff at Point Fermin Park and do my swan dive again. But this time I'll do it right, and that will be the end of it.

What is the purpose of learning, if not to access wisdom?

"What's your point, Old Man, that all my learning has made me wise? Yeah, well, I've been doing nothing else but learning all this time, and what good has it done me?"

Knowledge begins with learning, and then proceeds to understanding.

"Yeah, and then it ends with death. So what was the point of all that learning?"

Logic is the method. Wisdom, the organization of knowledge that comes through the method, is the outcome.

"So, the point of it all is wisdom? And what good will wisdom do me? What good will it do anybody?"

Opportunity will come.

"Opportunity will come? What the hell does that mean? Opportunity to do what? To do something for the world? How is that going to happen if I'm just an all-alone *hikikomori* stuck inside my grandmother's house with no money, barely able to walk, and now with no other prospects?

Opportunity will come.

I think the old man has gone round the bend. He never says things directly like that. Normally, he only gives speeches. I bet I know what he's up to; he's trying to talk me out of going back to my cliff. I suppose he's right about that; it was a stupid idea and it left me crippled. Back then, I thought there was no point to life, and it's true, there isn't. But now, I know there's no point to death either. Ah, the hell with it. I might as well just go home and get back on the computer and never come outside again. I get a good grip on my cane, and slowly start down the long hallway toward the front entrance. I guess I might as well listen to the old man this time. I'll just go back to studying on the internet. Maybe I'll find something there that will tell me what the point of my life is.

12
Phenomenological Features of Experience

I wake up in my own bed. The bus ride back home seemed to take forever. The pain in my chest from that damn stab wound isn't so bad now, but I'm feeling a hell of a lot of pain in my legs from walking so much. But so what? I'm used to pain, and if I can't take classes from Derrida, I won't have to do any more walking. I'll just stay right here in Grandma's house and study interesting things on the internet. I had reconciled myself to that before. I should have stuck with it. Studying will be my purpose in life, my only purpose, my giant boulder to push up the hill. Forever, or until . . .

I get up off my mattress and get into my wheelchair. I wheel myself into the kitchen to fix Grandma's breakfast, just like I do every morning, just like I'll probably go on doing until it's time for me to die.

Pretty Boy flies down from his lampshade to land on my shoulder. He turns his head sideways to look me in the eye. "Pretty Boy?"

He's curious about where I went yesterday. "Nothing to worry about, Pretty Boy. Just a little trip down south. It doesn't matter."

"Pretty Boy?"

"No, I won't be doing that again. I'll just stay here with you and Grandma."

That seems to satisfy him, so he gets busy trying to pull my shirt collar to pieces. He's making good progress, but I suspect he's not happy that I've put on my same old shirt again, the one I wear every day. I'm sure he would prefer a new challenge, but I'm afraid he's just going to have to make do with the one shirt I give him to work on.

As soon as Grandma's morning meal is taken care of, I get on my computer to look up how Professor Derrida died. It says he died of pancreatic cancer, and that he had only been diagnosed with the cancer the year before. Surprisingly, he's still listed as a professor at that university in Irvine, and there doesn't seem to be any notice at the university site about him dying.

"Well, Pretty Boy, if I don't want to study about Derrida anymore, what should I study?"

Pretty Boy's only response is a shrill whistle right in my ear.

"Yeah, I know you're right. I should go back to studying pain."

But haven't I read just about everything the internet has to say about pain? Well, maybe not everything. I haven't studied pain that's permanent, maybe because I just couldn't face the fact that I'll have to live with this much pain for the rest of my life. But now, I know I will. I Google "chronic pain," and it gives me a list of all kinds of sites. One of them is supposed to be about unusual pain, but when I click on it, I find it's about imaginary pain. Well, I can assure you the pain in my legs sure as hell is not imaginary. I go to another site that's about writer's cramp. Is writer's "cramp" really considered to be pain? Isn't it just the kind of pain your get in your hand from writing too much? I keep reading, and it turns out that although sometimes writer's cramp *is* just a muscle cramp, there is another type of writer's cramp that becomes permanent. Supposedly, it also affect typists, seamstresses, painters, and musicians. The site says that although their activities are different, they are all suffering from the same thing, a type of neurological disorder that causes muscles to involuntarily contract. It's called focal dystonia. Now this what I'm looking for. It may not be directly related to the kind of pain I'm having, but it is about pain is controlled by the brain. The site says the cause of focal dystonia is not well understood. Some people believe that there must be some kind of misfiring of neurons. But what I want to know is what part of the body's pain system, and what part of the brain, is making it happen. I Google "focal dystonia," and it turns out that there's a lot of interest in it because it can become so severe and painful that professional musicians, like piano players or trumpet players, get so they can no longer make a living in their profession. Apparently, when the brain tells a given muscle to contract, its supposed to simultaneously stop contractions of any other muscles that would oppose that contraction. With focal dystonia, that doesn't happen, and it can get very painful. It says the condition might be caused originally by over-training, like with piano players that practice too much, but once the brain starts fouling up how the opposing muscles contract, the pain can become permanent. Oddly, the pain is usually quite task specific; that is, some piano players who can no longer play the piano because of the condition, he can still type on a computer keyboard. If you think that's weird, it goes on to say the affected piano players can actually play the piano music notes on fake piano keys that are drawn on a table top.

I stop reading and look at my fingers resting on my computer keyboard. How can that be? How could they be able to play on a fake piano, but not on a real piano? It's exactly the same movements of the fingers. It must mean it's a psychological thing: the piano player is just, I don't know, freaking out or something. Like when he has to play the piano in front of a big audience. But no, I keep reading, and it says it can happen even when the piano player is alone, just practicing, or even just playing for fun. Now that's weird. And the site says there are much more serious cases: it says the condition can start to spread to other muscles until a person's whole body can become racked by uncontrollable, and very painful, muscle spasms. It says the condition has been known by doctors for a long time, but in the old days, because of Freud and the worldwide influence of psychotherapy, it was considered to be a psychological ailment. People who suffered with it were told it was caused by the unconscious suppression of some childhood incident, and sometimes they were locked up in mental hospitals. Nowadays, however, based on the idea that the piano player can play just fine on a fake piano keyboard, people who suffer from the condition are sent to different kinds of psychologists who try to retrain the person to approach the task in a different way. Sometimes, small changes in the way a task is approached can help people overcome the neurological condition; for example, by having the piano player wear thin gloves or something. This is very interesting. It supports exactly what I've believed for a long time, that the brain can be retrained to not feel pain. So, who's to say I can't retrain my brain to ignore the pain signals I'm getting from my legs? Maybe the neurologists would think my theory is all wet, but what do I have to lose? From now on, whenever I'm walking and feeling pain in my legs, I'll try walking in a completely different way, and at the same time, I'll try to concentrate on some different kind of activity, like I'm walking on a soccer field or something. It might work. What the hell, it's worth a try.

I'm still reading about focal dystonia when I hear somebody come up onto the creaking old boards of the front porch.

I hurry and wheel to the front door, hoping to get it open before whoever it is knocks loud enough for Grandma to hear.

But nobody knocks.

I wheel over to the dining room window and pull aside the curtain. It's that kid, David, and there's a girl with him. A very thin dark-haired girl dressed in a halter top and tight white jeans. David is earnestly talking to her, gesturing with his hands.

I wheel to the door, shoo Pretty Bird off of my shoulder, and open it.

David is telling the girl, "All you have to do is—" He sees me and stops in mid sentence. He grins and runs over to shake my hand. "Hi there, Scotty old pal." He half turns and holds out his hand toward the girl. I want you to meet my sister, Lilly. Come here, Lil. This is Scotty. The really smart guy I told you about."

She comes forward and shakes my hand. She looks right into my eyes, but she doesn't say anything. I have the strong feeling she's sizing me up, evaluating me, probably trying to figure out if I'm anything like the person her brother described. Her eyes are alive, quick. I bet she's a perceptive person.

Not many people have alert eyes like that.

"Well, aren't you going to ask us in?" asks David.

"Why?" I say. "What do you want?"

David gets an overly surprised look on his face. "Why, just to say hello, that's all. We just figured we were in the neighborhood so we'd stop and say hello."

"You two whities? Just happen to be in *this* neighborhood? Not likely."

His sister grabs his sleeve and tries to pull him away. "Come on, David. Let's go. Can't you see he's busy?"

She again leans down to shake my hand, still looking me right in the eyes. "We'll come back some other time."

But I'm not quite ready to let go of her hand. I don't know why. Maybe it's just because it's such a nice soft hand. And it's a small hand. I have the thought that it's like *she* grew up, but her hands didn't. That makes me curious about her. "Well," I say, "since you already *just happen* to be in the neighborhood, you might was well come in."

I wheel my chair back, and David hurries right in. But his sister is still a little hesitant. David goes back and grabs her arm. He roughly pulls her inside.

"We have to be quiet," I whisper. "My Grandma's sleeping."

They both look toward the back of the house where the TV is blaring. If they wonder how anybody could sleep with all that racket going on, they don't say anything about it.

I lead them into my bedroom and close the door.

David runs right over and points at my computer. "See, it's just like I told you. He spends all his time reading philosophy and shit like that on the internet. Well, what're you studying today, Scotty?" He leans down to look at the screen. "The neurology of focal dy-ston-ia." He signals his sister to come look. "See here. Neurology. I told you. He studies everything."

His sister nods, but she doesn't go any closer.

I say, "Sorry, I don't have any chairs in here. David, go out and get a couple of the dining room chairs."

Lilly waves him off. "No, don't bother. I'll sit on your bed." She sits down on my mattress, but then acts like maybe she's about to get up again. "I mean, if that's all right with you."

"Sure," I say. "Sit. You can sit down too, David."

He glances at his wrist, even though he's not wearing a watch. "Uh, no. Gotta go. Important appointment. But Lil can stay. Show her what you're learning, Scotty. Tell her about that . . . that neurology stuff. And tell her about that philosophy stuff you were telling me about."

He starts to leave the room, but I say, "Wait a minute, David." I point toward his sister. "She has to go with you. You don't want her walking to the bus stop by herself. Not in this neighborhood."

David waves my words off. "No problem, Lilly can take care of herself."

But I'm not about to let him get away. "A white chick alone on this street? And a damn pretty one at that. No way."

David grins and leans around me to look at his sister. "See, there, Sis. I told you he'd think you were cute. Didn't I tell ya?"

She frowns, but she doesn't seem quite ready to get up to leave.

I move my wheelchair to block David's way. "Damn it, David. You're not listening to me. You're not leaving here without her."

He gets ahold of the handles of my chair and rolls me out of his way. "No problem. No problem. I'll go do my business and come back and get her."

He heads for the front door, and all I can do is call after him. "How long will you be?"

He stops with his hand on the doorknob. "Not long. I'll be back before you know it."

"You'd better be. And you be careful out there. If any of those gangbangers try to talk to you, just run away. Run away fast. They'll just laugh at you. Got it?"

He gives me the thumbs up, and then he's gone. At least he remembered to close the door quietly so Grandma wouldn't here him leave.

I close my bedroom door again and wheel my chair around to face Lilly.

She's looking at the door and smiling, probably thinking about what an idiot her brother is.

She has a nice smile. I suspect not everybody would find her all that pretty, but to me, she looks . . . interesting.

She looks toward the front door and shakes her head. "You can't talk sense to him. Nobody can. But he'll be all right. Some of those gang guys, pretty young kids actually, called him names when we were about a block from your house. He just laughed and agreed with whatever they said."

"Good idea. They need to think they came out on top."

She stares at me for a few moments and then says, "So, is that what you do when you go out? Let them think they came out on top? David said they stabbed you. He said that's where he met you. In the hospital."

I shrug. "Yeah, I guess I should have just kept my mouth shut that time."

"You don't seem like the type to keep your mouth shut."

How did she know that? Does it show? I shrug again. "I guess I do have kind of a . . . smart mouth."

There's an awkward silence for few moments, but then she laughs.

She's probably laughing at me. I guess I must look uncomfortable.

"So," she says, "David tells me you're supposed to be some kind of genius."

I shrug again, but then tell myself I've got to stop doing that. It probably shows how nervous I am to be talking to a girl. "Oh, you can't believe everything David says."

"But I do. If there is one thing David is not, it's a liar. At least when he's around me."

I stare at her. She has a kind of innocence about her, but she has to be at least twenty-one. Maybe older. What would she see in me? Then, I remember I should respond to what she said. "Oh, yeah. David said you two had some kind of pact."

She laughs a quick little laugh. "Yeah. Kind of silly, I guess. Goes back to when our dad took off, and Mom started drinking. We were on our own a lot."

"I can understand that. My Mom . . . Well, I mean, I was on my own a lot too."

She gazes at me.

What is she thinking? Did David tell her about my legs? How I fucked myself up? But I never told David that. I just said it was an accident, and surprisingly, he didn't ask questions.

Finally, she says, "David says you live here with your grandmother. So, where is your mom?"

"Beats me."

I expect her to ask a follow-up question about that, but she doesn't. She looks around the room. "No pictures or . . . anything like that?"

I glance at the computer screen. "Nope, just me and my computer. With the internet, what else does a person need?"

She nods toward the computer screen. "So you study neurology?"

This time, I force myself not to shrug. "Not really. I mean not usually. It's just something I was looking at today."

"Okay, tell me about it."

I'm not sure what she means. Does she want me to talk about what I study on the internet. Why would she want to know about that? "Uh, about what?"

She points at the computer screen. "About that. Neurology."

"Oh, I just ran across this site. It's about focal dystonia, how the brain controls our muscles. I'm interested in . . . that."

"Okay, tell me about focal dystonia."

I stare at the computer screen, thinking about how to explain it. "Well, the main thing is that when we learn a motor skill, the brain has to . . . "

I glance back at her to see if she's really interested and find her taking off her clothes. She's already got her halter top off.

"Hey!" I say. "What're you doing?"

She stops with her halter top still in her hand. She doesn't try to cover herself up. "Taking off my clothes. Isn't that what you want?"

"No! I mean . . . what?"

"David said you wanted to fuck me. Don't you?"

"No! I mean, I . . . didn't tell him that."

"No, you didn't tell him that, or no, you don't want to?"

"Well, I . . . uh, didn't think you'd really want to."

She lies back on the mattress and starts squirming out of her tight jeans. She pulls down her panties and tosses them onto the floor. Now she's completely naked, and I don't know what to say or do, so I just stare at her. She actually has a very nice body. Thin and athletic looking.

"Uh, is this that thing David told me about? That you have to do everything he tells you to?"

"That's right. We have an agreement. Goes way back. Like I said, we were alone together a lot."

"Well, you don't have to just because . . . uh, I mean David doesn't need to do me any favors."

She lies there, just looking at me, as if being totally naked in front of a stranger doesn't bother her at all.

This time it's her that shrugs. "Actually, David thinks he's doing me a favor. He thinks after my abortion, I need to get laid, so I won't start hating men and turn lesbian."

I'm not sure she would like it that David already told me about her abortion, so I just say, "Uh, you had an abortion?"

"Yeah. Couple of years ago. But don't worry, I'm on the pill now. In case you're worried."

She stares at me. "Well?"

I stay where I am and look at her. I suddenly realize I've never seen a naked girl before, except for in pictures on the internet.

She giggles. "You've never seen a naked girl, have you?"

It's like she's reading my mind. I have the feeling she'd know if I lied, so decide to be honest with her and nod.

"Well, come here," she says and holds out her arms. "I'll show you what to do."

The more I look at her, the prettier she seems. Maybe I should go along with this. I mean, if it's what she really wants.

I get up out of my wheelchair and hobble over to the bed. I sit down next to her, and she doesn't even wait for me to take off my clothes. She quickly unbuttons my shirt and strips it off of me. I lie back, and she pulls my pants off of me and throws them aside.

When she gets her first look at my legs, she lets out her breath so fast it's almost like a groan. "Oh dear," she says.

I sit up. "I understand. We don't have to go on. I know my legs are really . . . ugly."

She shakes her head and pushes me back down. "They're not ugly. I think they're . . . interesting. When we're done, I want you to tell me about how they got like that. I'm studying to be a medical tech."

I nod and lie still.

"I'll get on top, so it won't hurt your legs. Okay?"

I nod again and try to lie very still as she straddles me.

She reaches down and slips me inside of her.

The feeling takes my breath away, but I try not to look surprised.

She begins to move slowly. I close my eyes to try to hold back. I don't want to finish too quick. But then I realize this is something I want to see. I open my eyes and watch her move against me. She's not moving very fast, and that's helping me hold back. I concentrate on watching her body, focusing on how her muscles are working. I try to think about it logically, scientifically: we're just two human bodies, doing what humans have done for thousands of years.

But soon, I lose my scientific observation and get caught up in the feeling of it. She must sense it because she starts to move faster. I feel the mingling of our sweat down there and that does it: I can't hold it back any longer.

After it's over, she stays still for a few more moments before she rolls off of me.

The air feels pleasantly cool on my sweaty skin, so I lie still with my eyes closed, enjoying the afterglow of it.

When I open my eyes, I find her staring at me. "Well? Was it good?"

I nod and resist the temptation to ask her if it was good for her. It probably wasn't all that great for her. I decide, right then and there, that if we ever do this again, I'll be the one on top, making it good for her, no matter how much it hurts my legs.

"Well?" she says.

I turn onto my side to look at her. "No, really. It was very good."

"No, not about that. You're supposed to tell me about your legs."

"Oh. Well, there's not much to tell. An accident."

She looks doubtful. "An accident? Run over by a truck or something?"

"No, I . . . fell."

"Fell? Come on. That much damage from a fall?"

"I . . . sort of fell of a cliff. Out at San Pedro."

She nods, staring into my eyes. "Sort of fell, eh? Okay, I won't ask any more questions."

"No, it's all right. As you probably guessed, I didn't really fall. I jumped. Now, looking back at it, I'm not sure why. That night, it just seemed like . . . the right thing to do. Everything seemed like . . . you know, just . . . shit."

She nods. "David had pretty much the same idea. Cut up his wrists. Now I understand why he likes you so much."

"Actually, I didn't tell him. About the cliff, I mean."

"Maybe not, but David can be a lot smarter than he looks. Anyhow, I won't say anything to him. Or to anybody."

"Anyhow, the fall fucked my legs up good. The doctors did a lot of patching up, hooking the bones back together, but they couldn't quite make them right again."

She leans close to look. "Looks like there's metal in there. I guess they used screws and things."

"Yeah." I point at a couple of the lumps. "That's what those are."

She touches one of the lumps very gently and then she traces one of the scars with her finger. She looks up at me. "But you can walk, right?"

I shrug. "Sort of. With a cane."

She nods toward my wheelchair. "David told me you'd be in a wheelchair, but he said you can walk when you have to."

"Yeah, I can walk. I shouldn't use my chair so often, but I get . . . lazy. The pain . . . well, that's why I study things like that focal dystonia pain stuff. And . . . other things. I'm trying to learn how pain works, so I can control it better."

She again traces a long scar with her finger. "So you just stay here in this old house in the middle of Watts, studying stuff on the internet?"

"That's about it."

"You don't get lonely?"

"Naw. I've got friends. Sort of. My friends are Husserl and Sartre and Derrida."

"Who are they?"

I shrug. "Well, I didn't actually mean like . . . *real* friends. They're philosophers. Old dead guys I read about on the internet."

"What? Oh, you mean that's what you like to study. You're not even on Facebook?"

"Naw." I glance toward the computer. "I know about Facebook, but I've never bothered to sign up. I don't have anybody to . . . interact with."

She smiles and pats my bare hip. "You could interact, as you call it, with me."

Before I can come up with any reason to disagree, she stands up and pulls on her pants. She goes to the computer. "Come on. We're going to set you up a Facebook page right now. That way, I can send you direct messages. It's like email."

Before I even finish dressing, she's started creating me a Facebook page.

I go and stand behind her.

Her fingers are moving fast on the keyboard. She says, "I'm using one of my extra Yahoo email accounts to get you signed up. I set you up as Scotty Loner. That okay with you?"

She doesn't wait for my answer. "Now, I'm going to have your page friend my page. Then we can send each other direct messages."

I stand very close behind her, so close I can smell her sweat. I like the fact that she feels comfortable enough being with me that she didn't even bother to put her top back on. I reach around from behind her to put my hands gently on her nice small breasts.

She keeps her eyes on the screen and says, "You don't have to do that. David told me you don't like people much. So don't think you have to pretend this was anymore than just a convenient fuck."

I quickly pull my hands away. A convenient fuck? Is that what this is? Is that all it means to her? I quietly say, "I wasn't pretending. I liked . . . what we did. I like . . . you."

She still won't look at me. "So you wouldn't mind doing it again sometime?"

"Sure. I mean, if you want to."

"Okay with me. We can set up our fuck dates on Facebook. I'll send you a message to let you know when I'm free."

Some part of me doesn't want to think of them as only fuck dates. But then I remember how much older she is than me. Why would she be interested in a crippled kid like me? Maybe she's only doing what her brother told her to do. Both of them are probably just doing me a favor.

A voice from behind me: "Are you done?"

We both turn. It's David.

"David!" I say. "How did you get in?"

He laughs and points over his shoulder with his thumb. "You were so eager to get into her pants, you forgot to lock the door. I've been waiting on the porch, but you guys are so quiet, I couldn't tell if you'd done it yet."

Lilly goes to the bed to get her halter top and puts it on. "Yes, we're done, as you so crudely put it. Have a little sensitivity, would you?"

He pouts. "Sorry."

She points at my computer. "I set him up on Facebook so we have a way to communicate."

"Oh, friend me too, Scotty. Will you?"

Lilly says, "Come on, David. Let's leave this poor guy alone, so he can get back to his studying." She gets ahold of her brother's shirt sleeve, but he resists. "But I want to talk. What have you two been talking about? And what was that stuff you were studying on the computer?"

Lilly says, "Leave him alone, David. He's too busy studying to answer all your dumb questions." She gives me a quick kiss me on the cheek and grabs her brother's arm to drag him toward the front door.

I sit down in my wheelchair and follow them into the dining room. As Lilly pulls him toward the front door, David looks back at me and grins. He holds up both of his hands as if to say, What can I do? She's the boss.

And then, they're gone. I'm left staring at the closed front door. As I lock it, Pretty Boy comes flying to land on my shoulder. He stares at me, but doesn't say anything. Is that a reproachful look?

I turn to look back toward Grandma's room. I can hear the TV blaring away back there. Hopefully, Grandma didn't hear a thing. I realize that I never for one moment thought about the chance of her coming into my bedroom when Lilly and I were naked. Hard to imagine what she would have thought. I look toward my bedroom. If Lilly really is going to come back again, I'd better get some kind of lock to put on my bedroom door. That thought makes me realize I'm hoping she really *will* come back. But will she? I'm pretty sure it was like she said, only a convenient fuck, nothing more. I have to remember that and not get caught up thinking she's going to be my girlfriend or anything like that. She's older than me. She either just feels sorry for me, or else, as a medical technology student, she's just curious about my fucked-up legs. She's not my girlfriend and never will be. I will never have a girlfriend and don't want one. I'm doing fine, just as I am. I have a roof over my head. I have food. And I have my studies. When I get tired of that . . . well, then it will be time to go back to my cliff. Or something.

13
Trace Inscriptions

So far, no messages have shown up on my Facebook page. I have to force myself to not constantly check for a message from Lilly. And I've been going to her Facebook page to see what she's up to, but she never posts anything. I don't know why she's even on Facebook if she's never going to use it.

The problem is, thinking about her is distracting me from my studies. To try to focus, I've even tried to go back to studying the old guys like Kant and Hegel, but after the French philosophers, I find them boring. Even looking at my lonely mattress there on the floor is distracting because I can't keep myself from thinking about when I was on that mattress with her. I keep telling myself there's no point of thinking about that. She'll probably never come back. Why should she? One fuck, and I think I'm in love. It's dumb. Maybe every other person in the world feels like this after their first time, but I'm not like every other person. That would be ordinary, and I'm not ordinary. I should just forget about her and move on. I don't mean anything to her. She's probably fucked lots of guys. She's probably fucking some other guy right now. Maybe she likes fucking weird guys and then never contacting them again. Maybe it's her hobby, like collecting bugs or something. So as of this moment, I will stop thinking about her. If she wants to send me a Facebook message, she will. But she probably won't. I should just assume I won't ever hear from her again. From this moment on, I will move my mind away from thinking about her and focus on important stuff. Like philosophy and psychology. Those are the most important subjects in the world. Every student should be studying them, but they don't teach either one of them the public schools. No, that would make too much sense. That might even make it worth going to school.

That thought makes me remember being on that university campus down in Irvine. I wonder if you go to college to study philosophy, do you have to take other kinds of classes too? It would be better if you could just take the philosophy classes and skip all the other stuff.

That gives me an idea. Now that Derrida is dead, maybe other college teachers are teaching about his philosophy of deconstruction. I do a Google search for "Derrida deconstruction" at .edu sites and it gives me 177,000 hits. Jeez! I didn't realize there was that much interest in him at universities. Maybe there's even more interest in him now that he's dead. I've noticed that philosophers like to attack the theories of dead philosophers. Probably because they can't talk back.

But what led him to deconstructionism? The word deconstruct is an interesting word itself. It makes me think of a little kid tearing things apart to learn what makes them tick. I like that. I remember when I was little, I tore apart Mom's vacuum cleaner to see how it worked. But I couldn't put if back together right, and it never worked again. Mom was pissed off at me for breaking it. But so what? She hardly ever used it anyhow. Maybe Derrida was like that when he was little, tearing things apart just to find out how they worked, and then, when he became a grown-up philosopher, he invented deconstructionism so he could tear apart everybody's belief systems.

I'm still thinking about that when I hear somebody come up onto the creaking front porch. Before I can roll my chair out to the dining room window to see who it is, somebody knocks on the front door.

No salesman would dare knock on a door in this neighborhood, so it must be Denesa. Or maybe Lilly has come back. I wouldn't mind seeing Denesa again. I like her visits, especially if she brings her kids, but I have to admit that I'm really hoping it's Lilly.

I open the door. It's not Lilly. It's that gang guy, Jake. He doesn't look very friendly, but then again, he doesn't look unfriendly. Is he here to hurt me? But why would he do that? He said I was a citizen in "his hood."

"What do you want?" I say. But then I wonder if maybe I said it in too challenging a way. This guy could easily kick the shit out of me, and he probably wouldn't think twice about doing it.

He says, "May I come in?"

He actually sounds polite. "Uh, why?"

"Just let me in. Don't leave me standin' out here. Your neighbors are lookin'."

I figure I have no choice. Now that I've opened the door, this guy looks so damn tough he could easily force his way in, if that's what he wants to do.

I wheel my chair backwards, and he steps in and closes the door.

Pretty Bird immediately flies down from his lampshade and lands on Jake's shoulder.

Jake ducks and shoos the bird away.

"Don't mind him," I say, laughing. "It's only Pretty Boy, my killer attack parakeet. I keep him around in case of intruders."

Jake laughs, and I take that as a good sign. He's probably not here to kill me.

Pretty Boy must think it's a good sign too because he comes flying back to again land on Jake's shoulder.

"Well," I say, "Pretty Boy likes you, so you must be okay."

Jake turns his head to look at Pretty Boy. "Hello there, bird."

He seems to like birds. Another good sign.

Pretty Boy responds with a few loud tweets and flies back over to my shoulder. He's said his hello, but now it's time to get back to pulling at the many threads he's managed to tear loose from my collar.

I turn back to Jake and put my finger to my lips. "My grandma is back there." I point. "We have to be quiet."

"Okay," he whispers.

"Come in here," I say and lead him into my bedroom and close the door. "Okay," I say, "what do I owe this honor to?"

He's looking over my room, probably thinking about how stark it is.

He turns and looks down at me. "Were you makin' some kinda joke? I mean about it bein' an honor?"

"Isn't it an honor in this neighborhood to get a visit from the biggety big of the neighborhood gang?"

"I wouldn't call myself that."

"Really?" I'm curious about why he would deny being a gang leader, but I decide I'd better not ask.

He looks toward Grandma's room where we can still hear her loud TV. "So, you live here with your grandmother. You've been here what, coupla years?"

"Yeah, how do you know that?"

"I keep track of what goes on in my neighborhood. They call you Scotty, right? And you stay in this old house all the time. Don't go to school."

"I'm eighteen. I don't have to go to school."

He looks skeptical. "You don't look eighteen."

"Well, I am. About. So, what do you want? Are you the neighborhood welcome wagon?"

He seems confused by my joke, but he doesn't follow up on it. "The reason I'm here is to warn ya. My boys tell me cops are lookin' for ya."

"Me? Why?"

"They need you to testify 'gainst those Criminals that stabbed ya on that bus. But nobody found out your name. Not even at the hospital."

"Uh, so you came to warn me against the cops?"

He nods. "And not just the cops lookin'. That gang is also out lookin' for ya."

"Why?"

"To make sure you *don't* testify."

I try to keep a calm face. I don't want this Jake guy to think I'm scared of a bunch of stupid gang idiots, but it does worry me. If this Jake guy could find me, maybe they can too. "Aw, let 'em try," I say. "There's nothing they can—"

He leans closer to me and holds a finger up in front of my face. "Listen to me, Scotty. Those guys won't *try* to shut you up, they *will* shut you up. Permanently."

"Is that so? Maybe I should find out where they hang out and go confront them on the street. That way, they'd have to kill me right there in public. I'd be famous. Innocent little white kid killed on the streets of LA by viscous gang." I grin to let him know I'm making a joke. Sort of.

Jake looks right into my eyes. "I'm tryin' to figure you out, Scotty. I never know when you're kiddin' and when you're not. You tellin' me you're not afraid to die?"

I shrug. "Some days, I figure it doesn't matter one way or the other. But I don't want to get involved with the cops, so I think I'll just stay here inside this old house and forget about the whole thing."

Jake nods thoughtfully. "If you're tellin' me the truth, that you won't talk to the cops, I think I can get word about that to that gang."

"I always tell the truth. Why not? Sure. Tell 'em I'm not interested in testifying against their stupid little gang homies."

"Okay. I'll let 'em know." He smiles. "But I'll leave out the characterization."

Characterization. Not the kind of word I'd expect a gangbanger to use. "Fine. Tell them if they leave me alone, I'll leave them alone."

"Will do. You just lay low for a while. Don't go wanderin' 'round or nuthin'. They may be driving 'round lookin' for ya."

I shrug again. "I never go out anyhow."

He looks around my room. "You stay in here? All the time?"

"Pretty much. Since I fucked up my legs."

"Oh yeah? How'd that happen?"

Should I tell him? Why not. What difference does it make now? "Ever been to Point Fermin Park? Out in San Pedro?"

"Yeah. Why?"

"Did you happen to notice there's a rather sheer cliff at the ocean side of that park? It's a place where, you know, accidents can happen."

Jake stares at me. Then he nods. "Okay, I get it."

I wonder if he really did get it. Maybe he did. He actually seems like a pretty smart guy.

"So, you stay inside all day. Whatta ya do?"

I nod toward the computer. "I study."

"On the computer?"

"That's right. The internet."

"Study what?"

"This and that."

He looks thoughtful, probably wondering what it would be like to stay in a room all the time studying. He probably can't imagine it.

"I'm studyin' too." he says. "Business."

"Really?"

"Yeah. El Camino. Over'n Compton."

Interesting. This Jake is not at all like how I would have imagined a gang dude. "So you're studying business at the local junior college. You don't seem like the suit and tie type."

"There are other kinds of business."

"You want to start your own business?"

"Got one already. Actually, couple of 'em. Trying to learn how to manage 'em better."

Now he's got me curious "You're an entrepreneur? What's your business?"

"Various things. Sales mostly."

"Sales of what?"

"Cars. Some. And car parts. Shit like that."

I'm catching on. He probably sells stuff his gang steals. "Drugs too?"

He hesitates, then shakes his head. "Not anymore. Others take care of that. But I can get ya some if that's what you're looking for." He points at my legs. "For your . . uh, pain problem. Meds. Hard stuff. Whatever you need. I can get it."

"Aw, I'm dealing with the pain. Besides, I don't have any money."

"You need money? You want to make some money?"

"Me? How?"

"There are times I could use a white guy."

"You want me to go to work for you? What could I do for you?"

"You tell me. What're ya good at?"

I glance at my computer. "Actually, I'm not good at anything. I just spend all day on the internet."

"Do ya know how to sell stuff on eBay?"

"I guess I could figure it out."

"Okay, let's start with that. Can you set me up a business on eBay?"

"I suppose I could."

"Okay, here's the deal. I ended up with a shit load of motorcycle parts. Don't know how to get rid of 'em. Old stuff. But somebody might want that kind of old stuff. You know, somebody rebuilding an old bike, or somethin' like that. Let's try to sell that shit on eBay."

"And you'll pay me?"

He reaches into his back pocket and pulls out a large leather wallet that's chained to his belt. He takes out a hundred-dollar bill and hands it to me. "This is for settin' it up. Then, if you can sell the stuff, I'll pay you a commission."

"Well, okay, but I bet to set up a business account on eBay, they'll probably require a deposit. Or maybe a credit card."

"No problem." He pulls a half dozen credit cards out of his wallet and sorts through them. He hands one of them to me.

I look at the name on it. "I thought your name was Jake."

He winks at me. "One of the requirements of this job is that you don't ask questions."

"Got it," I say, but it does make me wonder what I'm getting myself into. But who cares? At least it'll be something interesting to do with my time. I'm on the computer all day anyhow, so why not? "And we'll need to set up a PayPal account. To take payments."

"What's pay pal?" he asks.

"It's a way to take payments online."

"Can you set that up too?"

"I guess so."

"Good. Do it." He glances toward the front door. "Well, gotta go now . . . partner." He reaches out to shake my hand.

I shake it, even though that word *partner* makes me a little nervous. As he heads for the door, I call after him. "Uh, how will I contact you? If I need information . . . or something."

He turns back. "Oh yeah. Let me give you my number."

"Uh, my grandma's got the only phone, but it's by her bed."

"No problem." He unzips his jacket pocket and takes out three fancy-looking cell phones. He looks at them for a moment, then hands me one of them. This guy seems to have multiples of everything.

He points to one of the buttons on the phone. "Press this button, and then hit the number one. That rings me. Got it?"

"Yeah. Okay."

"Gotta go. My boys'll keep an eye on your house. They'll tell me if they see any of those Criminals dudes in this area. Okay?"

"Okay."

"Let me know when you get the eBay thing set up. I'll bring you the motorcycle parts. Anything else you need?"

"Not that I can think of right now."

"Okay. See you soon, partner." He leaves quickly. A man in a hurry.

I stare at the cell phone in my hand. That means I can call anybody I want. That is, if I had anybody to call. And I have a job. I'm supposed to set up an eBay online business to sell the stuff Jake has "acquired." Maybe those young wannabe gang kids I saw him with on that corner steal the stuff for him. Maybe Jake is the gang's official businessman, the one who brings in the money. And he takes it seriously enough to take classes at the local JC to learn how to run his "business" better. Interesting. And now he wants to take his business online. Not the kind of thing I would have imagined a gang guy doing, but it makes sense; I guess in the twenty-first century, everybody has to go high tech if they want to make the real money.

I sit down and go to the main eBay web page. I click on "Start Selling," then I click on "Register." It asks me to enter my name and address. I can use a fake address, but what about a name? I look at the name on the credit card. Am I supposed to use that name? I suppose I have to because sooner or later it's going to ask me to enter my credit card info. But what if it shows up as a stolen card? I can only hope Jake knows what he's doing.

It only takes me a few minutes to get signed up to be an eBay seller and to take payments through the PayPal online payment program. Now, all I have to do is wait for Jake to show me what we're selling. This is going to be interesting. I wonder how much money I'll make.

14
Deconstructing Belief

The next time Denesa shows up, she's surprised to see my bedroom cluttered with motorcycle parts. "What's all this stuff?" she asks.

"Old motorcycle parts," I say. "I'm selling them on eBay."

"What's eBay?"

"It's a place on the internet where you sell stuff."

"Okay, but where'd you get the motorcycle parts?"

"Don't ask."

"What you mean, don't ask? What you gone and got yourself into?"

I feel like a schoolboy who's being bawled out. I shrug. "I met this guy. But I'm not doing anything wrong. I'm just the techie." I show her my new smartphone. "See, I take pictures of the stuff with this and upload them to eBay. I don't ask where the stuff comes from. Wanna see how eBay works?"

She frowns. "No, I got to go. I just came by to ask if you'd mind watching my boys for a few hours tomorrow."

"Sure. I'd love to see them again. Where you goin'?"

"Oh, hell, I got a subpoena. We all did. More trouble at the projects. Some white kid got himself shot over there. Can you believe it? They shot the kid right there in front of our building. In broad daylight. Cops are sayin' it was a drug deal gone bad, but cause the kid was white, they're makin' a big deal out of it. Callin' in everybody who lives in a street-side apartment. Anybody who mighta seen somethin'. They say we all got to go down and try to identify photos." She makes a "Hmpf" sound. "As if any of us would be crazy enough to finger a gang kid. Anyhow, we all got to go in, so I got nobody to leave the kids with."

I quickly say, "No problem. I'll be here. I'm always here, aren't I?"

"It'll be in the morning. I don't know how long they'll keep us."

"Uh, did you actually see anything?"

"Naw, I look out when I hear the shot, but car's already goin' away."

"Are you going to tell them that? About the car, I mean?"

"You kiddin'? I tell 'em I seen nuthin. I don't know what the other ladies are gonna say, but me, I mind my own business."

"Probably the safest thing to do. Safest for your kids, for sure."

"Right. That's how I look at it."

"Sure. Bring Zyrell and Javon right on over in the morning. Pretty Boy's been missing them. We'll have fun."

As if he just heard me mention his name, Pretty Boy comes flying in and lands on Denesa's shoulder.

She brushes him off, and he flies up to land on the curtain rod. He stares down at her. I can tell he's irritated with her, but he'll get over it.

She leans over to hug me around my shoulders. "Thanks, Scotty. You're a dear." She looks at my computer screen. "What's that?"

"It's a picture of a 1970 BSA gas tank. Two hundred bucks."

"You're gonna buy that? What for?"

"No, like I said, we're selling it. That's it right over there." I point toward the BSA gas tank that's sitting on my bedroom floor."

She looks at the gas tank and shakes her head. "You sure are some case. The things you get into. I'll bring the kids by in the mornin'."

She leaves, and I turn back to the computer to check each of our eBay sales pages. It looks like there are actually bids coming in on everything. Who knew there would be so much interest in old motorcycle parts? I wonder how much money I'm going to make. Jake never said how much of a commission he was going to pay me.

I hear Jake's secret double tap on my bedroom window. Was he out there waiting for Denesa to leave?

I roll to the front door to let him in. He grabs a dining room chair, and once we're in my bedroom, he points toward the front of the house. "Who was that woman? Your mom?"

"You makin' a joke?"

"You never know. There are some African-Americans in this neighborhood as white as you are. Have you seen those twins down the street? One white and one black."

"No. Really? Twins?"

"Yep. Black father, white mom. They had two little girls, one blonde and blue eyed, the other black as me. Everybody's talkin' about it."

Is Jake making a point about racism? I suspect he is, so I say, "Well, I guess that says a lot about racism, if you think about it."

Jake nods, watching me. "Sure does."

"No, my mom was a light-skinned person, like me. Very light, actually. She was a redhead. But now that you mention it, I read on the internet that I actually *am* African-American. At least in the same sense as you are. DNA studies show all of us humans came from Africa originally. And all of our ancestors had dark skin."

He nods, as if he's interested, but he's not smiling. "Yeah, but don't forget my ancestors were brought here as slaves. Against their will."

I realize maybe I shouldn't have said anything about those DNA studies, but so far, I've always been straight with Jake. I decide to go on. "Yeah, I get that. But I think it's weird that people in this country make such a big deal about skin color when those DNA studies show that every human on Earth came from the same dark skinned ancestors."

Jake thinks about that for a moment, then says, "So you're sayin' you're black as me."

"Right. Except my ancestors left Africa about fifty thousand years before yours did."

Jake chuckles at that. "You'd better not start tellin' people around here you're African-American. They might not be interested in hearin' 'bout some kind of DNA studies that prove it."

"I guess you're right. People are pretty mentally ill when it comes to the color of skin."

He gives me an odd look. "Mentally ill?"

I nod toward the computer. "I was just reading about that too. What I mean is, mental illness is my way of saying you believe weird things, even if other people don't think it's so weird. Hey, you might be interested in something I was just reading."

"Oh yeah? What's that?"

"Well, the concept of mental illness is interesting to me, so I did some searching on the internet about it. Listen to this. I found out there was an established definition of a type of mental illness in the South during the slave days. If a slave didn't want to be a slave anymore, that person was legally considered to be mentally ill."

Jake frowns. "Really?"

"Yeah. Remember, crazy is defined by the overall society. As a result, you get called crazy if you believe in stuff most people in your society don't believe in. And the opposite is true too: people can believe in crazy stuff, do crazy stuff, but if the society accepts it, well, then it's not considered mentally ill. Like the fact that, not all that long ago, people with skin as dark as yours were not even allowed to set foot in a lot of public places. The lighter-skinned people we call white thought there was something dirty about darker-skinned people. It was a kind of society-wide mental illness, but it wasn't defined as mental illness because so many people believed it."

Jake is staring at me.

"Uh, you don't mind me talking about black-white stuff do you?"

"Not at all. I'm interested. Go ahead."

"Well, here's the example I was just reading about. Back in the fifties, in Las Vegas, the casinos hired big name entertainers to draw in the suckers. They were willing to hire any famous entertainer, even if they had dark skin. People like Nat King Cole and Ella Fitzgerald and Louee Armstrong. They were paid big bucks to entertain the white people in the hotel showrooms. But guess what? They weren't allowed to stay in those same hotels. They had to go stay in the cheap hotels over in the black part of town. Get it? It was crazy thinking, but it wasn't called mental illness because everybody agreed with it. Eventually, people like Sammy Davis Junior called bullshit on it and refused to perform in the white-owned hotels unless he was allowed to stay there too. So, they had to find a solution. They decided to allow him to stay in the hotel, as long as he was willing to sneak in through the kitchen. They put him in a tiny, hidden-away back room. And after he left, they burned any sheets and towels he'd used. That was the mental illness of the time. One time, he decided he wanted to take a quick dip in the hotel pool. After he finished his swim, they immediately drained the pool and refilled it. See? Crazy. A kind of mental illness. But it wasn't called that because all the light skinned people—the ones who made up the rules back then—all went along with it."

Jake smiles. "You're an interestin' dude, Scotty. You never say black, you always say dark skinned."

"That's all it is, Jake. An excess of some stupid chemical, called melanin, that's what makes some people's skin darker. It's genetics."

He nods thoughtfully. "I guess that's true, but not many look at it that way. On either side."

"My point exactly, Jake. Mental illness is not confined to any group or race. It's something we learn when we're little kids." I touch the side of my head. "It gets into our brains, and after that, it's stuck in there."

Jake looks toward the front of the house. "All that was to answer my question about who that woman with the dark skin was?"

I chuckle to show him I appreciate his "dark skin" reference. "Oh, her. That dark-skinned woman's name is Denesa. She's on some kind of work-for-welfare program. She's supposed to come by and look after Grandma from time to time."

"She never stays very long."

I look up at him. "How do you know that? You been watching me?"

He smiles. "I got my spies"

"She's okay. I'm gonna watch her kids tomorrow. How about that?"

He seems surprised. "You're her baby sitter? Baby sittin' for money? You won't be needin' money now. We got our business deal, right?"

"Naw. I'm not watching her kids for money. Denesa doesn't have any money. I just keep an eye on 'em for her because, well, just because I like 'em. They're great kids. Two cute little boys."

He nods, thinking. Then, he points toward my computer's screen. "So, how's our business goin'. We sellin' anything?"

"Yeah. Actually, we're doin' pretty good. Gettin' bids on almost everything. We're gonna make some money, Jake. Serious money."

"Well, that's the idea, eh, Scotty?"

"Right, *partner*. And hey, you never said how much you're gonna pay me. You said I'd get a commission."

"Well, in the class I'm takin' at the college, they say sales commissions can vary from four to ten percent. I don't know about commissions for online activity. How much do you need?"

"Is that what they teach you at that college, to ask your employees how much they need?"

He chuckles at that. "Naw, they act like employees are the enemy. You know, unions. You aren't plannin' to start a union, are you?"

"Maybe I will. If you don't pay me enough, I'll do a sit-down strike." I tap the arm rests of my wheelchair.

He smiles at my joke, "In your case, you'd have to do a stand-up strike. But seriously, Scotty, how much do ya need? You're doin' a great job with this eBay thing. I can give you some cash if you need it."

I shrug. "Hell, Jake, if you pay me based on what I need, you wouldn't have to pay me anything. I just sit here in this house all day. I can't even think what I'd use the money for."

"Everybody needs money, Scotty. Here, let me give you another hundred. If you need to go anywhere, use the money to call a cab. I don't want my computer expert getting stabbed on any more city buses." He takes another hundred-dollar bill out of his fat wallet.

I take it and start to stuff it into my shirt pocket, but I feel the other hundred dollar bill he gave me is still in there. I pull it out and show it to him. "I haven't spent the first one you gave me. How could I? I haven't set foot out of this place in . . . I don't know. Quite a while."

"You never go out?"

"Where would I go?"

"What about on Sunday? You don't go to church on Sunday?"

A gang leader asking if I go to church? Does it mean he does? Do all gangbangers go to church on Sunday? Do they have a truce to not shoot each other in church? I say, "No, I don't. Do you?"

"Yeah. I have to take my mom."

I try to imagine a big tough guy like Jake getting all dressed up and taking his dear old mom to a church.

He sees me staring at him and says, "Didn't your mother ever take you to church?"

"Are you kidding? My Mom go to church? Not a chance. I've never once even set foot in a church."

"So, you're an atheist."

"An atheist? Naw. The truth is, I've never much thought about it. I think atheist means you don't believe there is any kind of god up there. It's probably a word made up by people who *do* believe in God, a word for those who don't agree with them. But I don't believe one way or the other. It just doesn't matter to me."

"But you probably don't actually believe in God?"

I'm not sure where Jake is going with this, but he's always been honest with me, so I decide to be honest with him. "Well, it seems to me if there really was a God, we'd know it. And it wouldn't be such a big deal. If there really was some kind of God looking down on us and interfering in our lives, then everybody would know about it. We wouldn't have to run around trying to prove it by building big fancy temples and wearing fancy outfits and doing complicated rituals. It would just be an ordinary thing. I read on the internet that people have been trying to prove there's a God for thousands and thousands of years. In just about every culture. Think about the opposite, Jake. What would it be like if there really *isn't* a God. What would people do?"

"Whatta ya mean?"

"I mean wouldn't people do exactly what they are doing? Doing all kinds of things to prove to themselves that there *is* a God. Wouldn't they build big fancy churches and have special rituals and everything, just like they do now?"

Jake frowns. "At the church my mom goes to, they don't have many special rituals. They just drink coffee and eat donuts and talk to each other. And then the choir starts singing songs, and everybody goes to the pews and starts in singin' and clappin' along with the spiritual music. Some of 'em even go out and dance in the aisles."

I nod. "Well, that's *their* church rituals. What little I know about it, I think every church has different rituals. I've been studying something called semiotic analysis. It talks about rituals within societies."

Jake is looking down at the floor. I can tell he's thinking about it. Finally, he looks up at me. "So you think my mom and all her friends go to church just to try to prove to themselves there is a God?"

"Well, I doubt if they're consciously thinking about it like that, but I've read that in all societies, throughout history, people always did their religious rituals together. Maybe it's just a social thing, but they could be getting support for their beliefs by seeing that other people believe the same thing."

"I think my mom would still call you an atheist."

"She probably would. Most religious people would probably call me that, and to them, it has a negative connotation. I'll tell you a story about what an atheist really is. My mother told me that when she was little, she had a great need to believe in God. She grew up in a small-town in Montana. In a strict Lutheran family. She believed everything the preacher preached on Sunday, about how, in the end, the faithful will rise up to heaven and the wicked will go down to be punished forever in hell. As a child, she believed it all so much that one day when she saw the cover of a magazine in their little local store that showed a female model in a bikini, she went to the police to report the store owner's immorality. Of course, the police laughed at her, but that only proved to her that they were immoral too. Later, after her father left them, her mother moved them here to Los Angeles. But she couldn't find a job, and they ended up homeless. They were barely surviving, just moving from one homeless shelter to another.

Jake points toward the back of the house. "Are we talking about your grandma? That one? Back there in her bedroom?"

"Yeah. She's had a rough life. Even had to sell her body at times to get food for herself and my mom. After a while, her daughter, my mom, started to believe God had abandoned them. But her mother kept on dragging her to church on Sunday, and every Sunday, she'd put what little money they had in the collection plate. My mom told me she tried and tried to get her mother to stop giving away their money to that church. She said God wouldn't want them to go hungry just so that church could maintain a big fancy building. But her mother wouldn't stop doing it. She said it was her way of proving she believed, and that God would see her sacrifice and eventually bring them lots of money. But it never happened. One Sunday, her mother gave their last dollar to that church, and Mom had seen enough. She walked right out of that church, and went out on her own. She was pretty, what with her nice red hair and all, so she was able to get money from men she met in bars. She no longer believed in God, but let me tell you something, Jake, she still had a great need to believe in things. I read on the internet that we have a part of our brain that's just for belief, and if that part gets developed when we're young, it creates a lifelong need to believe in things. My mom got that part of her brain developed in that Lutheran church when she was young, so from then on, she was a true believer. Always had to believe in something. After she gave up on God, she believed in atheism with all her heart. She believed absolutely that there was no God. And she found lots of other things to believe in too. First, it was flying saucers. She read everything she could get her hands on about alien beings. One time, a guy loaned her a car, and she dragged me all the way out to Roswell, New Mexico to see where the alien beings had once landed."

Jake chuckles. "Yeah, my Mom went for that one too. At least she never took me to New Mexico."

"Mom also took on a lot of weird beliefs about various government conspiracies. She was absolutely sure there had been a government conspiracy to kill Kennedy, and she believed the government controlled the weather to create droughts and floods and earthquakes. She belonged to a group that met in a bar to talk about a secret government conspiracy to spray some kind of poisonous chemical out of the back of Air Force jet airplanes. I was just a kid then, but I looked that one up on the internet. It said it was just water vapor coming out of those jets, contrails, something produced naturally by jet engines. I told her about that, but she didn't believe it for a second. She said every one of the world's scientists were in on the conspiracy, and she blamed those jet airplane "chemtrails" for every ache and pain she had. I asked her why the government and those scientists would want to do that. She said it was because they were evil. They hated us regular folks and wanted us to suffer. When I looked skeptical, she got mad, and for once, acted like a regular mother. She said, 'Who are you going to believe, me, or a bunch of scientists you don't even know?' Well, Jake, even though I was still pretty young back then, at that moment, I saw clearly what she was, a bleary-eyed drunk who slurred her words and believed in all kinds of strange shit. At that moment, I asked myself if I wanted to believe what the world's scientists were telling me, or did I want to believe a sad woman who was totally dependent on her booze and the kind of men who hang out in bars, a woman who spends most of her time chasing weird conspiracy rainbows and trying to look younger than she actually was? I didn't say that to her out loud, but I decided that from then on, I was only going to believe in science."

Jake doesn't say anything. I can tell he's thinking about my words. Finally, he says, "Well, ya know, Scotty, alcoholic parents are not all that uncommon around here."

"Yeah, I know, Jake. But it was weird. Growing up watching her take on one strange new belief after another. She went through them like she was trying out new styles of clothes. And she believed in every one of them with all her heart. She went to all kinds of weird meetings. She had criticized her mother for giving all their money to that church, and there she was, donating what little money we had to one weird cause after another." I stop talking, actually a bit amazed that Jake had sat silently listening to my overly long story. I shrug and say, "Well, anyhow. Sorry to go on and on about that crap, but when I figured it out, it was a big moment for me. Right then and there, I made a vow not to believe in anything that couldn't be proved scientifically. I told myself that not believing in anything was the true scientific way. In school, I was always watching for things that didn't seem to have any real proof. My science teacher marveled at the symmetry and beauty of atomic structure. He showed us drawings of what was supposed to be inside of a hydrogen atom, with the electron going around the nucleus in a perfect circle. He said it was just like how the moon circled around the earth, and like how the earth circled around the sun. Pure perfection. I sat silent in that class, thinking it sounded a lot like religion, God making everything nice and symmetrical. Later, quantum physics came along and proved all that symmetry and perfection was pure bullshit. So it didn't take me long to learn that even the most accepted science usually turns out to be nothing but beliefs. Some said the dinosaurs were killed by climate change. Others are trying say it was a damn meteor. Those so-called scientists are just like my mother, believing in whatever they want to believe in."

Jake is back to staring at the floor again. Uh oh, I did it again. Going on and on about shit he probably doesn't care about in the least. What's the matter with me? Am I lonely? Bending this poor guy's ear just because we're supposed to be "partners."

Finally, he looks up at me. "Scotty, do you think we can live like that? Believin' in nothing?"

I try to hold back. No use getting another long-winded diatribe going. But I guess I should at least answer his question. "Well, why not, Jake? Why can't we study everything, but believe nothing? I think the best way to live is doing what I call fostering doubt. I try to doubt everything I hear. I try to think it through for myself, no matter what anybody else says."

Jake nods. I'm not sure he's accepting everything I'm saying, but I can tell he's thinking it through. He says, "But if everybody did your fostering doubt thing, there wouldn't be any religion anymore. What about all the good things religion does? Charity and stuff."

"Sure, some of them do good things. Real good things. Because it makes them feel good. That's why there will always be religion. Remember what I said about that belief area in people's brains?"

"Jesus, Scotty, have you told anybody else about this? I'd be a little careful talkin' like around here."

I say, "Yeah," but I think I've again gone too far. But he doesn't seem mad a me. Maybe he just thinks I'm weird, which, of course, is true.

He says, "What do you think of the Bible?"

"The Bible? Even the Christians admit it's a book written by humans, not by God. But they have a vague sense that it contains information passed down from God to man. The Muslims also think the stuff in their book was passed down from their God. But I read on the internet that if you trace the Bible back, it's pretty clear its a collection of older religious stories that were passed down through the generations. And there's usually some guy who goes up into the mountains and comes down claiming he talked to God. Christianity had Moses and others. The Muslims had Mohammed. The Mormons had Joseph Smith. They all did that go up onto the mountain and talk to God thing. But today, anybody who claims they talk to God get written off as kooks, but back then, a few were convincing enough to get some people to believe them, especially if the people are in desperate straits at that time. But if you think about it, why would God talk only to one guy and not anybody else? That should have been suspicious right off the bat."

Jake holds up both hands. "Okay, Scotty. I know you're smarter'n me, smarter'n anybody I've ever known. But somethin' inside me says there must be some kind of God up there. Otherwise, how did everything get started? How did we even come to exist?"

I know what I should say to him. I should tell him about evolution and about the quantum physics I've been studying, how everything blew up in a big bang, or a series of big bangs, and then the blown-up matter cooled down and coalesced into the physical material we have today. But I don't think being honest with each other means I have to tell him things that will upset him more than I already have.

Jake is waiting for my response. I think he wants some kind of reassurance from me. It means he respects me, respects my opinion. I should honor that.

I shrug. "But that's the thing about religion, Jake. Nobody knows for sure, so you just have to decide for yourself whether to believe it or not. And how about this? People who say they're atheists are also saying they believe in something. They're saying they are absolutely sure there isn't any God. But they don't have any proof of that either."

He nods at that and glances toward the door. Maybe he's getting tired of me going on and on.

"Well, that was interesting," he says. "How'd we get onto that?"

"Beats me," I say. I look back at the computer screen. "Maybe we were hoping God would help us sell more motorcycle parts."

He laughs. "Don't hold your breathe for that. I think he's got more important things in this world to worry about right now."

"If you mean the current state of the world, that's for sure."

He nods toward the computer. "So, how long?"

"The final auction deadline is tonight. Then, I'll notify the winning bidders and tell 'em to do a payment via PayPal. As soon as PayPal says the money's in our account, you can mail the stuff to the buyers."

"Good. And I got somebody to do the shippin' part. I delegate. That's what they're teachin' me in my class."

"Sounds like you're actually getting something out of that class."

"Well, it's all pretty common sense stuff."

"When you're a multimillionaire, you should teach the class."

He chuckles. "That'll be the day."

We're both silent for a few moments, and then he says, "Well, gotta go. Things to do, people to see."

"Ah yes, the busy businessman."

He smiles. "Right."

"Tell me, Jake, before you go, what're you gonna do with all this money you're gonna make when you're a big time businessman?"

He rubs at the side of his neck. "First thing is to get these tattoos off of my neck" He rubs at them again, as if he wishes he could just rub them off with his hand. "My teacher at the college took me aside and said I was a really good student, but that I wouldn't get far in the world of business with gang-looking tattoos on my neck. He said he knew a place where they'd do a good job of taking 'em off, but it's expensive."

"I guess he's right about how business people would look at you. But what about the other side of your business? Your, uh, suppliers. Wouldn't they wonder why you're getting rid of your gang tattoos?"

"Yeah, some of the older guys are already gettin' a bit suspicious of me. 'Specially since I backed out of the drug business. They think I'm slowly pullin' out of the gang."

"Are you?"

"Thinkin' bout it. Been thinkin' bout it for quite a while. But, man, I grew up with those guys. They took care of me after my dad took off, and my mom had to go to work. When I got shot by another gang, my boys paid em back for me. Paid em back in spades. One of my guys went to jail for it, but he never said my name to the cops. He got a long stretch in the pen for doin' it. I owe him. I owe em all. Not so easy to just say so long, guys, I'm gonna go become a big time businessman."

"Jeez, Jake. You got shot?"

"Yeah." He pulls up his shirt to show me.

There's a round scar in his side, and he puts his finger on it. "This is where the bullet went in. Little hole." He turns to show me a ragged scar on his back. "And this is where it came out. Bigger hole."

"Jesus."

He grins at me. "So now you *are* a believer in Jesus."

I smile at his joke and nod to show him I got it.

He stands up. "But so much for stories of the good ol' days. Gotta get a move on. Call me if you need anythin'."

He takes his chair back into the dining room and then comes back to pick up the motorcycle parts.

He heads for the front door, and I roll after him. "I'll let you know tonight how much we made. Maybe it'll be enough to start getting those tattoos off."

He shrugs. "Well, maybe. Anyhow, catch you later."

As he goes out onto the porch, I notice a fairly new black BMW parked in front of the house.

"That your new ride?" I ask as he heads down the steps off of the porch. "You show up in a different car every time you come here."

He stops and turns back to wink at me. "Like I said, don't ask."

I give him a thumbs up and say, "BMW? What BMW? I never saw any shiny black, new-lookin' BMW."

He heads for the car without looking back.

As he drives away, I think about him driving a fancy car like that in this neighborhood. And in broad daylight. Wouldn't the cops notice a black guy with gang tattoos driving a car like that in Watts? There are a lot of things I'd like to ask him about his various businesses, but if he says don't ask, I won't ask. Interesting to have a friend like Jake.

I close the door, wondering if Jake really is my friend. I rambled on for a long time about all that black and white mental illness stuff, and about religion too. He stuck around, and he listened. I guess I was talking to him like he was a friend, but actually, I know very little about him. We both grew up in a poor section of LA, and we both come from so-called "broken" families, but the different darkness of our skins means we probably had very different experiences growing up. Because of the kind of mental illness I was talking to him about.

So why did I talk so much? Maybe I'm more lonely than I thought. Maybe I just needed somebody to talk to about all the stuff that I've been filling up my head with for the past few years.

I head to the kitchen to start fixing Grandma's lunch.

Pretty Boy is on the counter, pecking away at his pile of birdseed.

I stare at the silly little bird. "You like him, don't you?"

Pretty Boy looks up and lets out a loud tweet.

"I'll take that as a yes."

He goes back to pecking at his seeds.

As I fix Grandma's lunch, I wonder if it's actually possible for a light-skinned kid and a dark-skinned gang leader to be friends. Those young gang dudes that like to hassle me on the street think being friendly to a white person should be taken as a joke. Maybe Jake just needs a computer guy, and he's smart enough to act friendly to get what he wants. But the more I think about that, the less I believe it. We just had a serious conversation about beliefs. In fact, we shared our beliefs. He asked me if I believed in God, and I told him the truth. I had a strong feeling that throughout the whole conversation, we were both being honest, and we were both interested in what each other thought. That has to be more important than the darkness or lightness of our skins. It just has to be.

15
Subrepresentative Passive Syntheses

The next morning, Denesa shows up with Javon and Zyrell. As soon as they are inside, Zyrell runs to give me a big hug. Then he's off to find Pretty Boy. "Pretty Boy, Pretty Boy," he calls, holding out a finger.

Pretty Boy comes flying in from my bedroom and dutifully lands on Zyrell's shoulder. Zyrell gives the silly little bird a smooch on the beak, and Pretty Boy responds with a loud approving, "Pretty Boy."

Denise and I both laugh out loud, and even the usually somber Javon has to laugh at that.

"Now you boys listen to me," says Denesa. "You do whatever Mister Scotty says. If he's busy, you leave him alone."

"I'm never too busy for these two," I say. "I really do like having them here."

"Well," she says, "anyhow, if you have things to do on that computer of yours, they can occupy themselves. I'll be back in a couple of hours. I don't see how they can keep us down there any longer than that."

She opens the door, and I wheel over to see her out.

There's a beat-up old car idling at the curb. Several dark-skinned women's faces peer out at me, and I quickly duck behind the door.

Denesa stares at me. "What? You don't want 'em to see you? It's only my neighbors. My next door neighbor borrowed her son's car to drive us down to the police station."

"I don't know why I ducked. I guess I just like my privacy. But how come the cops didn't send a car for you?"

"Are you kiddin'? You want I should let the people see us gettin' inta a police car? No way."

Then she's out the door and hurrying down the stairs.

I close the door and lock it behind her.

I guess she's right. No use broadcasting to the gang types that live in her public apartment complex that she's talking to the police, even if it's not by choice.

I turn to the boys. Pretty Boy is parked on Zyrell's shoulder and Javon is rubbing its fuzzy chest with the back of his finger, something Pretty Boy doesn't especially like, but for these two, he puts up with it.

"Well, what should we do first, boys? Hungry?"

They both nod excitedly, and Zyrell doesn't wait to be invited. He runs for the kitchen causing Pretty Boy to have to flutter his wings and hang on tight.

I follow, and Javon walks alongside me, looking serious, trying to act more grown up than his impetuous younger brother. I see that he's still wearing the Tow Mater T-shirt I ordered on the internet, but it's frayed and its bright colors have faded. It makes me wonder if it's his only shirt for school. I glance at Zyrell and see that he's wearing a plain blue T-shirt, also worn and very faded. Did he completely wear out his prized Cars cartoon shirt? I decide I'd better get on Amazon and get them both new Disney shirts.

"Well, what'll it be, boys? Toast and honey again?"

"Toast and honey," shouts Zyrell. "Yum!"

"Shh," I say with my finger up to my mouth. "Remember, Grandma's sleeping."

But it's too late. She must have heard them because soon she comes shuffling in wearing her old green bathrobe. She stops and stares at us, her hands on her hips. "What's going on here?" she demands. "What are these black kids doing in my house?"

"It's okay, Grandma," I say. "I'm just watching them for their mother for a little while. You can go back to bed."

She shakes her fingers at me. "I don't want any black people in my house, Fitzgerald. You know what they're like."

"Now, don't say that, Grandma. They're just little kids."

"Well, get rid of them. And then I want to talk to you. You can't be doing things like this without asking me."

She turns and shuffles away down the hallway back to her bedroom.

I turn to the kids. They're wide-eyed and looking a little scared.

I smile and say, "Don't mind her. Grandma gets a little grumpy when she gets woke up. But we have to be quiet."

They both look worried, and Javon looks toward the front door. Is he thinking about leaving, or just wondering how soon his mother will be back? It's too bad Grandma had to act like that. It will only reinforce their feeling that white people don't like them.

But soon, we're busily making our toast and honey, and they seem to have forgotten about Grandma's sudden appearance. Once again, Zyrell gets to be in charge of squeezing the honey out of the plastic bear-shaped jar. He does it very carefully, the tip of his little tongue sticking out the side of his mouth. I guess it must help his aim. He's so damn cute, I can't imagine him growing up to be a gangbanger, even if he does live in the projects.

Once the toast and honey eating is done, we adjourn to my bedroom to get on the computer. I decide not to order the Disney T-shirts in front of them. Their mother might have warned them not to let me buy them anything. I know her pride, and now that I've watched her kids twice, she'll think she owes me instead of the other way around. But I do go to the Disney site to ask them which are their favorite Disney characters. They both still like the Cars-movie characters best, so I decide that later, after they leave, I'll try to find some T-shirts for them with different characters from that Cars cartoon movie. If I give it to them as a surprise the next time they come over, it'll be like birthday presents or something, and it'll be too late for Denesa to make me send them back.

After they've decided which Disney characters they like best, I ask the boys what they want to do next.

In unison, they say, "Games."

I get it. They were ready for me. They don't just want to look at cartoons this time; they want to play computer games.

The trouble is, I'm not interested in games, so I haven't downloaded any. But there are some online chess sites that I play sometimes when I get tired of studying. Would they be interested in playing chess? "Well, boys, the only game I've got on this computer is chess. Do you know how to play chess?"

They look confused. Apparently, they've never heard of chess.

"It's a really fun game. Let me show you."

I go to the computer online chess site and pick the layout with the most interesting looking pieces. The pawns are pretty normal, just foot soldiers, but the bishops are dressed in fancy long coats and pointed hats. The king has a sword at his side, and the rooks are elephants with some kind of fancy box on their backs.

The kids lean forward to get a closer look at the weird little figures on the computer screen.

I point at the screen. "Here's how it works. See, it's a board with white and black squares, and those little characters are like two armies facing each other. We're the white army, and we have to try to capture the members of that black army on the other side of the board. Got it?"

They both nod their heads eagerly.

Good. I've got them interested.

I set the game controls to the easiest beginner level, and say, "Okay, we get to move first. We can move these little soldiers. They're called pawns. Or we can move one of the two horses. What should be we do?"

"Let's get 'em with our soldiers," says Zyrell.

"Okay," I say. "Move a soldier forward. They can move one or two spaces straight ahead."

"How do I do it?" asks Javon.

"You use the mouse to click on the piece you want to move. Try it."

Javon grabs the mouse and clicks on the pawn that's in front of the queen. The two squares in front of that pawn light up.

"See there? It's showing you can move forward either one or two spaces."

He looks at me. "Should I do it?"

"Sure. Click on one of those two lit-up squares."

He very carefully clicks on the second forward square. The pawn slides forward until it rests on that square.

The computer instantly responds by moving out its queen's knight, a rearing horse with a knight in armor mounted on it.

Zyrell get excited and points at the computer screen. "He moved that horsy."

"That's right. He did."

Zyrell turns to look at me. Can we move our horsy too?"

"Sure we can."

"Can I do it? Can I?"

Javon doesn't seem all that willing to relinquish the mouse, so I intervene. "How about if we let Zyrell move the horses? He can be our horse expert."

Javon shrugs and reluctantly lets Zyrell take control of the mouse.

Zyrell grabs the mouse and clicks on the knight. The three squares that the knight is allowed to move to light up.

I say, "Which lit-up square do you want to move the horse to?"

He seems puzzled. "Can it jump over the little soldiers?"

"Sure. Horses are good jumpers. He can hop to any one of those three lit-up squares."

Zyrell decides on the square that's right in front of the queen. Probably not a good move because it blocks future movement of both the queen and the queen's bishop, but I don't say anything. That's the way I learned chess, by making mistakes and seeing what happened.

The computer responds by moving it's queen's pawn forward.

Javon takes back the mouse. "I'm gonna get 'em with the elephant." He clicks on the king's rook, but no squares light up.

I point that out. "No squares lit up because the elephant can't move forward or sideways when there are other pieces blocking it."

He frowns. "But Zyrell's horse jumped over those little soldiers."

"Horses are very good jumpers," I explain. "Elephants aren't."

He studies the board and decides on moving out the queen's rook pawn. He's determined to free up his elephant.

Of course, with those kinds of moves, it doesn't take the computer long to beat us, and Javon is not happy about that. He turns to me. "How come we lost?"

"The computer is very smart. It's hard to beat. But if we keep trying, we'll beat it sometimes."

"I want to win," says Javon.

"Me too," chimes in Zyrell. "We should win."

"We will," I say. "If we keep learning from out mistakes. That's one of the best things about chess. It's not a luck game, like dice games. It's a type of game where you have to get smarter to win."

They both look doubtful.

"But you two boys are about the smartest two kids I've ever met. If anybody can beat the computer, you can. What do you say? Shall we try it again?"

They both nod their agreement, looking very serious.

I restart the game, again choosing the easiest beginner level. This time, as the game progresses, I give them some tips. Luckily, this particular computer chess game lets you take back moves, which gives me a chance to explain the problem with their moves, so they can take back that move and try a different one.

This time, we win and the boys let out whoops of joy.

I laugh, but I put my finger to my lips to tell them we have to be quiet.

They look nervously toward the door, but they are quickly back to looking at the computer screen. They're ready to play again.

We manage to complete two more matches, winning one and losing one. We're just about to start another match when I hear footsteps on the front porch.

"I bet that's your momma," I say.

They sprint to the front door and have it open before Denesa can even knock. As they hug her, Javon says, "We played chess, Momma."

"We won, we won," says Zyrell. "We beat the computer."

"Is that so," says Denesa, looking at me.

"Yep," I say. "It's true. They learned all the moves, and they beat the computer twice."

She squats down and kisses both of their foreheads. "Now aren't you two the smartest."

"They are smart," I say. "They picked up the game very quickly."

She comes to lean down to give me a hug too. She puts her hands on my shoulders and looks into my eyes. "I don't know how to thank you, Scotty. "You've been—"

"No need to thank me, Denesa. I really like having them here. Bring them by anytime."

She looks toward the door. "They're waitin' for us in the car. We gotta go. Thanks again, Scotty."

As she herds the boys toward the front door, I ask, "How did it go?"

She frowns. "Buncha dumb questions. Took us in one at a time. What'd we see? What do we know about gang activity in our projects? As if we're dumb enough to answer them questions. Waste of time." Again, she looks at the door. "Well . . . "

"Right," I say. "You'd better get going." I look at the boys. Okay, guys. See you later."

They start to go out the door, but Zyrell runs back to give me a goodbye hug. Javon hesitates, but then he comes to hug me too.

I tousle his hair.

He frowns and re-combs it with his fingers.

And then, they're gone. I roll to the window to watch them drive away. The street seems unusually quiet out there. If any of Jake's boys are watching me, I can't see where they might be hiding.

I roll to the kitchen to begin fixing Grandma's lunch. I hope she's not too upset with me for letting Denesa's two boys come into her house without asking her permission. But of course, had I asked her permission, she wouldn't have given it. It's clear she doesn't like dark-skinned people. Probably because everything in the neighborhood has changed so much. When she and her new boyfriend bought this house a long time ago, it was probably a quiet, mostly-white neighborhood. She must have seen it gradually get more and more run down, and that was when crime started to increase. It makes sense that she feels like it's the dark-skinned people that caused it. I think about explaining to her that the slums of every big city in the world have crime and gangs, and it has nothing to do with skin color. I look toward her bedroom where the TV is blasting and realize I might as well save my breath. She doesn't care about that. All she cares about are her TV soap operas. Maybe she's already forgotten about those two little dark-skinned kids that she saw in her kitchen. Maybe she thinks it was something she saw on TV.

Anyhow, it's over and done with. No use worrying about it. What *does* have me worried is why the police dragged Denesa in today. They must know she wouldn't tell them anything. Nobody in the projects is going to cooperate with the police. Maybe they're doing it to put pressure on the gangs. Trying to get somebody in the gang to squeal. The cops must be under a lot of pressure to quickly solve the murder of a white kid that took place in Watts. In this neighborhood, dark-skinned kids get killed all the time. But a light-skinned kid getting killed is different.

I take Grandma's lunch in to her, and even though the TV is turned up very loud, she's sound asleep and snoring. I leave her food on the bedside table, and wait next to her bed to look at her. She's looking old, and her face looks worried, even thought she's sound asleep. Mom told me Grandma had a tough life, so why shouldn't she now be allowed to do nothing but sleep and watch TV? It's really not much trouble for me to fix her meals and keep the house sort of clean. It's the least I can do to pay her back for letting me just hide out here and be a *Hikikomori*.

16
Death and Ontological Anxiety

Jake surprises me by showing up in the middle of the night. After we do our usual fist bumping thing, he takes off his backpack and dumps its contents on the table next to my computer. "Think we can sell this stuff on eBay?"

I look it over. It's mostly jewelry, rings and necklaces and such, with a few fancy watches and silver coins mixed in.

I look up at him. "Uh, not exactly old motorcycle parts."

He doesn't react to my joke. He seems unusually serious tonight, maybe even a little irritated. When Pretty Boy leaves my shoulder and tries to land on his, he brushes him away. Pretty Boy flies up to sit on his curtain rod and pout.

I sort through the jewelry. "So your gang homies steal the stuff and expect you to get them money for it."

"Remember, I told you not to ask? Well, I don't ask either. Maybe their grandmas gave it to 'em."

I pick up a silver bracelet. "I'm not sure I can sell this stuff if I don't know what it's made of. Feels heavy. Might be silver, but who knows."

"Can't you research it on your computer?"

"That won't tell me what it's made of. Better take it to one of those places that buys gold and silver. I read on the internet they have a chemical they can put on it to tell."

He holds up a couple of the coins and two Rolex watches. "What about these?"

"Rolexes could be a problem. They probably have serial numbers on them, and there may be a list of stolen watches."

"Can't you check that out on the computer?"

"Maybe. Let's see." I turn to the computer and Google "Rolex watch serial numbers." One of the hits that turns up is a YouTube video. The video shows how to find the serial number on a watch. The video also shows how to tell if it's a fake Rolex. I go back to Google and type in "How to tell if a Rolex watch is stolen." Several links pop up, and they all say the same thing: the Rolex company keeps a list of watches that have been reported stolen. "Uh oh," I say, "if these watches are stolen, that's gonna be a problem. If you're gonna work your way into being a legit businessman, you'd better not let yourself get caught fencing stolen goods. You don't want to get yourself a felony record."

"Too late for that."

"You've already got a felony record?"

"Shit, Scotty, when I was a dumb teenager, I was in and out of the pen all the time. Who in my set wasn't?"

"But then you got smart."

"Right."

I decide not to ask any more about that. I pick up some of the coins. "Anyhow, here's what I think. I can sell the coins, but you should sell the jewelry at one of those places that buy and sell gold and silver. And they might also buy the watches."

Jake winks at me. "I'll get somebody to do that. Delegate, right?"

"Right. If possible, I'd delegate it to somebody outside this city. Know anybody in Chicago?"

He nods, smiling. "I'll take care of it. But what you're telling me is that if I bring you more silver coins, you can sell them?"

"Right. No problem."

He scoops up the jewelry and the watches, and I think he's about to leave, but then he hesitates. He looks toward the dining room. "Mind if I drag in a chair? I need to talk to you about something. Or were you about to go to sleep?"

"Sleep? What's that? Sure, go get a chair."

He drags in a chair from the dining room and sits down close to me. "I talked to my mom about what you told me about people makin' up things to try to prove God exists. You said if God would make himself known, then religion wouldn't be such a big deal. Let me tell you, she's not very happy with what you said. She says I got to go tell you you're wrong. God does reveal Himself to us. She showed me pictures in some of the religious magazines she gets, pictures of Jesus's face in lots of places. In the melting snow on a roof, and there was one picture of Christ in the bark on the side of a tree. Thousands of people had been bringing flowers and candles and praying at that tree."

"How did she know it was the face of Jesus?"

"Well, it did look like him."

I turn to the computer and Google "images of Jesus." It shows us a large number of pictures that people have claimed to be miraculous appearances of Jesus in unexpected place like on trees, or in food, but most of them are just vague images of something that may or may not look like a face, depending on how you look at it. One of them, a rusty stain on a wall, shows a hippie-looking face with a light-colored beard and long hair.

"Like this one?" I ask Jake.

"Yeah," he says. "Her Christian magazines have lots of pictures like that."

"All right," I say. "Let's do some internet research." I Google, "the historically accurate face of Jesus," and it leads me to a site that shows a somewhat round, Arab-looking face with somewhat dark skin, a close-cut black beard, and closely-cropped dark curly hair. I point to the picture on the screen. "This is what the forensic anthropologists say Jesus would have looked like. Based on the region he was born in and the tribe he belonged to."

Jake leans close to the computer screen to look. "What? That doesn't look anything like the pictures of Jesus I've seen."

"Right. The most famous painting of Jesus was done by Michelangelo in the middle ages. He was probably required to satisfy the church leaders who were paying him to do the painting, so he made Jesus look like their idealized son of God, a handsome, tall, light-haired man with gentle light-colored eyes. Other painters of that period did the same thing, and it's those images of an idealized Jesus that have come down to us today. When people think they're seeing Jesus in tree bark, or in their toasted cheese sandwich, they're actually seeing that idealized image created by those old-time painters. It's another example of people desperately trying to find things that will help them keep on believing what they were taught as kids. But it says in the Bible that Jesus looked like any ordinary man in that area of the world. In fact, it says that when the authorities came to take Him away, they couldn't tell Him from the other criminals. The historians say Jesus would have been a Galilean Semite, an Arab, and He would have been short, only about five feet tall.

Jake is still staring at the picture on the screen. "An Arab?"

"That's right. But most people don't want to think of him looking like that. They really *want* to think of him as he appears in those famous old European paintings, an angelic-looking, tall young white guy."

Jake continues to stare at the picture for quite a while before he turns to look at me. "Scotty, you can be cruel. You know that? You're smart as hell, but sometimes I think you learn stuff on the internet, and you memorize it, just to prove you're smarter than anybody else."

I turn to look at my computer screen. The "historically-accurate" picture of Jesus stares back at me. Could that be true? Do I spend all my time studying just to prove I'm smarter than other people? No, that can't be because I never expect to have an opportunity to discuss it with anyone. But maybe I *do* want to be smarter than anybody else, even if nobody else will ever know it. Is that what's motivating me?

I realize Jake is waiting for my response. "I don't know why I study all the time, Jake. But it's not to show off. I don't ever leave this house, so who would I show off to?"

"Me."

"I'm not trying to show off to you, Jake. I just like talking to you, and the stuff I read on the internet is all I have to talk to you about."

Jake nods thoughtfully, and it makes me wonder if I've made a mistake, not in *what* I talk to him about, but *how* I talk to him. He's older than me, and a lot more experienced than me, but here I am talking like I'm the teacher, and he's the student. He's the one who is taking college classes, and I'm the one who didn't even finish high school.

"Listen, Jake, don't let my rambling on about all that stuff mess up our friendship. I get carried away with ideas and don't know when to stop. Sorry."

Jake slaps me on the back (maybe a little too hard), and says, "No sweat, Scotty. It's just that you read all that stuff and you get me half convinced, and then, when I tell my mom about it, she gets mad and gives me no end of grief."

"Aw, just tell her it's a bunch of weird ideas your crazy friend makes up. It's just that at some point . . . I guess it was when I was in the hospital after I fucked up my legs, I promised myself to be absolutely logical about *everything*. So now, I analyze everything to death. Sorry. But if I'm showing off, I think it's only to myself. I guess I'm trying to convince myself that I'm smart enough to figure all this stuff out on my own without going to any damn school."

"You *are* smart, Scotty. You're the smartest person I've ever met, but I bet you rub people the wrong way. I think you probably try to."

"Yeah, maybe so. But don't let me do it to you. If you didn't come over here to see me once in a while, I'd probably go crazy in this old house. If I haven't already."

Jake stands up and punches my shoulder (not as hard this time). "Hell, Scotty, no problem. We're partners, aren't we?"

He carries the chair back out to the dining room, but then he comes back and pats me on the shoulder. "Actually, I like listening to you, Scotty. You're learning about interesting stuff on that computer of yours, and I like to hear about it. Just spare me the talk about religion, okay? For my mother's sake."

I hold out my fist. "Deal."

He bumps fists with me, and then says, "Gotta go. Let me know how the sales of those coins go. I think my boys can get more."

"Will do."

After he leaves, I sit there staring at the image of Jesus on the screen. I'm sure most Christians wouldn't want *their* Jesus to look like this ordinary-looking Arab guy. This supposedly historically-accurate picture has probably led to a lot of heated arguments, maybe even to some lost friendships. I'll have to be sure stuff like that doesn't come between Jake and me. I don't want anything to mess up our friendship. That thought makes me realize that as different from each other as we are, I really am starting to think of him as my friend, the only real friend I've ever had in my life.

After he's gone, I get on the computer to post the silver coins. They won't bring in much, just their silver value, but they'll be easy to sell.

That done, I feel sleepy. How long since I slept? I can't remember. I decide to lie down on my mattress for a quick nap. But as soon as I lie down, I feel wide awake. Every time I lie down on my mattress, I can't help but think about that day when Lilly was here with me. She said she'd send me a direct message on Facebook, but she hasn't. Maybe she's waiting for me to send her one first. But I'm not going to do that. I don't want her to think I'm pestering her. Most likely, it was a one time thing for her. If she wants to contact me, she will. If not, so be it.

But then I change my mind. Maybe she's forgotten the name she gave my Facebook page. Just to be sure, I'll send her a quick message to say hello. I get up and go back to the computer. I get on Facebook and go to her page. I click on the message option.

But then I can't decide what to say. Remember me, the weird guy you fucked, the one with a bunch of screws and shit stuck inside in his torn up legs? No, that would be stupid. I'll just say hello.

I type in "Hello, What've you been up to?" I send it and wait to see if there is a response. There isn't. Well, what did I expect, that she would be sitting there at her computer just waiting for a message from me?

I lie back down on my mattress again and stare up at my black sky ceiling. I must have slept a little last night because I woke up remembering a weird dream about being in a cemetery. Somebody was being buried, and a small group of people, all dressed in black, were gathered around an open grave. I didn't know any of them, and when I looked down into the grave, there was a skeleton down there. No casket or anything, just a grinning skeleton lying there on the dirt. What a weird dream. But wait, when I was reading about Freud on the internet, didn't it tell me about his having a dream about a cemetery? I decide to get up to see if I can find that site again. I get on the computer and search for "Freud dream interpretation." I find a site that says Freud came up with his theories about dreams after his father died. Evidently, after his father died, Freud had troubling dreams about arguing with his father. He wrote about a dream in which his father was trying to go into a cemetery, but got stuck at the gate. The gate was open, but he couldn't force himself to go in. Freud decided it meant that he was actually subconsciously angry at his father, and from that one dream, he came up with his whole theory about dreams being manifestations of things going on in your unconscious, all of them repressed issues with regard to your parents. Although it seems like a silly reason for coming up with a whole new theory, it might explain why I had that dream. Maybe I'm mad at my mother for leaving me alone. Maybe I subconsciously wish she was dead. I don't like that thought, so I quickly go back to Google and start looking for other sites about dream interpretation.

Pretty Boy comes flying in to land on my shoulder. He must have noticed I'm out of bed and on the computer. He lets out a few loud whistles right in my ear. I tell him to pipe down, so he shrugs and goes to work pulling threads out of my collar.

"Today, we're going to look up dreams," I say.

He ignores me. Guess he doesn't care about dreams. Maybe birds don't dream. I'll have to look that up later.

I Google the words "interpretation of dreams" and "cemetery." Google links me to a site that gives brief interpretations of what dreams mean. It says dreams about cemeteries mean you subconsciously either want somebody to be dead, or you're afraid somebody is going to die. Well, duh. That seems too obvious an explanation. I'm beginning to think dreams don't mean anything about the subconscious. Maybe they're just triggered by something you were thinking about before you went to sleep. I decide to forget dreams and study something else.

But before I can decide what to study next, I hear somebody come up onto the porch. Is it Jake with more stuff to sell? No, he always taps on my bedroom window before he goes up onto the porch.

Somebody knocks on the front door.

Now who could that be? It didn't sound like Denesa's timid tap; it sounded more like somebody who isn't going to go away, even if I don't answer the door.

Sure enough, the knocking comes again, even louder this time, and more insistent. I quickly wheel my chair to the front door, trying to get there before whoever it is starts knocking so loud they wake Grandma up. I push Pretty Boy off of my shoulder, and wait until he's safely over on top of his favorite lampshade. Then, I open the door and discover it's two men in wrinkled suits, a tall dark-skinned guy with a somewhat friendly face and a short light-skinned guy who, for some reason, seems pissed off. Both of them are holding out leather wallet-type ID cases, but they didn't need to bother; I could already tell they were cops.

Uh oh, this could be something about my "business" with Jake. I glance back toward my bedroom. I'm glad there's a site about dream interpretation on the screen and not pictures of the stuff I've been selling for Jake on eBay.

The tall dark-skinned cop holds his ID closer to my face and says, "I'm Sergeant Johnson. LAPD." He uses his thumb to point to this partner. "This is Officer Kelly."

I stick out my hand to Cop Kelly. "Nice to meet you Officer Kelly. Maybe you can tell me why every cop you read about in novels is always named Kelly."

He frowns and doesn't shake my hand. "You live here?"

I say, "Yeah, but I didn't do it."

He looks puzzled. "Do what?"

"Whatever you're here to accuse me of."

"What makes you think we're gonna accuse you of something?"

I guess Cop Kelly is not too big on jokes. "Just kidding," I say with a shrug. I put a grin on my face that I hope looks silly—and very innocent.

But Cop Kelly doesn't change his hard-ass expression one bit. He's still staring at me with narrowed eyes.

A loud motorcycle passes by out on the street, and it makes him quickly turn.

The guy seems jumpy.

I lean to the side of my chair to look around him. Some of the dark-skinned folks across the street have come out to see why there's a cop car parked on *their* street.

For some reason, white Cop Kelly's nervousness strikes me as funny, but I guess it actually isn't all that funny; being a whitebread cop in this neighborhood, he probably has good reason to feel nervous.

But the dark-skinned cop, Johnson, still seems friendly enough. At least he's smiling. Maybe he appreciates the quality of my jokes better than his partner.

He says, "We're not here to accuse you of anything, son. We're looking for a redheaded woman. Does a redheaded woman live in this house?"

Redheaded? Like my mother? Are they looking for my mom? Is she back from South America? I shake my head. "Nope, no redheads here."

Cop Kelly abruptly steps forward, bumping his knee into my knee which makes my wheelchair roll back a little. His knee banging trick hurt like hell, and I'm pretty sure he did it on purpose, but I manage to keep a straight face.

"Don't lie to us kid," says Cop Kelly, shaking his finger in my face. "We know who you are." He pulls a folded-up picture out of this pocket. "You gonna tell us this is not you?"

It is a picture of me. Taken maybe three or four years ago. I remember my mom had that same picture stuck to the mirror in her bedroom. Where the hell did this cop get it?

I shrug. "Must be my long-lost twin brother."

He shoves the picture right up close to my face. "It's not any Goddam lost brother. This is *you*. We know all about you, kid. You used to live over in Inglewood, didn't ya? With your mother."

Uh oh, they must have been talking to that asshole landlord. I shake my head again. "Not me. You must have me mixed up with somebody else."

Cop Johnson takes the picture from Cop Kelly and shows it to me. "Now, don't be like that, son. We know this is you. We got this picture from your former landlord. He says you stole money from him."

So that's what this is about. That son of a bitch. He got the cops to track me down because I took a few lousy coins out of his jar. I cross my arms in front of my chest and get ready to deny it. That jerk landlord didn't see me break into his place. He can't prove it was me. "Stole money?" I say. "No way. Not me. And why don't you go back and ask him where he got that picture of me. He's the thief. He stole all of our stuff. Our clothes. Our furniture. Everything. Why don't you ask him about that?"

Cop Johnson puts the picture in his pocket. "Listen, son. We're not here about a few stolen coins. We just need to ask you some questions. When was the last time you saw your mother?"

Uh oh, does this mean she *is* back in LA? What has she done now? "Uh, it's been a while."

"How long?" demands Cop Kelly. "Exactly, kid."

"I don't know. A few years, I guess. She took off, and I haven't seen her since."

"She just left?" asks Cop Johnson, more politely. "Without telling you where she was going?"

"Yeah. Just took off. I'm pretty sure she left the country. Down to South America, I think."

The two cops look at each other. Then, Cop Kelly says, "Enough of your jokes, kid. We wanna know what you know about her disappearance. Right now!"

He leans down to stick his angry face right in my face, and I think I smell meat on his breath. Maybe pepperoni. It's still early morning. Did this cop have pizza for breakfast? No wonder he's acting so pissed off.

Cop Johnson puts his arm out to hold his partner back. "What makes you think she left the country?"

Should I mention how that bastard An-hell was always talking to her about going down there? Did he get her involved in something illegal? I decide to keep it vague. "Uh, 'cause she was always talking about it. And looking at maps. Maps of South America, especially."

Cop Johnson nods thoughtfully. "Listen, son. We may have some bad news for you. We found a body. A woman. Red hair."

At first, I'm not sure how to take his words. A body? Is he saying my mother is dead? No, that can't be. I shake my head, hard. "Yeah, she has red hair, but it couldn't be her. She's not even in this country anymore. It has to be some kind of mistake."

He nods, as if he's agreeing with me. "Sure, that's possible, son. But we found an envelope with the body. A bill. It had your address in Inglewood. The owner of that house said a red-haired woman had lived there but skipped out on the rent. He said her son broke into his place and stole some money. He gave us your picture. Now, does that sound like a mistake?"

I stare at him. Could it be? My mother? Dead? I'm confused. Did she come back from South America? Maybe she never even went to South America.

I feel something touch the front of my shoulder, and I look up. It's the dark-skinned cop, Cop Johnson. He says, "Are you all right, son?"

Am I all right? No, I'm not all right. If Mom is really dead, that would mean she didn't really leave me. It would mean . . .

"Well?" says Cop Kelly.

I look up at the two cop. They're waiting for an answer. But I'm having too many thoughts all at once to know what to say. If my mom is really dead, then what the fuck does anything mean? I knew the world was shit, but this is like extra, throw-shit-in-your-face proof of it. What's the point of living in such a world? Why couldn't I have died that night out there at that Point Fermin cliff? Then I wouldn't have had to find out she was dead.

But wait, they only said they found a body. So far, it's just *a* body. It doesn't have to be her. It could be that somebody that got ahold of her stuff. Stole her purse maybe, with that envelope in it. "You said you found a body? Where was . . . I mean, how did she die?"

Cop Kelly says, "We need to talk to you about that. You have to come with us."

"Come with you? Why?"

"Don't give us any trouble, kid." He looks down at my legs. "Can you walk?"

"Uh, yeah. With my cane."

The white cop reaches around me and grabs my cane off of the back of my chair. He hands it to me. "Let's go."

"But why? Where are you taking me?"

The two cops get ahold of my arms and stand me up.

I shake them off. "I can walk, God damn it. Leave me alone."

I look toward the back where Grandma's TV is blasting away.

"You don't need to bother to turn off your TV," says Cop Johnson. "We won't be long."

I get a good grip on my cane and shuffle out onto the porch. Quite a few of the neighbors are outside of their houses, watching to see what the cops are up to.

Once again, the two cops get on both sides of me and all but carry me out to their black and white cop car and put me into the back seat. Cop Johnson gets behind the wheel and we start down the street.

I look out the car window and see that the little dark-skinned girl next door is staring at me through the railing of her front porch. She has her thumb in her mouth, and her eyes are wide and curious as we pass by. I wave goodbye to her, and she surprises me by waving back. She's probably thinking it all makes sense: the weird person with the white skin is being removed from her neighborhood of dark-skinned people.

I look back and see that most of the neighbors are going back into their houses. A few stay out on the sidewalk to talk. They're probably wondering what I did to get myself arrested.

I sit back and think about if I've ever been in the back of a police car. I guess not, except for that time when a truant officer picked me up. But that truant cop's car had a regular back seat. This one is damn uncomfortable. It's made of molded plastic with some kind of depressed area behind my back. I turn to look it over and see that the depressed areas in the plastic are roughly the shape of human arms. It makes sense: most people that get stuck in the back of a police car are handcuffed, so the cops provide a depressed area so "the suspect" isn't leaning back against his arms. My, how considerate of them. But why is the entire back seat made of molded plastic? The car's floor is also plastic. Actually, when I think about it, that makes sense too: they must hose these cars out at night. After all, this is LA. I can just see some low-level worker at the police garage coming in on the night shift to hose down and scrub out the scum of LA. Vomit. Blood. Who knows what.

The car is moving fairly fast, and the cops are talking about something that I can't hear very well because of all the chatter on their police radio. I lean forward to try to hear them, but I can't make out much. Something about having to act fast on this one. I can't get any closer because there's a thick mesh screen between me and the two cops in the front seat. Thinking it through, I realize they must be taking me downtown to have me identify the body. To a morgue or something. But if that's what they're doing, why didn't they just say so? But the good thing is if they want me to identify the body, it means they're not sure. Maybe it *is* some kind of mistake, a mix-up. There must be thousands of redheaded women in LA. Tens of thousands even. And there could be lots of ways one of them got ahold of some of my mother's papers. I try to move my mind away from the idea that Mom is dead by trying to remember some of the philosophy I've been reading on the internet. What did it say about death?

Death can tell us nothing about our reality. Only life can reveal that path.

"Uh, maybe so, Old Man, but if—"

"You got somethin' to say, kid? You ready to talk now?"

It's Cop Kelly. He's turned around to look back at me, and for some reason, it still looks like he's pissed off at me.

I shake my head and go back to thinking. But it's hard to focus on things like life and death and reality in a philosophical way right now. All I can think about is how long I've been blaming my mother for abandoning me. But maybe she didn't. If she's dead, then maybe . . .

No, no, I don't want to go there. Not yet. It still might just be some kind of mistake.

I feel the car speed up. I sit up and see that we're now on a freeway, heading east. What the hell? Where are we going? This isn't the way downtown.

I lean forward and put my fingers through the screen mesh. "Why are we going in this direction? Aren't we going downtown?"

"Just sit back and relax," says Cop Johnson.

"It looks like we're heading out of town. Where the hell are you taking me?"

Cop Kelly smacks my fingers where they were protruding through the wire mesh. "Shut your face. Sit back and be quiet."

I sit back and rub my fingers where he hit them. It doesn't hurt all that much. This asshole cop has no idea how much I know about pain, real pain. I have control over my own brain; I can make it not hurt if I want to.

But I do wonder where they could be taking me. I lean forward again to try to hear what they're saying.

Cop Johnson says something about how they shouldn't be breaking the rules like this.

Cop Kelly says, "It's no big deal. We need to find out what he knows."

Find out what I know? What the hell does that mean? Know about what?

Johnson doesn't answer. He just keeps on driving east, still moving fast.

"Besides," says Cop Kelly, "rules don't matter this time. She's been dead since who knows when. No real evidence left up there anyhow."

Cop Johnson still doesn't respond.

What the hell are these cops up to? Where are they taking me? And what was that about rules and being dead for a long time? I decide there's nothing I can do but just sit back and watch the scenery go by. I don't much care what they do to me. If Mom really is dead, then why should I care about anything? I feel numb, and I know it's better to be numb. It's actually more logical to be numb. I lie down on the hard plastic seat and stare up at the car's ceiling. It's speckled and spotted. Spit? Vomit? There are some dark spots too. Probably blood. Do these cops beat people up in the back seats of these cars? Is that why it's made of plastic? So they can wash away the evidence?

After a while, I can tell we're going uphill. I sit up and see we're still on the freeway, but we've left the city. A long line of cars and trucks are ahead of us, moving slowly on the long hill, but as we approach them, the vehicles move out of our way. I'm not hearing a siren, but maybe Cop Johnson has turned on his flashing red lights.

We pass a freeway sign: 15. Now I know where we are: this is the 15 freeway, the one that goes to Las Vegas. Takes us up out of the LA valley into the desert. But why would we be heading for Vegas? None of it makes any sense, but after getting my fingers rapped, I'm pretty sure there's no point in asking where we're going. Neither one of these damn cops seems interested in telling me anything.

People in the cars we're passing stare at me. They probably think I've been arrested. Actually, being in the back of this cop car, I *do* feel like a suspect, even though I know I didn't do anything. Do these cops actually see me as a suspect? Do they think I'd kill my own mother?

I lie back down, but before long I feel the car going over a series of bumps. Did we go off the highway? I sit up and see that we're in the desert, driving on a rutted dirt road. The car is raising a huge cloud of dust behind us. Pretty soon, we come to an area that looks like an old dumping ground: half-buried tires, pieces of sheet metal, bottles, rusty tin cans. We come to a stop. There are other cop cars parked all over the place.

Cop Johnson gets out and opens the back door for me.

"What are we doing here?" I ask.

"Just keep your trap shut," says Cop Kelly.

Cop Johnson tells him to stay in the car and listen to the radio.

Cop Kelly shrugs and does as he was told.

"Come with me," says Cop Johnson. "This won't take long."

He helps me out of the car, and we start up a short hill.

My cane keeps sinking into the soft dirt, so Cop Johnson gets a tight hold on my elbow to help me along.

At the top of the rise, yellow police crime-scene tape is stretched between the bushes.

It hits me that his must be where they found my . . . found that red-haired woman's body. Am I going to have to look at it?

A couple of uniformed cops seem to be standing guard in front of the yellow tape. They stare at me as we approach.

When we get there, they nod to Cop Johnson and lift the yellow tape for us to pass under it.

Ahead, a few men in suits are standing around a dug-up area. They're all wearing blue plastic gloves.

One of them turns to look at Cop Johnson, "Who you got there?"

Cop Johnson says, "Could be her son. Took us a while to find him. He was at another house, but we tracked him down. Claims his mother ran off a while back."

The man in the suit frowns. "He shouldn't be here."

Cop Johnson tells me to stay put, and he leads the man in the suit a short distance away. They whisper together for a few moments, and then the guy in the suit jabs Cop Johnson's chest with one finger and says, "Okay, Johnson, one quick look. Then you gotta get him outta here. Before the lieutenant comes back."

I hear a shout. A uniformed cop is waving from the top of a nearby small rise. "We got another one," he yells. "And this one hasn't been dead very long."

"Like this one?" shouts back the man in the suit.

"Yep. Another redhead. Smashed in the backa the head. The same."

The man in the suit turns back to Cop Johnson. "Looks like we got ourselves a serial killer who likes redheads. I bet we'll find others buried here. I'm gonna tell the lieutenant we need to bring in a sniffer dog."

Cop Johnson comes back to me and takes my arm. "Now, son, I know this won't be easy, but we need you to try to identify the dead woman. She's over here."

He leads me close to a hole in the ground that's surrounded by freshly dug-up dirt. "There's not all that much left of her," he says quietly, "but I want you to tell me if you see anything familiar. Like her clothes maybe."

He keeps ahold of my arm to help me over the mound of dirt, and he keeps a good grip on my arm as I look down into the hole. It's dark in the hole, but I can see what looks a body.

"I can't tell," I say. "It's too dark down there."

Cop Johnson calls to the two cops down by the yellow tape: "Anybody got a flashlight?"

One of the cops jogs up and hands him a large flashlight. He clicks it on and hands it to me. I shine the light down into the hole, and what I see takes my breath away: the woman's face is little more than a horrible grinning skeleton. There are no eyes, only two black holes with hanging bits of flesh. But the skeleton really does have red hair.

Cop Johnson catches me as I stumble backwards.

"Well?" he says.

"How can I tell? It's a damn . . . skeleton."

"Did you look at the clothes?"

"Uh, no. I forgot."

"Look again. Don't look at the face. Just look at the dress she's wearing."

I cautiously edge forward and shine the light down into the hole, making sure it doesn't shine on that horrible skeleton face, only on the dress. The dress is dirty, and it's falling apart, but I can tell it used to be blue. And it has a pattern to it, like crushed blue flowers. I do recognize it. It's my mother's favorite dress, her going-out-on-the-town dress.

I have to turn away to keep from throwing up. I try to get away, but Cop Johnson won't let me go.

"Well?" he says.

I want to answer him, but my throat feels like its stuck. I suddenly have a panicky feeling that my throat is so stuck I'm not going to be able to breathe. I put my hand against my chest and gasp for air.

Cop Johnson still has ahold of my arm, and I realize he's the only thing keeping me from falling down.

"Easy now," he says. "Breathe. Take one breath at a time."

I do what he says, and after several wheezing breaths, I realize my throat is not entirely closed off. I can breathe, but it feels too tight. I'm sure something has gone wrong with my throat.

"Well? Did you recognize anything?"

I can't talk. I just nod my head.

"What? Her clothes?"

"It's . . . her dress. Her . . . favorite." But then I realize I shouldn't have said that out loud because the memory of her going out the door wearing that pretty dress is going to make me cry, and I don't want to cry in front of all these damn cops.

"All right, son. That's enough. Let's get you back to the car."

He leads me back to the car and tells Cop Kelly I identified the woman as my mother. He tells him to take me home.

Cop Kelly is not happy about that. "Now wait a minute. Shouldn't we take him downtown? Like I told ya before, this kid knows something. I can feel it."

Cop Johnson puts me into the back seat and hands me my cane. He slams the door closed and goes around to the driver's side to talk to Cop Kelly. "He thought his mother ran off. That's all he knows. Take him home. If we need to, we can talk to him later." He turns away and hurries back up to where they're finding the bodies.

Cop Kelly starts the car and looks at me in his rear-view mirror. "So, it was your old lady after all."

Old lady? What an asshole. She may have been a drunk, and maybe I never saw that much of her, but she was my mother. What would this asshole cop think if it was his mother buried in the dirt? I'm not going to answer him. On the way up here, he wanted me to be quiet, so I will. I won't say a damn word. I want to just be left alone so I can think. That dress. It was her favorite. She was wearing it the last time I saw her. It means she really is dead. She's not down there in South America, she's dead. Then it hits me. It has to be that bastard, An-hell. He must have lured her up here and killed her. The cops said the other body they found also had red hair. An-hell must have a thing about red hair. Picks them up in bars and—

"You listenin' to me, kid?"

Had he been talking to me? Who cares? I'm not going to listen this jerk cop. Why should I care about anything he has to say?

"I was asking you what you know about this deal. I know you know more than you're lettin' on."

I hesitate. Should I tell him about An-hell? No way. I shake my head. I have no proof that An-hell was the one that did it, only that he kept on talking to her about going off to South America with him. If I tell the cops, they'll pick him up. But with no proof, they'd have to let him go, and then he'd just take off back to his home country, down there in South America, or Mexico, or wherever he's from. He'd get away clean. I can't let that happen. I'll find the bastard myself. And if I find out he was the one who did it, then . . . well, then, I'll do the same God damn thing to him. I'll smash his fucking head in, just like he did my mom. See how he likes that. Maybe I'll bring him up here and bury him in the desert like he did my mom. The more I think about it, the more I'm sure he never intended to take her down to South America. Maybe the son of a bitch is smarter than I thought. Maybe all that looking at maps shit was just a cover story so I wouldn't report her missing.

But that gives me a worrying thought: what if he's already taken off? What if he's already left the country. No, the cops said they'd just found another woman's body. It means An-hell must still be out there looking for more lonely red-haired women like my mom. He's probably out there in some bar right now, showing some redheaded woman that same stupid map of South America.

That's it then. I'll go to those bars and find him. We'll see how he likes his head getting smashed in. Or maybe I'll get a gun and shoot the son of a bitch. I bet Jake can get me a gun. I'll ask Jake to get me a gun, and then I'll find the guy and kill him.

"Okay, kid, I think it's time we had a little talk."

I see that he's pulled the car off onto a dirt side road.

"Why are we stopped? You're supposed to be taking me home."

He gets out and opens the back door. "Get out."

I shake my head. "No way. You were told to take me home." I try close the car door, but he grabs my arm and pulls me out.

I try to stay on my feet, but without my cane to lean on, I fall flat on my face.

The cop laughs. "Clumsy, aren't ya?" He puts his foot on my back to keep me down. "Now let's have that little talk, shall we? I'm going to ask the questions, and you're gonna give me the answers. Now, what do you know about your mother's disappearance? And don't tell me you don't know. You know somethin'. I can tell."

I turn my head to look up at him. I try to keep a very calm look on my face. "Listen, Kelly, I hardly ever saw her. I don't know what she did with her life. All I know is she up and disappeared."

"You're lyin'. A kid knows what his mother is up to. How'd the two of you get along? Not so good, I bet."

"We got along fine. What little I saw of her."

"Come on, kid. Let me have it. Were you in on it? Or are you protecting somebody else? We're not leaving here until you open up."

"So are going to try to beat it out of me? Oh, good. Hey, do me a favor and beat me up real good? I need the money. I read on the internet that Rodney King got three point eight million bucks out of you guys. I'm not black, but maybe I could get a million or so."

"You're some smart ass, aren't ya, kid?"

"Yep, sure am. Here, hit me right here." I point to my cheek. "Make sure you hit me hard enough to leave a good bruise. Or break my nose. Go ahead and do it. I've got a photographer standing by."

He gets red in the face. "Smart ass, eh?" He gives me a good kick in the side.

Trying to keep a straight face, I say, "Come on, that hardly hurt at all. Kick me harder. That one might leave a bruise, but a bruise like that might only be worth a few thousand bucks."

He bends down and snarls into my face. I smell that weird pepperoni-like smell again. Maybe this dumb cop doesn't eat pizza for breakfast, maybe he just naturally smells like that. That strikes me as funny, and I giggle. I try to concentrate on the image of him as a big fat round pepperoni pizza.

He grabs my hair and jerks my head up. "You think that's funny, do you? Listen kid, I been doin' this a long time, and I can tell when somebody is lyin'. We're not leaving here 'til you start talking."

"I am talking. I'm saying words all over the place. You want me to talk some more. Okay, how about this? How about a poem about cops? I read a good one on the internet the other day. There once was a cop from Nantucket, with a dick so long he could suck it. He looked in the mirror, saw a hole in his ear, and—"

He doesn't let me finish the funny limerick. He kicks me in the side again, harder this time. I close my eyes. Time to put my mind in some other place. I imagine him with a head like a round pizza. With pepperoni for eyes. Now that's really funny. I laugh out loud.

He kicks me again, but I'm not going to let it hurt. I'm going to think about my poor mom getting her head bashed in by that An-hell bastard. I try to remember what he looked like. Pudgy. Dull eyes. Mean eyes. I try to imagine how he'll react when I shoot him right in the middle of his fat face.

The cop is saying something about spilling it, but I don't care. I'm no longer listening. He's a fool if he thinks he can hurt me. What are a few kicks in the side compared to what that bastard An-hell did to my poor mother. Her face was nothing but a skeleton. How long had she been buried up there? It makes me wonder how long it takes for us poor humans to turn into a skeleton, and why skeletons no longer have eyes, only black holes. Was it bugs? Are our eyes the first thing bugs go after?

Death is simply no longer being, no longer being something that was.

"Yeah, Old Man, I guess that's one way to look at it. We were not. Then we were born and we were. Finally, when we die, we—"

I feel another kick. "What's that, kid? What'd you say? Maybe you really are a little nutty. Or are you puttin' on some kind of act?"

Death is a concept that is part of being. It is always there, always standing before us, always impending.

"Yeah, Old Man, I get that. Death has been part of my being for a long time. I know it's impending, and I know it's under my control."

The cop is saying some words at me, but I'm not hearing them. I'm thinking about death as a concept. Derrida said words like death can only have meaning with regard to the concept of *being*. We *are*, but we are always in the process of moving toward *not being*.

Now the cop is standing me up. Maybe he's going to kill me now and throw me in the ditch. How long will it take before I'm nothing but a skeleton, like my mother?

He pushes me into the back seat of the car, and I end up lying on my side. It's the side he was kicking and it hurts. I turn over onto my other side, facing toward the back of the car. I must deny the pain. I'm the pain expert, so there's nothing this asshole cop can do to hurt me. He knows nothing about pain. Only I know about pain, and only I know how to move my mind to the place where there is no pain.

I hear him start the car. We're moving again. At first, I wonder where we might be going next, but then I realize I don't care. Now that I know my mom is never coming back to get me, what does anything matter? Ever since I jumped off that cliff that night, I always wondered what she would think when she found out I was dead. Thinking that would have made her unhappy was about the only reason I was glad I didn't succeed in knocking myself off that night. Now, it looks like she was probably already dead. It makes me wish even more that I would have succeeded that night.

I turn over onto my back and stare up at those weird stains on the car's ceiling. Is that what you call the inside of a car's roof, a ceiling? I'll have to look that up on the internet. Terms and linguistics. Derrida's thoughts on linguistics are a real puzzle. But then, he died too. By now, maybe he's a skeleton too. Or maybe he got himself cremated. I sure wish I could have talked to him before he died. Maybe he would have told me what it all means, all this being, this being alive and then being dead.

I feel the car stop.

Cop Kelly pulls me out of the car, and I barely have time to grab my cane before he's dragging me up some concrete steps. You'd think it would hurt my legs, but I hardly feel it. That's interesting. I say, "Hey, this isn't my house. This is a big stone building. My house is quite a bit smaller. You are one confused cop, Cop Kelly. You know that?"

Cop Kelly stops to catch his breath. He grabs my chin to make me look into his stupid eyes. "I know exactly what to do with a white smart ass like you. You'll soon be singing like a little birdie. You'll beg to come out and talk to me."

I think about pointing out what a cliche his bird-singing simile is, but then I get to wondering why he mentioned the fact that I'm white He's white too, so what was his point?

Inside the building, I see it's some kind of cop station. Cops all over the place.

He pulls me along a corridor until we get to a wall that's made out of bars. The whole wall. It's like a cage. A policewoman in a fancy blue uniform is inside the cage, and she's looking at me like I'm some kind of insect.

I smile at her and say, "Good morning, Cop Lady. Would you mind explaining to Cop Kelly here that this is not my house?"

She doesn't laugh. She doesn't even smile. Don't any of these people have a sense of humor?

She makes me give her everything in my pockets, which is not much except my house key, some change, and the two hundred-dollar bills Jake gave me. She takes it all, and even makes me hand over my cane.

"No ID? She asks.

I shrug.

"Name?"

"Scotch."

She looks irritated.

What, she doesn't believe my name is really Scotch? I'd better explain it to her. "My mother named me after her favorite drink."

She doesn't even look up from the paper she's writing on. "Last name."

"Doe. Scotch Doe."

I have no idea whether she believes me or not. She probably doesn't care one way or the other. She just writes it down.

Another cop, a big one, comes to get me. As he leads me away, Cop Kelly calls after me, "See ya, smart-ass, I'll be waitin' 'til you're ready to come out and talk to me."

I holler back, "Don't hold your breath, pizza face."

The big cop leads me past some cells full of prisoners. The inhabitants stare at us as we go by. One big fat guy shoves both of his fat hands through the bars and says, "Put him in here, Come on, give him to us."

I'm about to suggest to the big cop that I'd prefer not to be put in there, but I don't need to say that because he keeps me moving right on past that cell. His iron grip on my arm is very helpful, keeping me upright as well as keeping me moving, but his grip is so tight it's probably going to leave bruises. I have the feeling that this cop is not as mean as Cop Kelly, just impatient with my slow walking pace.

Who cares? I'll just keep my mouth shut and let myself be dragged along.

We turn down another long hallway that's covered with stains. Blood? "Hey," I say, "this place is in bad need of a paint job."

He ignores my clever comment and keeps on dragging me down the hallway.

We arrive at another cell and stop in front of it. I look through the bars. A dozen or so young dark-skinned guys are inside. They're gathered in two separate groups, one in each of the two back corners. Is this cop going to put me in with these dark-skinned dudes? A white kid in an all-black cell? They're all obviously gangbangers, every one of them covered in gang tattoos.

As he unlocks the cell door, I get it: this is what Cop Kelly meant when he said he knew what to do with a white smart ass like me.

The cop pushes me inside and closes the cell door behind me. I barely manage to keep from falling by grabbing onto the bars.

All of the dark-skinned gang dudes in the cell are staring at me. They seem as surprised as I am to see a white guy put into an all-black cell.

One of them quickly approaches. He's smiling.

Friend or foe?

He's a tall guy with a tattoo of a black widow spider on his neck. I've never seen anything like it. It's so well done, it looks like a real spider is actually clinging to the side of neck.

He grins. "Well, lookee here what they gave us to play with."

Okay, foe.

He looks me up and down and lets out a low chuckle. "What the fuck you do ta get yourself tossed in here with us, whitey?"

I shrug and grin at him. "I guess they just like me."

This time he doesn't laugh, so I add, "Doing me a favor, I guess. Put me in with the . . . uh, more experienced set."

He still doesn't laugh. He doesn't even smile. In fact, nobody in the cell is smiling at my jokes. They're going over like the proverbial lead balloon. Don't any of these dudes have a sense of humor?

The other gangbangers in the cell are keeping their distance, but they're all watching.

"How bout if you start by sucking our cocks, whitey?" says the spider guy.

"Oh, sorry," I say, still grinning, "I wouldn't know how to do that."

He gets ahold of my arm. "Just come back away from these bars, kid. I'll teach you."

I keep a good grip on the bars. "Oh, are you an expert at it? Maybe I'll just watch and learn."

"Oh, a smart ass, eh? Just get your ass over there into our corner." He looks back at his pals. "This is gonna be fun, eh?" He reaches for his crotch and makes humping motions.

His pals laugh.

I stop grinning and look him right in the eyes. "You try to stick that thing in my mouth, and I absolutely guarantee you I'll bite the little tiny thing right off."

He grabs the front of my shirt and pulls my face right up against his. "Maybe we oughta just beat the shit out of ya and be done with it. You hear what I'm sayin'?"

I shrug and try to look bored. "Okay with me. Maybe you'll hurt me bad. Or maybe you'll end up killing me. Doesn't matter to me one way or the other. I'll be dead, and you'll get the needle." I gesture toward the others. "Look at how many are in this cell. They're what's known as witnesses. Think they won't rat on you?" I look at his pals. One of them is looking a little worried. I point at him. "Him, for example. You can see it in his eyes. He's thinkin' maybe he should try to find a way out of this. He's thinkin' his momma wouldn't want him to get involved in no bad shit, not in no jailhouse right in front of so many witnesses." I put a childish whine in my voice: "It weren't me officer. It was him." I point at the black widow dude.

He shakes his head and glares at me. "You sure do like to hear yourself talk, don't ya, whitey? What a smart ass. Okay, boys, teach him how it is in here."

Two of his henchmen come forward and try to pry my hands off the bars.

Oh crap. Now I've done it. They're gonna hurt me, and as much as I hate to admit it, my left side is already hurting more than I realized from where that asshole cop kicked me. Now that I'm actually paying attention to the pain, it feels like I might even have a couple of cracked ribs. Maybe if I tell these guys about getting beat up by the cops, they'll see that we're all in this boat together so they won't hit me quite as hard. "Hey, listen guys, as much as I'd like to play the role of punching bag for you fellas, the cops already took care of that for ya." I touch my side. "In fact, I think they broke a couple of my ribs."

But the two gang dudes are not interested. They pry my hands loose from the bars, and down I go.

One of them starts stomping on me, and I barely have time to turn over to make sure he's kicking the side Cop Kelly somehow overlooked. I try to push the pain away. I tell myself to think, be logical. I'm supposed to be so damn smart, there must be a way to talk to these guys. The next time the dude's foot comes down on me, I grab it and say, "Hey, wait. Listen, you're right, I am a smart ass. Sorry about that. Big D Jake says I can't help myself. He's always tellin' me I'm a born smart ass."

The black widow dude pulls the stomper back. He stands over me, staring down at me. What is that look? Disgust, for sure, but maybe a little doubt mixed in.

"How you know the Dog, asshole?"

I sit up and rub my side. "How do I know Jake? Good ol' Jake? Oh, me and Jake go back a long ways. I'm surprised he hasn't mentioned me to you. I'm the Scotch man. The fence."

He doesn't look like he believes a word I'm saying.

"No, really," I say with a grin. "You guys must not be up on the latest stealin' thing. These days, you gotta go high tech. You gotta have a computer expert to unload the stuff on eBay. You heard of eBay haven't ya? These days, most stolen stuff gets unloaded on eBay. That's where I come in. I'm Jake's eBay computer guy."

Black widow doesn't seem impressed. "You think we're gonna be scared just because you know the Dog? We--"

But he doesn't get to finish whatever he was going to say because a huge dark-skinned guy suddenly appears and pushes him away. I size up this new guy. Damn, he must be six-four and at least two-fifty. And he's got one of those street graffiti-style 99 tattoos on his neck, just like Jake's. Wow, maybe he's in the same gang as Jake. I begin to have the teeniest bit of hope that I might actually get out of this cell alive after all.

The big guy reaches down and pulls me to my feet. He does it so fast and easy it's like he's picking up a little child. Jesus, how strong is this guy?

He drags me into the opposite corner from where the black-widow dudes are. Do these guys create turfs even in jail?

He leans me up against the wall, and puts his face almost right up against my face. "You'd better really be a friend of the Dog's, motherfucker, or you're in deep shit."

Three other guys, all with those 99 tattoos on their necks, surround us. Are they trying to hide whatever they are planning to do to me from anybody who might wander past our cell?

I put the most innocent look on my face I can muster. "Sure. I only got a few friends in this world, but I'm proud to say Jake is one of them."

"A whitebread?" he snarls. "A friend of the Dog's?"

I realize I'd better be careful what I say. I don't want to get Jake in trouble with his gang pals. "Well, it's more of a business arrangement, if you know what I mean. Like I said to those guys, I'm just the fence. I unload stuff for Jake. On eBay, you see. Hey, listen, guys, I'm always looking for new clients. You guys need anything fenced, you come see me. I can unload just about anything."

They stare at me for a while, but then they turn away from me to glare at the black-widow guy and his pals over on the other side of the large cell. Am I going to get caught in the middle of a gang war in here?

I take advantage of their attention being diverted and let myself slide down the wall. I sit with my back against the wall and take stock of my injuries. Feels like the side that got kicked by Cop Kelly is hurt worse than the few kicks that black-widow gang dude got in to my other side. I cautiously probe my ribs on the Cop Kelly side to try to figure out if they're busted and floating loose. Far as I can tell, they don't seem to be completely broken, but they sure do hurt like hell.

None of the dark-skinned dudes are paying any attention to me now, so I lie down on the floor and close my eyes. I've got to get into my pain-control mode, and find something else to think about. What should I think about? The answer is obvious: I should think about how I'm going to get my revenge on that bastard, An-hell. First, I need to get a gun from Jake. Then, I'll go looking for An-hell. I sure hope he doesn't get wind that the cops have found his secret burying place up there in the desert. He'll take off across the Mexican border, and I'll never be able to find him. Thinking about that bastard getting away just makes my side hurt even more. Time to focus. I have to think about something else besides the pain. I'll think about . . . about Derrida. He talked about how we use words. Texts. He criticized some of the most famous philosophers.

It is always difficult for those who come after to recognize the contributions of those who came before.

"Yeah, but I bet he didn't give a shit."

I get the feeling he might have been one contentious son of a bitch. He criticized just about every philosopher that came before him, essentially criticizing the whole thrust of historical philosophy.

The thrust of historical philosophy is defined by those who came after.

"That's my point exactly. He scoffed at their attempts to pin down what knowledge was, even what reality was. I wonder if he believed there were limits to what we humans could deduce just with thought. Maybe he just believed—"

Somebody is shaking my shoulder. It's the big guy who saved me from the black-widow dudes. He's kneeling down next to me.

"Hey, kid. Are you listening to me?"

I blink to clear my eyes. Everything is a little fuzzy. "What?"

"I said what're ya whisperin' about?"

"Oh, just . . . things."

"Like what things?"

Is he really interested? He seems to be. His pals have also moved in closer. I guess they're curious about me. Okay, if they're all that curious, I'll tell them. "I was thinking about the nature of reality."

That seems to strike them as funny. Smiling, they look at each other. One of them does the spinning finger thing next to the side of his head. They think I'm crazy.

"No, really," I say. "I've been studying philosophy, and this one philosopher guy—his name is Derrida—seemed to think it's a hopeless task to try to do what all the other philosophers have been doing since . . . well, like since forever."

The others are still smiling, but the big guy still seems interested. He says, "Are you a student or somethin'? You go to college out there with the Dog?"

So they know about Jake's taking college classes. He said he was afraid they wouldn't understand, but maybe they actually admire him for doing it.

"No, he's studying business. I study philosophy. I mean, I'm not a student right now, but I might be later. Right now, I just read stuff on the internet."

The big dude sits down on the floor next to me. He doesn't look all that bright, but he does seem interested. Maybe he's smarter than he looks.

"Okay, tell me about what you're studying."

"You really want to know?"

"Sure, we got all night, don't we? My name's Joe."

He sticks out his big hand, and I shake it. "My name's Scott."

The others sit down in front of me. I look across the cell. The black-widow dudes are keeping a close eye on us. I decide I like these guys sitting all around me like this. It makes me feel a lot safer, and it sort of makes me feel like a teacher. I've never had that feeling before, and I kind of like it.

"Okay," I say, keeping my voice down so they have to lean in close. "I think about what I've been studying so I don't have to think about how that damn cop tried to bust my ribs. Do you think he did?" I pull up my shirt to show him.

"It looks okay," says Joe. "Look at this." He pulls up his shirt. His side seems all lumpy. Cops chase me down this alley, see. Catch me in a dead end. Kicked the shit outta me. Musta broke my ribs. Some of 'em anyhow. Feels like it."

"You didn't go to the hospital?"

"Why bother? What could they do? I got busted ribs before. Went in to the emergency room that first time, and they said there was nuthin' they could do about it."

"Didn't they at least take an x-ray?"

"Naw. I didn't have no money. But hell with that. Go on. You were gonna tell us what you thought about this philosopher guy. What was his name again?"

"Derrida. A professor. At a university. I went to see him once, but he was already dead."

"Somebody offed him?"

"No, cancer."

"So you never got ta talk to him."

"No, but I read his ideas. He thought a lot of philosophers, even Heidegger and Nietzsche, were barking up the wrong tree. But he was actually more interested in linguistics than regular philosophy."

"What's linguistics?"

"Well, it's like . . . sort of like a science of how we talk. And what language means."

They all stare at me.

"I also like to think about infinity."

Joe is frowning.

Doesn't he know what the word means? "You know," I say, "infinity. It's a mathematical concept. It means . . . uh, without limit."

They all nod like they know what I'm talking about. I guess they want me to go on.

"I got to thinking, what if the human race is lucky enough to stick around for infinity."

Joe shakes his head. "No way."

"Well, you're probably right. We're bound to blow ourselves up, or fuck up the planet so bad we'll all die off. But let's assume we do live forever. Us or some other human-like species. And given the fact that knowledge is constantly accumulating, somewhere out there at the far edge of infinite time, everything will become known. We, or whatever consciousness is still functional, will understand time and space and all reality. And we'll be able to control it."

"Will we be able to travel in time?" asks one of the younger ones, a thin young kid that looks kind of shy despite the evil-looking tattoo of a snake that snakes up out of his shirt collar.

"Sure we will. We'll be like gods."

"No shit?" says Joe. "Like gods?"

"Sure, we'll be able to do anything we want. And it'll be no big deal. Once you know everything, it all gets easy. Like quantum physics. I've been reading about this Qbism solution that takes into account the role of the observer, so when you run an experiment, you can—"

"Doe. Scotch Doe. Come forward."

We all turn to look. A cop is pointing at me.

"Shit," says Joe. "Just when it was gettin' good."

"Do I have to go?" I call out to the cop.

He scowls at me. "You making some kind of smart ass joke, kid? Get your ass over here." He's shaking a pair of handcuffs at me.

"When they go at ya, tuck yourself into a ball," whispers Joe. "Lay down on the floor and pull your knees up."

I shake his hand, and thank him for the advice. I also shake the hands of the others. "See ya, guys. Hope I run into ya back in the hood."

They all shake my hand vigorously, as if I'm some kind of long-time friend that's going away for good. Do they think the cops are gonna kill me?

Without my cane, I have to hand-over-hand along the bars until I get to the cell door. There, the cop makes me turn around and stick my wrists through the hole in the bars so he can put the handcuffs on me. After he lets me out, he leads me down the hallway, holding me up in order to keep me moving.

Where is he taking me? Do they have a special room where they take prisoners to beat information out of them?

But no, he leads me right back to that wall-cage. The same woman cop is inside the cage. She shoves my cane, my house key, and some change toward me. The hundred-dollar bills are missing, but I'm not about to risk another beating by complaining. I put the coins in my pocket, and even though I now have my cane back, the cop once again grabs my arm and all but drags me down the hall. He takes me right to the front door and unlocks the handcuffs. He turns away without a word and disappears back down the long hallway.

Does this mean I'm free to go?

I look around. The only other people in the room are lined up at a window that's been cut into the wall. Behind the window is another uniformed woman cop. She's protected by thick glass, so the people trying to talk to her have to lean down and talk through a small cutout at the bottom of the glass. Nobody is paying any attention to me, so I decide I might as well just leave. I walk out, and for some reason, I had no idea it would be nighttime. I wonder what time it is.

I slowly make my way down the concrete steps and stop on the sidewalk. The street is busy with cars and buses and cabs. I must be downtown. The smell of smog in the humid night air tells me I'm back in LA, alive, and not hurt all that bad. My ribs hurt, but I can take it. I'm the expert on pain aren't I?

I watch the cars go by. A bus pulls to the curb, and the people inside the bus look out at me. Do they know I just got out of jail? Do I have that look? No matter, the important thing is to figure out how to get back to grandma's house. If I'm anywhere close to the center of town, it's going to be a hell of a long walk back to Watts, especially with my slow limp. But those cops took my money, so I guess I have no choice. I start my slow shuffle, heading south, keeping my eyes on the nearly-full moon looking down on me through the smoggy evening sky.

A parked car across the street flashes it's lights several times. I stop. It's a new-looking, very shiny black car. I think it's a Mercedes. Is it flashing its lights at me? I move closer to the curb to look, but I can't see who is inside that car. I'm about to go back to my slow shuffling down the sidewalk when I see the driver's side window come down. The driver puts out his arm and waves at me. Is it Jake? He yells something at me, but because of the traffic noise, I can't tell what it was. I wait for the traffic to go by, and now I can see that it *is* Jake. Good old Jake. He must have been the one who got me sprung from jail. How else would he know when I was getting out? Does he have a contact in the police department? Somebody he's paying off maybe?

He points to the intersection ahead. I guess he wants me to cross over so he can pick me up.

I hurry to the intersection as fast as my clumsy shuffle and my hurt ribs will allow. When the light changes, I try to make it across the wide street, but as usual, I'm hardly more than halfway across before yellow "Don't Walk" light starts flashing at me. The light turns red and the cars start edging toward me. One of them honks. I give him the finger and yell, "I'm going as fast as I can, God damn it!"

I make it almost to the curb before the cars take off fast, passing very close to my heels.

Jake's black car pulls up next to me and stops. There's a squeal of brakes as the car behind him slides to a stop, and there's more honking as Jake flings the passenger door open for me. I climb in, and he burns rubber to make it through the light before it turns red.

He looks over at me and grins. "Well, Scotty, you got yourself into one this time. What'd they get you for?"

"Nothing. Some cop was just pissed off at me." I reach out to touch Jake's arm. "Listen, Jake, I need a gun. You have to get me a gun."

He looks surprised. Then, he laughs. "The cops threw you in a cell with my homies, and you say you didn't do anything, but now you need a gun? Hey, aren't you the guy who never sets foot outside your grandma's house? The guy on the computer all day? Is this the same guy who now needs a gun? What're you up to, Scotty?"

I stare straight ahead. The traffic is heavy, but we're moving. A little.

"Well?"

"I can't tell you. Can you get me a gun, or not? If you won't do it, I'll buy one on the street. I bet I can get one over at the projects."

He shakes his head. He seems disgusted with me. "You do that, and it's you that's liable to get shot."

"I don't care."

Jake reaches across and grabs ahold of my shirt sleeve. He pulls me closer to him. "Hey, shithead, this is me. Your friend. Tell me what the fuck is going on."

I pry his hand off. His pulling at me hurts my side where that damn Cop Kelly kicked me. I look straight ahead. I can't tell Jake what I'm going to do. I can't tell anybody. But by God, I am going to do it. If I can find that asshole An-hell, I will kill him for what he did to my mother.

Jake pulls off the main street and stops in a quiet side street. He shuts off the car. "I saw ya wince, Scotty. You hurt?"

"Aw, the damn cop kicked the shit out of me. Doesn't matter."

"The cops beat you? Why?"

"Aw, the stupid cop thought I knew something."

Jake nods. "So that's why they threw you in that cell. To scare you."

"They don't scare me."

"But somethin's got you all freaked out. Got you so stirred up, you think need a gun. Okay, maybe I can get you a gun, but first you got to tell me what you need it for."

"I don't want you to know. I don't want you involved."

"If I get you a gun, it'll be a cold one. No way they can trace it back to me. Tell me what's going on."

I look at him. If I tell him, will he try to talk me out of it? I realize it doesn't matter. He's not going to talk me out of it. I'm going to kill An-hell, and nobody is ever going to talk me out of it. Then maybe I'll use the gun on myself. So what? What do I have to live for now that I know Mom is never coming back?

Jake is still staring at me, waiting.

I decide I have to tell him, or he won't get me the gun. "Okay. This is it. Remember I told you that my mom ran off. I thought she left the country with some South American bastard who kept on showing her maps of where he used to live down there. Well, I just found out she didn't run off with him. He killed her."

I'm not sure Jake believes me. He just stares at me, frowning.

"That's why I need a gun. I'm going to kill him."

"You know for a fact she's dead?" Jake's voice is flat, and scary calm.

"Yeah. The cops showed me her body. The bastard smashed her head in and buried her out in the desert. And they're finding other bodies up there too. That son of a bitch, An-hell, has been killing redheaded women. I think he looks for lonely and vulnerable women who're comin' up on middle age. Women like my poor mom."

"An-hell?"

"He said that was his name. It's spelled like Angel, but he's no Goddam angel. He's a damn killer."

"How can we be sure it was him?"

I like the fact that Jake used the word "we." Does it mean he's going to help me get a gun?

I think about how to answer his question. Am I sure? I shrug.

"So you're not sure." Jake is not smiling or looking doubtful. He may question whether I'm sure, but at least he's taking me seriously.

"Who else could have done it? Think about that story he gave her. Sayin' he was gonna take her down to South America? He was just making sure I wouldn't report her missing."

"Could be, but you can't go around killin' people on a hunch. Maybe you just want to get back at somebody for your mother's death."

"I know he did it. I always suspected he was up to something no good. He killed her, and now I'm gonna to kill him. And what about those other redheaded women? He's probably out there right now, finding new victims. What about them?"

Jake starts the car. "Let's go find out. Where do we start lookin'?"

"I know the bar my mom used to hang out in. They used to call me when she got too drunk so I could come get her. I bet that's where he finds his victims."

Jake nods. "Tell me where to go."

I direct him to the sleazy bar in Inglewood where Mom used to hang out. As we drive on through the night, I try to think what I'll say to the guy if we find him. I turn to Jake. "What if we find him? Have you got a gun on you?"

"We'll worry about the gun later. If you find him, don't talk to him. Don't even let him see you. If he's in that bar, you come right back out and tell me."

"Then what?"

"We'll see what he does."

"Okay, but I don't want the son of a bitch to get away."

"Don't get ahead of yourself. First we have to find him."

We drive on in silence.

When we come to the bar, I tell Jake to park a little ways down the street.

I start to get out, but Jake grabs my arm. "Be careful. And don't get carried away. You gotta be calm. Ever follow anybody before?"

I think about that. Of course I've never followed anybody.

Jake doesn't wait for my answer. He says, "You're headin' into a different world now, Scotty. This is more my world than yours. Just go in and take a quick look around. Try to find a place to stand where nobody will notice ya. You look too young to be in there, but in this neighborhood they won't care about that as long as you got money in your pocket. But don't order a drink. Just get in, look, and get out."

"Got it."

Jake still has ahold of my arm. "If you see him, don't get emotional and make a mistake. Make sure he doesn't see you. Just come back out here and tell me."

"Okay. I understand."

I decide to leave my cane in the car. That's something that might make people notice me. I get out of the car and test my legs. My right leg is doing pretty well, but my left leg still hurts like hell every time I put weight on it. But so what? It doesn't matter how much it hurts; it will support me long enough to get to that bar. I close the car door softly, so as not to make too much noise, but then I wonder why I did that. The street is heavy with traffic and plenty noisy. I have to think about what I look like. If I do something suspicious, like closing the car door in an unusual way, people might notice something like that. Shit, Jake is right, I really don't know how to do this kind of thing. But I will do it. I need to get this done and get it over with. Nothing else matters. I *will* find An-hell, and I *will* kill him. And not just for my Mom; I could be saving other lonely women like her.

I limp toward the bar, getting better at it as I go. I tell myself there is no pain. Pain doesn't matter anymore.

Inside the bar, it's crowded, noisy, and smoky. I thought it was against the law to smoke in public places in California, but in this kind of bar, I guess nobody gives a shit. I stay by the door and try to spot An-hell. But it's a long narrow bar and damn smoky. I can't get a good look at the people in the back. I think about Jake's advice. Find a place where nobody will notice you. I look around. There are no empty seats at the bar, but Jake told me not to order a drink anyhow. Besides, I suddenly realize I don't have any money. Those bastard cops stole it. All I have in my pocket is a little bit of loose change.

But I spot a pinball machine near the bar's front window. Perfect. I go to it and feed in a quarter, it registers one credit. I send the steel ball on its way, and I pretend to be focused on the game. But actually, I hardly notice the ball bouncing its way down through the colorful lit-up posts; I'm leaning this way and that, trying to get a good look at everybody in the bar. I don't see An-hell. I look for redheaded women. I spot one sitting at the bar, but her hair is way too red. Must be dyed.

She notices me looking at her and winks. Is she a hooker?

I turn back to the pinball game. I've got to be careful not to stare at people in these bars. A lot of them are just looking to make eye contact with somebody. Otherwise, why would they waste their money coming to a bar instead of just drinking at home?

By the time I finish the pinball game, I'm pretty sure An-hell is not in this bar. I put my head down and head for the door.

Back outside on the sidewalk, I feel a tremendous letdown. Is this going to be a wild goose chase? There are hundreds of bars in LA. Probably thousands. An-hell could be in any of them, looking for lonely red-headed women. And that's assuming he's still in LA.

Jake's car is idling in front of the bar.

I get in the car and shake my head.

"Okay," he says. "Where to now?"

I try to think. Maybe he wouldn't go back to the same bar where he picked up my mom. Maybe I need to look for just that same type of bar. "Let's just drive around this area," I say. "Let's check some other bars."

Jake heads on down the street while I watch for a bar that looks right. He slows in front of one that has neon beer signs in the window, but from the people hanging around outside smoking, it looks like a place that's haunted by a younger crowd. I tell him to drive on.

A few blocks farther on, he slows again, but this bar has outside seating. Too fancy. I shake my head, no.

"I know a bar district farther south," he says, and he turns in that direction.

The next time he slows, the bar is on the other side of the street. If it wasn't for the tattered green awning above the door with pictures of cocktail glasses on it, you'd hardly know it was a bar. The building itself is a faded gray color, and the front window has been painted over with the same gray, used-to-be white paint.

"Yeah," I say. "I'll check this one out."

Jake waits for the traffic to die down and makes a U-turn. He parks a little ways down the street from the bar.

I start to get out, but he grabs my sleeve. "Be careful in there, Scotty. This is kind of rough neighborhood."

"You mean like the one I live in?"

He smiles. "Not quite that rough."

"At that last place, I played a pinball machine. You got any quarters? The cops took all my money. Even those hundreds you gave me."

"Of course they did."

He unzips his leather jacket pocket and takes out a handful of change. I pick out several quarters. He takes out his wallet and hands me a couple of twenties and a hundred-dollar bill. I only got a quick glance at his fat wallet, and I can't even guess at how many hundred-dollar bills he has in there, but one thing for sure, he can't be making that much money selling stolen crap on eBay. For the first time, I notice the new-car smell of the car and the squeaky clean feel of the leather seats. Is this a brand new Mercedes? Where could he be getting all these brand new cars? Are they stolen? And if they are stolen, how does he unload them after he's done driving them? None of my business, I guess.

As I pocket the bills, he says, "If anybody gives you trouble, just slip 'em the hundred and get the hell out quick."

"Okay."

"Now, same routine as that last bar. Low profile. Right? If this guy really is killin' people, he'll be watchful as a nervous coyote. Constantly lookin' over his shoulder. And don't forget, he knows you."

I get out, and this time I slam the door like normal. Once I make it to the bar, I hesitate at the door. I need to think about what I'm going to do. If there are not many people in there, and if An-hell is in there, he might be watching the door. Nothing I can do about that. I have to go in. I'll just try not to attract any attention. I put my weight fully on both legs, push away the resulting pain, take a deep breath, and push open the door. Inside, it's like I've gone right back into that first bar. Same long narrow configuration. Crowded, smoky, noisy. The same. But there's no pinball machine. There's a pool table in the middle of the place, and quite a few of the patrons are watching the ongoing pool game.

There are two stacks of money on the pool table, one at each end. The players must be betting, and maybe the other people are also betting on the outcome. Good. It means they won't pay any attention to me. I start to move through the bar to get a better look at who might be in the back of the place, but before I take two steps, I spot him: An-hell is at a back table, and he's leaning forward, talking to a woman with red hair. I freeze. It's just like I imagined it would be. She's even older than my mom was, and she seems very drunk.

He looks up, and glances around the bar. He seems nervous, just like Jake said he would be.

Damn! Did he see me?

I quickly turn away and pretend to look at a stupid picture on the wall. Dogs playing poker. Dumb.

I'm afraid to look back to see if An-hell saw me. Shit. I told myself not to stare at anybody, and then I stood there like an idiot staring at the very person I shouldn't let see me. I know I have to get out of this place quick, like Jake told me, but there's something wrong with my eyes. They're all wet, and I can hardly see where the front door is. The damn hanging cigarette smoke in the air seems to be settling down all around me. It's too hot in this place, and too stuffy. Makes it hard to breathe. I feel so shaky, I'm not sure I can even manage to make it to the front door. I tell myself to just walk. Focus on the front door. Get outside and you'll be able to breathe.

By feeling my way along the wall, I do make it to the front door. I push it open and stumble out onto the sidewalk. I lean up against the building and try to catch my breath. It's like all that cigarette smoke has gotten stuck in my throat, and I can't get enough air. Every breath makes a wheezing sound. What the hell is wrong with me?

Somebody grabs my arm. I spin around, fists up.

But it's not An-hell. It's Jake.

"What's wrong, Scotty? Was he in there?"

I can't seem to get the words out. I nod.

"Did he see you?"

I whisper, "Not . . . sure."

He grabs my arm. "Let's get you back in the car."

He leads me to it and opens the door. I get in, and he slams the door closed. He runs around and gets in the driver's seat. He puts the car in gear and we slowly roll away down the block. He hasn't turned the headlights on. Suddenly, he makes a wild U-turn across the traffic and pulls up to park across the street from the bar. He switches off the engine and turns to me. "So he was in there. What was he doing?"

I'm still having trouble with my throat. I try clear it, but it doesn't help. I feel like it's closing off and I'm not going to be able to breathe. Am I going to die?

Jake touches my shoulder. "What's the matter?"

"Can't breathe," I whisper.

Jake shakes his head. He looks disgusted with me. "So this is the hotshot who was gonna get a gun and kill the bastard. And now, just seein' him's got you all freaked out and wobbly."

I stare at him. It feels like he slapped me in the face. He's right. I'm a fucking wimp. Seeing that guy talking to that drunk redheaded woman *did* freak me out. That stupid old woman made me think of my mom: I could just see her in a bar like that, drunk on her ass, listening to every bullshit word some asshole feeds her, a mean bastard who only wants to get her out into the desert so he can kill her. Poor Mom. It makes me want to start crying and never stop.

But no, God damn it! I'm not going to cry. Not in front of Jake. I jumped off a God damned cliff and fucked my legs all up, and I never cried once. My mom is dead, and if I have to cry about that, I'll do it later. Right now, I know what I have to do.

I pull myself together and say, "I'm all right now." I take a several deep breaths.

"You sure?"

He's still touching my shoulder.

I push his hand away. "I said I was all right, didn't I?" My voice is a bit hoarse and shaky, but I'm not going to let him treat me like a wimp.

Jake looks surprised at my fast recovery, but he doesn't know what I've been through. I'll show him how tough I really am. "Are you going to get me a gun, or not?"

He raises his eyebrows. "You gonna walk right inta that bar and shoot him?"

"Yes, I am. He's talking to another redheaded woman. He's gonna kill her. I'm gonna stop him. Right now."

"So, you're gonna be the hero and save her."

I think about his words. It's not true. I'm not trying to be any kind of hero. I'm actually not thinking about that poor woman in there at all; I'm only thinking about my poor mom. Just because she was a sad drunk, she didn't deserve to die.

I look right at Jake. "He killed my mom, God damn it. I'm not letting him get away with it. Would you?"

Jake looks out the front window and thinks about that for a moment. Then, he looks back at me. "Okay, let's say you go in there and shoot him. Then what? Even if they can prove he's the one who's been killin' those women, you'd still do some time in prison for killin' him. You said he was Hispanic. What do you think the Hispanic gangs will do to you once you end up in prison with 'em?"

"I don't give a shit about that. It doesn't matter."

Again, he stares at me, and again he reaches out to touch my shoulder. "Scotty, are you thinking about shooting yourself? You gonna storm in there and blast him and then turn the gun on yourself."

I shrug. "Maybe. I hadn't got that far yet."

Jake stares at me. Is he going to try to talk me out of it?

But no, he turns to look out the window. "Let's wait here until he comes out."

"Then what? We can't let him get away."

"He won't."

We wait, and it doesn't take long before Jake points. "Is that him? The guy coming out of the bar? The guy in the leather jacket?"

I turn to look. It *is* him. An-hell has walked out of the bar's front door, and he's got ahold of the red-headed woman's arm. As he leads her down the street, he's talking and laughing. She's sort of laughing too, but she's staggering all over the place. He gets his arm around her waist and leads her on, trying to keep her from falling down.

I turn to Jake. "Now! Give me the gun."

"Look," he says, pointing, "they've got a car."

He's right. They're standing next to a beat up old Ford sedan, and the woman is fishing in her purse. She must be looking for her keys, but she can't seem to find them.

An-hell takes her purse and quickly finds the keys. He puts the woman in the passenger seat and gets into the driver's seat.

I say, "No! We've gotta stop him. He's gonna take her up to the desert. He's going to kill her."

"You said the cops were up there looking for other bodies. They'll still be up there."

I reach across to grab his sleeve. "That's even worse. If he sees the cops up there, he'll know they're onto him. He'll kill the woman somewhere else and make a run for the Mexican border."

Jake points again.

I look and see their car is moving. "Follow them. Follow them," I yell.

"Take it easy, Scotty. "They won't get away from me." Jake starts the car.

"But what if they get lost from us in all this traffic?"

"Not a chance. I know what I'm doing."

He makes a U-turn and follows them, but there are two cars in between us.

"Don't lose them, Jake. Please don't lose them."

"I won't. Calm down."

We continue to follow them for several blocks.

I point. "He's speeding up. I knew it. He's heading for the freeway entrance. He's going to take her up to the desert."

Jake nods and the car's engine roars as he pulls around the two cars in front of us.

He says, "Get down on the floor?"

"What?"

"Hurry. Sit down on the floor, and keep your head down. Don't get out of this car no matter what happens."

I do as he says and sit on the car's floor with my back against the door. What is Jake going to do?

I feel the car speed up, and then I hear my passenger side electric window going down. I glance back at Jake. He's holding out a silver badge. He yells out the window, "Turn at the next corner. Pull over."

I feel the car turn.

Jake yells, "Pull over, asshole. Now!"

I feel the car slow and then stop.

Jake is hurriedly putting on a pair of black leather gloves, and then he reaches way up under the dash and pulls out a small pistol. He grabs a heavy sweater from the back seat and wraps it around the gun.

"No," I whisper. I try to get up off the floor. "I want to do it."

Jake points the gun at me. "Stay right where you are. Don't move."

He gets out, and closes the door quietly. I squirm to get up on my knees to see what he's going to do. Is he going to kill the son of a bitch for me? Does he think he's protecting me or something? I don't need his help. It was my mother that An-hell killed. If anybody gets to kill the bastard, it should be me.

I open the door and get out. I head for the other car as fast as my clumsy shuffle will allow.

Jake is holding the pistol against An-hell's neck, and he's walking An-hell around to the other side of the car. I don't hear Jake say a word before he wraps his sweater around the gun and fires.

The sound of the shot is muffled, but the woman's scream is loud.

As An-hell goes down into the gutter between the car and the curb, Jake points the gun at the woman inside the car.

"No!" I yell. "Don't shoot her."

Jake gestures angrily for me to stay back.

I pull my shirt up so it covers all of my face except for my eyes. I move in closer.

Jake tells the woman to move over into the driver's seat. He keeps the gun pointed right at her head.

She's shaking, but she does as he says.

Jake leans into the car's open window. "He was gonna kill ya."

She's wide-eyed, and stammers, "Wha? Kill me?"

"He was gonna kill ya and bury ya in the desert. He's been killin' redheaded women. You'll hear about it on the news. Go home. Drive slow. Take the back streets. If the cops come, say you don't know nuthin. You came home from the bar alone. Went right to bed. Got it?"

She nods, her hand up to her mouth. She's shaking badly.

"I saved your life lady, but if you say one word to the cops, or to anybody else, I'll find you. I'll kill you. Do you understand me?"

The woman nods again.

Jake says, "Go." He steps back and the woman quickly drives away.

We watch her go. She's driving pretty straight. Maybe Jake scared her sober.

Jake says, "Help me drag this guy."

We drag An-hell back to Jake's car that's still idling by the curb. Jake pops the trunk. There's a blue tarp inside. He unfolds it, and we roll An-hell into the trunk and wrap him up. Jake quietly closes the trunk lid and looks around.

I don't see any lights coming on in any of the nearby houses. Good.

Jake puts his fingers to his lips, and we get back in the car. He starts down the street, moving slowly, lights off.

Back on the main street, he turns the headlights on and speeds up. He looks at me. "You all right?"

I nod. I feel shaky and still a little out of breath. But overall, I feel good, and it's easier to breathe, as if a huge weight has been lifted off of my chest.

Jake smiles and reaches over to shake my shoulder. "Revenge. Feels good, eh?"

I nod again. It does. It really does. I wonder what kind of person that makes me. But then I decide I don't care. The son of a bitch killed my mother. And he was going to kill that drunk redheaded woman. We only did what had to be done.

Jake holds up a large ball-peen hammer. "Check this out."

I stare at the hammer. "Where did you get that?"

"He had a special pocket for it sewed inside his jacket."

"You think that's how he killed my mom? With that hammer?"

Jake nods. "Spect so."

"Can I hold it?"

He hands it to me. If feels unbelievably heavy in my hand. I get ahold of the handle and shake it. I try to imagine him hitting my mother with this very hammer. But the image of him hitting the back of her head, hitting her beautiful red hair, is too much for me. I don't want to hold the hammer anymore. I drop it to the floor and look out the side window to make sure Jake can't see the tears welling up in my eyes.

When I've recovered, I turn back to him. "Where we goin'?"

Jake grins. "Feel like doing a little diggin' out in the desert tonight? I know a place way out past Palm Springs. Turnabout's fair play, right?"

"Right," I say, and I don't feel one bit sorry for that An-hell bastard. Not one bit.

17
The Existential Reconciliation of Death

After Jake drops me off, I go in to check on Grandma. Of course, she's mad at me for disappearing without telling her. She takes her eyes off her blaring TV long enough to accuse me of trying to starve her to death, but I can see that she's been into her stash of cookies and potato chips, so she hasn't exactly starved. I say, "Sorry, I had to go out."

"You always say that. You keep on leaving me alone."

I sit down on the edge of her bed, something I don't recall ever doing before. "The police came, Grandma. They took me to identify a body. I think it was Mom."

For a moment, she seems confused, but then she turns back to the TV. "I knew it. As soon as you told me she went to South America, I knew she'd get herself in trouble down there."

I try to decide whether to tell her Mom never made it down to South America. I'm not sure how much Grandma even understands these days. Her mind is going, and she's so lost in her world of TV soap operas she doesn't much care about the real world anymore. I decide I've told her the important fact, her daughter is dead. Now, it's up to her to deal with it in her own way, just as I have to deal with it in my own way.

I go out to the kitchen to fix her something to eat, and while I'm fixing her food, I try to remember how long it had been since I sat down to have a meal with Mom. A long time. We hardly ever ate together, except maybe when I'd heat up her crappy weight watcher meals in the microwave and bring them to her in front of the TV. I tried, I really tried a few times, to stay there and watch TV with her while we ate, but the stuff she was watching was so stupid and so boring, I always retreated to my room to get on the internet. The last time I tried to watch TV with her was when I was . . . what? Maybe about fourteen or so. It was about then when she started going out to bars at night, and I didn't see much of her after that. At least now I know she didn't abandon me. I think about how many times I got mad thinking about her leaving me to go down there to South America. It wasn't her fault that she was lonely and got hooked on alcohol and going to bars. I remember she was always talking about how she was going to find a good man who would be like a father to me, a man who would take me fishing and stuff like that. I wasn't at all interested in fishing, but I didn't tell her that. At that age, I didn't really care what she did, so I guess

I never gave her much reinforcement for her big plans. Now, I wonder if I should have watched TV with her. Maybe I should have tried to keep her from going to those bars every night. Maybe then she wouldn't have got so lonely and wouldn't have even met that An-hell bastard. I try to shake off those kinds of thoughts. What does it matter now? I have to be logical about it all. This is no time to let down and get all emotional. And I sure don't want to be mad at her anymore. She did what she did, and now she's gone. Maybe it was fate or something. Her mother, my poor old grandma, led a tough life too. She too spent her time in bars with men. Maybe that life style was all either one of them knew. At least Grandma was lucky enough to meet a guy who bought her this old house before he decided to take off and leave her alone.

I take Grandma's meal in to her. She's focused on the TV. I put the food down on her bedside tray and sit down on the edge of her bed again. She ignores me. I stare at her. I hadn't noticed how gray her hair has gotten. I reach over and tuck a loose lock of her hair behind her ear,

She slaps my hand away. "Can't you see I'm watching TV?"

"I'm sorry about Mom, Grandma. We both thought she'd run off and left us, but she hadn't. It wasn't her fault."

Grandma still won't look at me. She hasn't even asked me how her daughter died. I guess she doesn't want to think about it.

I watch her stare at that TV. She's so focused on some TV show, I swear she thinks she's inside the TV along with those actors. She looks tired. Old and tired. I know from old photos that she used to be pretty good looking. Now, it's like she's decided she wants no part of the real world outside of her TV set. In a way, I guess I'm a lot like that too. Except my place to retreat to is the internet.

Oh well, if she doesn't want to know what happened to Mom, I'm not going to force it on her. I go back out to kitchen and open the refrigerator. But standing there, staring at what little food there is, I decide I'm not really hungry. I close the refrigerator door and go back to my bedroom. I stare at the computer for a while, but I can't really think of anything I want to study right now. Besides, my side is hurting where that cop kicked me. I decide to lie down on my mattress for a while. Tomorrow, I'll try to sort out what it all means. And maybe I'll be able to cry then. Right now, I only feel numb.

But then I think about the cops up there in the desert digging up bodies. I get back on the computer and go to the LA news sites. As I expected, somebody in the police department has leaked the story. The local TV news sites are all over it with bold headlines: multiple murders, bodies buried in the desert near LA. Live video from their breaking-news team shows police holding everybody back behind yellow crime-scene tape, the same yellow tape that I saw stretched between the bushes up there in the desert. The TV cameras zoom in close enough to show several dug-up areas. Men in hooded white crime-scene suits are kneeling. The commentator says, "Looks like they're removing bodies, but so far, they won't say who was killed."

As I watch the jerky video on my computer screen, I find myself hoping that redheaded woman we saved last night is watching this. Maybe it will make her keep her mouth shut. I decide I don't want to see any more. I'd better just get back to doing internet research and stop thinking about all the shit that goes on out there in the world. Besides, it's all in the past now, and what does the past matter?

Of course, the first thing I do is check to see if Lilly has sent me a Facebook message. I don't know why I bother. I haven't heard a word from her since that day she was here. I bet she's forgotten about me. Probably forgot about me the moment she walked out the door.

But when I check my Facebook page, it tells me I have a message waiting. I click on the message icon and the message box opens up. It's a response to my message to Lilly. It says, "Fuck you!!!"

Well, at least she's succinct. And with three exclamation points to boot. But why is she so mad at me? All I did was send her that one line message asking her what she'd been up to. Oh well, this must be her way of saying don't bother me. Okay, fine with me. It doesn't matter. I had already figured she was done with me, so I need to forget about her and get back to my studying. I go to Google. What should I research today? But I can't seem to focus. I keep on wondering why Lilly would send such an angry message? Those three exclamation marks don't feel like a leave-me-alone message; it feels like she thinks I did something wrong. But I didn't do anything. Is she thinking I should have contacted her sooner? I click on the Reply option and type in "What's the matter? What did I do?" I hit send and sit there staring at the screen. She probably won't respond. And if she does, it might take days. Or weeks. Most likely, never.

But all of a sudden, a new message pops up. "You know what you did. It was you who told him where to go find heroin."

What the hell is she talking about? Oh, wait, David was talking about suicide when we first met. I may have told him the easiest way would be to do an overdose of heroin. Shit. Did he do that? It was just a hypothetical discussion. I quickly type in "What are you saying? Did he get some heroin?"

She responds, "Are you saying you really don't know? You have to know. He gets killed a few blocks from you, and you didn't know?"

Oh my God. Denesa *did* say a white kid had been shot by gangbangers out in front of the projects. She said that's why the cops were all over it, just because the kid was white. A drug deal gone bad; that's what they said. It must have been David, trying to buy heroin. And now Lilly thinks it was my fault. Could she be right? Maybe I did mention to David that you could get heroin in this neighborhood. But I warned him, didn't I?

I type in "I admit we did talk about the better way to kill yourself. But only hypothetically. And I told him not to go looking for it on the streets."

The response comes back quickly. "You put the idea in his head. And you know David."

Do I know David? I only know him . . . knew him, from that one time after we escaped from the hospital, and then that other time when he brought Lilly here.

I stare at the screen. She's probably waiting for my response. But what am I supposed to say? I start typing: "I'm very very sorry, Lilly. I guess I should have tried harder to talk him out of the idea of killing himself. But I've been struggling with that concept myself. I . . "

I can't decide what else to say, so I just send the message. She probably doesn't care what I have to say anyhow. Her brother is dead, and that's that. No wonder she's pissed off at me.

This time there's a long wait before she responds. "Being sorry doesn't help. But forget it. He got what he wanted. Goodbye."

I quickly type in "Do you want to talk? You could come over here."

The response comes back almost as quickly: "No, I'm leaving. I met a guy who says he can get me a med tech job up in Alaska even if I haven't finished my degree. He's got a big ass truck, and he says we can drive up the Alaska highway. So, see ya."

It makes me think about what happened to my mom. As fast as I can, I type "Who is this guy? Can you trust him?"

I wait, but there's no response.

Grandma starts tinkling her damn little bell, but I'm afraid to take my eyes off the screen. But there's still no response. She's not going to answer me. She's lost her brother. And he was more than a brother: they were more like close pals. David said their mother didn't pay much attention to them. David was probably the only friend she had.

I hear Grandma's tinkling bell again, getting more insistent now. I push back from the computer, but I continue to stare a the computer screen. I say out loud, "Well, so long, Lilly. I hope you find what you're looking for up there in Alaska."

Tears fill my eyes, but I angrily wipe them away. My poor mom is dead. And now poor dumb David is dead too. What does it mean? Death is all around, just waiting for opportunity? But maybe it doesn't mean anything. Does anything mean anything? Probably not. Like the philosophers say, we're born, we live for a little while, and then we die. None of it means a Goddam thing.

But I now I'll miss Lilly. It feels stupid to think I'm going to miss a girl I only knew for a few hours, but I can't deny that I do. Shows what happens if you get soft and start thinking there's anything of value in this stupid world. I warned myself not to let that happen, and then I went ahead and did it. Well, I won't let it happen again. It's not logical.

And what about my mom? I feel like I'm going to miss her too. But why? When she was alive, for the last few years anyhow, I she hardly had anything to do with me. She spent all her time with her drunken friends. If she ever did come home, she'd be all fucked up. Why would I miss that? Sure, I'm sad she had to die. But then, we all have to die sooner or later, don't we? So what?

Death is the sole thing that is certain, and yet all deny it.

"Right you are, Old Man. Right you are. She lived, and then she died. I live, but before long I will also be dead. Everybody else wants to deny that reality, but not me; I will be logical and face it. I will look straight at it. It is what it is. I will stay logical about it, no matter what. And I will also be rational about it. I'll be rational about death, and . . . and all the rest of it. I will not cry because there's no point in crying. Mom is dead, and Lilly is gone, and I'm alone. Well, so what? Haven't I pretty much always been alone my whole fucking life? BFD.

Grandma is tinkling her bell even more frantically now. I roll my chair toward the kitchen and yell, "All right, Grandma, I hear you."

18
Objective and Subjective Representations

I'm awakened by somebody pounding on the front door. From the insistent sound of it, I'm guessing it's the cops again. There's no way they could have found An-hell's body because we buried it good in a such a remote place nobody will ever find it. But what if they're here about David getting killed? No, Lilly wouldn't have told them I put him up to it, would she?

I get into my chair and wheel to the dining room window. I pull aside the curtain. Sure enough, it's Cop Johnson and his asshole sidekick, Cop Kelly.

I unlock the door and smile at Kelly. "Are you here to kick me some more? Should I lay down on the floor?"

Cop Johnson turns to look at him. "You kicked him?"

Cop Kelly puts a disgusted look on his face. "I never touched him. I told you the kid was a born liar."

Cop Johnson turns back to me. "We have a few more questions, son. May we come in?"

I shake my head. "Do you have a warrant?"

Cop Kelly steps forward and bangs his knee into mine. I was pretty sure he did that intentionally last time, and him doing it again now proves it. I say, "Do you enjoy banging your knee into mine? Did somebody at the hospital tell you how much that would hurt me, or did you figure it out all by yourself?"

He grabs the front of my shirt and almost lifts me out of my chair. "You want me to show you what hurts, kid? I can show you a few things that—"

Cop Johnson pulls him back. "What's the matter with you, Sean? We said we were just going to ask him some questions, remember?"

Cop Kelly pushes me back down into my chair.

I can tell he's steaming. Maybe I can send him off the deep end. "No, it's fine. He can beat me up if he wants to. Maybe he has a deep-seated need to hurt cripples. Maybe he—"

Cop Johnson interrupts me. "Now, don't be like that, son. Nobody is going to hurt you. We just need to ask you a few more questions."

I point at Cop Kelly. "I don't much like the way he asks questions. I think you should leave now. I grab the edge of the door try to close it.

"No, wait," says Cop Johnson. He turns to Cop Kelly. "Why don't you wait in the car, Sean. I'll just be a few minutes."

Cop Kelly hesitates, then shrugs. "Whatever you say, sergeant. But don't forget I warned you. This kid will lie through his teeth."

He goes down the steps and heads for their car But some of my neighbors are coming out of their houses to see what's going on. Cop Kelly goes across the street to talk to them.

Now what's he up to? Probably asking them what they know about me. Asking them about my comings and goings. I hope they don't tell them about the black Mercedes that dropped me off late last night. But no, I suspect they're too smart to tell cops anything.

"Just a couple of questions," says Cop Johnson.

"Fine," I say. "Ask away."

"It would be more comfortable to talk inside."

I say, "I'm comfortable."

He seems frustrated, but he just says, "All right. No problem. We can talk here. First off, we need to know who your mother's dentist was. To help us with the identification. You understand."

"Sorry, I wouldn't know about that. If she ever went to the dentist, I never heard about it. But she did have a tooth missing." I point to one of my back teeth. "Back here. She was always complaining about getting food caught back there."

"Good. That will help." He takes out a little notebook. "Now, I need to know who her friends were. Did she have any friends? A boyfriend maybe?"

"Not that I know of. Listen, officer, it's like this. I hate to say it, but the fact is she was a drunk. She went out to bars. Most every night. She'd come back late at night, drunk and go to bed. That's all I know."

"She never brought anybody home with her?"

"Nope."

"That's not what your landlord said. He said he kept on seeing a middle-aged Mexican male coming out of your house. Sometimes not until morning."

I shrug. "If she brought home some Mexican, I never saw him. Like I said, she'd come home late at night. I would have been asleep."

The cop stares at me. I can tell he doesn't believe me. So what? That asshole landlord can't prove I ever saw An-hell.

"Are you telling me you're such a sound sleeper you wouldn't know if your mother brought a man home with her from one of those bars?"

"Right. Once my head hits the pillow, it's like clunk, I'm gone 'til morning."

"So, you're not going to help us find your mother's killer."

"Officer, if I could, I would. And what about those other dead women you found? Those other redheads. He might still be doing it. If I knew anything,

anything at all, wouldn't I tell you? To protect them."

He frowns and writes something else in his little book.

I wonder what he could be writing? The son is uncooperative? Or the son is out of it. Hopefully, he's only writing down that the dead woman's son doesn't know shit.

"All right, son. If you say you don't know anything, then I have to believe you. But I may have more questions. You're not planning on leaving town or anything are you?"

I use my thumb to point to my own chest. "Me? I hardly ever go outside this house." I tap on my knee. "Bad legs. Hard for me to walk, as you've seen. I just stay here and . . . read."

He looks past me. I realize Grandma's TV is blaring back there, as usual.

"And watch TV," I add. "I watch a lot of TV."

"All right, son. If you think of anything else, you call me." He hands me his card. "All right?"

"Will do, officer." I nod repeatedly to show him how sincere I am.

He leaves, and I quickly close the door and wheel myself over to the dining room window. Across the street, I can see that Cop Kelly is still talking to the neighbors. What are they telling him?

Cop Johnson calls for him to come, and Cop Kelly hands my neighbors a card before hurrying back across the street to get in the car.

They drive away, leaving the neighbors standing out there in their front yards staring at my house. I can just imagine what Cop Kelly told them about me. I bet he told them to keep an eye on me. But I doubt if they will. Why would my dark-skinned neighbors want to cooperate with an asshole white cop who likes to beat people up?

I roll back into my bedroom and get back on the computer. I try to get focused by doing yet another search for articles about modern philosophers. I need to focus on something, anything. What do I care about what the cops think? That asshole landlord could be a problem, telling them about An-hell, but he thought An-hell was a Mexican. He also probably told the cops Mom didn't have a car, so the cops will probably start hitting the bars near the neighborhood we lived in. I bet An-hell stopped going to those bars after he killed Mom. That bar where we found him was a long ways from that neighborhood. In the end, it won't matter what the cops find out. When the killing of redheads stops, they'll assume the killer has run off back to Mexico. They'll forget all about it. I bet I won't see them at my door again.

I try to focus on the list of articles about philosophers, but I can't keep my mind from drifting back to my poor mother. She was always dreaming of somehow getting "discovered" and becoming a famous Hollywood movie star. She drove herself crazy because she didn't know how to make it happen. And then she ends up getting killed by some maniac, just because she wanted someone to pay attention to her. It makes me wonder if I could have done more for her. Mostly, I just let her do "her thing," her boozing and her bar-hopping, because it was what she wanted to do. The few times I questioned what she was doing with her life, she said it was "necessary." I wonder why I never asked her what she meant by that. Did she mean it was necessary in order to get money from the men she met in those bars? So we could eat? Or was it necessary because she needed men to pay attention to her? Probably it was both.

I try to refocus on the computer screen. I guess I have to admit to myself that I've been avoiding thinking about her death. Doing away with that bastard An-hell seemed like the end of the whole issue, and I guess it was. I really don't want to get caught up in any weepy sadness, or lamenting. (Remember my list of cool words? Lamenting is a good word, but not for me.). No lamenting for me. Better if I just remain logical. The cops proved to me that she was dead, and I dealt with her killer. End of story.

For the individual, death means the end of time.

"Yeah, I know that. But what about those of us who are left behind? How are we supposed to deal with it?"

Humans deal with the death of others by outer-directing it.

"What the hell is that supposed to mean?"

They avoid thinking about the absoluteness of their own coming death by adhering to rituals like religious funerals.

Oh, Christ, I hadn't even thought about a funeral. Why haven't the police, or somebody, contacted me about a funeral for Mom? I guess I really have been avoiding thinking about it. Funerals are probably damn expensive. I have no money. But then, I bet a lot of people in this town don't have enough money to pay for a funeral. So what do they do with the dead when people can't pay for a funeral? Where do they bury people who don't have any money?

I Google "Where do they bury people who don't have enough money for a funeral?"

As usual, when you do a search on the internet, a bunch of ads pop up advertising cheap funerals. But once I get past all that spam, I find the real answer: it says if bodies are left unclaimed at the city morgue, after thirty days, they get cremated. So they don't get buried. There is no funeral. It says they just write down the name of the deceased (if they know it). They must have some kind of ledger book. Your name gets written down, your body gets burned up, and that's the end of it.

I try to be logical and not get all freaked out about my mom being cremated all alone in some county furnace. I mean, what does it matter: once we're dead? Once you're dead, you're dead, and that's the end of it. If I had been successful in my attempted swan dive off of that cliff, I guess my body would have stayed in one of those drawers at the country morgue for thirty days, and because my Mom was already dead by then, and I intentionally didn't have any ID on me that night, nobody would have claimed my body. I would have been cremated as an unknown homeless kid. Another John Doe. Toss him into the furnace. But it doesn't say anything about burying the ashes. What do they do with the ashes? Do they just toss them in the trash? I do some more searching, but there's nothing on the internet about that. I guess they don't want anybody to know what they do. I bet at the end of the day, all the accumulated ashes of the burned up people go out to the dumpster in the alley. I know I should be a good existentialist and just admit that we all die, so what does it matter where we end up? But I can't force myself to be cool and logical when I think about my Mom being thrown out with the trash.

That thought gets me to wondering how much it would cost for me to get her cremated myself. I click on the back button to get back to those ads about cheap cremations. It says the average cost of a funeral in America today is over eight thousand dollars, but a cremation can be had for as low as six hundred dollars. Damn, six hundred dollars. That doesn't seem like very much, but for me, it might as well be a million. Where would I get six hundred dollars? And what about the burial plot? I read on, and it says you don't need a burial plot because you don't have to bury the ashes. They just give them to you in an urn, and you can do whatever you want with them. Oh, that's right. I remember a movie I watched on TV with Mom where some guy took his friend's ashes down to the ocean and scattered them into the water because his friend liked to sit on the beach. I could take her ashes to the ocean, like that guy in the movie did.

But where to get the six hundred? Grandma doesn't have anywhere near that much in her bank account. It takes just about all of her monthly Social Security check to pay the house bills and for the food we eat. Jake gave me a hundred that night we were looking for An-hell, but that won't even get me started. Should I ask Jake for the rest? I could tell him what the money was for and tell him he could take it out of my future earnings for selling his stolen stuff on eBay. But do I want to tell Jake about my plan? No, he's such a nice guy, he'd probably insist on springing for an expensive regular funeral. And I kind of like the idea of us humans turning into ashes after we die. The dust-to-dust thing. No, I'd rather just do this on my own. Maybe I can earn enough commissions by selling his stuff on eBay to pay for it myself. After all, I've got thirty days to get down there to the county morgue and claim her body.

The body is corporal, and life is ephemeral. It is the only truth worth contemplating.

"I don't know what you mean by that, Old Man, but I'm not going to let my Mom get thrown out with the trash. I'll get the six hundred somehow."

Staring at all the internet ads about funerals and cremations makes me think about David. He said his family had money. I bet he got a full-on funeral. David. The kid was a puzzle. Kind of happy-go-lucky, but determined to knock himself off. And then he went and got himself shot. Why was he in such a hurry to die? Was it because his mother didn't pay any attention to him? Or because he didn't have any friends? Should I have tried harder to be his friend? But then his sister Lilly was his friend, and that didn't deter him. And of course, that thought makes me think about Lilly. I wonder if she even went to her brother's funeral. I suppose she did. And then she said she was taking off to Alaska with some guy. In a big truck. I wonder what she's looking for up there. Hard to imagine a warm-weather LA girl up there in all that ice and snow. Maybe after her little brother's death, she just wanted to go somewhere very different. Maybe she went up there hoping to figure out what it all means. Is that what I'm doing? Spending all my time on the computer trying to figure out what it all means? Maybe she and I are a lot alike, both of us trying to find answers, even though we both know there aren't any.

I try to focus on the computer, but I feel irritable. With the way things are going to shit, feeling irritable feels right to me. I think feeling pissed off at the world's nonsense is the only logical way a person *should* feel, don't you? What I need to do is refocus on being logical. I should stop thinking about sad things like Mom and David and Lilly, and just get on with my studying. Being sad doesn't do me one damn bit of good. Like I told you before, my rule of life is to *foster doubt*—question everything and believe in nothing except that which has solid proof. If I'm going to survive in this shit world, I have to always be on my toes and ever watchful for the world's phony crap. Everybody thinks they know what's best, but the truth is nobody knows shit. They're just trying to convince themselves. Real truth lies in knowing you don't know, and that takes guts. The real truth is that we are surrounded by con artists and crooks, swindlers and charlatans. Hustlers, all of them. And TV is the worst hustler of them all. I remember those nights when Mom couldn't get anybody to take her out to a bar. She'd spend all night in front of that damn TV. If she hadn't got anybody to buy her a bottle of her favorite brand of Scotch, she'd spend the night drinking cheap gin in tonic water while she watched the sitcoms, which as far as I could tell, were nothing but old re-packaged jokes about sex, accompanied by cattle-prod laugh tracks that demand you guffaw on cue. When the evening sitcoms were over, the TV entertainment "news" would come on with all the latest gossip about who was screwing who and what new plastic surgery some star had. Mom was all caught up in that movie-star shit. She was sure that someday she'd get "discovered," and then she'd become a big star too. I think it was because we lived in LA, and even though our neighborhood was a damn slum, we weren't all that far from Hollywood. I guess watching that entertainment news must have given her some kind of weird hope. There she'd be, curled up on the couch in front of that TV, fussing with her long red hair while the TV commentators rambled on about all that movie nonsense. The truth is, those TV shows, and even the TV news, had only one purpose, to sell her crap—cars and car insurance, plastic baby diapers and dumb-looking clothes that nobody in their right mind would ever wear. And what is it with all those different brands of beer? Every one of them claiming to be better than all the others, even though they probably all came out of the same giant vat. Worst of all were the late-night TV ads: "Call right now and we'll double the offer." Mom used to keep the phone right next to her, and when she'd get drunk enough, she'd call those phone numbers and spend what little money we had buying magic house-cleaning sponges (even though she never did any house cleaning) and miracle food choppers (even though she hardly ever cooked anything that didn't come out of a can). Worst of all are the politicians on TV. They'll do anything or say anything to get themselves elected. They'll create phony enemies which always leads to phony wars. They're perfectly willing to send young Americans off to stupid wars that kill millions of innocent people, just to get elected. To keep their wars going, they encourage us to get into the good old you-versus-meism of patriotism: us "good" guys against all those "other" bad people who don't happen to live inside the dotted lines that define as "our" country. Like I was telling you before, patriotism is one of those grand narratives, and it's our grand narrative of patriotism that gets us involved in all those ridiculous foreign wars. It's our grand narrative of patriotism that makes it okay for us to kill all those "others," especially if we can do it by dropping bombs on them from airplanes or pilotless drones so we don't have to get our hands dirty. It's our grand narrative of patriotism that tells us that "those" people are not like us; therefore, they are *less than* us. And the people of this fine country, like a bunch of hypnotized guppies, go for it every time.

But not me. I know it's all a bunch of crap made up by lying politicians who want to get elected and lying military generals who only want to get another row of medals on their stupid chests. Flags and parades as we march off to yet another glorious war. How stupid can people be? But I *will not* be stupid. I will foster doubt and be smart.

I hear somebody come up onto the porch. Then comes the impatient knocking that means the cops are back. But why would they come back again? Did they find out about what Jake and I did? No, how could they? We buried that asshole An-hell and his bloody hammer real good, way out in the desert.

I roll my chair to the dining room window and pull the curtain aside. Cop Kelly is standing out there on the porch staring at me. He knew I would look out the window before I opened the door. Maybe he's not as dumb as he seems.

"Now what do you want, Kelly?" I say through the glass.

He raps on the glass. "Go open the door, kid." His voice is muffled by the glass, but I can tell he's pissed off about something.

He points toward the door. "Now, kid!"

I'm not letting that son of bitch in without Cop Johnson here to protect me. I yell, "No way. I don't have to let you in unless you've got a warrant."

"You want me to kick in this window? Is that what you want?" He steps back and lifts his boot.

I don't think he'll do it. The broken glass would prove he forced his way in without a warrant.

Then a dark-skinned woman appears from behind him. She grabs his arm and pulls him back. "Let me talk to him," she says. She holds a card up to the window that I can't read through the dirty glass. "I'm from county services," she says. "I need to talk to your grandmother."

Why would somebody from the county be coming to see Grandma? And why is she with Cop Kelly?

I decide I have to let them in. If I don't, they might try to make trouble for Grandma.

I roll to the front door and open it. "Yeah, what do you want?"

Cop Kelly pushes the county services lady out of the way and shakes his stupid finger in my face. "Don't lip off to her, kid. We know what you been up to. Livin' off your poor old grandmother. Stealin' from her. Hell, for all we know she might already be dead and you're—"

The county services lady steps in front of him. "Now, now. Let's not get all upset here until we know all the facts. I just need to talk to your grandmother, son. I need to make sure she's all right."

I say, "Why shouldn't she be all right?" I point to her back bedroom with my thumb. "Hear that TV blasting back there? She watches her soap operas all day long. I make sure she's taken good care of. I fix her food. She's happy just staying in bed most of the time watching those silly—"

" Nevertheless," says the woman, "I just have to talk to her. There have been some complaints."

"Complaints?" I look over her shoulder at Cop Kelly. "From who? Him?"

She glances back at him. "No, from your neighbors. Officer Kelly talked to them."

I'm still keeping my eyes on Kelly. "Complaints from my neighbors? They've hardly ever seen me." I look hard at Kelly. "Did you have to kick the shit out of them like you did me to force them to make a complaint?"

He again pushes the county services lady out of the way and gets in my face. "You want to resist a legal process, kid? Is that what you're doin'? Resistin'?"

Again, the county services lady steps in front of him. "You say she likes to watch TV? Back there?" She points. "I'll just go in and say hello."

I back my wheelchair out of her way. "Go right ahead. Maybe she'll talk to you. Unless some stupid soap opera actress is about to get her heart broken again for about the hundredth time. If so, you'll have to wait for the commercial."

The county services lady squeezes past me. "I'll just be a minute."

"I'll be right behind you," I say. "You're not leaving me out here with *Officer* Kelly. He likes to kick us cripples."

The three of us head down the hallway, the county services lady leading the way. I stay close to her, and I swear I can hear low growling coming from behind me, like Cop Kelly has turned into a damn pit bull dog or something.

In Grandma's bedroom, the TV is blaring as usual, and as usual, Grandma's eyes are locked on the TV screen as she munches on her favorite snack, the chocolate chip cookies I order for her from Amazon.com..

The county services lady goes to grandma's bedside and says, "Excuse me, ma'am. Can I talk to you for a minute?"

Grandma won't even look at her. She just waves her away. It's like she thinks the county services lady is a pesky fly.

On the TV screen, a very tall man in a military uniform and a very short woman in a flimsy bathrobe are locked in a passionate embrace. But the man in the uniform seems to want to leave. He has his hand on the doorknob of the front door. Neither of the actors are speaking, but violin music is starting to build in the background. Grandma seems to be holding her breath, waiting to see what's going to happen. I glance at the county services lady. She also has her eyes on the TV screen. Is she holding her breath too?

Cop Kelly pushes past us and turns off the TV. "All right. I've seen enough.

This kid is holding his poor old grandmother captive in this dark room while he steals all her money. Probably keeps her drugged up back here and feeds her sweets so she'll die soon."

Grandma has a stunned look on her face as she continues to stare at the blank screen. She must think the world has just ended, leaving her alone in a void without TV soap operas.

"Let's go," says Cop Kelly. He takes the county services lady by the elbow and tries to lead her out of the room.

But the woman is tougher than she looks. She shakes off his grip and stares him down. "You brought me here to talk to his woman, and that's exactly what I'm going to do."

She sits on the edge of Grandma's bed. "I'm sorry to disturb you, ma'am. This will just take a minute. I need to know if you are being well taken care of. Are you?"

Grandma finally seems to realize the TV has been turned off. She looks at the county services lady. "He left her, didn't he? I knew he was going to."

I'm not sure the county services lady even understands that Grandma is talking about the soap opera show on the TV. Grandma hasn't made the adjustment back to the real world yet.

The county services lady nods and says, "We'll be leaving in just a few minutes. I just need to know if your grandson here is taking good care of you." She points at me.

Grandma looks at me, still bewildered.

I say, "She wants to know if you're all right, grandma. Just say you're fine, and then she'll leave, and you can go back to your TV show."

Cop Kelly gets ahold of the back of my chair and jerks me backward. "Don't be trying to stop her from talking, kid. Just shut your trap."

"I mean are you getting enough to eat, ma'am? Does he feed you all right?"

Grandma frowns and looks back at the blank TV screen. "Only mushroom soup."

"There. Didn't I tell you," says Cop Kelly.

"It's all she likes to eat," I say. "That and toasted cheese sandwiches."

Cop Kelly grabs the back of my neck and leans down to snarl at me. "Didn't I just tell you to shut up?"

As usual, I smell pepperoni on his breath. Does this guy live on pepperoni pizza?

"Mushroom soup?" asks the county services lady.

"Yes. But half the time he goes gallivanting off, and I have to ring my bell like this." She picks up her little bell and shakes it. "He doesn't come for a long time."

I quickly say, "The only time that even happened was when Cop Kelly here dragged me off to the desert so he could kick the shit out of me."

"That's it," says Kelly. He gets ahold of the handles of my wheelchair and rushes me out of the room.

When he gets me back out to the dining room, I say," Do you want me to lie down on the floor to make it easier for you to kick me?"

He gets in my face and grins. "So you're still playin' the smart ass. How about this?" He leans down to put his hands on my knees. "Didn't you say your knees were all fucked up? Which one? This one?"

He squeezes my right knee, the one that's not hurt quite as bad, but I pretend it hurts like hell and yelp as loud as I can so the woman in the other room will hear. "Quit that," I yell. "That hurts, you sadistic bastard."

"It's supposed to hurt, asshole. And it's gonna keep on hurting until you tell me what you know. Guess what I found out?"

He squeezes my knee again, and I yelp again.

"Remember that Mexican guy your landlord told us about? Well, it seems him and your mother hung out at a certain bar, and they often left together. We go lookin' for the guy, and guess what we found out? His landlady says now *he's* disappeared. Didn't come home the other night. Quite a coincidence, eh? You find out your mother's been murdered, and next thing we know, our main suspect disappears."

He squeezes my knee again, and I dutifully do my yelp sound again. "A Mexican is your main suspect? He probably heard you were looking for him and took off across the border. You'll never see him again."

"Bullshit. He didn't take any of his clothes. Not even his toothbrush. If he took off, he took off fast. And I bet you know why, don't ya? What aren't you telling me, kid?"

He squeezes my knee again, even harder, but this time I don't bother to yelp. Instead, I say, "You know, officer, when I first hurt my legs and was in the hospital, a couple of queer guys came to my room to try to shake me down. One of them was a real character. You shoulda seen his weird tattoos. He did that same thing. Squeezed my hurt knee to try to get me to pay him off. You and him outta get together. I think you'd make a fine couple."

That puts him over the edge. He lifts his hand to give my face a good smack, but unfortunately for him, the county services lady chooses that moment to come out of Grandma's bedroom. She says, "What's going on here?"

"Oh, nothing out of the ordinary," I say. "Officer Kelly just likes to hurt people."

Kelly, drops his hand and tries to look innocent. "Well, what did you find out?"

"She seems okay. She could use a more complex diet, but she seems healthy enough."

"Bullshit," says Cop Kelly. "I think she looks about half dead. And what about how she hardly knew we were there? She's out of it."

The county services lady nods. "Yes, dementia does seem to be setting in. Not all that unusual at her age. I'll have a county nurse come by and evaluate her more fully."

Cop Kelly looks at me. "What about him? I think he's been neglecting her. Aren't you gonna put that in your report?"

The county services lady puts a hand on my shoulder and looks me in my eyes. "Are you really capable of taking good care of her, son? I mean with you being in a wheelchair and all."

"That's right," says Cop Kelly. "The old lady belongs in a home or something."

The county services lady shakes her head. "No, not, at this time. Overall, she seems to be doing all right here."

I jump in before Cop Kelly can try to talk her out of it. "Of course she is. I take good care of her. In fact, that's all I do. My screwed up legs mean I can't go out or anything, so I just stay here and take care of her. I try to get her to eat better. I really do. But like I said, she only eats what she likes. If I fix her anything else, she won't eat it."

Even though Cop Kelly is scowling at her, the county services lady seems ready to accept what I'm saying. She nods and says, "All right. I'll have a nutritionist come by to talk to you about her diet. And I'll schedule a nurse to come by periodically to check on her."

I quickly say, "Good. Thank you. That would be a big help."

The county services lady heads for the front door, leaving Cop Kelly fuming. He leans down close to my face. "I know you know a lot more than you're sayin', asshole. From now on, I'm on your case. And you can forget about stealing your grandma's money from now on. I'm gonna talk to her bank and make sure they cut you off. For good. You hear me, asshole?"

I give him a snappy salute. "Loud and clear, officer."

He gives my right knee a seemingly friendly pat, but of course it's plenty hard enough to hurt.

I just smile at him and wave goodbye. "See ya."

He shakes his head in disgust and follows the county services lady out the door.

I hurry to lock it and roll to the dining room window to watch them as they leave. She goes to a car with some kind of official county seal on the front door.

Cop Kelly follows her. He's pointing at my house. I think he's trying to talk her into something, but she isn't going for it. Luckily for me, she's got a mind of her own. She gets into her car and drives away.

Cop Kelly goes to his cop car and opens the door, but he doesn't get in. He stares at my house, probably trying to decide if he can figure out a way to justify running me in. Finally, he gets into his car and drives away. I roll my chair back away from the window, and Pretty Boy uses it as a signal to fly down from his perch on the curtain rod to land on my shoulder. He turns his head sideways to look at me.

"Well, Pretty Boy, glad to see you're smart enough to stay away from that sadistic asshole. Unfortunately, I don't think it's the last we're gonna see of him."

19
The Structural Features of Consciousness

I'm on the computer, reading about new ways to look at the world at the quantum level, when I hear a knock at the door. It turns out to be a Hispanic-looking nurse from country services. As soon as I let her in, Pretty Boy tries to fly down and land on her shoulder, and although she shoos him away, I take it as a good sign: if Pretty Boy likes her, she can't be all bad. Maybe she'll see I'm taking good care of Grandma and not bother us anymore.

I follow her into Grandma's bedroom, and we find her sound asleep even though the TV is blaring. I go over to turn the volume down, and that wakes Grandma up. She stares at me, blinking, and then turns to look at the county nurse. It's like she's not sure if this is a real nurse or one of the many nurses she sees on her TV soap operas.

The nurse introduces herself, and says she just needs to do a few tests. She opens her bag and puts a blood pressure cuff on Grandma's arm. Then, she takes Grandma's pulse.

Grandma ignores her and continues to watch her TV.

The nurse writes down the results of her tests, and then shines a little light in grandma's eyes.

Grandma doesn't like that and tries to wave her away.

The nurse takes out a little piece of paper and says, I'm going to read you a few words. I want you to try to remember them. All right?"

She slowly reads a short list of words, but Grandma ignores her and keeps her eyes on the TV where, by chance, it's yet another soap opera about a nurse. The TV nurse is talking to her boyfriend on the phone, telling him she's sure she's carrying his baby.

The real nurse tries again to get Grandma to memorize the words, but Grandma is fully involved in what the fake nurse in the TV show is saying.

The real nurse finally gives up and waves for me to follow her out to the dining room. There, she carefully explains to me what I already knew, that grandma seems to be fairly healthy, but is clearly showing signs of dementia. The real nurse somberly suggests it might be the early signs of Alzheimer's disease. She asks me a bunch of questions about how long Grandma has been having memory issues.

I tell her it's been gradual.

The nurse asks if I've noticed any changes in her behavior or eating habits lately.

I tell her no, that's just the way Grandma is. She likes her TV and her cookies, and that she mostly likes to eat mushroom soup and toasted cheese sandwiches.

That seems to satisfy the nurse. She makes some notes, tells me to get Grandma some multivitamins, and then she leaves.

I roll to the window and watch her get into a car and drive away. I hope that's the last we'll see of her.

I roll back to my computer and Google Alzheimer's disease. It gives me 83,400,000 results. I read about it on Wikipedia, which says it's a hard-to-diagnose degenerative neurological disease first noted in 1906 by a German psychiatrist named Alois Alzheimer. It says there is no cure, and its symptoms —caused by the disease's increasing physical damage to the brain—include confusion, mood swings, and progressively worse memory loss. Doesn't sound like Grandma; she *is* out of it, but she's been like that for a long time, and I haven't noticed her getting much worse. But I decide I'd better keep a closer eye on her to try to determine what she can remember and what she can't.

That reminds me, that woman said I should get some multivitamins for Grandma. I'd better put in a new food order at Amazon. I log onto the Amazon website and put the usual food stuff into my shopping cart. I add a couple of big bottles of multivitamins and select the "pay by electronic check" option, as usual. But it instantly comes back saying the transaction was not approved. What the hell? I try to put through the order again, but I get the same result. Damn it! Cop Kelly said he was going to stop me from using Grandma's money. Did he go to Grandma's bank? How the hell did he even find out which bank her account was at? The son of a bitch is so eager to get me, he must have gone to every bank in the neighborhood until he found the right one. Probably told them there was some kind of police investigation going on about money being illegally withdrawn from Grandma's account.

Now what? How am I going to get money to pay for our food? I've still got the two twenties and the hundred Jake gave me, but I'm going to need that for Mom's cremation. It means I'll have get Grandma used to writing out checks to me for cash. More important, it means I'm going to have to leave this house to get us food. Damn that Cop Kelly. Why did he have to stick his nose in?

When it comes time for lunch, I make Grandma's food and take it into her bedroom. Of course, she's totally engrossed in yet another stupid soap opera. I put her lunch on her bedside table, but she hardly seems to notice. Maybe that nurse lady is right. Maybe Grandma's mind really is going. But there's no way

I'm going to let them put her in some kind of home. She'd hate that, and besides, I bet those places are expensive. Her dole money would run out real quick, and then what? What do they do with old people like her if they have no money? Put them out on the street like all those people I saw downtown on skid row? I don't even want to think about that. I'll find a way to take care of her. I'll call Jake and get him to find us more stuff to sell on eBay.

I stand by Grandma's bedroom door and watch her. She doesn't seem interested in eating. I can tell from the violin music on the TV that the soap opera is building to a crescendo. She won't eat until the commercial comes on.

I go to her dresser and get her checkbook out of the top drawer. "I say, "Time to pay the bills, Grandma. I fill out the usual checks and make one extra with the payee and amount lines blank. I can fill in my own name and the amount later and take it to the bank to get some cash. She dutifully signs the checks, the way she always does, with one eye on her TV show. She doesn't seem to notice the extra blank check. I tell her I have to go out shopping, and to be sure to eat her lunch before it gets cold. I'm not even sure she hears me because she's watching a man and a woman on the TV argue. The woman seems pissed off about something, and she's crying into a very clean little white hanky. Same old crap.

I go to my bedroom to get my cane, but as soon as I stand up, I realize I shouldn't have been depending on my wheelchair so much. My legs may be pretty well healed up, but it still hurts like hell to put much weight on them, especially the left one. I take a few deep breaths and try to put my mind where the pain isn't. Ready or not, I have to go out. No choice. I use Jake's cell phone to call a cab and head for the front door, telling myself over and over, there is no pain, there is no such thing as pain.

At the bank, as soon as I try to cash Grandma's check that's made out to me, the teller sends me to a woman who's sitting at a nearby desk. She seems overly polite as she tells me my grandmother will have to come in and cash the check herself. I tell her my grandmother is bedridden, but the woman says there's nothing she can do about it. Rules are rules.

I ask her if I can talk to the person who makes up those rules.

She says the person is not available.

I ask her if it's a mystical person that is never available, and while she's fumbling for an answer, I suggest she might need to see a shrink if she's been imagining mystical people who make up rules.

Between gritted teeth, she says that if I don't leave right now, she's going to call the police.

So I leave. Pointless to talk to a robot.

After I go out, I look back through the glass doors. She's on the phone. Calling Cop Kelly, I bet.

I hobble down the street to the supermarket. As soon as I go through the automatic doors, it hits me: man, how long has it been since I was in one of these places? Endless rows of packaged and canned food. And a produce section too. At first, I just look. They've got just about every kind of vegetable and fruit you can think of. I pick up a tomato. How long has it been since I had a fresh tomato? I decide I should get one just for the experience. But then I notice the price. Jesus! That much for one tomato? How can people in this part of town afford any of this stuff? I decide to stick to the usual stuff I order online from Amazon, canned soup and canned tuna fish, jars of peanut butter. Oh yeah, and some cheese and bread and honey. That'll do. Eating that kind of stuff hasn't killed Grandma or me yet.

After I've finished the shopping, I use Jake's cell phone to call a cab. After I prove to the driver that I have just enough cash left to pay the fare, he delivers me right to Grandma's front door. I could get used to this cab way of getting around. A lot less painful than having to walk to the bus stop. On the other hand, it costs a lot more, and if I'm going to have to be going out to do the shopping from now on, I'd better get Jake to find me more stuff to sell. And then there's the problem of getting enough money to pay for Mom's cremation. The thirty days before the county cremates her and throws her into the trash are slipping away fast.

As I put the groceries away, I start to wonder why I haven't heard from Jake lately. In fact, I haven't heard from him since that night we buried An-hell out in the desert. Is he avoiding me because of that? He didn't seem mad at me for getting him involved that night; in fact, he was the one who took charge, but maybe he's had second thoughts.

I decide I'd better call him. But when I dial his number, all I get is an automated answering message. That's never happened before. He always answers his phone. I leave a message for him to call me.

I check on Grandma. She's sound asleep with the TV blaring. I sit down on the edge of her bed and look at her. She looks . . . old. And her face looks tired, even though she's been sleeping a lot lately. She's always had streaks of gray in her hair, but now, her hair has turned so gray it looks more like she has streaks of brown in it. It makes me wonder what would have become of her if I had been successful at knocking myself off that night at the cliff. And what about when that gangbanger stabbed me? He could have hit something vital inside of me, and then she'd have been left here all alone. I again wonder what happens to old people in LA if they are all alone and have no money. I should look that up on the internet. But after I roll into my bedroom and get on the computer, I change my mind; I don't want to know. There's no *need* to know: I'm not going anywhere. I'll take care of her, for as long as she's got left.

I stare at the computer screen. I can't concentrate on anything to study because I keep thinking about what Cop Kelly could be up to. He's probably still out there looking for An-hell. I hope that as soon as he realizes there are no more murders of redheaded women taking place, he'll decide An-hell took off for Mexico, and he'll move on to other cases. In a city like LA, he must have plenty of other murder cases, so it shouldn't take him long to forget about a few lonely redheaded bar-type women that got themselves knocked off. What's a few more unsolved murders in a place like LA? Everybody will forget about it, and life will go on.

I suddenly remember the last time I saw Mom. She came into my bedroom to tell me she was going out. I just said, "Who cares?" and turned back to my computer. She frowned at my attitude, but kissed my cheek anyhow. Now, I wonder why I acted like that. But why not? How could I know that would be the last time I would ever see her? She was always going out at night, and she always came back, eventually.

I go to the Google site and get ready to type in a new search subject. But I can't think what to study. I wonder why my brain isn't working right. Maybe I'm betting burned out from studying too much. Maybe I should take a break from studying for a while. Maybe I should write something. Maybe I should write a novel about my shitty life.

But then I notice a spider on the table. He's walking along right next to my computer. "Well, hello, mister spider."

He stops. Did he hear me? Is he looking at me? How can you tell what a spider is looking at?

"What kind of spider are you?" I ask.

He doesn't move. Just sits there, looking up at me.

I decide to look up spiders on the internet. This old house is full of spiders, so I guess I should try to find out what type they are. Some of them might be dangerous. This one looks kind of tough, shiny black and bulbous, with some kind of orange shape on its back. I find a bunch of sites on the internet with pictures of spiders. My spider turns out to be the black widow type. It says it's poisonous, and if it bites you, you might have a strong reaction, depending on how allergic to its venom you are. It says the black widow spider is one of the few spiders that has fangs strong enough to bite through human skin. But it also says they are not especially aggressive. If you leave them alone, they won't bite you. It says they only eat bugs. In fact, the site says that without spiders, we would be overrun with bugs. It says some of the spider webs they use to catch bugs are so strong they can catch full-grown butterflies, and if you could weave the web strands into a rope, it would be stronger than any rope in the world. I lean down to get a closer look at my spider. "Okay then mister black widow spider, it says you eat bugs, and that you won't bother me if I don't bother you. So I won't. In this old house, anything that helps get rid of bugs can only be a good thing." But then I think about my mattress being on the floor. It he came over there for a visit, I might roll over onto him in my sleep. In that case, he probably *would* bite me. I think about getting something to swat him with, but then I realize there isn't any reason to kill him. I decide to go find a bottle and catch him. I could feed him bugs. Pretty Boy and I can watch him to see what he does.

I wheel into the kitchen and find a bottle under the sink. But when I come back, he's gone. Where the heck could he have gone so fast? I look under my computer, and sure enough, there he is. Maybe he likes it under there. Maybe he likes the heat it produces. I use the bottle to scoop him up, and then I screw the lid on tight. I put the bottle down on the table and lean forward to watch him. He walks around the bottom of the bottle a few times, but soon, he seems to figure out he's just walking in circles. He stops and just sits there. He's staring at me again, probably pissed off at me for putting him in a bottle. Maybe he'll get bored in there. I wonder what he'd do if I gave him a friend. Would they get along, or would they fight like humans do when you put them together in a prison?

I wheel to the closet and open it. Plenty of spiders in there, but all of them are spindly little things with long skinny legs. The internet said the black widow spider was the only poisonous spider in California, so these can't hurt me. I grab the biggest one by the legs. He squirms to get away, but I hold onto him and take him back into my bedroom. I open the jar and drop him in. He takes one look at my black widow and scurries to the other side of the bottle. After that, they just sit there watching each other. Neither of them moves. Boring. I decide spiders are not very interesting and go back to surfing the internet.

What now? Wasn't there something I was about to do yesterday? I was reading up on how humans perceive time. One site said we humans experience what is known as the "arrow of time," the sense that we are in the present, have moved out of the past, and are moving into the future. But is that real?

I Google "perception of time," and some of the sites talk about *presentism*, a philosophical doctrine in which only things that occur in the present moment exist. What does it mean? I read on, and it says the Buddhists believe in something like that, a sort of spiritual presentism. They think that since everything in the past is no longer real, and everything in the future is not yet real, the only real reality is the present moment. I like that. Maybe I should try to live like that. Maybe it would make me stop thinking about my mom up there in the desert in that shallow grave, nothing left of her except a skeleton in a fancy going-out-on-the-town dress. But no, I might as well face the fact that I'm never going to forget that sight, no matter what I study.

I read on. I wonder if the concept of presentism could be related to Einstein's theories of relativity. He said that no matter what our senses might be telling us, we are actually at a specific point in space *and* time. He said motion changes reality—not just our perceptions of reality, but actual reality. It's his famous "frame of reference" concept. As we move faster, he said time would not appear to be slowing down, but it really would be slowing down relative to anyone who is not traveling that fast. He called it *time dilation*. I'm not sure where that leads me with regard to the philosophical concept of presentism, but it's interesting.

Searching on, I find a site that talks about an opposing group who believe in something called eternalism, which is the belief that all points in time are equally real.

I think about that. It seems like Einstein's theory of relativity could also support that idea. He said time was just another dimension, a fourth dimension in addition to our usual observable three dimensions. If time itself speeds up or slows down, depending on how fast we are moving, then time is *relative*. Could that mean everything is happening simultaneously, and we just *perceive* it as time passing? I wonder what quantum mechanics might have to say about this, and I'm about to look that up when Pretty Boy flies in to land on my shoulder. He gives me a few loud tweets in my ear. I know what they means: he's trying to get my attention.

I look at him. "Okay, Pretty Boy, what do you want?"

He says, "Pretty Boy," louder than usual.

I'm not sure what he means by that, but he's staring at me fervently (good word, eh?), obviously trying to tell me something. I glance toward the other room. "Is there something wrong out there?"

He says, "Pretty Boy," and then he repeats it, which always means something significant, although I can't always tell what it might be. But if Pretty Boy says something needs my attention, I'd better go check it out. I back my wheelchair up and roll out into the other room. Maybe Pretty Boy is just upset because he's running low on bird seed.

But no, he doesn't fly into the kitchen, he flies down the hallway and into Grandma's room. What the hell? He never goes in there because he knows Grandma doesn't like him.

I follow, but when I get to Grandma's bedroom, I don't see Pretty Boy anywhere. Grandma, of course, is watching her TV and doesn't even seem to notice I'm there. But where did Pretty Boy go?

I look toward Grandma's bathroom. The door is open. Did he fly in there? But why?

I wheel my way around the end of Grandma's bed and past her TV.

She's watching me, wondering what I'm up to.

I roll into her bathroom, and I'm shocked to see that her bathroom window is wide open. Pretty Boy is sitting on the sill looking out.

"No," I shout. "Pretty Boy! Don't go out there."

But he's not looking at me. He's caught up in staring at something outside the window.

I roll toward him, but I don't want to move too fast. If I scare him, he might fly out, and then who knows what would happen to him? Would he come back, or would he get lost out there in the great big world, a place he knows nothing about?

I roll up to the window and slowly stand up, being careful not to make any sudden movements. Now I can see what he's looking at our there: several large crows are sitting in a tree. I doubt if Pretty Boy has ever seen another bird. Maybe he's thinking about flying out there to join them. Does he have any conception of how big those birds are compared to him? I carefully put my finger up against his little chest, and he dutifully climbs up on it. I hold him at arm's length, away from the window, while I reach back to close it.

Pretty Boy let's out a few tweets and flies right back to the windowsill. I'm not sure if he's upset that I didn't let him go out there, or if he just wants to look some more.

I again force him up onto my finger, and this time I pinch his little toes to make sure he can't fly away again.

He complains with a few loud tweets.

"Yes, I know, Pretty Boy. Those big birds are interesting, but it's dangerous out there."

Keeping ahold of his toes, I use one hand to clumsily wheel myself out of Grandma's bathroom. I close the door behind me and place Pretty Boy on my shoulder. He continues to complain with another round of loud tweets in my ear.

I turn to Grandma. She's still watching me.

"You left your bathroom window open, Grandma. You can't do that. Pretty Boy almost flew out."

She frowns at me. "I had to open it. It was stinky in there."

"Well, if you have to open the window, keep your bathroom door closed so Pretty Boy can't get in there."

"I'll do whatever I want to. This is my house. It's not that stupid bird's house."

I roll closer to the bed. "Listen, Grandma. I know it's your house. But I'm the one who has to take care of things around here. Don't I take care good care of you?"

She looks at her TV, refusing to look at me. "You'd better. You think you can live here for nothing?"

"Grandma, listen to me. If you want your bathroom window open, just keep the door closed. Okay? Besides, I wouldn't think you'd want to leave that window open. What if a burglar climbed in? You wouldn't want that would you? Think about all those gangbangers out there."

She still won't look at me, but I think she got the message.

I leave her to her TV and wheel back to my bedroom. Pretty Boy stays on my shoulder, but from the way he's staring at me, I can tell he's waiting for an explanation.

"It's hard to explain, Pretty Boy, but the fact is, there's a bigger world outside this house. It's a different kind of reality out there, a reality you wouldn't understand."

He turns his head sideways to stare at me with his unblinking little black eye.

"There's a big bad world outside that window, Pretty Boy, and there are some big bad birds in it. They might hurt you."

I can tell he doesn't believe me, or at least not that part about there being bad birds. To make his point that he doesn't believe me, he flies off of my shoulder and goes up to perch way up on the curtain rod.

"Well, you can sit up there and pout if you want to, Pretty Boy, but it's the truth."

I go back to my computer, but now, I'm worried that he's curious about those other birds out there. I'd better check often to make sure Grandma doesn't leave that window open anymore.

I resume my reading about the concept of time on some physics sites, but I'm not finding much of interest. Looks like physicists are a hard-nosed bunch; they like to speculate about the nature of matter, but they don't seem all that interested in the nature of reality.

I glance at my spider bottle. Speaking of the big bad world outside of this house, I should throw those two spiders out. I bet they'd be a lot happier outside where there are more bugs to eat. "Okay, you two, time for you to go out." I pick up the bottle, but I can only see one spider in there, the black widow. Where is the other one? I figure he must be hiding up under the lid. I carefully unscrew the lid, but he's not under there. I look down into the bottle and mister black widow looks up at me. I ask him, "What happened to the other spider? Did you eat him?"

He just stares at me. I can tell he doesn't care what I think. If he wants to eat another spider, it's up to him, but how did he do it so fast?

"Well, if you ate him that fast, you sure are a quick eater. Tell you what, I'm going to put you outside. Out there, you can eat all the spiders and bugs you want to. How about that?"

He just continues to stare up at me.

I make sure Pretty Boy is nowhere around, and I open the front door just enough to shake the spider out of the bottle onto the front porch. "So long little spider. Have fun out there in the big bad world."

20
Introspective Reflectivity and Experience

I wake up from a bad dream. I know it was bad because of the anxiousness I'm feeling, but I can't quite remember what the dream was about. Something about being trapped in a dark place.

I look toward the window and see that it's still dark outside. How long did I sleep? Not long, by the look of it. By the light of my computer's screen, I can see that Pretty Boy is still up on the curtain rod. Did he stay up there all the time I was sleeping? He usually spends at least some of the night out in the dining room on the top edge of his lampshade. If he stayed up on that curtain rod staring down at me all night, it must mean he's still mad at me. On the other hand, maybe it's because I scared him with my description of the big bad world outside, and he's staying close to me for assurance. After all, I'm the only thing he's got in this world. He depends on me for food and water, and most of all, for companionship. Maybe I made him feel insecure with all my talk about the world outside this house. I hope so. It might convince him to stay away from open windows and doors.

I get up and get back on the computer, but before I can decide what to study today, I remember what my bad dream was about. I was trapped in a dark place, a basement I think, and there was somebody, or something, down there with me. For some reason, it seems like it might have been David. Maybe he was a ghost that hung around down there in that dark basement. Dumb dream. I don't believe in ghosts. But in the dream, there was something scary about him, so I kept on trying to get out of that dark place, trying to get away from whatever it was. But every time I went through a door, it only led to other dark rooms. It was like the basement was enormous, with more and more cold dark rooms, and in every new room, the David-like thing was there. But now that I think about it, I never actually saw him; it was more like I sensed him.

I shake off that stupid dream. I should think about something else. But it does get me to wondering why I dreamed about David. Am I feeling guilty that I offhandedly told him he could buy heroin on any street corner in this neighborhood, and that comment ended up getting him killed. Lilly blamed me, but how could I know he would do something as stupid as going to the projects to buy heroin? Thinking about it logically, I know I'm not really to blame, but maybe in my subconscious, I think I am. They say dreams are about what your subconscious is trying to tell you. I know better than to look up dream interpretation on the internet; I've looked at those kinds of web sites before, and I know they're all a bunch of nonsense. Besides, I can interpret this dream myself. I've got death on my mind. No surprise there. And I'm thinking about how to get enough money to pay for Mom's cremation. I can only hope Jake hurries up and brings me more stuff to sell on eBay. But what if he doesn't have anything for me to fence right now? I really might have to ask him to loan me the money, against future sales. Six hundred bucks wouldn't mean anything to him, but I'd have to be sure he doesn't try to pay for it himself. Look what happened the last time I got him involved.

I call him again, but again, I get only his automated answering message. That seems odd to me. Shouldn't a businessman like Jake always answer his phone? Maybe he's avoiding me. I leave another message asking him to call me when he gets a chance. That done, I sit and stare at the cell phone. Not only haven't I heard from Jake for a while, I haven't heard from Denesa either. Why doesn't she ever come by anymore? And why hasn't she asked me to watch her kids? I miss them. It's like everybody in my life is disappearing. My mom. David. And now Lilly has run off to Alaska. Not only that, for some reason, Old Man isn't talking to me either. What the hell is going on? Is everybody avoiding me? Maybe it's time to get back on the internet and spend some time with the old-time philosophers again. But before I can decide which one I want to talk to, I hear somebody pounding on the front door. Loud pounding. That means it can't be Denesa, and it can't be Jake either because he just taps on my bedroom window before he goes to the front door. That only leaves the cops. I hope it's not Cop Kelly again. Hasn't he caused me enough trouble?

I roll out into the dining room and peek out of the front window. Sure enough, it's Cop Kelly.

I roll to the door and talk to him through it. "What do you want this time, Kelly?"

"Let me in. I need to talk to you."

"Are you by yourself?"

"Yes, I'm alone."

"Then I'm not opening this door. My ribs are barely healed up from the last time you decided you wanted to *talk* to me."

"Open this door, kid. I'm not going to hurt you. I have some information you'll wanna know about."

"No thanks, Kelly. Like I told you before, I don't know anything. Leave me alone."

"Open this door, or I'm gonna kick it in. Your old grandma won't like that too much, would she?"

I decide I'd better let him in. Hopefully, he won't hurt me too bad, not with Grandma in the other room. He doesn't know she's so focused on her TV, she probably wouldn't hear a thing.

I open the door. "Okay, Kelly, what do you want?"

He pushes his way in and closes the door.

Uh oh, what's he up to now?

He leans down close to my face. Oddly, he doesn't smell like pizza this time. It's late afternoon, so maybe he decided to have something different for lunch today.

He grins at me. "Guess what, kid. We got a witness."

"Oh yeah? A witness to what? Did somebody catch you beating up your prisoners?"

"Very funny, kid. You know what I'm talkin' about." He pauses for effect. "I'm talking about what you and that gang dude did to that spic."

I quickly say, "I have no idea what you're talking about, Kelly. I never go outside this house. Didn't you know? I'm a *hikikomori*."

"A hicky what?"

"Never mind. It just means I don't go out."

"Well, you went out *that* night. We got a woman who told us all about it. They picked her up on a DUI. Drunk as a skunk and weaving all over the road. And guess what? A redhead. Whatta ya think of that?"

"Yeah, so you picked up a redhead. Must be plenty of them in LA."

"Yeah, well it turns out this particular redhead had a little bitty pistol in her purse. Said she'd just got it. For self protection 'cause somebody was gonna kill her. That's when they called me in. Get it? Redhead? Somebody tryin' to kill her?"

I just stare at him, trying to keep a straight face. It must be that woman we saved from An-hell. How much did she tell him?

"Got your attention yet, kid? Well, it gets even more interesting. After I put the screws to her a bit, she starts singin'. Said she'd tell me something we needed to know real bad if we'd drop the DUI and weapons charges and give her protection. Long story short, we make the deal, and she starts tellin' me that one night some black guy forced her car off the road, and then he killed the guy she was with. A man she met at a bar, a guy known around the bar scene as "the Angel." She claimed this Angel guy told her he was from somewhere down in South America, and he was gonna take her down there, all expenses paid. But then this black guy shows up and shoots the Angel, right in front of her, then carts him away with some other guy helpin'. We show the woman some pictures, and she fingers the black dude. Turns out he's well known to us. A known gang member. Gang leader, actually. Record as long as your arm. Goes by the name of Jake the Dog. And guess what. He's known to hang around this very neighborhood. How about that? You wouldn't happen to know the guy, would ya?"

I shrug. "Doesn't ring a bell."

"I bet."

He stares at me, and I stare right back at him, trying not to show any emotion at all.

"Here's what I'm thinkin', kid? I'm thinkin' this Angel guy was the so-called Mexican your mother was hangin' around with. The guy that magically disappeared, you know? So, you got anything to say about that?"

I shrug. "About what? About some crazy drunk woman with a story about a shooting? And the dead guy supposedly gets carted away, which means you got no dead body to prove she isn't making the whole thing up. Why would I have anything to say about something like that?"

Kelly grins at me. "Okay, kid, if that's the way you wanna to play it. No skin off my nose. Fact is, if you paid some gang dude to get revenge for your mother's murder, fine with me. One more scumbag off the street is okay with me. Especially if he really was the one who was killing all those redheads." He leans down to look me in the eyes. "Listen, kid. Like I said, if you got this gangbanger, Jake, to kill the spic, it's no sweat off me. That's assuming this Angel dude really was the guy who killed your mom. You know, if no more redheaded women turn up dead, I might just decide to put this case to bed and move on. I got other cases to work on, ya know."

I shrug.

He straightens up and looks toward Grandma's bedroom.

What is he thinking?

He leans down close to me again, and whispers. "But listen, kid, when we find this Jake character and put the screws to *him*, he may talk to save his own skin. If that happens, I can't protect ya. Understand?"

I nod.

"Say it out loud."

"I understand."

He straightens up and takes a step back. "As long as we understand each other, you probably won't be seeing me again. That all right with you?"

"Yep."

He turns and heads for the door.

"Uh, officer. Could you also tell the bank to release the hold on my grandmother's account?"

He partially turns back. "You got a problem at the bank?"

"You know I do."

He grins at me. "Well, then maybe it's time you went out and got a job. Can't just sit here spongin' off your poor old grandma forever, now can you?"

He doesn't wait for my response. He's out the door and heading down the steps before I can come up with a way to try to get him to change his mind. Doesn't matter. Probably a waste of time to try to convince that asshole of anything. Better to leave well enough alone.

I wheel to the door and watch him get into his cop car. Some of my neighbors are out in their front yards, probably waiting for the show, waiting for the cops to drag me out in handcuffs. Too bad I had to disappoint them again. For now, they're stuck with a teenaged whitebread as a neighbor, whether they like it or not.

Kelly starts his cop car and heads off down the street, moving fast. I can only hope he's true to his word, and that's the last time I'll see him.

As soon as I get back into my bedroom, I decide I'd better call Jake to warn him. I punch in his number and get the automated answering message again. I say "Hey Jake, you remember that sadistic cop I told you about? Well, he came by this morning with a story about a woman squealing about something that happened." I hesitate. Should I say more? I don't want him to think I gave anything away to the cop. I add, "The cop had your name. They're looking for you. But listen, Jake, I didn't say a thing. Call me back to let me know what to do. If you can't call me, try to find a way to let me know you're okay."

I click the phone off. Now, at least he knows they're after him, and he knows it wasn't me that talked. I sure hope he can get away. Maybe he already knows the cops are after him, and that's why I haven't heard from him. He must be laying low.

I get back on the computer, but pretty soon, I hear a car pull up outside. Is it Jake? I roll to the window and pull back the curtain. It's a low rider, shining black and lowered more in the back than in the front. A gang car. Is Jake in there? The car has darkened windows all around, so it's hard to tell how many are inside. The car's rumbling exhaust pipes sound ominous, which I suppose, is exactly the sound they want.

This time, the neighbors don't come outside. Can't blame them. They also know what a gang car looks like.

A hefty dark-skinned guy hops out of the car and hurries up onto my front porch. I don't recognize the guy, but it's for damn sure he's a gang member. Tattoos all over him. Is he in Jake's gang?

He bangs on the door.

Damn, that was loud. I hope he didn't wake Grandma up.

He bangs on the door again, even louder.

I have to decide quick whether or not to open it. I did leave that message on Jake's phone telling him to find a way to get in touch with me. Maybe this is his way.

I open the door.

The gang dude looks me over. "You Scott?"

I nod. "That's me."

"Jake sent me."

Thank goodness. Jake must have got my message. I say, "Where is he? Is he all right?"

"He's okay, but you got to come. Now."

"He wants me to come to where he is?"

The gang dude nods and points back at the car. "Jake say to come. All I know." He looks at my wheelchair. "Can you get outta that thing?"

"Yeah, just let me tell my grandma I have to go out." I wheel my chair around.

But the gang dude has ahold of my wheelchair. "No! You got to come. Now!"

I try to push his hand off my chair. "I'm coming. But first, I have to make sure my grandmother has something to eat."

But he won't let loose of my chair. What's the urgency? Is Jake in trouble? Did he tell them to come get me fast? Before I can decide what to do, the guy jerks me up out of my chair.

"Wait," I say. "I can walk. Just let me get my cane. It's in my bedroom."

But he won't let me go. He pulls my arm over his shoulder and drags me out the front door and down the stairs. Jesus, this guy is incredibly strong. I'm sure he could break me in half if he wanted to.

"Wait," I say. "I have to lock the door."

But it's as if I hadn't even spoken. He's all but carrying me to the car.

"Well, it sure is nice of you to help me, dude. Maybe from now on you could hang around and carry me wherever I need to go."

Still no comment.

The car door opens and the big gorilla pushes me into the back seat and piles in next to me. As we roar off down the street, it's only me and the big gorilla in the back seat, but he's so huge it feels crowded. There's another guy in the front seat next to the driver, but nobody says a word.

I lean forward to ask the driver where we're going, but the gorilla pulls me back. I grin at him, like I'm not worried, but this situation doesn't feel right at all. If they really are taking me to meet with Jake, why are they being so stony silent about it? I assess the situation. If they're taking me to see Jake, I might as well just relax and go along for the ride. If they're taking me somewhere to kill me—well, there's nothing I can do about it.

It's starting to get dark outside, and the traffic is heavy. All I can tell is we're heading west.

Somebody in the front seat turns on some music, if that's what you call it. Rhythmic rap, unintelligible words, and so incredibly loud inside the closed-up car I can feel it in my body. A rhyming rap tune, rhyming repeated stanzas about violence, something about lighting a fuse, can't lose, bury you deep, kill you for keeps. Over and over. Simple words, simple non-tune. Can't these gangster rappers manage to come up with rhymes of more than one syllable? When I get out of this, I'm going to have to get on the internet and study rap music. *If* I get out of this. The rap is so loud, I have to put my fingers in my ears. How can it be so loud? Have all these guys destroyed their hearing? I keep my fingers in my ears and lean back in the seat. Might as well relax; whatever is going to happen, is going to happen.

Pretty soon, I realize that wherever we're going, it's not close by. We've been driving for quite a while, and now we're on the freeway. From the direction of the setting sun, I figure we must be going south. I try not to think about where they're taking me. Maybe I should think about something else. When Cop Kelly was kicking the shit out of me up there in the desert, I thought about Derrida. Derrida asked What is the I? He said we don't even understand ourselves, so how can we hope to understand others? Why did he say that? What was the referent? I've read so much about him, it's all starting to get jumbled together. He must have been talking about how we keep secrets from ourselves. I think it was that article he wrote about how we become a new person with every new experience. It makes me think about everything I've gone through since that night I jumped off the cliff out at Point Fermin Park. Derrida would say it's all made me who I am at this moment. But who am I? Who do these gang dudes think I am? Do they think about me as an individual, or do they just think of me as some whitebread? Maybe they don't even think about such things. They all have skins much darker than mine, and in our society, that seems to be a barrier to believing we have any hope of understanding each other. But that's not true. My friendship with Jake proves skin color doesn't matter. Maybe it's just that nobody *wants* to understand somebody who looks different from them. The root cause of all racism could simply be the you-versus-meism we all have in our brains. Maybe it goes all the way back to our caveman days: it's safer not to trust anyone from a "different tribe." It could be why light-skinned people in LA don't care about the dark-skinned people that live only a few miles away in the south central part of their city.

That thought makes me think about the first time I met Jake. At first, I saw him as just another local gangbanger. I saw his gang tattoos instead of seeing *him*. But he turned out to be a really nice guy, a guy who wants to better himself by going to college, a guy who cares about his mother and takes her to church every Sunday.

I shouldn't have started thinking about Jake because now I'm worried about him. Why didn't he come get me himself? Something about these guys supposedly taking me to meet him isn't right.

I feel the car make a series of turns. I sit up to look out. We're off the freeway, but it's pretty dark now, so I can't see much. We're going down a wide street. Lots of cars on the street. We pass a gas station. A bank. Some stores. I have no idea where we are. We could be in any part of LA. We turn onto a dark street. A residential neighborhood. Where the hell are we going?

The car stops, and I look out the window. Other gang dudes are gathered around a bench in some kind of park. In fact, it looks a lot like Point Fermin Park. Could it be? What the hell? Could they have somehow found out that this is where I tried to do myself in? If so, why would they bring me here?

My big seatmate climbs out and pulls me out too. Without my cane, I have to lean back against the car to keep my balance, and instantly, one of the gangbangers—the driver, I suppose—is on my case for leaning against his car. He pulls me away from the car, and I almost go down. Some of the gang dudes laugh at that.

And then one of them, a guy standing back in the shadows next to a tree, calls to me. "Hey, Scotty. Come over here."

Do I know that guy? How does he know my name?

I limp closer to him. I do know him. It's Joe, from the city lockup, the big gang dude that was genuinely interested in my rambling on about philosophy when we were in the same cell together. I'm damn glad to see him. I was starting to get worried about why they brought me here.

I painfully limp over to him and stick out my hand.

He shakes my hand with his iron grip, and he doesn't let it go. He doesn't seem to be trying to hurt me, but he won't let go of my hand. He says, "So, Scotty, long time no see."

I guess that must have been a joke. It hasn't been all that long since we were in the city jail together. His words seemed friendly enough, but his face doesn't look friendly. In fact, he looks worried. What could he be worried about? He's surrounded by his gang buddies. What's going on here?

"You don't mind me callin' you Scotty, do ya? That's what Jake calls ya."

I shrug. "Fine with me, Joe."

Still holding my hand in his amazingly strong grip, he says, "Hey, less you're worried that Jake gave you up, he didn't. We got the word from a cop we know that they were lookin' for Jake, cause he and some white kid offed a Mexican. I figured it might be you, beins how you and Jake were doin' some business together. Then you called and left him a message." He takes out a cell phone. "This is Jake's phone. You left that message about a woman squealin'. You said the cops were after him."

I quickly say, "Hey, listen, Joe, don't blame Jake. It was my deal. Jake was just helpin' me take care of the bastard who killed my mother."

He loosens his grip on my hand. "Your mother got killed?"

"Yeah. I wanted to take care of it myself, but Jake wanted to help me."

Joe finally lets go of my hand and pats me on the shoulder. "Sorry to hear that, man. Tough deal, losin' your mom like that. But Jake knew the rules. He brought the cops down on all of us just to help out some whitebread, and that ain't right."

I reach out to grab Joe's arm. "Listen, Joe. Don't blame Jake. It's all my fault. You can do whatever you want to me, but leave Jake out of it. I'll go to the cops and tell 'em it wasn't Jake. I'll tell 'em I did it myself. Alone."

Joe shakes his head and looks down at the ground. "Too late for that. The word I get is that they're gonna use this murder rap to take us all down. Say it was a conspiracy. That's what my snitch is tellin' me."

"No. Listen to me, Joe. I know this one cop. He's the main cop on the case. I can tell him—"

Joe steps forward and get right up in my face. "Can it, Scotty. Too late for that shit. We got no choice. You can't go talkin' to the cops anymore. Lil G here told us a cop has been to your house. More than once." He points at Lil G, one of the gang dudettes from the neighborhood, the one that liked to show me his fancy silver gun.

I wave at him. "Hey, Lil G. How're ya doin'? Still got that fancy silver pistol?"

He reaches for his waistband. "Yeah, asshole, you wanna see it?"

I grin at him. "Why, thanks, kid. Hey how 'bout I borrow it for a little while."

He looks surprised. "You makin' some kind of joke, asshole?"

I keep on smiling. "As a matter of fact, I was, kid. And you almost got it. I'm proud of you. You must be gettin' a lot smarter than you look."

Lil G is not happy with the way I'm talking to him. He pulls out his fancy pistol and points it at me.

I grin even bigger. "Go ahead, kid. Do it. You'll spend the rest of your life in jail, but at least you'll get your name in the paper. It just might be worth it."

"Put that gun away," snarls Joe.

Lil G puts the gun back into his waistband, but it's obvious that he's not happy with my smart-ass comments.

Joe turns to the others. "Now, listen, God damn it. All of you. We're gonna do this right. Accordin' to the rules."

He comes to me and takes my arm. "Come on, Scotty. I'll help ya."

I allow him to help hold me up as we head toward the cliff. Now I know where we're going and what we're going to do. Jake must have told them about my jumping off the cliff, so they're going to help me finish the job. This time I really will die. To the police, it will look like I came here to kill myself. Out of remorse, probably, for killing An-hell. What a laugh.

Joe is not hurrying me, but his forward pressure is persistent. He whispers, "Hope you understand, Scotty. This is the way it has to be."

I nod. "Don't sweat it, Joe, I do understand. It probably would have come to this, sooner or later anyhow. Remember that philosophy stuff I talked to you about when we were in the county lockup?"

"Sure," he says. "I think about what ya said all the time. Interestin' stuff."

"Well, the main message is that life is just what it is. We live and then we die. That's what it means to be a human. No more, and no less."

Joe nods thoughtfully.

We go on, getting closer and closer to the cliff.

So this is it. My night to die, and in the same way and at the same place as where I tried to do it the last time. And this time, there's nothing I can do about it so there's no need to contemplate it any more. Maybe it's the right thing. Now that just about everybody I know is dead, what's the point of going on anyhow? My mom is dead, and poor David is dead too. Even old Derrida is dead. Grandma probably won't last long, and without her Social Security checks to pay the house bills, I'd just end up homeless again. No place to get out of the weather, and more important, no way to access the internet. So, why not end it all tonight? What good am I to the world anyhow? No one will miss me. What does one less *hikikomori* matter to anybody? The county will turn Mom's body into ashes, with or without me, and Grandma will go on watching her TV soap operas and go on retreating more and more into her world of overly-dramatic fantasy until she dies. She'll probably hardly even notice I'm gone.

My thoughts are interrupted when we arrive at the fence next to the cliff. Joe gets ahold of both of my shoulders and looks me in the eyes. "Sorry about this, Scotty. I like you. I really do."

"I know, Joe. Listen, no reason for you guys to get in trouble for throwing me off. Let me go, and I'll do it myself."

Joe looks down at the ground. "I wish it was that easy, Scotty. But there are certain . . . rules." He lets go of my arm and nods to the other members of his gang.

They begin to close in around me.

Joe grabs my hand, leans close to me, and whispers, "Remember what I told you when we were in the slammer. Get down on your side. Knees up. Cover your head with your arms."

He tries to let go of my hand and step away, but I keep ahold of him. "Not that I don't appreciate that advice, Joe, but if this is going to be my last few minutes on this stupid planet, I want to feel all of it."

He frowns, but nods and lets go of my hand. "Suit yourself, philosopher. See you in the next go around."

I grin at him. "If there is one, which I doubt, I'll be waiting for you there." I turn to face the others. They're closing in on me. I grin at them too. "I'll be waiting for all you gangbangers there, and I bet I won't hafta wait long."

Little G gets in the first blow. He punches me in the stomach, but I hardly feel it. I laugh at him. "That's it? That's all you got? Why shit, I could do better than that with one hand tied behind my—"

I don't see the next one coming, and I find myself on the ground looking up at a big guy who has most of his front teeth missing. He has quite a right hook. He starts kicking me in the side, and the others join right in.

"No wait!" I yell. "Give me a chance to stand up."

Amazingly, they do let me get up. As I struggle to my feet, I try to assess how bad I'm hurt. But then I realize it doesn't matter. What the fuck, I'm about to die anyhow.

This time when the missing-teeth guy nails me, I'm ready for it, and although I stagger backwards, I somehow stay on my feet. For some reason, tonight, my legs are feeling fairly strong.

"Good one, buddy," I say. "You got a solid punch there. But it didn't hurt. Not a bit. Try again."

He looks surprised, but I'm telling him the truth. I'm not feeling much pain at all. Maybe this means I've finally mastered it: I'm actually able to tell my brain to turn off most of the pain. That little bit of success actually makes me happy, and I'm feeling more at peace than I have since that night I jumped off this very cliff. All my studying and all my mediation is finally paying off.

The same big guy hits me in the face again, harder this time. But again, I manage to stay on my feet. My teeth on the side he hit feel loose, but that doesn't matter either. I grin at him. I hold out my arms and turn in a full circle, facing all of them, grinning. "Well, come on. What are you waiting for?"

And then they're all over me. I go down hard, and as soon as I try to get back up, somebody kicks me in the side of the head. That makes things pretty hazy. More kicking, but I think one time I did make it back up onto my hands and knees for a few seconds. I hear laughing, and it takes me quite a while to realize that it's me that's doing the laughing. It's a weird sounding laugh, even to me, so I can't imagine how it must sound to them. They start kicking me harder, pissed off, I guess, because I'm laughing. They think I'm laughing at them. I wish I could tell them I'm not laughing at them, but I have a mouth full of blood and can no longer talk. If only I could talk, I would explain to them that I'm laughing at the absurdity of it all, laughing at all those crazy old-time philosophers, from Plato to Kierkegaard to Kant, all of those old guys who thought there was a higher realm of reality, some kind of metaphysical place beyond this plane, a place where morality and the rule of order prevailed. No way. They were all wrong. This is the real reality, death by pointless and meaningless violence. For most humans, this is the way it always ends, death in fights, death in wars, death at the hand of their fellow humans. The modern existentialists had it right: we poor humans have been dying in this pointless way for thousands and thousands of years, ever since we stood upright and learned how to pick up a club or a rock.

After some unknown amount of time has passed, I hear a voice say, "Okay, boys, that's enough."

They stop kicking me.

I'm not sure, but I think I'm still quietly chuckling. I'm pretty sure I'm still alive, but it's hard to tell because I'm not feeling anything. No pain, no regrets, nothing.

But I can tell one thing for sure: they've fucked me up good. Things inside of me are definitely not right, not fitting together the way they should. But I refuse to call it pain; it's just some other odd type of sensation.

I open my eyes and look up. I see Joe leaning down to look at me. My eyes are not working so good right now, but I'm pretty sure it is Joe.

He says, "Time to go, Scotty."

He gets ahold of one of my arms, and somebody else gets ahold of the other one. They stand me up, and amazingly, my legs still seem to be working. For some reason, they were mostly just kicking my midsection. Not one of them ever kicked my legs. I wonder if Joe told them not to.

They walk me toward the cliff, but by the time we get to the fence, my eyes are starting to work a little better. The weirdest things is that my legs are working just fine. It's as if they have suddenly become healed. I can actually walk, and it doesn't hurt at all.

I try to shake off the hands that have ahold of my arms. I try to explain it to them, but my mouth doesn't seem to be working right. I manage to mumble, "Do it . . . myself." I think about trying to explain to them that the trick is to do a perfect swan dive, but I decide against it. Too complicated. Mouth not working right. Doesn't matter anyhow.

Somebody is helping me over the shaky old fence. I feel somebody pushing me out toward the cliff, but I push away from them. "Leave . . me . . . alone. Have to do . . . swan dive."

I hear Joe's voice: "Let him go."

The hands are still on me, and somebody says, "He won't jump. He'll chicken out."

Joe says, "Yes he will. He'll do it. Let him go."

The hands go away.

I put both of my hands out to the side for balance and edge my way out onto the broken-off sidewalk. I look straight ahead, out into the blackness of an endless ocean. I'm a bit disappointed that I can't see any lights moving out there. I guess no ships coming in tonight. But whales must be out there, just swimming along under the water. Good old whales. I silently say goodbye to them.

I'm ready to do it. I shuffle my way out to the end of the diving-board-like broken-off sidewalk. This time, I'll do it right. I'll do a perfect swan dive, and then I'll be out of this stupid world once and for all.

I'm right at the edge now, and I'm feeling amazingly strong. They kicked me as hard as they could, and they couldn't hurt me. I'm stronger than any of them.

I lean forward and look down. It's dark down there, but I can see the whiteness of the surf as it crashes into all the dark rocks below. The crashing sound of those waves hitting those rocks is not scary this time. In fact, it's inviting.

I'm ready to take that last step out into nothingness, but then I remember something Joe said about Jake knowing the rules. Jake! Where is Jake? Why isn't he here? I'd like to say goodbye to him. I'd like to tell him how much I appreciate his friendship. I can't believe I never said that to him. I'd also like to tell him to tell his mother I'm sorry if my ranting about religion and such upset her.

I turn back to look at the gangbangers who are gathered at the fence, all of them watching me. "Joe," I say, "tell Jake . . . sorry. And tell his . . . mother—"

"Tell him yourself, asshole. You'll be seeing him soon enough."

That voice. I think it's Lil G. Why did he say that? Is he saying Jake is down there? Did they throw him off this cliff before I got here?

I turn back and look down into the darkness. There *is* a dark shape down there. It looks like a body.

I turn back to Joe. "No, Joe. Tell me . . . isn't."

Joe nods, looking very sad. "Like I said, Scotty, Jake knew the rules. I'm sorry. He was my friend too."

Lil G pulls out his fancy pistol and aims it at me. "Jump, motherfucker, or I shoot."

Joe pushes the kid's arm down. "He'll do it. Give him a second."

I turn my back on them. Fuck them. Fuck them all. Fuck everybody in this stupid world. Jake was my friend, and he died because of me. He's down there, and I'm happy to be joining him. There's nothing left for me here. I imagine myself doing a perfect swan dive, enjoying the fall down and down through the cool night air, almost as if I'm flying, and then hitting the rocks down below head first. A perfect ending to all this nonsense. I lift my foot to step out.

"Freeze, all of you!"

Who said that? Is somebody telling me to freeze? I freeze with one foot in the air. Isn't that interesting. All of a sudden, my right leg feels very strong. I'm able to freeze with my left foot in the air, not moving at all, as if it's some kind of kid's stay-frozen-in-place game.

I hear a shot, and then another. Who the hell is shooting?

I step back from the cliff edge and turn to look. People are running. More shooting. A lot of yelling. A lot of screaming.

I turn back toward the ocean and look down into the darkness. It's not fair that Jake is down there. Why should a good person like Jake have to die when so many other bad people get to live? It's absurd, I should ask Old Man about it. "Tell me this, Old Man, why should good people have to die? What about fairness?

There is no such thing as fairness, no such thing as good or bad. The terms are normative, of no value in and of themselves. The concept of good is relative only with regard to its relationship to the concept of bad, and both are evaluated only through the perceptions of an individual.

"You're right, Old Man, I guess I did know that. And you want to know something? You're starting to sound a lot like Derrida even though he was a hundred years after your time."

"Hey, what the hell are you doing out there? Get back here."

Is that voice talking to me?

I turn around. A cop is pointing a gun at me. A bunch of other cops behind him, pointing their guns at the gangbangers. Some of the other gangbangers are lying on the ground, face down. Are they dead? Is their death important? Should it matter to me?

I notice a body of a person lying next to the fence. Is it Joe? I have to know. I shuffle my way back to the fence, but before I can tell who is lying there on the ground, two cops grab me by my arms and drag me back over the fence. For some reason, they're not letting me see who is dead and who is not. They're hustling me all the way across the park, back toward the parking lot.

I try to get my thinking organized. Who was that lying on the ground back there? The body was face down, but I don't think it was Joe. It was a smaller person. Must have been Lil G.

The cops are making me move too fast, and it's hard to think straight. Red lights are flashing. Along the sidewalk, more bodies are lying in the dirt.

A cops puts me into the back seat of a cop car and start asking me questions. What's this all about? Some kind of gang initiation? What are *you* doing here, whitey?"

I don't know how to answer him. It probably doesn't matter. Or does it? What does matter? How do you tell?

If there is no such thing as a value system, then nothing matters. Things only have meaning in reference to the individual's set of values. And even then, what matters to that individual can shift, thereby moving meaning to a different position along the value scale.

"Yes, it has to be true, Old Man. We create values, and in so doing, we create what matters and what doesn't."

The cop shakes his head and goes away.

Soon, another face appears.

"Looks like they tried to kill you, eh? Had to shut you up, I guess. I was afraid this would happen."

I blink my eyes to try to clear them. I think it's Cop Kelly. How did he get here?

I try to answer him, but my mouth isn't working right.

"No need to talk, kid. We'll get you to the hospital."

I shake my head. "No . . . hosp. Need . . . go home."

Cop Kelly's face goes away. I hear him say, " I know this kid. He's not part of the gang. They were trying to kill him. I'll take him home."

Somebody again has me by the arms. Why can't they leave me alone?

I'm in another car. Somehow, I feel like I know this car. The smell of it . . . or something. I lie down on the hard plastic back seat and look up at the car's ceiling. There are spots up there. What are those spots? Spit? Vomit? Blood? Have I had that thought before?

Now the car is moving.

"So, they thought you'd squeal on 'em."

All I can mumble is, "Rules."

"He says, "What was that?"

I can't explain it to him. There are rules in this world, and the rules make things happen. Jake had to die because of rules. I had to die because of rules. But I'm not dead. So what happened to the rule?

"You sure you're all right, kid? Maybe I'd better drop you at the hospital. Have them check you out."

"No. Hadta . . . go . . . home."

"Well, okay then. Suit yourself. I'll take you home. You know, when I heard all the radio calls, neighbors reporting a big gang fight out at Point Fermin, I had the oddest feeling it might be you. When you get to feelin' better, I want you to tell me what the hell was going on out there. And why the hell did they start shootin'? Doesn't make any sense. Shootin'? Just for us breaking up a fight?"

I say, "Jake."

"What'd you say, kid?"

"Jake . . . dead."

"Dead? Oh, now I get it. They killed the gangbanger who did in the Mexican. Makes sense. Listen, maybe instead of taking you home, I'd better take you downtown. Call it protective custody. Until this all calms down."

This time I make sure my mouth and my teeth are set in the right places before I say, as loud as I can, "No . . . jail."

Cop Kelly laughs. "Okay, okay. I guess you're right. Jail might not be the safest place for you either."

He says some more things, but I'm having trouble understanding his words. They all seem to be merging into one long sentence with none of it making any sense at all. Might be better just to sleep. Maybe dream.

I feel the car stop, and then Cop Kelly has ahold of me. He's damn strong. Was he always that strong? Somehow, he gets me out of the car and up the steps onto the front porch. He tries the front door, but it's locked. He bangs on it and waits. Nothing happens, and he again bangs on the door, louder this time. If he expects Grandma to get out of bed and come open the door, he's got a long wait ahead of him. I again have the overwhelming feeling that this is all some kind of absurd dream, as if we're not actually standing on Grandma's front porch but on some other porch, maybe in another kind of world where—

The door opens, and there's Grandma, standing in the doorway, wide-eyed and staring. I guess she's pretty surprised to see me being held up by a cop. She's wearing her ratty old blue bathrobe. I wonder how long she's had that old bathrobe. I'd like to ask her that, but Kelly pushes past her and takes me into my bedroom. He carefully lowers me down onto my mattress and turns to Grandma. "He got beat up. Better keep an eye on him. He starts lookin' pale or anything, call 9-1-1."

Grandma looks confused.

Cop Kelly says, "I'll be back to check on him in a few days. Okay?"

Grandma still hasn't said a word. She just stares at him.

Kelly looks back at me and shakes his head. "Well, good luck, kid. From what I saw out there, you're damn lucky to be alive." He looks back at Grandma. "Like I said, keep an eye on him."

And then he's gone.

Grandma is staring down at me like she thinks I did something wrong. But I didn't do anything wrong. I was just—

"What did he mean, Fitzgerald? Beat up? What have you gone and got yourself into this time?"

"Little . . . hurt," I mumble. "Be okay. Couple . . . days."

She shrugs and turns away. I hear her padding her way back to her bedroom.

I guess she just wants to get back to her bed, back to her TV soap operas.

"Grandma," I call after her. "Could you get me some water?"

No answer.

Doesn't matter. Nothing matters, and I'm too sleepy to care anyhow. My mind seems to be working a little bit better now, but my brain is insisting that I should go to sleep. Maybe it means I'm dying. If I die in this bed tonight, I wonder what Grandma will do. Will she pay for a cremation? No, she'll probably just sweep me out with the trash. She'll think, What a lot of bother that boy was.

21
Pre-reflective Self-Consciousness

I wake up to find Grandma hovering over me. She's holding something out to me.

She says, "Here, take this."

I manage to get my eyes cleared up enough to see that it's a pill and a glass of water. I try to sit up, but the pain in my midsection makes me plop right back down. What that hell is wrong inside of me? Then I remember: Joe's gang dudes kicked the shit out of me. For some reason, they seemed to focus on my stomach and back. My face hurts too, but I don't remember getting hit in the face too many times. Then there was the cliff. Jake down below. Then came the shooting. Bodies lying in the dirt, face-down, bleeding.

"Well, do you want it or not?"

She's holding out a pill and a glass of water. Hard as it is to believe, this is not a dream; Grandma is actually out of her bed and here in my room. I think she trying to help me. As far as I can remember, this is the first time she's ever come into my room.

I take the pill out of her hand and look at it. A fairly small, light blue pill. Is it for pain? She has so many prescriptions for pills, it could be just about anything. I say, "What . . . is?"

She says, "How should I know? Whatever it is, it makes me feel better."

I decide to take the pill, if for no other reason than to show my gratitude that she's here and that she's worried about me. The way my insides are feeling, I don't think I'm going to be able to get out of bed to take care of myself, at least not for a little while. Will she actually stay away from her TV long enough to help me?

I toss the pill into my mouth and wash it down with the entire glass of water. Man, I was really thirsty. How long has it been since I had anything to drink? I say, "Thanks . . . Grandma. I'm . . . sorry."

She takes the glass out of my hand and frowns at me. "Well, what was it this time?"

Is she really interested? This is the closest thing to a conversation we've had since I moved in here. Maybe her TV's broken.

"Gang dudes. Beat . . . up. No . . . big deal."

"Gangs. Figures. What did you do?"

For some strange reason, she really seems to want to know. But there's no way I'm going to answer that question. She's been so out of it lately, I'm not even sure she remembers I told her that Mom is dead.

"What did you do, Fitzgerald? Is this about your mother? Are they the ones that killed her?"

So she was paying attention after all. I wonder why she didn't react back when I told her. "No. Just . . . gang . . . deal."

"But why did they beat *you* up?"

I do an exaggerated shrug, which was a mistake because even that little movement hurts like hell. What happened to my ability to push away the pain? When those assholes were kicking the shit out of me last night out at Point Fermin Park, I hardly felt it.

Grandma is glancing back toward her bedroom. She turns back to me. "So, how long are you going to lay in here?"

Ah, now that's the Grandma I know and love. Maybe one of her soap operas is about to start, and she doesn't want to miss it.

I say, "Just give me . . . few days."

She points her bony old finger at me. "Now don't start feeling sorry for yourself, young man. I can get my own food. And I can take care of you too. Heaven knows, I took care of you often enough when you were a baby. Whenever your mother went gallivanting off to who knows where. And don't think I haven't seen this kind of thing before. I can't tell you the number of times she'd come dragging herself home all beat up, expecting me to nursemaid her. So, I'll fix your meals for a while, and you can have some of my pills too, if you need them. But mind you, it's only until you're back up and around. Our bargain is that I let you live here, and you take care of my needs. A deal is a deal."

She turns and shuffles off out of my room. I hear the slap of her old slippers on the linoleum kitchen floor. Is she really going to fix me something to eat? This is the side of Grandma I've never see before. She's turned back into the tough old girl my mother used to talk about. From what Mom told me, Grandma lived a hard life after she landed in LA, so I guess she knows about things like getting beat up. I guess I was wrong about her, thinking she only cared about her damn old TV soap operas. For the moment at least, she seems to care that I got hurt. Or maybe it's just part of our bargain: whichever one of us is stuck in bed is the one that gets taken care of.

22
The Phenomenology of Self-Awareness

I'm back to the routine I had after I got out of the hospital the first time with my busted-up legs. I spend most of my time lying on my mattress with my laptop computer propped up next to me. Pretty Boy is back to his job of pulling threads out of my shirt collar, although he does seem to be staring at me more than usual. I guess my face must look pretty beat up.

But I am getting up three times a day to fix Grandma's meals. After taking care of me for several days, she decided I was just loafing and told me it was time to get out that bed and make myself useful. As before, I fix her meals sitting in my wheelchair, and as before, when I roll them into her bedroom, she keeps her focus on her TV and hardly even glances at me. I guess she's had enough of the real world, a world I made her face for a few days. Now she's ready to get back to her world of soap operas.

Because it hurts too much to sit up in my wheelchair for very long, I'm spending quite a bit of time lying down while I concentrate on pushing the pain into the background. With the help of handfuls of ibuprofen, I can force most of the little pain guys to retreat back to their hiding places deep within my brain, but once in a while, they break out and act up a bit, rampaging around, causing trouble, mostly attacking my busted-up ribs, and of course, going to work on my legs whenever they get the chance. When that happens, I have to get out my mental whip and chair and force them back to wherever they hide out. They whimper a bit, taking a last few jabs at the side of my head where one of the gangbangers must have punched me, but eventually they leave me alone with my thoughts.

A lot of my thoughts are about Jake. I miss him. I guess I didn't really get to know him all that well, but I considered him a friend—actually, my only friend. I'll never get over regretting that it was me that got him killed. I can't stop thinking about him lying dead at the bottom of that cliff. I keep thinking, why him and not me? I should have never let him get involved in my revenge. I should have taken care of An-hell by myself.

There wasn't much on the local news sites about what happened out there at Point Fermin. A few small stories about the police being called to quell "a gang fight in a park." Four dead. Of course, they don't say it was the police that did the killing. But then, I was so out of it, I'm not actually sure what happened that night.

One thing I am sure of is that Jake's gang is probably out there somewhere looking for me. They probably still think I might talk to the cops. Maybe they'll break into this house and kill me. I hope they don't kill Grandma too.

Sometimes I think I should go get myself a gun. But I don't want to go down that road. Besides, guns cost money, and I don't have any.

That thought reminds me I still have to figure out how to get enough money to pay for Mom's cremation. Jake was my only chance to get my hands on that much money. Mom's thirty days down there in that county morgue are running out, and I don't know what I'm going to do about it.

I give up thinking about it and chase Pretty Boy away. I lie on my back and stare up at my black ceiling. I should try to get a little sleep.

But sleep won't come. I'm still staring up into the darkness, trying to keep the little pain guys at bay, when I hear somebody come up onto the front porch. I quickly crawl out of bed and get into my wheelchair. Doing that hurts like hell, but I push the pain away. I hurry and roll myself to the front door, trying to get there before they start knocking. If they've come to kill me, I'd rather get outside so they have to do it on the front porch.

I take a deep breath and open the front door.

But it's not the gangbangers; it's Denesa. And she's got Javon with her. I'm glad to see her. I've been hoping she would come by so I can give her the new Disney T-shirts I bought online for Javon and Zyrell before Cop Kelly cut off my Amazon account.

But where is Zyrell? And why is Denesa just standing there on the porch staring at me? She's got a cold hard look on her face, but her eyes are red as if she's been crying.

She pushes Javon forward. "Here, you take him."

Javon looks scared, and I can tell he's been crying too.

She turns and starts down the porch steps.

"No, wait!" I say. "What's going on?"

She stops and turns back, but she stays where she is, halfway down the steps, as if she doesn't want to get too close to me.

She says, "I'll be back for him. You just . . . keep him."

Javon says, "Mama, I don't want to."

She glares at him. "Do as you're told. Stay here with Scotty until I get back." Her voice is shaky, but cold and distant, almost as if she's in some kind of trance.

"Denesa," I say, as gently as I can, "what's wrong? Come in and tell me what's going on. Why are you here in the middle of the night? And where's Zyrell?"

Her lower lip begins to quiver and tears well up in her eyes. "Where do you think he is? He's dead. What did you think? That they would ever leave us alone?"

She seems angry. Her eyes are wild, darting left and right, as if she thinks something or somebody is about to pounce on her from out of the darkness.

But what is she talking about? Who is dead? It can't be Jake. She doesn't even know Jake.

"Who is dead, Denesa? I don't know what you're talking about."

"Zyrell!" she screams. "Zyrell! They killed him. They shot up all the apartments that face the street. They thought we told on 'em. But we didn't, Scotty. We didn't say a word."

My mind is having trouble comprehending what she's saying. Is she saying her child, little Zyrell, is dead? But how can that be? He was innocent. He wasn't in a gang. He was the sweetest little kid in the world. My mind is trying make sense of it. Somehow, it feels like it's my fault, as if I did something to make all this killing happen. I got Jake killed, and now maybe I also got Zyrell killed. Zyrell, the most wonderful little boy in the whole wide world, the little boy who always stuck his little tongue out of the corner of his mouth as he concentrated on carefully squirting the honey onto the toast. How can such a beautiful child be dead?

Javon runs to her and throws his arms around her. "No, Mama. He's only hurt. You said."

She pries him off and squats down to look him in the eyes. "No, Javon. I lied to you. Don't you understand? I told you he was hurt, but that was a lie. As soon as I pulled him out of his bed, I knew he was dead. I knew it even before they came to take him away. They shot him in the head, Javon. The bullets came right through the wall. I lied to you, Javon. I lied to myself too. I'm a liar, but there's no use lyin' anymore. He's dead, and . . . and none of it matters anymore. You have to stay here with Scotty until I come back to get you. Then we'll go to Mississippi like I said. I promise we'll go. We'll stay with Grandma down there, until . . . until I can decide what to do."

She pushes him away and turns to hurry down the steps.

"Denesa," I call after her, "I'll take care of him. Don't worry. Just go do . . . what you need to do. I'll, uh, get him something to eat."

That was probably a dumb thing to say to a grieving mother, but it probably doesn't matter because it looks like she didn't hear me.

Javon tries to run after her, but luckily I'm just able to catch his arm and hold him back. I keep a tight hold on his arm even though he fights me. I pull him back inside and close the door.

As soon at I let go of him, he immediately tries to get out. But I won't let him. I take ahold of his shoulders and force him to look at me. "Javon, listen to me. You have to mind your momma. She said you have to wait here until she comes back."

He has a panicked look on his face, and I feel his shoulders tremble. Finally, he bursts into tears and puts his head against me. "He's not dead," he whispers between sobs. "Not really. He's only hurt. Only hurt bad."

I put my hand on top of his head. "Let's hope so, Javon. But for now, your mama wants you to stay here with me until she finds out for sure. Don't worry. She'll be back soon. We'll just wait here until she comes back. We can get on the computer and do things if you want to. And we can get you something to eat if you're hungry."

"What's going on here?"

I turn. It's Grandma. All the yelling has awakened her, and she's standing in the hall doorway in her old blue bathrobe, her hands on her hips.

Javon turns to face her, but leans back against me, obviously afraid of her.

"There's been a shooting, Grandma. This is Javon. His little brother got shot, so Javon will have to stay here with us for a little while. Just until his mother comes back."

Grandma doesn't seem all that surprised, and happily, this time she doesn't seem angry at me for letting Javon stay here. She says, "Gangs again, I suppose."

"Yes, Grandma. I think it was gangs. There was a white kid killed down at the projects recently. The police have been nosing around. Maybe the shooting was a warning to make sure nobody talked. I think little Zyrell must have got hit by a stray bullet."

"They shot out our windows," says Javon, his voice soft and shaky.

Grandma shakes her head. "I knew it. I saw it coming years ago. Whole neighborhood going to pot. The black people moved in, and then the trouble started."

"Grandma!" I say, pointing at the top of Javon's head.

"Well, I'm not saying it's this little boy's fault, but it's true. They come in and take over the neighborhood and trouble follows." She comes to Javon and grabs his hand. "Well, come on, kid. Let's get you something to eat. You're so damn skinny, you look like you haven't had a decent meal in who knows how long."

Javon obediently follows her into the kitchen, and soon he's explaining to her that he knows how to make toast and how to squirt honey onto it.

She seems totally attentive to what he's saying, seemingly not in the slightest hurry to get back to her TV.

I watch in amazement. This is a side of Grandma I've never seen, a seemingly fully aware woman who is willing to take time out from her TV world to help a little boy get something to eat.

I go to the dining room window and pull aside the curtain. There's nobody outside, and no suspicious cars on the street. Good. Maybe after the shootings out at Point Fermin Park, Joe's gang is lying low for a while. But I know they'll be coming, sooner or later. As I stare out at the street, it finally hits me: little Zyrell really is dead. I was so concerned about taking care of Javon, it didn't actually sink in that a beautiful child is dead, and for no damn reason at all. The little boy who was probably the happiest and most innocent child in this whole damn world is now gone. What does it say about our godforsaken world when an innocent child like Zyrell can be so pointlessly cut down? Now I can see why his mother seemed so cold and emotionless. It was like she was hypnotized, too tired to go on. I feel exactly the same way. It's all so stupid. Mom got herself killed for no reason, and Jake ends up dead because he broke some stupid rule, and now it's Zyrell. If something like this can happen, then whatever hope I might have had for the human race has been completely drained out of me. If something like this can happen, then nothing is too horrible to contemplate. And it means for damn sure there is no God. No merciful God would let something like this happen. No way. The world is shit, and there is no meaning to any of it. The existentialist and the absurdists had it right all along: the only truth of life is that it's completely absurd. Absurdity and pointlessness is the only reality. The only meaning in this stupid life is that there is no meaning.

I turn to see that Grandma and Javon are sitting at the old dining room table. The toast has been eaten, and neither one of them are saying anything. Grandma looks tired, so I guess I'd better go rescue her. I roll over next to Javon and ask him, "You had some toast, did you? That's good. Can I get you anything else?"

He shakes his head and stares down at the table.

I can tell he's trying not to cry. He's just holding on, waiting for his mother to come back, hoping she will tell him everything is going to be all right.

I turn to Grandma. "I'll take care of him now. You can go back to bed if you want to."

She glances in the direction of her bedroom, and I can hear the sound of her TV in there.

"Maybe I'd better lie down for a while," she says. She puts her hand on her lower back and says, "My back you know."

"Good idea," I say.

She struggles to get up from her chair.

I roll over to help her, but she shakes my hand off. "I can do it," she says. "I'm no cripple."

She seems irritated, and I wonder if her use of the word "cripple" was aimed at me.

No matter. I'm feeling nothing now. Nothing she or anybody else can say or do can possibly hurt me now.

I watch her shuffle down the hallway back to her bedroom, and soon I hear her turn up the volume on her TV.

Good for you, Grandma. Go back to your fantasy-land of meaningless soap opera nonsense. Turn off the world. Take it from me, the real world is as meaningless as that crap you watch on TV.

I look back at Javon and discover that he has his head down on the table and seems to be falling asleep.

I get up out of my wheelchair and go to him, but when I try to rouse him, he leans toward me, still more or less asleep. I pick him up, and as I cradle him in my arms, he puts his head against my chest, now fully asleep. I guess he too wants to retreat from this horrible world.

I carry him into my bedroom, not at all worried about the pain in my legs or in my chest. None of that matters anymore. In fact, Javon feels light as a feather, and I'm hardly feeling any pain at all. It makes me wonder what has happened inside my brain to make all the pain go away. Is my cold feeling of pointlessness doing something inside my brain that's incompatible with pain? It may be the answer I've been looking for all this time.

I carefully put Zyrell down on my mattress and stand there looking down at him. He turns onto his side without opening his eyes. His soft breathing tells me he's found the refuge he was looking for, blessed sleep. I wish I could do the same, but I know I have to stand guard. Now, I not only have to worry about Jake's gang coming in here and killing me and Grandma, but now, some other gang might be looking for Javon and his mother. They are both potential witnesses to the shooting that killed poor little Zyrell.

I go back into the dining room and get back into my wheelchair. I roll to the window to keep watch. Nothing is moving out there. It's a warm night, but none of my neighbors are out on their front porches. Maybe they've heard about the trouble down at the projects.

I keep watch until it starts to get light, and then I see Denesa hurrying up the sidewalk. As she comes up the front steps, I open the front door and ask her, "Is he?"

She shakes her head grimly.

"I'm so sorry, Denesa. Is there's anything I can do?"

She stares at me with those cold black eyes. "You got any money?"

Do I? Did those gangbangers that beat me up take my money? Funny that I didn't even think to check. I reach into my shirt pocket and pull out the hundred-dollar bill Jake gave me. I hold it out to her.

She looks me in the eyes. "That's it? That's all you got? They said the cheapest funeral was—"

I can see she's fighting back tears. I reach out to touch her arm. "It's all I've got, Denesa. Maybe I can—"

"Never mind," she says. "They got to do something for folks that got no money, don't they?" She angrily pushes the money away. "Don't worry about it."

I point toward my bedroom. "He ate a little. Now he's asleep."

She goes to my bedroom and gets Javon up. He's still sleepy, and he resists waking up, but Denesa jerks at his arm. "Wake up, Javon. We have to go."

He sits up and rubs his eyes with the backs of his hands. He says, "Where's Zyrell, Mama?"

"Not now!" says his mother sharply. "We'll talk about that later. We have to go now. Say goodbye to Mister Scotty and let's go." She still seems to be in that state of cold self-hypnotism, trying not to feel anything.

Zyrell looks at me, blinking his sleepy eyes, and then he comes up next to my wheelchair and throws his arms around me. He pushes his head against my shoulder and says, "Bye, Mister Scotty." His voice is full of tears. I guess he realizes he may never see me again.

I say, "Bye, bye, Javon," trying to keep my voice from shaking. "Don't worry. I'll see you later."

At the door, there's an awkward moment when both Denesa and I stand there looking at each other, unable to think what to say. Finally, I say, "Well, let me know if you need anything."

She waves away the idea. "No, we'll be all right."

Her voice is harsh, but I understand: she's barely holding on, but trying to tough it out for Javon's sake.

She starts out the door, but turns and comes back. She gives me a quick hug, and then she takes Javon's hand and leads him down the steps. Javon looks back and waves goodbye, but Denesa hurries him on. They go off down the sidewalk, moving fast.

I close the door and sit there staring at it. Finally, I turn and wheel into the kitchen. The loaf of bread and the honey are still sitting there on the counter. That makes me remember how little Zyrell so carefully squirted the honey out of that stupid little bear-shaped honey container with the tip of his tongue sticking out of the corner of his mouth. And that finally makes the tears come. I'm crying like a little baby, and I can't do a damn thing about it.

Finally, after several minutes of unstoppable crying, I angrily wipe away the tears with the backs of my hands. No more of that, damn it. I have to think clearly. Crying like a stupid little baby isn't going to help.

Pretty Boy comes flying in and lands on my shoulder. Where has he been? All the tension in the air and people coming and going must have scared him into hiding out somewhere.

He asks, "Pretty Boy?"

But I have no answers for him. The whole thing has got me so emotionally exhausted, I can't even pretend to play along with the game of talking to him. I shoo him away and don't even bother to look to see where he goes.

I keep on thinking that this kind of thing will just go on and on. That nobody will do anything about it. An innocent little child has been killed, but will the police just ignore it? Will they see it as yet another black kid getting killed in gang violence "down there" in Watts.

I should do something. But what? I'm not sure what good I can do, but I can't just hide out here and do nothing.

I go in to Grandma's bedroom to tell her that I have to go out for a while. But she's sound asleep. Coming out and facing the real world seems to have worn her out too. I turn down her TV and creep out of the room. If I don't make it back, well then she'll just have to call the welfare people to get somebody like Denesa to come take care of her until it's her time to go too.

I grab my cane and go out the front door. As I start down the sidewalk, I'm amazed at how strong I feel. There *is* pain in my legs, and in my side where those gangbangers were kicking me, but it's not near as intense as I would have expected; it's more like a notification, a message sent up to my brain about something that should be attended to, but it can be ignored if necessary. I increase my pace, heading straight for the corner where the wannabe gangbangers always hang out.

But I can already see they're not there. Did the shootout in the park change everything? I'm pretty sure one of the bodies I saw lying face down at the park that night was Lil G. Maybe Little G's death has made them think twice about wanting to be big time gangbangers.

When I get to the projects, I see two little kids playing with a toy truck on the front sidewalk. I go up to them and ask if they know a gang dude named Joe.

They stare at me, probably wondering how a whitebread could be so brave to come here, let alone be asking about gangs. They grab their toy truck and go running off between the buildings.

I follow them and see they're heading for a playground. They run up to talk to some teenagers that are playing basketball on a blacktop basketball court that has so many cracks and weeds that it's a wonder they can even dribble the ball. The basketball players turn to stare at me, but then they too run away.

I wait next to the basketball court. As soon as those kids pass the word that I'm out here waiting, Joe, or somebody else from the gang, will come. They have unfinished business with me.

It doesn't take them long to show up. It's Joe, followed by three of his henchmen. I think I remember at least one of them from that night out at Point Fermin Park. A big guy with most of his front teeth missing. I think he was the first one to hit me.

When they get to me, before they can say anything, I reach out to shake Joe's hand. "Damn, Joe, I'm glad to see you. I was afraid you mighta got shot."

He stares at my hand for a long second, but he won't shake it. "I didn't have no weapon on me, so they had to let me out on bail."

"Well, good," I say. "I need to talk to you. Joe. It's about that little kid that got shot here last night. Listen, Joe, I don't much care what you do to me. Maybe I deserve it, but that doesn't matter now. Don't you see, Joe? We can't stand by and see innocent little kids get killed. I know you didn't have anything to do with that, but we have to do something, don't we?"

He shakes his head. "*We* have to do something? What's it to you?"

"I knew the child. I baby-sat for him sometimes. A wonderful, sweet little boy."

Joe glances toward the nearest building. "Yeah, that's what everybody says, but we don't need you buttin' in. We'll take care of it."

"Take care of it? Like more killing? How's that gonna keep it from happening again? How's more shooting gonna keep little kids from getting killed in the crossfire when everybody keeps on doing the revenge thing?"

Now, Joe looks pissed off. He takes a threatening step toward me. "Didn't I just say we'd take care of it?"

"Yeah," says the big guy. He steps forward and grabs the front of my shirt. "It's none of your fuckin—"

"Back off, Bull," says Joe.

The big dude, Bull, let's go of my shirt, but as he does it, he gives me a shove backwards.

I stagger, but then I recover and go right back to Joe and get up in his face. "Joe, you gotta listen to me. There has to be another way. I don't know if you or any of your boys here even know who that kid was. His name was Zyrell. He was Denesa's youngest child, the cutest, cleverest little boy you'd ever wanna see. A cute, happy little tyke. Who knows what he could have grown up to be? And now, for no good reason, he's gone. Dead. And what about that white kid who got shot right here a while back? I bet you know about that too. His name was David. He didn't know his ass from a hole in the ground, but why should he have to die for that? His death is what brought the cop trouble down on you all in the first place. Don't you get it? If the only solution is shooting the shit out of each other, then it's never gonna end."

Bull steps in front of Joe. "Maybe you don't hear so good, motherfucker. Get your ass out of here before you're the one who ends up dead." He pushes me toward the street.

This time, I'm ready for him, and I don't even stagger. I jab my finger into his big chest. "Butt out, asshole. Your brain might be the size of a pea, but Joe here has some smarts. That's why I'm talking to him, not you."

Apparently, Bull doesn't like me jabbing my finger at him. He pulls out a really big knife and pushes it against my stomach. I think I feel the tip of the blade go in, but I don't think it penetrated very far. I doubt if he'd have any qualms about killing me, but maybe he doesn't want to do it right here in plain sight in the middle of the day.

I grin at him and lean into the knife. "Go ahead, dimwit. Stab me. But it won't bring back that little boy, and that's all I care about."

He seems confused. He can't figure out why I'm not acting scared.

I grab ahold of his hand, the hand that's holding the knife. "Better yet," I say, "give me the knife, and I'll do it myself. If that's what you all want, if I need to be stuck, then fine, I'll do it. Maybe I should die right here in front of you. Maybe then my point will sink in. What I'm trying to tell you guys is that when little kids get shot, they die. They really are dead, for Christ's sake, God damned for sure dead. What's his mother gonna do now? And his poor brother. Both of 'em lost and confused and scared to death. Jesus, Joe, don't you get it? We have to find a way to stop this shit."

Bull pushes the knife a little harder into my stomach. "You sure do like to hear yourself talk, don't ya, asshole?"

"Talk is the only thing I can think to do, Bull." I look past him at Joe. "Listen to me, Joe. I came here today because I felt like I had to do something. Damn it, don't you see where this is going? If we don't stop it right now, these shootings are gonna go on and on, and more innocent little kids are going to end up dead. How about this? Let's make it a rule that if you want somebody dead, you have to kill them like this." I touch the big guy's hand that's pressing the knife against me. "You have to stab them to death. Okay? That way, everybody will know it wasn't a mistake. That way, if you want some poor little boy to die, you have to just walk right up to him and cut his fucking throat. Maybe you should also cut open his insides and pull out his heart and eat it. How about that? That make you happy? At least that way, little kids won't get shot. Only cowards would shoot up somebody's apartment in the middle of the night, not even knowing who's inside."

I stop talking because thinking about poor little Zyrell is threatening to make the tears start up again, and I don't want these assholes to think I'm just some kind of softhearted wimp.

Big Bull still has the knife against my stomach, and I'm putting pressure on his hand, making the knife stick a little bit more into my stomach all the time. I can tell he's confused.

"Back off, Bull," says Joe.

Bull pulls his hand back. I think he's happy Joe got him out of the situation. But he still wants to wave the knife in my face. He says, "What the fuck's the matter with you, man? You tryin' to get yourself killed?"

I reach for his hand again. "Give me the knife. You want to kill me? I'll show you how."

He pulls away. "What the fuck? No way."

Joe quietly says, "Give him the knife."

Bull says, "What?"

"You heard me, Bull. Give him the knife."

Bull drops the knife at my feet and backs away.

The others back up a little also.

Only Joe stands his ground.

They must think it was some kind of trick to get a weapon. Or else, they just think I'm crazy. Either way, they don't want to stay too close.

I roll up my sleeve and pick up the knife. "Look here," I say. "This is what I mean." I run the knife across my forearm. "You cut somebody, they bleed. See?" The knife is surprisingly sharp, and the cut feels pretty deep. Blood comes pouring out and runs down onto my hand. I cup my hand so it fills up with blood, and hold it out to them. "You see? This is what you get when you stab somebody. Blood. Real blood." I pull up my shirt. The place where the big guy stuck me is bleeding a little. I jab the same spot with his knife, and then do it twice more until those spots are also bleeding pretty good.

Bull turns to Joe. "The motherfucker is nuts."

Joe ignores him. He's staring at me.

More blood leaks down into my hand. I cup it to catch as much of the blood as I can. I hold it out to Joe.

Joe nods thoughtfully. "Scotty may be nuts, but he has a way of making his point." He reaches out and shakes my bloody hand. He turns to show it to the others, and then he turns back to me. "All right, Scotty, let me tell you how it went down. We don't know who the trigger man was exactly, but we know it was small-time drug dealers. Not one of our bunch. A while back, they come here sellin' dope and end up killin' some white kid right on our turf. We been lookin' for 'em ever since, but they been layin' low. Then, they come back last night to shoot up the place. We sent people out lookin' for em right away. When we find out who did it, we'll deal with 'em."

I hold out both hands to Joe. "That's exactly what I'm tryin' to stop, Joe. You do that, and it'll just go on and on. Listen, tell you what. You find out who it was, then you tell me. I can get 'em put away for a long, long time."

"Bullshit," says Bull, pointing at me. "You gonna bring the cops down on all of us." He turns to Joe. "We should take care of this ourselves."

I ignore him and keep my eyes on Joe. "Listen to me, Joe. I got a connection. In the cops. I will guarantee you that the cops will leave your bunch alone if you give me the name of who did it. They don't give a shit who gets shot down here, but they gotta deliver whoever killed David, that white kid. If I give them those guys, they'll leave you alone."

Joe is staring at me. "You can guarantee that?"

I nod right back at him. "I can."

"And if you can't?"

"Then you know where to find me. If I fuck up, I'll be waiting for you. You saw what I did our there at Point Fermin Park. I was willing to jump right off that cliff, wasn't I? Shit, if I fuck up, I'll go straight there and do it by myself."

Bull steps forward, and it seems like he's about to say something, but Joe pulls him back and says, "All right, Scotty, we'll do it your way."

"Now wait a fuckin' minute," says Bull.

Joe raises a hand to shut him up. "I said, we'll try it his way. Then we'll see." He smiles as he holds his bloody hand up for the others to see. "I think we can take Scotty here at his word. Blood oath, right?" He turns back to me, still smiling. "Go home, Scotty. Wrap up those cuts. When I find out who did the shooting, I'll let you know."

On my way back home, I'm amazed not only that I'm still alive, but my demonstration of hacking on myself up actually worked. Looking back on it, it now almost seems like I pulled off some kind of circus act: come see the kid hurt himself, come see the blood flow. It sure did get their attention.

23
Non-Objectifying Self-Awareness

As soon as I come into the house, Pretty Boy flies down to land on my shoulder. I can tell he's happy to see me. Was he worried I might never come back?

I head for the bathroom to see how bad I hurt myself. I pull up my shirt to assess my injuries. Pretty Boy gets a good grip on my shirt and leans forward to look. He asks, "Pretty Boy?"

"Yeah, Pretty Boy, I got stuck with a knife. No big deal."

And I realize I'm not lying to him. I did get some cuts on my stomach and on my arm, but thinking back on it, it didn't hurt at all. While I was doing it, I felt like a dispassionate doctor doing surgery, as if wasn't my flesh that I was cutting on. The bleeding has mostly stopped, but the cut on my arm is still seeping. It looks pretty deep. Maybe it will leave a scar. That might not be a bad thing. Maybe a few scars will make people listen to me. But do I want people to listen to me? I guess I'm still thinking I have to do something, not only about poor little kids like Zyrell getting killed, but also about all the other shit that's going down in the world. Does that mean I'm no longer a *Hikikomori*? Am I starting to think I should go out into the world and try to make a difference? But what can I do? Who would listen to me?

In the bathroom closet, I find an old pillowcase and cut it up to make a long thin bandage to wrap around my arm. The few holes that I poked in my stomach aren't all that bad. Shouldn't require anything other than large Band-Aids.

That done, I chase Pretty Boy away and put on a fresh, non-bloody, shirt. I go into Grandma's bedroom to see if she needs anything. She's sound asleep, probably still worn out from her brief time of coming out of her bedroom to see what terrible things are going on the "real" world. Her TV is blasting away, as usual. I turn it down and go out to the kitchen to start making her lunch. As soon as she wakes up, she'll be tinkling her little bell, and I don't want her to have to wait. She said we have a bargain, and she's right. She provides me with a house and food, so it's only fair that I take care of her as well as I can.

I take her food back in to her, and find her awake. She's watching TV, of course, but she hasn't turned the volume up to it's usual blasting level. I wonder why.

When I put her food tray down on the table next to her bed, she actually turns her head to look at me. "That black kid gone?"

"Yeah, Grandma. He's gone."

"Good. I don't like those people in my house. Don't let them come back anymore."

"They won't, Grandma. His mother is going to take him out of the state."

She points down at my legs. "How come you're not in your wheelchair?"

"Oh," I say, and I also look down at my legs. When I got back from my confrontation with the gangbangers, I didn't even think about getting into my wheelchair. I don't think my legs could have gotten that much better that quickly, it's just that I can't seem to feel them anymore. In fact, I'm not feeling much of anything.

"Well?" she says, bringing me back.

"Oh, well, my legs are feeling a lot better these days, Grandma. Less pain anyhow. I guess walking around more is making them stronger."

"Good. So you're going to get me my food on time now? And you're not going to go running off to who knows where anymore?"

I point to the food tray. "Your lunch is right here, Grandma. I brought it in while you were still sleeping. And no, I'm not planning to go anywhere. I'll be here as long as you need me."

She glances at the food. "Well, all right then. But the soup probably won't be hot."

"I think it is, Grandma, but if it's not, I'll take it back out and reheat it for you. I don't mind."

She waves me off and goes back to watching her TV.

I go back out into the dining room, thinking about why I'm not feeling very much pain in my legs. In fact, I'm not even noticing my new cuts on my arm and my stomach, not unless I actually stop to think about it. Has something changed inside my brain? Has everything that's been happening, all the killing and death, finally turned off the part of my brain that feels pain?

"Well, how about that, Pretty Boy? I think I've finally figured it out."

But he's not up on his favorite lampshade. Now where did he fly off too?

I go into my bedroom, but he's not there. When did I seem him last. Seems like it was when I was in the bathroom looking at my wounds. Maybe that scared him.

I go into Grandma's room to see if, for some reason, he flew in there. And that's when I see that her bathroom door is open. No! Could it be? I point at the door to try to get Grandma's attention. "Grandma! Did you leave your bathroom window open again? Pretty Boy might fly out."

She shrugs. "It's not my responsibility to keep track of him. It's your bird."

I hurry into her bathroom, and sure enough, the window is wide open. I rush to the window and look out. At first, I don't see him, but then I hear his voice out there somewhere, a very shrill, "Pretty Boy."

I can't see him, but I can still hear him: "Pretty Boy. Pretty Boy."

I put my head out the window and look up. There he is, way up high in the neighbor's tree. There are other birds in the tree too, a couple of very large crows. I hold my finger out the window and call, "Pretty Boy. Get back in here." But he's not looking in my direction. He lets out a few shrill whistles and then another very clear, "Pretty Boy." What the hell does he think he's doing? Is he trying to make contact with crows? He must have flown into Grandma's bathroom to sit on the window sill like he did that time before, but this time, instead of just looking out at the other birds, he must have decided to go out there and have a talk with them. I keep calling for him, but he's ignoring me. He's still trying to talk to those crows: "Pretty boy. Pretty Boy." But they just stare down at him. They seem puzzled by the odd sounds the little bird is making. Or maybe they're just trying to figure out if the colorful little thing really is a bird.

I keep on trying to call him back in, but he's much too interested in the two crows to pay any attention to me. He keeps on trying to talk to them, and he's getting more shrill. I can tell he's frustrated that they won't respond to him.

From behind me, I hear Grandma calling: "Fitzgerald, what are you doing in there?"

"I'm trying to get Pretty boy back. You left your window open again, and he flew out into a tree."

"Well, isn't that where birds belong?" she says. "Close that window. I'm cold."

I know she's not cold. She just doesn't care if Pretty Boy gets away.

But I do care. I can't let him go. What would I do without him? It's like the last straw: death and dying all around me, and now this. I know the loss of a stupid little parakeet is nothing compared to the loss of my fellow humans, my friends, but this stupid situation is threatening to penetrate my numbness and bring back my pain. I can't let that happen.

I hurry out of the bathroom and go past Grandma's bed without saying a word to her. If I admitted to her how important Pretty Boy is to me, she'd just make fun of me. A grown up person making friends with a stupid little bird. Ridiculous.

But even if he is only a bird, he's my friend. He was with me when I went through a lot of shit. Besides, I know he won't last long out there. I should at least try to save him.

I hurry out the front door and go to the house next door. But there's a tall chain-link fence that keeps me from going into their backyard. I hear Pretty Boy still chatting away up there in their tree. Thank goodness, he hasn't flown away, not yet anyhow.

I go up onto the neighbor's porch and bang on their front door.

At first, nobody comes, but then the door opens a crack. A thin dark-skinned woman peers out at me. After all the time I've lived next door, why haven't I ever seen her before? She's got a security chain on the door that keeps it from opening any farther.

I lean forward and say, "Listen, lady, my name is Scott. I live right next door. My parakeet escaped, and he's up in your tree. I need to—"

"Your what?"

"My parakeet. It's a little blue and white bird. He's up in your tree. I need help getting him down."

She slams the door closed.

I frantically pound on the door and shout, "Please, lady. Just let me come through. I'll climb up and get him." But even as I say it, I wonder if I really could climb way up there. Maybe they have a ladder or something.

"Go away." Her voice is muffled by the thick door.

"Please. If I go under your tree, maybe I can call him down. Let me at least try."

"Go away, or I'll call the police."

Her words give me an idea. Maybe I should go back in and call the fire department. Maybe they'd be willing to use their tall ladders to get Pretty Boy down. I've heard of them rescuing cats out of trees. But would they come just to save a little bird? No, they probably don't even like coming into this neighborhood when there's an actual fire.

I go down off their porch and stand at the fence looking up at the tree. I hold out my finger and call, "Come down here, Pretty Boy. Right now! Aren't you hungry?"

But then I see that the tree is empty. The two crows are gone, and so is Pretty Boy. Those crows flew away, and Pretty Boy must have tried to follow them. The tree looks bare and empty. Is the tree dead too, like everything else in this stupid world?

But then I have a glimmer of hope. Maybe Pretty Boy flew back in through Grandma's bathroom window. Maybe he got tired of being out in the big world where nobody talks to you.

I hurry back inside and go down the hall to Grandma's room. "Did he come back?"

"How should I know?" she says. She won't take her eyes off of her TV.

I go into her bathroom and look out the window. The tree still looks bare and empty. No Pretty Boy.

I try to think what to do. Maybe he'll get hungry and come back—if he can find his way back.

I hurry out to the kitchen and scoop up a handful of bird seeds from the counter. I bring the seeds back to Grandma's bathroom and line them up all along the windowsill.

I go back into Grandma's bedroom. "Leave your window open for a while, Grandma. Maybe he'll come back."

"She says, "First you tell me not to leave it open, and now you tell me not to close it. What do you expect me to—"

"Damn it, Grandma. Just leave it open!" But then I'm, sorry I spoke so sharply. "Just leave it open for a little while. Let's see if he comes back."

She shrugs and goes back to focusing on her TV.

I go to my bedroom and sit down at my computer. I stare at the screen. What am I going to do without Pretty Boy? I feel like everybody and everything is being taken away from me, one buy one.

I don't even feel like looking up anything on the computer, so I lie down on my mattress and stare up at the ceiling. How long since I slept? Does sleep matter? Does anything matter?

It doesn't take me long to be absolutely sure I'm not going to be able to sleep. I get up and shuffle my way down the hallway to Grandma's bedroom. She's asleep, and her TV is off. Now that's a rarity.

I go into her bathroom. The window is still open, and the seeds are still there on the windowsill. It doesn't look like they've been disturbed. I look out. It's getting dark out there. The two crows are back in the tree, but Pretty Boy is not. Did they lead him astray? Or maybe they ate him. Do crows eat other birds? Hawks do, that's for sure. If poor little Pretty Boy ran into a hawk, he'd probably fly right up to it and try to talk, and that would be the end of one little too-talkative parakeet. It'd be like when I put those two spiders in the same bottle. Only one came out alive.

I hear somebody come up on the porch. I get up and hurry to open the front door, but all I see is a black low rider car disappearing down the street. Whoever it was, they left a piece of paper propped up against the side of the house next to the front door. I pick it up. There's a name on the paper. Is this the name of Zyrell's killer?

I go back inside and get on the computer to look up the phone numbers for the Los Angeles police department. There are a bunch of phone numbers under the heading, "How to Submit a Crime Tip." There are phone numbers for reporting everything from child abuse to drug crimes to stolen vehicles. But there's no phone number for murder. However, there is a 24-hour tip line. I take out Jake's cell phone and dial that number. I tell the woman who answers that I have a crime tip, and I need to talk to Officer Kelly. She asks who is calling, and I hesitate. But then I realize it doesn't matter if they know who I am. I give her my real name. She puts me on hold, and it's a long wait, but eventually Kelly comes on the line. He starts with, "So it's you again. You're the last person I expected to hear from."

"I'm not all that excited about talking to you again either, Kelly, but remember that night out at Point Fermin Park? The night you brought me home? You helped me out, and I appreciate that."

"So that's why you're calling me, to ask why I didn't come to make sure you're okay? Hey, kid, I've been busy keeping this city safe for punks like you. Besides, I didn't think your neighbors liked a white Irish cop like me hangin' around your place."

"I don't want you hanging around here either, Kelly, but this is not a social call. I've got a tip for you. I think I found out who killed that little boy the other night. Down the street at the projects. His name was Zyrell."

"Oh yeah? Since when did you start taking such an interest in community affairs? Black kids get killed all the time out there."

"Let's knock off the cynicism, Kelly. I knew that little boy. I baby-sat with him. A couple of times. He wasn't in a gang. He was just a sweet little boy. When he got killed, I knew I had to do something. So I went and found out who killed him."

"So you've changed your spots? Now you're gonna be the good citizen?"

"I've always been a good citizen, Kelly. I just keep to myself. I stay here and surf the internet, minding my own business."

"You only surf the internet, eh? Did the internet tell you how to hire a gang to do your revenge killings for you."

I start to come back at Kelly with a sarcastic response, but I stop myself. I can't let him write off Zyrell's death as just another gang killing. "I don't care what you think of me, Kelly, and I don't much care if the local gangbangers want to play cowboys and Indians and shoot the shit out of each other, but when wonderful little boys like Zyrell start getting killed in the crossfire, it's got to stop. You can't just ignore this as one more gang shooting. This is different."

"Okay, lighten up, kid. I didn't say I was gonna ignore it. We been out there a bunch of times since that little boy got killed, but everybody in the projects is locked down tight as a drum. You really think you know who did the shooting?"

"I've got the actual shooter's name." I read him the name off the paper. "I bet you know him, don't you? A drug dealer?"

"Yeah, we know him. Brought him in on drug charges a couple of times. In fact, as I recall, he's out on parole right now. And we even questioned him about the shooting of that white kid that got killed down there at those projects a while back. You sure he was the actual trigger man that killed that little boy?"

"I'm sure."

"Not that I don't believe you, but first you got to tell me how you found out. You got some kind of an in with the gangs out there? First they try to kill you, but now you're all buddy buddy with 'em?"

"Not exactly. What matters is that I went out and got that name for you. You need to nail somebody for killing that white kid, David. Right? Well, I'm pretty sure he was in on that one too. Now what're you gonna do about it?"

"What can I do? You got no proof."

This whole conversation is dragging me down into a very dark place. It's pretty clear that the cops just don't much care what goes on in this part of town. I've given him the name of the actual killer, but he just doesn't seem all that interested.

"You still there, kid?"

"I was just thinking about your response, Kelly. Here I give you the name of a killer on a silver platter, but it sounds like you're not gonna to do a damn thing about it."

"I didn't say that."

"What will you do?"

"Tell you what, kid. You tell me you're damn sure he really is the shooter, and I'll haul him in. I'll see what I can get out of him."

"All I know is what I was told. I was told he was the one that shot up the projects the other night. Tryin' to scare the residents to keep 'em quiet about what they might of seen the night that white guy, David, got killed. Zyrell just got hit by accident. Jesus, Kelly, the little kid was sound asleep in his bed. We can't just let that kind of shit go on, can we?"

"Do you think this guy acted alone?"

"I doubt it. Weren't there a lot of shots that night?"

"Well, if he wasn't alone, that makes it better. I'll pull his whole gang in and do the separate rooms trick. One of 'em will always squeal to save his own hide."

"Good."

There's a long silence before Kelly says, "How you doin', kid?"

I'm not sure I want to tell Cop Kelly anything, but it sounds like he really is willing to at least try to get Zyrell's killer. "Well, to tell you the truth, Kelly, I'm not doin' so hot."

"Still hurtin' from that beatin' you took out there at Point Fermin?"

"Naw, I'm getting over that okay. But after you took me up there to the desert where you found . . . you know, where you found my mom, I've been kind of . . . down. And now, with what happened to little Zyrell . . . Well, I guess I'll just say it's . . . getting to me."

"Yeah, I know. Tough thing all the way. I guess I never did say sorry. I mean about what happened to your mother, and how I acted. I just had to find out if —"

"I guess I'll get over it, Kelly. Just nail the son of a bitch that killed little Zyrell. That's all I'm asking of you."

"Okay. I'll see what I can do."

He hangs up without saying goodbye.

I turn off the phone and put it down. I stare at my computer screen. Now what? I can't think of anything to look up on the internet. In fact, it feels like I've been wasting my time doing all that learning. What good is it? I stare at the wall. The room feels cold and way too quiet. I pound my fist on the table. "Come on, Old Man. Why aren't you talking to me anymore?"

There is no such thing as value.

"Value? Are you talking about the value of learning, or the value of anything?"

Any and all actions are meaningless, except in terms of value.

"Wait a minute, Old Man. We've talked about this a thousand times. You told me doing anything is pointless, meaningless."

There is value in how your actions impact other humans.

"What do you mean by that? Action that impact other humans is the one thing that has value? Why?"

Life is finite.

"Life is finite? What is that supposed to mean?"

Human life is finite.

"Where are you going with this, Old Man? What does that have to do with value?"

No answer.

Why did he clam up all of a sudden? And what is he trying to tell me? As long as I've known him, he's been telling me that my actions are meaningless, but now, when I remind him about that, he gives me a riddle—human life is finite. What is that supposed to mean? Is he talking about how *my* actions affect others?

I turn and look toward the front door. Is he talking about my trip over there to the projects to talk to Joe and his gang buddies? I guess he's saying there *was* a point to that because it changed the behavior of other humans. It got me the name of Zyrell's killer, so maybe that time at least, my demonstrating that we humans are made of flesh and blood did have an impact. Is Old Man trying to tell me there is value in making other humans understand that life matters? And what about the life is finite thing? Is he telling me that I should face the fact that our lives are of limited duration, and therefore I should produce something that will have lasting impact on others even after I'm dead. Like what? I guess I could write a book about how I tried to kill myself by jumping off of a cliff, and how all that did was turn me into a cripple and give me a lot of pain. Yeah, I could write a book about that. I sure as hell know a lot about that. But who would want to read a book like that?

24
The Purpose of Existence

I've spent days and days thinking about the value of action in terms of it's impact on other humans. I've decided the old man is right: I should do something that has impact on people. When I went down to the projects to meet with those gangbangers, they paid attention to me because I made my point by cutting on myself. I keep on remembering the look in their eyes when I did that. As soon as the blood started to flow, their attention was riveted on me, like I was some kind of weird circus performer, doing something they couldn't take their eyes off of. And it helped me get through to them. They understood I was trying to say a human life has value. When the old man reminded me that life is finite, he was telling me to stop and think about what I'm doing with my life. When I went over there to talk to those gang guys, for that moment at least, I had a purpose out in the real world. I went outside this house and did something meaningful.

And that's got me thinking that maybe I could have impact on other people, regular people, if I showed them the same thing. It's got me to wondering how regular people would react to me cutting on myself like that? Would I be able to teach them something about the value of life? I've never thought of myself as a teacher. In fact, I made fun of the teachers in school. But all they did was talk. Talk, talk, talk about crap that didn't matter to me, shouldn't matter to anybody. But what if I've found a better way to teach, a way of teaching without talking, by teaching through demonstration? How would people react?

I roll my chair to the window, and pull back the curtain to look out. The world is out there. What does it want from me? Do I really have something to teach them? If I went out there and showed them I was willing to hurt myself as a demonstration of what it means to be alive, to be a human, would they pay attention? Or would I be like poor Pretty Boy, trying to talk to a bunch of crows who have no idea of what he's saying? And what would I be trying to say? That we're all the same inside our skins, only flesh and blood, no matter how hard we try to pretend otherwise? Maybe they would be surprised to learn that at least one person on this earth has learned how not to feel pain. But so what? Would they take that to mean anything about themselves? Descartes said, "I think therefore I am." He meant we're self aware, and that's what makes us human. But the fact that we all have feelings and emotional pain is another thing that makes us human. We are self aware of our own pain, whatever the cause. I remember when I first started reading Derrida's ideas, he talked about how hard it is to nail down what humanness is. He wrote a whole book about it, *The Animal That Therefore I Am.* The title was obviously referring to the Descartes assertion about self-awareness, but he was also exploring other things that make us human. Can I also get people to think about what it means to be human?

I decided there was only one way to find out, so this morning, I went through the house looking for sharp things. I found an assortment of kitchen knives and an X-Acto knife. I found some razor blades, and I created a bunch of broken glass. When Grandma was asleep, I went through her stuff and found a variety of pins and needles. Then, I dug into the back of the hall closet and found one of Grandma's old purses. It's a black leather thing, probably expensive in its day, from back when she was out in the world chasing after men. Now I've put my collection of sharp things into that purse, and I'm ready to go out into the world and see if the world will pay any attention to my little demonstrations.

The sun is setting. Time to go. I fix Grandma's last meal of the day and take it in to her. She's sleeping. She sleeps a lot these days.

I go back into my bedroom and pick up my purse full of sharp things. I grab the blanket from my bed and my cane, and a large bottle I found under the sink.

I go out the front door and hobble down the front porch steps. I head for the bus stop. I don't think about what I'm about to do. Old Man would probably tell me to stop and think more about it, but I'm not going to ask for his permission. I will do what is necessary, and I will have no regrets.

As I approach the corner where the young gang wannabes hang out, they turn to stare at me. I wonder what they've heard about me. Do they know about what happened out at Point Fermin Park? And did Joe tell them how I cut myself up on the playground out behind the projects they all live in?

One of the gang dudettes steps forward as if he's ready to hassle me. I recognize him. It's the tall dancing pretend-boxer who used me for a punching bag that night I was heading for my cliff at Point Fermin Park. Man, how long ago was that? It seems like a hundred years ago.

Before he can say a word, I say, "Are you going to kill me?"

That seems to confuse him.

"No? Then get the fuck out of my way."

He backs off, and they all stare at me as I go past. They must have heard about me, the crazy white kid who cuts on himself.

At the bus stop, the old dark-skinned people stare at me. That's unusual. Have they heard about the white kid that got stabbed on a bus? Or is it just that they can they tell there's something different about me tonight?

When the bus arrives, I sit by myself in the back. On the bus ride downtown, I think about what I'm about to do. How will the people react? That's the only unknown. I'm going to do what I do, so I guess it doesn't matter how they react.

When we arrive at the downtown train station, I wait until everybody else has gotten off the bus, then I get off and make my way to the train station's main entrance. People stream by me, all of them in a hurry. They're probably happy to have finished their long boring day at work and are eager to get home.

I take a deep breath and go inside.

I've never been in this building before. The amazingly high ceilings and the fancy marble walls are impressive, but none of it means anything to me. All I need is a spot to do my thing.

I find a good spot across the room from the information booth.

I lay out my blanket and sit down on it cross-legged. I take my sharp tools out of the purse and carefully lay them out in a neat row.

A few people, curious, stop to see what I'm up to.

A middle-aged man in a dark blue suit stares at my tools, I size him up. He probably works in one of the high-rise office buildings downtown. Probably just getting off work.

He leans down and says, "What's all this? You selling that crap?"

I pretend I don't hear him. I roll up my right sleeve.

I touch my tools, one at a time, while I watch his eyes.

He seems to react when I touch the razor blade.

I pick it up and cut my forearm with it. Not much blood comes out, so I slice it again. This time, I get a little more blood, and he reacts by pulling back, a shocked look on his face.

I point to the open mouth of my bottle that's at the front of my blanket.

He seems puzzled. "What the hell? You do this for money?"

I again point to the bottle.

"You want money? For cutting the shit out of your arm?"

I keep quiet and wait, staring past him.

The guy shakes his head and walks away.

Well, that wasn't such a great start, but other people were watching. Some of them are staying close by—but not too close—probably waiting to see what I'm going to do next.

Two older ladies were watching while I did my thing with the razor blade. They're both dressed in old-lady pantsuits, one a sort of pinkish color, the other, traditional trailer park lime green. The one in the lime green outfit says to the pink lady, "Did you see that? What, is he crazy?" They don't bother to keep their voices down.

I smile at them, and that draws them a bit closer.

Again, I reach out to touch each of my tools while I watch their eyes. When I touch Grandma's fancy long hat pin that has a fake diamond on the end of it, the lady in the pink outfit points and says, "That one."

I oblige her by picking the hat pin up. I hold it up high to make sure the onlookers that are starting to crowd in can see it clearly. I pinch up some skin on the top of my wrist and slowly stick the pin in.

I hear a gasp from one or two in the crowd.

Good, that's what I'm looking for. If they make some noise, it will draw others in.

The two old ladies cringe and clutch at each other as they watch the pin slowly go into the skin of my wrist. When the somewhat dull hat pin pushes the skin on the other side of my wrist up into a small tent shape, they lean closer.

I pause and point toward the tip jar, but they pull back, frowning.

Another guy pushes forward.

I'd put him at about forty, overweight and balding. He's wearing a well-worn dark suit.

He leans down and drops a dollar bill into my jar.

I nod, and go back to pushing the pin through. But it's too dull to get all the way through. I have to push it harder to get it to pop out through the skin on the other side, and when it does, a spurt of blood squirts out.

The two old ladies hurry away, but the guy in the suit doesn't. He has a bemused smile on this face. He says, "You do this for a living?"

I nod, but I don't say anything. I hold up my arm to give him a better look at the hat pin sticking through the skin of my wrist. I hold it up high so they all can see. I want to make sure that none of them think this is any kind of trick. I want them all to know the pin is real, and that the blood is real, and that I feel no pain at all.

"I'll be damned," says the guy in the suit.

I touch my tools again, but the guy walks away.

Others crowd forward to take his place. Without me needing to say a word, they all get it. All they have to do is let me know which sharp tool they like, and I will use it to "hurt" myself—as long as they put money in my jar. Cop Kelly said if I need to buy food for Grandma and me, I should go out and earn some money. So, here I am, out earning money.

I touch each of my tools and stare at the people.

When I get to the large safety pin, a woman says, "Do that one."

I point to my jar.

She fishes a dollar out of her purse and tries to hand it to me.

I point to my jar, and she drops it in.

I pick up the safety pin and quickly pin it to my wrist, next to the hat pin.

There is hardly any blood, and she seems disappointed.

A big guy in a somewhat dirty gray T-shirt laughs and says, "Hey, what would happen if you used a safety pin to hook two of your fingers together?"

I smile and point to the jar.

He drops in a couple of dollars, and I oblige by picking up another large safety pin. I use it to slowly and carefully hook the skin of my little finger on my left hand to the skin of the finger next to it.

I hold up my hand to show them.

The guy in the gray T-shirt says, "Christ, doesn't that hurt?"

I just smile and go back to pointing at my tools.

By the time the cops show up, I've got quite a bit of money in my jar. There are two of them, both uniformed LAPD patrolmen, both young, one dark-skinned and one light-skinned. As soon as I see them coming, I grab the money out of my jar and stuff it into my pants pocket.

The white cop pushes through the crowd that's gotten quite large. All right, break it up," he says, trying to put on a gruff voice that I suspect is intended to sound older and more sure of himself than he actually is.

The people take a few steps back, but they don't leave.

Good. I want them to see this.

He leans down to look at the various pins and pieces of razor blades that are stuck into my arms. He frowns. "What the hell you up to, bud?"

Making sure my voice is completely calm, I say, "It's my art, officer. I'm the pain artist. You want a demonstration?" I pick up a small paring knife and poke my arm with it a few times, not too hard, just enough to draw blood.

"Oh, for Christ's sake," he says. "Now I've seen it all."

"It's performance art," I say. " I'm the pain artist."

"Performance art my ass," he says. "Hurting yourself is art now? That's it, buddy. Stand up." He takes out his handcuffs.

I say, "You can't arrest me. I'm not hurting anybody but myself."

He just shakes his head, frowning. The two of them get on both sides to stand me up.

I say, "Wait. My art tools." I manage to break free long enough to grab my cane and most of my tools and stuff them into my purse before they jerk my arms behind me and put the cuffs on.

Outside, they drag me to their cop car and push me into the back seat. The dark-skinned cop dumps my blanket and my purse into my lap.

Thank goodness they let me keep my tools. I'll have to make sure I get them back when I get out of jail And I know I *will* get out of jail. I looked it up on the internet before I started this: there's no law in LA against street performances.

"Hurting" myself, as they called it, is my street performance, and it said on the internet that there's no law against setting out a tip jar, as long as it's considered a donation.

At the police station, a woman cop who's behind a counter takes my purse and my blanket and makes me remove the pins from my skin.

She cringes as I take my time pulling out the long hat pin. They also take my cane, and they make me take off my belt and my shoes. Do they think I might try to kill myself? That makes me laugh. If they only knew how bad I am at that.

The cops go through my pockets and dump the wadded-up bills on the counter.

"Hey!" I say. "That's my money."

"You'll get it back," the woman says.

"I want a receipt for that exact amount."

She shakes her head. She looks disgusted, but she does write it down in a book. She turns the book around to show me: fifty three dollars. "Hey," I say, "fifty-three bucks. Not bad for a first day."

That done, they walk me down a long hallway and put me in a cell. It's quiet, not at all like that other noisy cell block where I got put in with those gangbangers. There don't seem to be any other prisoners in this whole area. I wonder if this is where they put the nut cases.

Soon, a light-skinned woman cop comes and stares at me through the bars. She looks at me for a long time. Her face seems distressed. I'd like to tell her not to worry about me, that I'm doing fine, but I keep my mouth shut, and after a while she goes away without saying anything. To her, I must be some kind of sideshow freak. But then I guess that's what I've set myself up to look like. I decide to think of her as a *fan*.

I lie on my side on the hard cot, staring at the flaking-paint wall. I sense other cops are coming to stare at me. I ignore them. They leave, but soon I hear heavy footsteps coming down the hall. More fans, I suppose.

"So it is you."

I turn to look at the voice. It's Cop Kelly. Despite myself, I have to admit I'm glad to see him. I sit up. "Well, hello there, Kelly. Come to beat me up again?"

That makes him frown. "Hey, kid, lighten up. I thought we were past all that game playin'."

I get up and go to the bars. "Sorry, Kelly. Force of habit. Some of your *compadres* have been comin' by to stare at me. Curious about the monkey they've got in the cage, I guess." I grab the bars with both hands and try to shake them.

"What the hell have you been up to this time, kid? When everybody upstairs started talkin' about a crippled kid they brought in that calls himself the pain artist, I figured it could be you."

"Yep, it's me, the pain artist. In the flesh, so to speak. Hey, Kelly, check this out." I pull up my sleeve to show him the cuts and the smeared blood on my arm. "I made fifty-three bucks in only a couple of hours. How about that?"

He stares at me. "Are you saying people paid you to cut the shit out of yourself?"

"Yep. Pretty good, eh?"

Now it's his turn to grab the bars. He seems pissed off at me.

"What do you mean, good? It's stupid. Hurting yourself just so people will give you money."

"Hey, you were the one who said I should go out and get myself a job. So, that's what I did. I created a new occupation. I'm a pain artist."

He shakes his head. "I don't know where you're goin' with this, kid." He uses his thumb to point back over his shoulder. "But I can guarantee you one damn thing, they won't let you do it."

"They can't stop me, Kelly. I'm not doing anything wrong. I looked it up. Performance street art is not illegal in this town."

He's still staring at me. "You've changed, kid. What's up with you?"

I shrug. "Listen, Kelly. It's just that I finally found something I'm good at, and then they go and throw me in jail for doin' it."

"Well, I don't think they actually want to arrest you. They're just tryin' to make sure you stop doin' it. If you'll just promise never to do it again, I think I can get them to let you go. I'll tell 'em I know you and how you've had a hard life. Mother murdered and all. You tell 'em you're sorry and you'll never do it again, and I don't think they'll bring charges."

"Charges? For what? I didn't do a damn thing to hurt anybody but myself. Like I said, it's performance art. My performance art. I'm the Pain Artist, and I'm good at it. It won't be long before everybody knows about me. I'll be famous."

He smacks my fingers where they're holding onto the bars.

I quickly pull my hands back, even though it didn't hurt, not a bit.

"Knock that shit off, kid. You aren't fooling me. I know you. You like to play games You think you can put one over on the dumb cops. Well, you keep that shit up, and they'll keep you here as long as they want to. They're already talkin' about sending you on over to the hospital. To the psych ward. Let 'em do that, and it'll be a long spell before you get out, and you can trust me on that one."

Uh oh, not that damn psych ward again. I didn't count on that. And this time, I might not have somebody like David to help me escape.

Kelly shakes his finger at me. "Know what they do to people like you over on that psych ward?"

"Uh, no."

"Well, trust me, you wouldn't like it. You just hang tough here for a while, and I'll go upstairs and see if I can get you out on your own recognizance. So far, all they've charged you with is doin' a business without a permit. No big deal."

I just nod and keep my mouth shut.

That seems to satisfy him, and he walks away down the long hallway.

I sit on the cot to wait. A few cops com to look at me. I smile at them.

They don't smile back.

Pretty soon, Cop Kelly comes back and they let him into my cell. He sits on the edge of my cot next to me. "Okay, here's the deal. I got you a bail hearing. Now listen up before we go to the courtroom. I know this judge. She's heard a lot of my cases, and she owes me a favor or two. So let me do the talkin'. All they've got on you is doin' business without a permit. A misdemeanor. All we have to do is make sure the judge focuses on that, and doesn't make you out to be a nutter. You apologize and say you'll never do it again. They let you go, and I take you home. Got it?"

Again, I only nod. No need to tell him what I'm really going to do.

He goes away, and all I can do is wait. So I'm going before a judge. This should be interesting.

After a short time, two cops come to get me. Did it take two of them? Are they afraid of the nutter?

The cops stand me up and put a chain around my waist. It has handcuffs attached to it. They put the handcuffs on my wrists, and they also put chained shackles on my ankles. Looks like something out of the dark ages. I say, "Hey, what's with all this hardware? Am I dangerous?"

They don't smile. They get ahold of my elbows to lead me out of the cell, but with the clumsy chain that's got my ankles hooked together, it forces me to put too much weight onto my weak left leg, and I almost go down. The cops catch me just in time. One of them says, "What's the matter? Can't you walk?"

I say, "My legs are all fucked up. If you don't believe me, pull up my pants legs and look for yourself."

He does pull up my left pant leg. He takes one look and says, "Jeez."

They both get ahold of my arms, and they half drag, half carry me out of the cell and down the long hallway. It doesn't seem too hard for them to hold me up, and that makes me again wonder how much weight I've lost. I've hardly thought about eating lately, and I was thin to start with. I notice how thin my wrists are, and that gives me the weird thought that they look about as thin as in those pictures of poor starving people in the Nazi concentration camps. Hey, maybe looking so thin will help my Pain Artist business. I'll have to make sure I don't put on any weight.

But I know I have to push those kinds of distracting thoughts away. I have to start planning what I'm going to say to the judge when we get to the courtroom.

The two cops take me into the courtroom and put me behind a floor-to-ceiling clear plastic barrier. Oh no, the damn plastic wall might mess up my whole plan: how will the judge be able to hear my explanation? Damn. Maybe the prisoner is not allowed to talk in a bail hearing. Maybe only the lawyer is allowed to talk. But I don't have a lawyer. Or is that guy in the dark suit sitting at that table next to Cop Kelly supposed to be my lawyer?

I watch as a man in a police uniform goes forward to talk to the woman judge who is behind a high bench.

She looks up and waves Cop Kelly forward. They have a short conversation, and then Kelly gestures to the two cops.

The two cops get ahold of my arms and lead me out from behind the plastic wall and into the courtroom. They stand me up in front of the judge. As soon as they back off, Kelly gets ahold of my arm to make sure I don't tip over.

"Judge," he says," this is the young fellow I was telling you about. The crippled kid who lost his mother. The woman that was murdered, remember?"

The judge stares at me, and then looks back at Cop Kelly.

"Anyhow, judge," says Kelly, "they picked him at the train station downtown. He was doin' stuff to try to get people's loose change."

She stares at him. "Doing stuff?"

"Well," says Kelly, "he got this idea that if he stuck pins and stuff into his arms, people would give him money. The kid is crippled, like I said, and he's been havin' a hard time gettin' a job, your honor. But I think if he agrees never to do it again, we should drop the charges and let him go. I'll take him home and make sure he stays away from that train station."

The judge turns to me. "That right, son? You were sticking yourself with pins. Why were you doing that?"

She waits for an explanation, staring at me, and just for a moment, I think about going along with Kelly's plan. I know he's only trying to help me. But I know I'm going to have to tell her the truth. It's the only way now. Nothing else matters. "Judge, or your honor, or whatever I'm supposed to call you, the truth is I was down there practicing my art. I'm a performance artist, you see. I'm the

Pain Artist. I'm not crazy, your honor. I'm just trying to demonstrate to people that we're all human, nothing but flesh and blood."

The judge seems interested. "How to you do this so-called demonstration?"

"I penetrate my flesh with things. Pins and such."

"Doesn't that hurt?"

"No, your honor, I've learned how to turn off pain."

"Is that right? How did you learn to do that?"

I try to think how to explain it. I know what I say next will either make her understand or make her think I'm nuts and order me locked up in the nut house. "It took a long time, your honor. But in time, the deteriorating state of the world, the violence of us humans against our fellow humans, led me to not want to feel it anymore. I studied the neurology of pain, and for a while I tried meditating like the Eastern gurus do, but when that didn't work, I—"

"All right, young man. I don't need to know all that. You claim you were doing your so-called performance art, but I'm told you were asking people to give you money. While they watched."

"That's not true, your honor. I admit I had a tip jar sitting out, just like the street musicians do, but I never asked anybody for money. I read that street artists can legally put out a tip jar."

She looks past Cop Kelly at the man in the dark suit sitting at the big table. "You're charging him with operating a business without a license? Doesn't sound to me like he was running any kind of business."

The man at the table stands up. "Well, he was cutting himself. And people were, uh, paying money to watch him do it."

The judge shakes her head. "But that's not a business. Not if the giving was voluntary. Like he said, what about street musicians putting out tip jars? Are you going to start hauling them in here too?"

The man looks nervous. "But your honor, he was cutting himself with razor blades and things. He was—"

"He calls it his art."

"Art? Cutting yourself is art?"

She turns back to me. "I'm not so sure I'd call what you do art either. The way you describe it, to me, it sounds more like free speech. You say you're making a statement about the state of the world, so maybe you'd like to rephrase what you said to me. Maybe you'd like to tell me you were exercising your first amendment right of free speech."

I don't hesitate. "Yes, your honor, that's actually the way I look at it. I call myself a performance artist, but in fact I'm using my art to try to make a statement."

She turns back to the man in the suit who is still standing behind his big table. He can't seem to come up with a way to respond.

"Well then," says the judge, "if you're not interested in taking this first amendment case to the Supreme Court, then I suggest we drop the charges and let him go. Do you agree?"

The man shrugs.

The judge turns to Cop Kelly. "Listen, Kelly. I don't like what he's doing to himself any more than you do, but I don't think the prosecutor would have a chance of convicting him of breaking any law I can think of. You tell your people to leave him alone. Case dismissed."

Kelly starts to say something to her, but seems to change his mind. He pulls me away and helps me limp back out through the door and into the busy hallway. He tells the two waiting cops to unhook me.

They start to protest, but he says, "The judge dismissed the case against him. She says his so-called performance art is actually exercising his right of free speech. She said that from now on, we're supposed to leave him alone."

They both shake their heads in disgust, but they do unhook my handcuffs and shackles. They head off down the hallway.

Kelly looks at me, not smiling. "The judge may be right, kid. Maybe hurting yourself isn't against any law, but I want you to stop it. Will you do that for me?"

I shake my head. "Listen, Kelly, I wasn't bullshittin' that judge. I think I do have something to say. How do you think I got those gangbangers to give me the name of the shooter who killed that little boy?"

"By cutting yourself?"

"Yes. It got them to pay attention. It made them stop and think about the fact that we're all in this together, that we're all humans, all made of the same flesh and blood."

Kelly stares at me, frowning. I can tell he's not going for it. "You know what I think, kid. I think maybe they should have locked you up in that nut house. You keep on cutting on yourself, you're gonna end up dead. Ever hear of infection?"

I look him right in the eyes. "Does it matter, Kelly? Think about it. Would it really matter to anybody if I'm alive or dead? At least I should try to make them listen in the time I've got left."

"And what about your old grandmother? If you die, who's gonna take care of her?"

"My old grandma is a lot tougher than you think. She's a bit out of it, but she's healthier than you think. Besides, I'm not planning on dying anytime soon.

Tell you what, you offered to drive me home. On our way, let's stop at a drugstore, and I'll get myself some alcohol and salve and any other stuff that wards off infections. That satisfy you?"

"No, but it's better than nothing. After that, I'll take you home, and then I hope this is the last time I ever hear about you."

25
The Meaning of Existence

Cop Kelly didn't get his wish. He heard plenty about me. In fact, everybody heard plenty about me. It didn't take long before the word about what I was doing got around. The Times sent a reporter and a photographer down to the train station, and the next day, there was a big story about me, the Pain Artist, in the "entertainment" section of the newspaper. Next thing you knew, a couple of TV stations came down to film me in action. Then, the people who'd seen me on their TVs started arriving early for their trains just to watch me. Eventually, the celebrity tour buses added me as a regular stop so the tourists could come and gawk at me.

Through it all, I remained aloof. I refused to play along with the phony TV and radio interviews because they always asked the same two dumb questions: Why are you doing this? And Doesn't that hurt? All I would say is, "My actions are my statement. I am the Pain Artist. If you don't understand what my actions are saying about what it means to be human, then there's nothing more I can possibly add that will help you 'get it'."

Of course, the call-in talk radio people got all worked up about what I was doing. Those radio stations had a field day, getting people to call in and rant about me, for or against.

But that only made more people come to see me. They put more and more money into my tip jar. So much money, I got enough to pay for my mother's cremation. They gave me her ashes in an urn. For a while, I put the urn next to my computer so I could look at it often and think about her. But then, I decided what I should to do with her ashes: I went downtown and sprinkled them over those stars they have embedded in the Hollywood sidewalk of fame. She always fantasized about having her own star in that sidewalk, so it seemed like the place she should end up.

Unfortunately, some of the TV media people must have been following me, because they were there with their video cameras that night to catch me "in the act." The talk show people thought there should be a law against doing that too, but the cops continued to leave me alone.

But in time, people will get bored with anything. I still have a few regulars that come by to give me money, but usually they don't even stick around to watch me hurt myself anymore.

Tonight is the slowest night yet. The station is so quiet, even the soft cooing of the pigeons high up in the rafters seems loud. I watch them up there as they flutter and pace and coo, living out their pigeon lives up there. Somehow, they found their way into the station, and now, like me, they're stuck here, dependent on crumbs from strangers. Do they know that is their fate? Were they born in this station? Do they even know there's an "outside" world. It makes me think about Pretty Boy. Did he feel trapped in Grandma's old house? Did he think I was also trapped there? Is that why he escaped when he got the chance? Was he trying to tell me something? I look up and wonder if any of those pigeons up there ever met Pretty Boy.

It's getting on toward midnight, and there is hardly any money in my tip jar. I'm beginning to think this chapter of my life has about run its course. I come here every night and sit here cross-legged on my blanket, mostly ignored by the streams of people passing by. I watch them go by and try to imagine what their lives are like.

At Grandma's house, I still get on the internet and read about philosophy, but Old Man hardly ever talks to me anymore. I'm not sure why. Maybe he thinks now that I'm the famous Pain Artist, I don't need his guidance anymore. Or maybe he's just given up on me. Without him to help me make some sense out of everything, the days just go by, one after the other. I make Grandma her meals, and then when it starts to get dark, I make her supper, and then I take a cab down here to the train station to do my thing. But I rarely get a chance to do my thing anymore. Nobody seems to care about my "message" anymore. Maybe they never did. Maybe they watched me in order to *not* think about what their own shitty lives were like. I suppose their lives are difficult enough without me reminding them that we're all fragile human beings. I guess they were just curious, just wanted to see "the weirdo" in action. I was probably nothing but some weird sideshow down at the train station.

Well, so be it. What does it matter? More and more these days, I'm thinking about going back to my cliff. Not literally, of course; I'd probably fuck that up again. Like I told David, there are easier ways to kill yourself. I could use what little money I have left and go down to any street corner near the projects and buy some heroin. Or maybe they would just kill me, the way they killed David when he went there to buy heroin. Maybe that would be better. Another white kid killed in Watts trying to buy heroin. It would make the news: "Pain Artist killed on the street in Watts." Maybe then people would pay attention to what goes on in South Central Los Angeles.

But they wouldn't pay attention for very long. It made the news when David got killed, and it briefly made the news when poor little Zyrell got killed. But the news, and therefore the people, quickly forgot about them.

I see an oddly-dressed young couple come in through the main entrance.

Ah ha, potential audience. By now, I can usually tell the types that will be attracted to my act, and these two look like the type. They stop in the middle of the wide expanse of polished floor and look around.

What are they looking for? A mark? A drug connection? They both look like they're already on something, probably heavy downers. Both of them are dressed in goth black. The girl is dressed in a long black gown that drags on the floor, and the guy is wearing a black T-shirt that has several holes torn in it, each hole undoubtedly torn intentionally to get just the right look. On one of his arms, a snake with a vampire-looking human face wiggles down out of his cut-off sleeves.

The girl clings to the guy's arm, staring up at the pigeons. She's pretty, and maybe a little older than him. Despite the fact that her face is all whited out with some kind of makeup, and she's got painted black stuff all around her eyes, she looks familiar. Has she been here before to see me do my act?

The guy notices me. He comes closer, leaving her standing there in the middle of the station, looking up at the pigeons.

As he gets closer, I see that his shiny, tight black pants look like snakeskin. Could be real, but more likely fake. He has way-too-black spiky hair, a silver nose ring, and a matching eyebrow ring. The whole goth getup. It's clear these two are both heavy "into" the goth thing. Sitting here night after night, I see a lot of nose and belly button rings, and other body "ornamentation," but I don't see much goth. I read on the internet that goth was big back in the sixties and seventies. Maybe it's making a comeback.

The guy leans down to look over my tools. He says, "What's this stuff, dude?"

Of course, I don't answer him. I just point to each tool and then to my tip jar.

"What, are you selling this shit?"

He still doesn't get it. I pick up a few thumbtacks and stick them into my arm.

The boy raises his eyebrows and squats down for a closer look. "Cool," he whispers, not to me, to himself. He grabs my arm and looks closely at the two thumbtacks. I don't like people touching me, but he has a strong grip, so I decide to just wait him out while he examines the various scabs and healed-over scars on arms.

He stands back up and goes to get the girl.

He brings her back by the arm, and says, "Check this out."

But she doesn't seem to hear him, or even notice I'm here. She's still staring up at the pigeons, lost in her drugged-out haze.

Now that she's closer, I realize her long black gown is made out of some kind of thick black netting. The way it clings to her body creates an odd effect, as if she's been painted black, but with evenly-spaced flesh-colored spots left unpainted. I'm pretty sure she doesn't have anything on underneath that gown: I can see her pale white skin through the holes in the netting material, but where her nipples should be, there's just two dark circles. Has she also painted them black?

"Watch what he does," says the guy.

The girl glances down at me, surprised to see me, as if I've just appeared out of nowhere.

She stares at me, and it suddenly hits me that I do know her: it's Lilly. My god, how she's changed. Underneath all that white and black face paint, her face looks years older. I wonder if she really did go up there to Alaska with that trucker guy, and if so, how did she get back here, all dressed like a seventies goth girl, and with a new guy.

Seeing her gives me the oddest feeling; it's like some kind of old ache deep inside my brain is being activated. I try to push the memory of my time with her away. Memories are pointless, mere collections of neurons hidden away somewhere deep in my brain, long-lost reminders of the old dark days back when I was still "in" the human race, back before I learned how to turn everything like that off.

Just for her, for old times sake. I dig out one of my longest hat pins, the one with a bright pink plastic bead on the end. I show it to her and then push it through the skin of my wrist, making sure I do my usual pause as the no-longer-very-sharp end of the pin pushes out the skin before breaking out through the other side. The blood runs down my wrist, and like always, I hold up my arm for them to see the blood. Got to make sure she understands this is real; it's not a trick.

The boy grins. "All right!"

But Lilly seems puzzled by what I have just done. Does she remember me?

"Good one," says the guy, grinning. "Do another one."

As usual, I just point to my tip jar.

He doesn't seem to get it, so as always, I will have to wait him out.

While I wait for him to cough up some money, I stare are Lilly. Damn, it seems so long ago since we were together in my bed. Like in another lifetime, long, long ago.

She stares back at me, and I suspect she is also trying to remember, trying to clear away the cobwebs of whatever drug she's on, trying to make sense of seeing me here on my blanket in this train station, sticking pins into my arm.

The guy wanders away. Probably bored with my hat pin trick. Or maybe he just doesn't have any money.

But Lilly stays. She moves a little closer, a concerned look on her face.

I make sure I keep my usual impassive look on my face, determined not to give anything away. I have to be sure there is no longer anything *to* give away: the human named Scotty who cared about another human named Lilly is long gone. If she wasn't so stoned, maybe she'd realize that I am no longer that person.

She reaches out toward me with both hands, but I pull back. I can't let this happen; I must remain completely logical. It's not logical to care about anything in this shit world. It would be better if she just went away.

For a moment, I think she's about to speak, but she seems to change her mind and instead kneels down in front of me.

What is she up to?

She reaches out toward my arm, but I pull it away.

She scoots closer and gets ahold of my wrist.

I decide to let her do whatever she is going to do. I don't care. It doesn't matter to me one way or the other.

Carefully, she extracts the pin from my arm and uses an edge of her black gown to very gently wipe the blood off of my arm. When more bloods seeps out, she again wipes it away.

What the hell? Does she think she can get through to me by wiping away a little blood? If she only knew how much blood I've lost sitting here cutting and poking and piercing myself, night after night, in this lonely corner of a train station. What do I care about losing a little more blood? And why would I care if somebody I used to know wants to wipe away a tiny bit of my blood?

I push her hand away. If she likes blood, I'll show her some real blood.

I pull up my shirt and pick up my X-Acto knife. I hold it up to show her how cruel and sharp the long pointed blade is. I quickly make a short cut across my stomach, a few inches long. The blood seeps out.

Okay, I think, what are you going to do about that, Lilly? Are you going to try to wipe that blood away too?

She stares at the blood seeping out; then she looks back up at my face.

What does that look mean? Concern? Maybe, maybe not. She's not reacting at the sight of that much blood the way most people do, none of the usual hypnotized fascination mixed with disgust.

She just stares into my eyes.

I know what she'll do next. I've been doing this long enough to know how people react. She's not one of the sadistic ones who actually like seeing somebody hurt, and she's not one of the angry ones who put their hands on their hips and say they're going to call the police. No, any moment now, she will just get up and walk away. She'll try to forget the weirdo who sits on an old blanket in the train station, grossing people out by cutting on himself.

I wait for her to get up and leave, but she doesn't. Instead, she sits down cross-legged in front of me and lightly touches my wrist. What is she doing? Oh, I get it: she's trying to take the X-Acto knife out of my hand.

After a moment of hesitation, I let her take it.

The silver metal of it must feel cold to her. Does she know what that particular tool can do to human flesh? Does she care?

I know what she will do next. She will put it down on my blanket and try to talk me out of hurting myself anymore. Despite her big show of dressing up all gothy and hiding her face behind a bunch of ghoulish face paint, I suspect she's still the same old Lilly, the girl who was studying to be a medical technician, the girl who felt sympathy when she looked at what those damn surgeons did to my legs.

But she does not put the tool down. She runs her thumb over the blade.

Is she testing it to see how sharp it is? I can guarantee her, it is *very* sharp. I put in a new blade after just about every performance.

She pulls up the front of her net garment. As as I suspected, she's naked under the net dress. I look at the dark triangle of her pubic hair, remembering. But then I force myself to stop remembering. I don't want to remember. There's no point in thinking about the past. The past is gone forever. It means nothing.

She puts the point of the blade against her own stomach and looks into my eyes.

Why is she looking at me like that? What does she expect me to do, stop her? But it is not for me to either encourage her or stop her. We make our own reality, each of us. Beyond that, there is no meaning to anything.

She makes a quick cut on her own abdomen, not all that deep, but some blood does seep out.

The cut in her stomach is almost exactly the same as the cut I made in my own stomach. What point is she making? That she can do what I do? She can't. I'm the Pain Artist, the one and only Pain Artist.

Or is she trying to tell me something about pain, that things *should* hurt? Well, it may hurt her when she cuts herself, but it doesn't hurt me when I do it to myself. Not a bit.

She hands the knife back to me.

Why did she do that? I look at the X-Acto knife in my hand. Then, I look up and see that she's watching me. She seems to be waiting for something. Is she saying it's now my turn?

I look around to see if anyone is watching. Her boyfriend seems to have wandered off, and the place is mostly empty, only a few people on the benches up by the ticket counters, and they don't seem to have noticed what is going on over here.

I look back at Lilly. She's still holding up the front of her garment, but from the back she must appear fully dressed.

All right, if she wants to play, I know this game better than anybody. I make a cut on my stomach, lower down, longer and deeper than the one she made on herself.

She smiles. What does that smile mean? Is she gloating? Is she saying she won by making me be the follower instead of the leader?

But it doesn't seem to be the smile of a dominant winner. It's more of an innocent smile, a little girl smile. I suspect in her stoned state, she's just happy to be playing this game, happy to be a participant.

But I don't want any participants. This is *my* game. I'm the Pain Artist, not her. My interaction with the audience is supposed to be one way: I demonstrate; they are supposed to observe and learn. It is the only contact with humans I need.

So why do I hand the instrument back to her?

She makes another cut on herself to match mine, but much wider and much deeper. As her blood flows down into her public hair, I suddenly become aware of her femininity. Why am I allowing myself to notice that? Is she trying to make me remember that day when she made love to me and made me care about her. But I don't want to remember. I don't want to care. There is pain in caring, and I don't want that anymore. I don't need that anymore. Sure, I know that I'm male and she's female, but I don't care about that. Grandma's TV soap operas are full of that kind of crap—men and women playing at the game of sex, interleaved with endless ads telling you how they can make you a winner in that all-so-important game of sex. No, I will not participate. I am above all that. I am a mind, not a body. I must remain logical.

She tries to hand the X-Acto knife back to me, but I refuse to take it. I know what she wants, but I don't want to continue this game.

When I refuse to take the knife, she again presses the blade against her stomach. She waits for my reaction.

But I will not react. She can't make me react. I am the Pain Artist. I make them all think about pain, but I do not feel pain like they do. They feel pain because they are weak, but I am not weak. I refuse to be crippled by emotion like they are. I am logical, and because I am logical, I am stronger than they are.

It places me above pain. It places me above any possible human feeling, physical *or* emotional. As a stupid child, I felt emotion toward my mother, and what good did it do me? She mostly ignored me. She went out every night and got drunk, showing off her beautiful red hair until, in the end, it was her fancy red hair that got her killed. And I felt emotion toward poor little Zyrell. But then he too was gone. A stray bullet. Nobody else cared, so what good did it do if I cared? I even felt something for Big Jake. He was a paradox: a thoughtful gangbanger who wanted to be a businessman. He died too. Because of me. A lot of good caring about him did. And then, once upon a time, I even felt emotion toward this girl, this Lilly who got mad at me because her stupid brother got himself killed because of something I said. Should I care about that? All of them are dead now, so what was the purpose of all that caring? There was no purpose. Those existential philosophers were right: we live and then we die. There is no other meaning to it, no reason to care about any of it.

She is still holding the knife against her stomach. I can't keep my eyes off of that knife blade, but I know I must not care about it. That would not be logical.

I see the point of the knife penetrate her skin. I see the blood begin to flow.. She pushes it in deeper, and more blood flows.

What does she think she's doing? Showing she can take the pain? But I am the Pain Artist, the one and only Pain Artist. I have to stop her.

I reach out and grab her hand. I take X-Acto knife away from her. I look at it. Now there's blood all over it, on the shaft as well as on the blade. *Our* blood, mixed together. Was she trying to tell me she knows about pain too? About loss? Is that true?

She moves closer to me, but I don't want to look at her. I don't want to be reminded of that day when I looked at her naked body and . . . cared. I close my eyes.

I feel the slightest brush of her hair against my cheek, and it brings with it a strange odor, a kind of musky smell, like in a cave, but I'm sure there's also another paradoxical odor behind it, something like . . . dead flowers?

She whispers into my ear: "I want to see you, Scotty. I'll come by your house tomorrow."

And then, before I can protest, she's gone. I watch her as she walks away across the wide expanse of polished floor. She's probably looking for her ridiculous goth boyfriend.

She said she wanted to see me. She said she would come to my house tomorrow. But will she? Not likely. She's so stoned, she probably won't even remember anything that happened this night.

I look around. Nobody seems to have noticed what just happened.

But what did just happen? Lilly played a game with me, a game of you-cut-yourself, so watch me-cut-myself. But what did the game mean? And why did she say she would come to my house and see me tomorrow? Does she want to make love with me again? Does she want to be naked in bed with me like she did that time before when we . . .

No, I can't let myself think about that. It was a long time ago, and it doesn't matter anymore. Nothing matters.

I need to get out of here, right now! In fact, I should leave and never come back here again. What I'm doing here is stupid. Nobody cares anymore, so why should I?

I leave my blanket and my purse on the floor and gather up my tools. I take them to the nearest trash can and drop them in.

I head for the door.

Outside, the dark streets are almost deserted, and the air is cool. What time of year is it? Odd that I don't even know. Or care. Why should I care?

For some reason, my legs are hurting, and my stomach where I cut myself is also hurting. A little. Maybe I'd better use what little money I have left and take a cab home.

No! I am the Pain Artist. I can make the pain go away. I just have to find that place in my brain where the pain isn't, the not-caring place. I won't take a cab. It's not all that far to Grandma's house. I will use the walking time to make the pain go away.

As I start down the street, I try to push away the image of Lilly cutting on herself. What was she trying to say? Was she trying to prove that I really do care about her? But I've learned the only way to not feel pain, is to not feel those kinds of human emotions. If I do start caring again, won't the pain come right back?

In humans, consciousness produces moral value. Once you accept moral value, you must be influenced by the world.

"What are you saying, Old Man? That as a human, I have to care? I have to have feelings? But weren't you the one who told me reality is nothing but a product of my brain? Doesn't that mean I get to create my own reality? What good did caring and having feelings ever do for me? No, I don't believe you. I won't accept it. Caring only exists in trace elements of memory, a few scattered neurons that lie somewhere inside my brain. By tomorrow, if I will it so, this night too will be nothing but a fading memory. By tomorrow, I'll be back to normal, and everything will be as it was. All this stupid caring and feeling will be gone. Aren't I right, Old Man?"

He doesn't respond.

Does that mean he thinks I'm kidding myself? That I won't be able to get back to normal tomorrow? But if I start to care again, won't the pain come back? "Talk to me, Old Man. You have to help me. You have to tell me what happens to people in this world that *feel*? How can they go on? How can they continue to . . . *be*?"

He does not answer.